GUILT B

A HAZARD AND SOMERSET MYSTERY

GREGORY ASHE

This is a work of fiction. Names, characters, places, and incidents either are the product of the author's imagination or are used fictitiously, and any resemblance to actual persons, living or dead, business establishments, events, or locales is entirely coincidental.

Guilt by Association
Copyright © 2018 Gregory Ashe

All rights reserved. No part of this book may be reproduced in any form, stored in any retrieval system, or transmitted in any form by any means—electronic, mechanical, photocopy, recording, or otherwise—without prior written permission of the publisher, except as provided by United States of America copyright law. For permission requests and all other inquiries, contact: contact@hodgkinandblount.com

Published by Hodgkin & Blount
https://www.hodgkinandblount.com/
contact@hodgkinandblount.com

Published 2018
Printed in the United States of America

Version 1.03

ISBN #:9781720187462

CHAPTER ONE

**FEBRUARY 12
SATURDAY
9:47 PM**

EMERY HAZARD NEEDED TO BREAK UP with his boyfriend.

As soon as the thought surfaced, Hazard buried it, turning his attention to the sights and sounds flooding his senses. The music in the Pretty Pretty seemed louder than usual to Hazard. Everything seemed worse tonight: the music was louder, the swiveling lights were brighter, Hazard's headache was angrier, and he was definitely more drunk than usual. Even his dancing—which mostly consisted of swaying in place while his boyfriend, Nico, moved around him—was off. He'd just about broken Nico's toes when he accidentally took a step.

Nico, aside from a yelp, had borne it all pretty well. He didn't seem to notice that the music was louder, that the lights were brighter, that Wahredua's only gay club was somehow worse than normal. Tall, slender, with skin the color of toasted grain and with his shaggy dark hair, Nico didn't need to notice anything—everybody noticed him, and that was enough. Nico could just dance up on Hazard, peppering the grinding with long kisses that tasted like appletinis, and enjoy life. For Nico, the Pretty Pretty was heaven.

Hazard needed to break up with him.

There it was again, that thought worming its way through the pounding in Hazard's head. The pounding, too, had gotten worse tonight. Ever since an unfortunate collision with a baseball bat—wielded by the last killer Hazard had apprehended as part of his work for the Wahredua PD—he'd suffered from periods of severe headaches. Over the last six weeks, bruises and abrasions had healed; the gunshot wound to his shoulder and the deep slice across his palm had closed; but the headaches, although they had grown less frequent, persisted. And tonight, they were persisting like a bitch.

Nico, his shirt unbuttoned to the center of his chest, his skin gleaming with sweat, pressed his mouth against Hazard's, his tongue forcing a path between Hazard's lips. The kiss was hot, especially in time with the feel of Nico's muscled body thrusting against Hazard's. Everything about Nico was hot. He was an underwear model; well, to be fair, he was only a part-time model, and most of the time he was a graduate student in theology who didn't like to pick up his socks. But he was hot as hell. And kind, Hazard forced himself to remember. Nico was kind; he wasn't just a pretty boy. And smart. And funny. Not the kind of jokes that made Hazard laugh, not usually, but plenty of people thought he was funny. Plenty of people like—

—not Somers—

—well, plenty of people. And what the hell did it matter what Somers thought, anyway?

As the kiss broke, Hazard took the opportunity to shout over a thunderous bass line, "I'm headed to the bar." He pointed at his head. "Need to sit down."

Something flickered across Nico's face, but it was gone almost as soon as it had appeared. He nodded, kissed Hazard again—more coolly, this time—and as soon as they parted, a crowd of eager, attractive young men surged towards Nico. A second crowd surged towards Hazard, but most of them veered off when they saw his face. The few who didn't, the few who tried to talk to him, the few who might have thought they had a chance at a dance, bounced off him—one of them, literally.

Propped on a stool at the bar, Hazard nursed a Guinness. He didn't want it, not really. He definitely didn't need it. And it sure as hell wasn't doing anything for his head. What he wanted was to be back home, the lights low, his eyes closed as he listened to a book on tape and waited for the pain pills to kick in. What did he have from the library right now? *Munitions of the Spanish Civil War, Small Caliber*? Had he finished that one? Large caliber? God, his head.

This was the price of a relationship, though. After his last blow-up fight with Nico, Hazard had been forced to make concessions. No more staying at home on the weekends. That had been the biggest one. Nico, almost a decade younger and far more social than Hazard, thrived at the Pretty Pretty. Yes, thrived was the right word. Nico seemed to come alive here.

From his post at the bar, Hazard watched his boyfriend, glimpsing him through the crowd. Nico danced well. He was sexy in just about every way imaginable. He was kind. He was funny—yes, goddamnit, even if Somers didn't think so. He was—

Hazard groaned and rubbed a big finger between his eyes, trying to massage away the headache. He was making a list. Jesus, he thought, shoot me now.

This was how it had been with Alec. This was how it had been with Billy. The lists. List after list after list. Pros and cons. Plus and minus. Some lists that went on and on and on, only the good things. And the other lists that he never dared put on paper where Alec might see, where Billy might come across it. But lists. So many goddamn lists. And here he was again; it all started with the lists.

It was all because of the Pretty Pretty. Hazard just needed one weekend of quiet. One night of calm. That's all—and then things would be all right again. Things would go back to normal.

But Hazard couldn't quite get free of his own thoughts. It always started with the lists. Every time—well, to be fair, there had only been two—his relationships had gone bad, he'd started the lists way in advance. With Alec, it had been early. Hazard had started the lists before Alec had ever used the belt, back when he just used his hands, when he'd still laugh and pretend it was a joke, when he'd land a slap, when he'd leave a handprint like a neon sign, when he'd growl and say how sexy it was. Even back then, the lists had started.

With Billy too. With Billy, the lists had started—God, what? Eight months ago? Ten? Before Hazard had lost his job. Before he'd left St. Louis and come to Wahredua. Before, and this was the real bitch of it all, before Hazard had suspected, before he had let himself suspect, what was going on between Billy and Tom. Tom was just a friend. Tom was just a good friend. Sure, Billy and Tom were close, but Billy had lots of close friends. Sure—sure, sometimes Tom stood a little too close. Sure, sometimes, after parties, when Hazard had had too much to drink, sure, sometimes there were fights about Tom. But he hadn't known. God, he hadn't suspected, hadn't even let himself think those thoughts all the way to their conclusion. And before any of that, he'd started with the lists.

Hazard rocked his glass of Guinness, unsure if he could stomach any more of the dark liquid. Like chewing a sponge, that's what it felt like tonight. Normally Guinness was his drink of choice, but tonight—it had to be his head. The music had gotten louder if that were possible, and the pounding in his head was off-beat. Hazard didn't want to be here. There. He'd managed to think it to himself, which was one step closer to saying it out loud. Hazard never wanted to be here.

And Hazard wouldn't be here, he wouldn't have had to give up every weekend if he hadn't fought so hard about the apartment. The fight had dragged on close to eighteen hours—not steady going, but on and off. Hazard hadn't wanted to move. He'd liked his place, the place he shared with another detective, John-Henry Somerset, his partner. Somers. He hadn't wanted to move.

Fast forward, and here Hazard was: he'd lost the fight about the apartment, and he'd lost his weekends too. He dug his finger deeper into his forehead, as though he could punch through the bone and massage away the worst of the ache. Just shoot me, he thought again. A list, a fucking list all over again, just shoot me.

Things were going to turn out the same, a dark voice told him. Things were going to get worse. It was a matter of time. It was only, always, exclusively a matter of time before they saw—

—the real Emery Hazard—

—whatever it was inside him that had made Alec reach for the belt, that had made Billy reach for Tom, that was going to make—

"Nico is looking good out there." The voice was familiar: catty, warbling, a contrived lisp on the only S. Marcus, dressed in a sleeveless t-shirt and cut-off jeans in spite of the February cold, slumped against the bar next to Hazard. "Better be careful."

"Go away, Marcus."

Marcus sniffed. "I'll tell Nico."

"Tell him whatever you want."

Marcus stayed right where he was, swishing his hips to the beat, and Hazard could feel the younger man's eyes on him. "He's got good taste," Marcus said. With a twirl of his wrist, Marcus traced a finger down Hazard's arm.

"Keep that up and you won't be able to use that hand for a month."

"You're always so mean to me." Marcus sidled closer. He had finally shaved his ridiculous mustache, and he wasn't a bad-looking guy, even if he wasn't Hazard's type. His hip bumped into Hazard, and then again, and then again as Marcus swayed to the music. "I could be really nice to you. Nico wouldn't mind. We've shared before."

"Get lost."

"Let me blow you."

"I'll say it a different way: fuck off."

"Only if you're doing the fucking," Marcus hissed, arching an eyebrow.

Hazard got to his feet, and Marcus must have finally caught a hint because he scuttled backward, his eyes wide.

"This isn't smart, Marcus."

He must have expected something else because fresh confidence rushed into his face. "If you think Nico will be mad, I promise, he won't. We've—"

"I don't care. I don't care if the two of you fucked your way through City Hall together. You think I don't know what this is about? You don't like me. Fine. No, don't try to deny it. You think I don't remember back at Christmas when you called Nico and tried to rat me out?"

"You were—I thought maybe the two of you—"

"Bull. Shit. You like stirring things up. And now you're doing it again. If I say yes, you run straight to Nico with a story about how I'm cheating on him. If I say no, you run straight to Nico with a story about how mean I am, how I can't take a joke, how I'm boring, how he deserves so much better. How am I doing?"

The change in Marcus's expression was immediate and remarkable: his eyebrows knitted together, his mouth thinned into a line, and he bit his lower lip so hard that it turned white under his teeth. "You aren't good enough for him. You're—you're a phony. You're a joke, that's what you are. You're one of those butch gays who thinks he's better than everybody else. Repressed. You're trying to play it straight, but you moan like a bitch when Nico's inside you. Yeah. He told me. He told me how you screw up your face when he really sticks it to you, just like a good bitch—"

It wasn't really a punch, but Hazard's fist was closed, so maybe it technically counted as one. It was more like knocking on a door. He rapped the side of Marcus's head, that was all. Sure, maybe it was a hard knock. Harder than Hazard knocked on a normal door. But it was still just a knock.

Marcus staggered sideways. He clutched at the bar, but wood and metal slipped out of his grip, and he hit the ground. He scrambled to his feet again, and he didn't seem to know what to say or do. He just stood there, frozen, eyes wide. Hazard guessed nobody had ever hit him before.

"Run," Hazard said in his best cop voice.

Marcus ran.

When Marcus had disappeared into the dance-floor crowd—there would be hell to pay when Nico heard about it; Jesus, Mary, and Joseph, there'd be hell—Hazard dropped back onto the stool. Party boys watched him, their expressions a mixture of shock at the outburst of violence and persistent interest, but Hazard ignored them. In a matter of minutes, they went back to dancing and drinking and humping, although plenty of them still turned eyes toward Hazard now and then. He ignored them. His headache was worse than ever, and now his knuckles throbbed with heat.

9

He slid the Guinness across the bar, but he couldn't bring himself to take a drink. Thick as a fucking sponge tonight. He was done drinking. Throwing up—throwing up a lot, in fact—was climbing his to-do list.

"Don't tell me," a voice said. "He bought you the wrong drink."

The man was tall, well-built, dressed in a sports coat and tie that made him look sexy instead of officious. He had the classic good looks of a politician—of a Kennedy, for that matter—the kind of good looks that run straight through the bloodlines at Yale and Harvard. Dark hair in a conservative cut, strong jaw with a cleft, muscular without being a meathead. He probably rowed. He probably played squash. He probably owned a polo horse. Outside of the Pretty Pretty, Hazard would have hated him. Inside—well, inside, Hazard suddenly found his head wasn't hurting quite as bad. It was hard to focus on a headache when a perfect smile flashed your way.

"He thought I wanted a Bud Lite," Hazard said, not quite sure why he said it.

That perfect smile glowed about ten degrees brighter. "That was stupid of him. You're obviously a—" The man paused. His dark eyes darted to the half-drunk Guinness and then to Hazard. "You're obviously an Old Fashioned man." He tipped a hand at the bartender and then moved into the empty seat next to Hazard.

Hazard raised an eyebrow. "You saw what happened to the last guy."

This man laughed, and even his laugh sounded like it had cost a couple of grand. "I like taking chances."

"There's no chance here, buddy. I've got a boyfriend."

"I don't mind talking. Half of the guys out there look like they're still in college, and about seventy-five percent look like they're trying to find a daddy." His eyes were almost smoking as he studied Hazard. "Boyfriend, huh? Not that guy you gave a concussion, I hope."

"No, he's—oh, you've got to be fucking kidding me."

Across the room, Hazard watched another guy shove his tongue down Nico's throat.

CHAPTER TWO

FEBRUARY 10
SATURDAY
10:04 PM

HAZARD DIDN'T REALLY THINK about clearing a path across the crowded dance floor. He was out of his seat, charging across the room before he had a chance. He didn't think about a lot of things. He didn't think about his headache. He didn't think about the need to toss his cookies. He did think, briefly, of Billy. He did think, slightly longer, about Tom. In his head, in his fantasies, his fist connected with Tom's nose, cartilage crumpling, blood hot between his fingers. Then he only had room in his head for the snapshot he'd seen. It had lasted only a moment before the crowd closed again, but it had been clear: Nico pressed against another guy, making out like a horny teenager.

To Hazard's credit, even though he didn't think about clearing a path across the room, he still managed to do it well. Some of it came down to his hard, efficient shoves that sent gay boys sliding out of his way. Most of it, though, was what Somers would have called pure Hazard: a brooding, hulking thunderstorm of dark hair and muscle. Dancers hurried to get out of his way. They damn well scurried.

And then the crowd parted. Nico was fending off a guy who looked like he was trying his hardest to pry Nico's mouth open with his tongue. Hazard shoved the guy. He had an impression of the guy, just a flash, but the guy was clearly frat material: hair buzzed down on the sides, long on the top; a red tank top that showed just how much time this guy spent toning and flexing and grooming; and expensive sneakers that probably cost more than Hazard's car.

"What the hell is going on here?"

"Nothing," Nico said, drawing his hand across his mouth, the movement reflexive and furtive and guilty.

"Yo," the frat boy yelled. Yo. That's what he said, not ironically, not mockingly, but like he meant it, like that was the only word he knew. "Yo, what the fuck?"

Hazard ignored him and spoke to Nico. "It didn't look like nothing."

"It was a misunderstanding. It was—" Nico's shoulders curved inwards, and he dropped his hand. It looked like it took a lot of effort, prizing his hand away from his mouth, and he couldn't look Hazard in the eyes. "Let's get out of here. Let's go, all right?"

"Yo, motherfucker," the frat boy said. He walked like an ape. He walked like he was all shoulders, and Hazard saw the punch coming about five years before the frat boy threw it. When it came, Hazard moved, and the punch went past his chin.

Hazard caught hold of the frat boy and tossed him before the guy even knew what happened. Five yards. Six if you counted where he stopped sliding. Hazard rolled his shoulders, conscious of a new ache; he was getting old.

Frat boy was picking himself up.

"Stay down," Hazard said. He turned back to Nico. "Why should we leave? We're having a nice time."

"Emery, come on, we've got to go, he's—look out!"

This time, the punch was wild. Frat boy, red-faced and swearing, swung his hands like he was trying to catch flies. Hazard ducked one punch, bobbed out of the way of another, and planted his fist in frat boy's solar plexus. With a wheeze, frat boy collapsed.

"He wasn't doing anything wrong," Nico said. "He didn't know, goddamn it."

The music continued to pound, but around them, the dancing had stopped. In spite of the throbbing beat, the space was dead. The Pretty Pretty's patrons stood and watched. Two of the bouncers were working their way through the crowd, and Hazard knew they only had moments before they were dragged out of the place—and, if he were really, really lucky, banned for life.

Frat boy had gotten to his knees. A long strand of saliva hung from his mouth. He was still wheezing, but it sounded like more of the air was reaching his lungs now. He looked like he didn't know what time zone he was in. Hazard walked towards him.

"What the fuck are you doing?" Nico shouted, and it took Hazard a moment to realize Nico was talking to him.

"Getting that guy off your ass."

Nico glanced around. It was hard to tell in the darkness and with his complexion, but he might have been flushed. "He's just some drunk jerk-off. I don't need you to do that. He can't even stand—Jesus Christ, Emery, I'm talking to you. Stop. You can't do that."

Inside, Hazard was thinking, he isn't Billy, and that isn't Tom, and whatever the hell is going on you'd better get a hold of yourself fast, but it didn't matter what he told himself. He was thinking of Billy. He was thinking of Tom. He could practically see Tom, see his face overlaying the frat boy in front of him, the two faces swimming together in his vision. And he heard himself say, "Yes. I can."

The frat boy was trying to pick himself up. Hazard looked at Nico. Then he looked at the frat boy and planted his heel in the center of frat boy's back. He shoved down hard enough that he heard frat boy's jaw click against the floor even over the music.

"Stay down," Hazard said.

Nico, shaking his head, said, "You're unbelievable." He pushed his way into the crowd.

Over the heads and shoulders of the crowd, Hazard saw Marcus emerge, as though sliding out of nowhere, and enfold Nico in a hug. The bouncers came next, ignoring Marcus and Nico and beelining for Hazard. Hazard watched as Marcus urged Nico towards the door. He was holding Nico's hand and speaking into his ear. They were gone, vanishing out of the club before Hazard could take a second step.

"Let's get some shots out here," a familiar voice called from the bar. The guy in the suit and tie jerked a thumb at the bottles lining the wall. "On me until the first guy pukes."

The stillness broke. Many of the men surged towards the free drinks. A handful picked up frat boy, still limp and floppy, and dragged him away. Some of the boys—Hazard noticed that they were exclusively young, with the kind of gleaming skin that vanished around twenty-two or twenty-three—clustered around Hazard. They grabbed at his arms, his ass, his crotch, and they talked over each other, telling him how brave he was, how hot it had been to see him trash the frat boy, what they'd do to Hazard if he gave them half a chance.

At the bar, the guy in the suit and tie tipped a shot glass at Hazard—an invitation, or perhaps a salute. Or perhaps, Hazard thought when he glimpsed the man's smile, a kind of commiseration.

"Detective Hazard," one of the bouncers said, as the two big men finally worked their way through the last of the crowd.

"Are we going to have a problem?" the second one said. They looked like they came as a matching set: bald, tall, and built like cement trucks.

"I'm leaving. Anyway, he took the first swing. You tell Bradley that. Tell Will Pirk too." The Pretty Pretty's manager and owner weren't Hazard's friends by any means, but Hazard knew he had enough status as a local celebrity to buy him some wiggle room.

"Are you walking out of here?" the first bouncer said.

"I'm walking."

"Will might ban your ass," the second bouncer said. "Doesn't matter who you are."

"Tell him not to do me any favors."

Hazard worked his way free of his clinging admirers, gave the man in the suit and tie a last glance—he was still watching Hazard, and his interest was obvious—and found his way out of the club. The February air was cold. Dead cold. It snapped into his lungs like a rubber band, and the shock doubled Hazard's headache. At least it was cold, though. At least it smelled clean. It didn't taste like sweat and vinyl and a hundred different colognes. It tasted sweet like car exhaust and sweet like upper-crust snow.

Nico and Marcus huddled at the end of the block, with Nico facing the length of the sidewalk, staring right at Hazard, and with Marcus between them like a bodyguard. Hazard's steps sounded like explosions. It's the cement, he thought. It's frozen. That's why I'm hitting it so hard. I wouldn't walk like this. I never walk like this.

"Move."

"Fuck you," Marcus said.

"I'm not telling you again."

"Stop it," Nico said. His eyes were red, but he wasn't crying. The cold, maybe. And that must have been why he hunched his shoulders, why he was practically folded in on himself.

"I'm not going to stop it. Not until he gets lost."

"See?" Marcus said in a harsh whisper. "This is what I'm talking about."

"Emery," Nico said, "just stop. You're being a jerk."

"I'm being a jerk?" Hazard's head was pounding. Not a drum. Nothing like that. It was bigger. Much bigger. Like somebody standing inside an abandoned freighter with a jackhammer and giving it hell. That kind of huge. "Some guy's got his tongue down your throat—"

"You don't know what you're talking about."

"Some guy's got his tongue down your throat, and I get him off you—"

"You're an asshole."

"And I get him off you, and somehow I'm the jerk. That's it, huh?"

Nico didn't say anything; he was staring out of those red eyes like he'd gone to a week's worth of funerals, but he wasn't crying. Marcus didn't say anything either, but he looked pretty happy, pretty goddamn happy, like he was watching Hazard eat shit by the shovelful.

"I'm staying at Marcus's tonight."

"You're fucking kidding me."

"No. I'm not. We can talk about this tomorrow. Marcus, let's—"

"You're not going home with him." Hazard took a step forward, knocking Marcus aside, barely even feeling the impact. Seizing Nico's arm, he yanked him a step towards his old VW Jetta. "You're coming home, and we're going to talk about this like adults whether you—"

The blow to his head wasn't that hard, but combined with the headache, it felt like it had cracked Hazard's skull. He had the dizzied worry that somehow the punch had collided perfectly with the still-healing fracture and his brains were sliding out the back of his head. Hazard lost his grip on Nico and staggered.

By the time he'd pulled himself half-upright, Marcus had an arm around Nico and was hustling him down the block. Hazard watched them go, partly because his bell had just been rung like fucking New Year's and partly because he had absolutely no idea what to do. After fifteen yards, Nico stopped and looked back.

"We'll talk tomorrow," he said, his voice so thick that Hazard barely understood the words. Or maybe that was the headache again. Or maybe something was really wrong, something inside Hazard's head. Aphasia. That's what it was called. When words didn't make sense anymore. That's how it felt, tonight. Like they were talking nonsense at each other, and Jesus, how had it all gone sideways?

Emery Hazard thought he might have an answer, but before it could fully materialize, he dropped forward and sicked up all over his shoes.

CHAPTER THREE

**FEBRUARY 11
SUNDAY
11:15 AM**

THE PHONE'S RINGING went through Hazard's skull like a couple of inches of good steel. One minute he was asleep. The next, awake and feeling like someone had shoved a spear through the back of his head. It went on for a long time. Then it went quiet. Later, it rang again. A fragment of memory— *not for us, the flashing bronze,* was that Homer?—because the noise was like the blade of a fucking spear going into his brain. And then, again, blessed silence. The pillow, he thought drowsily as he tried to sink under the headache and into the gray stillness of sleep, smelled like Nico.

For a while he was there again, inside that grayness, while a part of his brain recycled the past night. The hammering music inside the Pretty Pretty. The smell of sweat and superheated lights and Guinness. Nico pressed against him—no, Nico across the room, far off, while Hazard talked to Marcus. No, to the hot guy in the jacket and tie. No, to the bouncers. And through it all, that mixture of headache and bass line, pounding, pounding, pounding—

Pounding on the door. Hazard jerked free of the tangled bedding. Immediately, he regretted it. The headache surged back to the front of his head, and he had to steady himself against the nightstand. The clock marked a bleary eleven. Whoever was knocking was really going to town.

"Just a minute," Hazard shouted.

Pants. And a shirt. But he had no memory of where anything had ended up last night, and he came up with a pair of shorts and a t-shirt. The shorts fit. The shirt didn't. It had to be Nico's, but it felt like a child's. A child's small. Jesus, maybe an infant's. It was choking the life out of Hazard.

And somebody was still trying to pound down the door.

Squeezed into the tiny shirt—had Nico bought it for a nephew? what the hell was it doing on the floor?—Hazard stumbled to the door and glanced through the peephole. Groaning, he turned back to the bedroom.

"I can hear you," Somers called from the other side of the door.

Hazard kept going.

"I'll keep knocking."

Hazard kicked aside Nico's empty laundry basket. His toes caught in the plastic mesh, and he swore as he ripped them free.

"I've got Big Biscuit."

At the bedroom door, Hazard stopped.

Somers had gone silent. Even without seeing Somers, even with a solid door between them, Hazard knew the bastard was smug. Probably grinning. Hazard knew he should go back to bed. He should take one of those pills for his head and pull the covers over his eyes and just go back to bed, and when he woke up, he'd call Nico, and he'd figure out what he'd done wrong last night, and he'd apologize the way he'd apologized to Billy, the way he'd apologized to Alec. He'd eat the same old shit out of this shiny new bowl. That was it. He'd just get into bed and ignore Somers. He'd—

By that point, he'd already unlocked the front door.

"Took you long enough—Jesus God, what are you wearing?"

"Shut up."

Somers, a plastic carryout bag hanging from one hand, appraised him. And it was exactly that: pure, fucking appraisal. Somers was hot. He was runway hot, swimsuit hot, blond and golden-skinned, even in the middle of winter, fuck him, and with eyes like Caribbean waters. Today, like every day, he managed to look like he'd just rolled out of bed—and like he hadn't been alone. His button-down was rumpled, his jacket was askew, his hair had that perfect messiness that made Hazard itch to run his hands through it. And he was still standing there, still appraising Hazard like he might buy him at auction. Now there was a thought. Hazard barely suppressed a second, very different kind of groan.

"What happened?"

"Give me the food."

"You look like shit."

Hazard tried to shut the door; he blamed his headache and hangover for the fact that Somers still managed to sneak inside. As Somers always did when he came to Nico's apartment—Nico and Hazard's apartment, Hazard amended—he made a show of considering the mess. Nico's clothes, Nico's books, Nico's shoes, Nico's latest shopping. There were about three square inches of space that weren't covered by something that Nico owned.

Somers went straight to the table and shoved a pile of unmatched socks onto the floor. Then, after a moment's consideration, he shoved a stack of textbooks.

"Hey."

"I'm messy."

"Please don't start."

"I know I'm messy."

"Somers, I've got the worst headache, and I'm tired, and I—"

"I mean, I know I'm messy. I know that's why you moved out. One of the reasons."

Hazard gave up and waited for the rest of it.

"But this," Somers gestured at the chaos—he paused, Hazard noted, when he saw a stack of some of Nico's more provocative underwear. Hazard shoved them under one of the sofa cushions.

"Pervert."

Somers, smirking, continued, "But this is insane. It's like you're living in a dorm. Or a frat. And as much as you might have enjoyed close quarters with all those rich, athletic boys, sharing showers, dropping towels, a few playful wrestling moves turn into something not quite so playful—"

"Somers, I swear to Christ."

"—you've got to admit you don't like living like this."

"Are you done?"

"Finished."

"You're sure?"

"Perfectly."

"Because if you've got more jokes, get them out now."

Somers spread his hands innocently.

"Any more comments about my—" He had been about to say boyfriend, but the word stuck in his throat. For once, his hesitance to acknowledge his relationship with Nico had nothing to do with how he felt about Somers. "—about my apartment?"

"It's not yours."

"Jesus."

"I'm just saying, it's not. It's Nico's."

"You're a real piece of work."

"I mean, I get it. You're living here now. But it's not like that's going to last forever."

The last words struck home hard. Hazard dropped into a seat at the table, head in his hands.

"Hey, what's going on?"

"Nothing."

"Ree, I was just teasing. Well, mostly. I mean, this place is a mess, but I'm not trying to—come on. What's going on?"

The pounding in Hazard's head had gotten worse. He needed one of those pills, but he couldn't drag himself out of the chair. Not yet. Just a minute, he just needed a minute.

"All right," Somers said. "Your hair is all loose and wild and sexy barbarian, which means you either just finished banging one out with Nico or you haven't showered yet. You're wearing a shirt that's about eighteen sizes too small, and those gym shorts—well, you're going commando, buddy. So again: either you just nailed Nico to the wall, or you're—" Somers whistled. "You're hungover."

"I'm not hungover."

"You are. You had a fight with Nico. You got plastered. You're wrecked."

"You don't have to sound so goddamn happy about it."

Neither man spoke for a moment. Then Somers touched the back of Hazard's neck, and Hazard flinched.

"He hit you? That motherfucking piece of shit put a hand on you?"

"What? God. No."

"You've got a bruise about a mile long back here. Doesn't he have any fucking brains? Didn't he even think about the fact that you're still healing, that you shouldn't even bump your head, let alone—and the little bitch hit you from behind, didn't he? Where is he?" Somers hadn't moved, hadn't raised his voice, hadn't so much as lifted his fingers from Hazard's neck. But it was like someone else had come into the room. It put a shiver down Hazard's back. And deep in his brain, at the surface of conscious thought, he realized he liked it. "Where is he?" Somers asked again. "That's all you have to say, just tell me where."

"You're acting crazy."

"All right. All right. You don't say anything. You don't have to say anything."

"You're out of your damn mind. Will you stop acting like this?"

"Don't worry about it. I'll find him myself."

"John-Henry, will you sit down and listen to me?"

Somers fell back into his seat. They sat that way for a moment, neither of them speaking, both watching the other as though seeing something new. Hazard had grown up in Wahredua. He had grown up hounded, persecuted, tormented by the man who sat in front of him. He had come back to this place, to this town he hated above all else, unwillingly, and he had found himself partnered with a man he had hated for most of his life—hated and, even worse, been attracted to. And instead of the bully, instead of the thug, instead of the cocky football star, he'd found an intelligent, funny, skilled detective who had wanted to make the past right. It hadn't hurt that Somers had grown up to be the kind of hot that, in a cartoon, would have made the mercury in a thermometer shoot up so fast the glass exploded. Somers's hand was still on the back of Hazard's neck. His fingers felt good there. They raised a strip of goosebumps down Hazard's chest.

"I'm listening."

So Hazard told him.

"He's just not that kind of guy," Somers said with a shrug.

"What kind? And don't say something asshole-ish. Don't say he's not the kind that's mature or something like that."

"Me? I meant he's not the kind that likes jealousy."

"I'm not jealous."

"You beat up a guy for kissing your boyfriend."

"I didn't beat him up. You make it sound like I'm in eighth grade."

"In eighth grade, you were so scrawny you could barely hold a pencil." Somers smirked. "Well, I guess you were definitely strong enough to hold your pencil, if you get what I—"

"I get it."

"I meant your dick. That's what I meant by pencil."

"Jesus Christ."

"Not everybody likes jealousy. Some people get off on it. Some don't mind—they might appreciate it, but they aren't looking for it. And some people don't like it. Hate it, even."

"I'm not jealous."

Somers fixed him with a look.

"All right, I shouldn't have hit that guy."

Somers waited.

"I definitely shouldn't have thrown him."

Somers shrugged.

"And I should have let Nico handle it."

"Yeah, well, you definitely shouldn't have done that."

"What's that supposed to mean?"

"Nothing."

"What did you mean?"

"I'm an idiot, all right? Stuff just comes out of my mouth sometimes."

"You meant something. You—" Before Hazard could finish, his phone buzzed. He pulled it out, and a message from Nico showed on the screen.

I'm staying at Marcus's place for a few more days. Can you tell me a time you'll be out of the apartment so I can pick up a few things?

"What?" Somers said.

Hazard dropped the phone on the table. Picking it up, Somers read the message. His eyebrows shot up, but he didn't say anything.

"Don't."

Somers put the phone back on the table.

"Don't fucking say you're sorry. Don't act like you're not thrilled. Don't act like this isn't what you wanted."

It took a moment before Somers answered, and when he spoke, his voice was carefully neutral. "I didn't want you to get hurt."

"Well, I didn't."

And it sounded so pathetic, like such an absolute, flat-out lie, that Hazard was blushing as soon as it was out of his mouth, and he was grateful Somers didn't even acknowledge the words.

"Let's eat. You're hungover. Your head hurts. You need food." Somers unpacked the clamshell containers of takeout from Big Biscuit, and then he touched the back of Hazard's neck again. "You've got to eat something. And you need a drink. Water, I mean. Lots of it. And those pills for your head, have you taken any today? Christ, of course you haven't."

Hazard knew he should get up. He could grab plates and forks. He could pour a glass of water. He could clean the rest of this shit, Nico's shit, so there was actually a decent space to eat. He didn't, though. He barely had the energy to turn the phone face-down so he didn't have to see that damn message any longer.

"Here."

Hazard swallowed the pills dry, and then a cool glass was pressed into his hand.

"Drink."

He drank, and when he'd finished, Somers opened the clamshells. Steam wafted off home fries, eggs over easy, and biscuits the size of dinner plates. Buttery, flakey, pillowy biscuits. Hazard waited for the smell to turn his stomach, but he was surprised that instead, he was hungry.

They ate, and as they ate and as the pills took effect, the worst of the pain—both emotional and physical—started to pass. It wasn't gone. It wasn't even close to gone. But it got better, and the world didn't seem like one big turd waiting for the flush. At least, not completely. Not—

—with Somers there—

—while the biscuits lasted.

It wasn't until Hazard had dragged the last home fry through a smear of ketchup that he noticed the third clamshell. Reaching over, he popped it open, and three delicate slices of strawberry french toast met his eyes.

"Are you shooting for three hundred?" Somers asked as Hazard speared the french toast and dragged it towards him.

"Screw you."

"You're not going to fit into your pants." A smile crinkled Somers's face, and it was so boyish, so genuine, that for a moment Hazard forgot about Nico and forgot about his cracked head and forgot, even, about the french toast dripping strawberries down his wrist. "You can barely fit into your shirt as it is."

"You're an idiot."

"An idiot who made you smile."

"I didn't smile."

Somers's grin got bigger.

"All right," the blond man finally said, shoving away the rest of his food. "We've got to think strategically." Hazard barely heard him; a half-eaten biscuit was staring back at Hazard. Half. Half of one of those perfect, heavenly creations. Half just tossed aside, like Somers was going to throw it in the trash. "Oh for heaven's sake," Somers said, knocking the styrofoam container towards Hazard. "Just eat it before you choke on your own spit."

Hazard did.

"They'll have to order one of those shipping containers to bury you."

"I'm recovering. I need to build up my strength."

Rolling his eyes, Somers said, "Here's what we're going to do: you're going to take a shower. I'm going to make some phone calls. Then we're going to do it."

The biscuit went sideways in Hazard's throat, and he began to choke. When he'd managed to clear his windpipe, he said, "What?"

A rakish grin peeled back the corners of Somers's mouth.

"You did that on purpose," Hazard grumbled. "Going to do what?"

"Get Nico back."

It took a moment for the words to sink in. "No."

"Come on."

"No. Whatever this is," he gestured at the phone, "however it works out, it'll be fine. I don't need you—"

"Do you want him to break up with you?"

Hazard hesitated. Yesterday, at the Pretty Pretty, he would have said yes. But now—now things were different. Facing into the loneliness, facing into the abyss, Hazard found himself unsure. Things were good with Nico.

Things had been really good. So they'd had a fight. So they'd had one little fight. All they had to do was work it out, figure where things went wrong, and things would be good again.

A little voice in his head, though, asked if that were true, then why hadn't he answered Somers yet?

"That's what I thought," Somers said. "So we'll take it from the top: flowers, a card, reservations at Moulin Vert. I bet if I ask, Cora will call him and get him to meet you there. She's good with people, she really is. And we'll have you dressed to the nines, and that poor boy won't know what hit him." Somers's grin tightened. "You're Emery fucking Hazard. He doesn't have any idea how lucky he is, but we're going to change that."

Hazard suppressed a grimace at the mention of Cora, Somers's estranged wife. "Look, this isn't—"

But Hazard never finished the objection. Somers's phone rang, and he glanced at the screen and answered it. His questions were short, sharp, and familiar.

When Somers ended the call, he shrugged and stood. "No time for a shower, I'm afraid, but you'll probably want to change out of the shirt. It's a little cold for that."

Hazard ignored the jab. "What is it?"

"Shooting."

"This isn't one of those fake shootings, is it? This isn't Batsy Ferrell calling because she's upset about the gun range at Windsor?"

"No. This is the real deal. Looks like a murder."

"Any ID on the victim?"

Somers blew out a breath. His eyes were very bright. They were bright like the sun flat on top of tropical water. But some of the color had left his face. "Oh yeah, plenty of ID. Just about everybody there ID'd him."

"Well?"

"The sheriff."

CHAPTER FOUR

**FEBRUARY 11
SUNDAY
12:11 PM**

SOMERS DROVE THE INTERCEPTOR, but he barely saw the streets. Autopilot, that's what it felt like. Autopilot on the way out to Sheriff Bingham's property at the edge of the city limit. Somers knew the streets. He knew all the streets in Wahredua; he'd grown up here, hadn't he? He didn't need to watch the houses shift, the cramped shotguns slowly giving way to sprawling houses with faded siding, and those houses in turn giving ground to larger, more substantial homes of brick and stone. It was a good thing, too, that Somers didn't need to pay attention. His brain was playing a video loop of the same fragmented moments over and over again.

Hazard set the phone down on the table. Somers read the message—that damn message, like the kid wasn't ripping out Hazard's heart, like he just wanted a favor, like he wanted to borrow a cup of sugar. For a long time, for four months now, Somers had been waiting for this. He'd been waiting for Nico to trip up, waiting for the kid to make a mistake so Hazard would shuttle him out of his life and—

—be Somers's—

—and when it happened, when it finally happened, what did Somers do? He wanted to groan. He wanted to bang his forehead against the steering wheel. He wanted to go back in time and kick himself, hard, right in the balls, to keep his mouth shut.

We're going to get Nico back. Jesus J. Christ, how had that come out of his mouth? Everything had been going right. Everything had been going the way it needed to go. Sure, Hazard was sitting there, moping, like a teddy bear with a thorn in his paw. Sure, those glittering, golden scarecrow eyes had lost some of their glow. Sure. Sure. But that was bound to happen, right?

That was just the way things went. Hazard, for all his gruff exterior, was sensitive. Maybe too sensitive, Somers worried, although he hadn't quite put it to himself that way before. Not in those words, anyway. Nico was taking the first steps to breaking up; Hazard was going to get hurt. That was life. That was every relationship in the world. All Somers had to do was wait it out. All he had to do was give it—what? A week? Two weeks? What were two weeks after he'd waited fifteen years? He could wait two weeks standing on his head.

But no. Somers wanted to scream. No, he hadn't kept his mouth shut. He'd opened his mouth, wide as he could, and shoved his foot right inside. We'll get Nico back. Fuck me, Somers thought. Somebody fuck me hard. That's the stupidest thing I've ever done. Why? Because of those big shoulders, because of that hangdog look, because of those eyes.

"What?" Hazard asked, breaking the silence in the car.

"Huh?"

"I thought I heard something. Like a noise in your throat."

"Nope."

"Are you sure?"

"Yes."

A few minutes passed. The roads had smoothed out; the asphalt here was fresh, newly replaced. These were the kinds of taxpayers that needed to be kept happy. Yeah, that was a good idea. Focus on the roads. On the streets. Just focus on finding your way to the sheriff's house. Don't think about Hazard. Don't think about how you just dicked yourself over.

"Somers, are you messing with me? I can hear it again."

"Yeah. I mean, nope. I mean, I don't hear anything."

"Are you grinding your teeth?"

"What is this?" Somers said, too loudly, too harshly. He laughed, but it was a shit job of smoothing over his outburst. "It's like a witch-hunt. How's your head?"

Hazard absently touched his temple and shrugged.

"You're not still thinking about him, are you? We'll get him back. Don't worry about it." What's wrong with me, Somers wondered. What the hell is wrong with me that I just can't keep my mouth shut?

"Yeah," was all Hazard said. Then, "Thanks."

"What are friends for?"

"Blowjobs," Hazard said.

Somers yanked the car back onto the road just in time. Barely.

"I mean," Hazard said, a humorless grin tightening his features, "if you ask Marcus, that's what he'd say."

"Oh. Oh, yeah. Right. He's a real bastard, huh?"

"He wants Nico. That's for sure."

"He—"

"Listen, can we not talk about this? I just need to clear my head."

"Yeah, sure. Yeah. Yeah, whatever you want."

And Somers didn't know if it was his imagination or not, but he was pretty sure that Hazard was starting to think something was up.

"You know much about the sheriff?" Somers asked hastily. "His reputation, I mean."

"I know he raised a real bastard," Hazard said. "And I know the sheriff didn't seem too bothered about little things like laws and justice when the truth came out."

Somers nodded. That much was definitely true. Their last major case had involved a shooting, and Sheriff Bingham's son—and granddaughter—had been tied to the mess. When those facts started to come to light, the sheriff hadn't hesitated to try to control the information. His first step had been blackmailing Hazard. Somers felt a satisfied smile part his lips. He'd taken care of that problem pretty neatly, though.

"What else? You remember anything from growing up?"

"Besides that the Binghams all seemed like royal assholes?"

"Maybe a little more pertinent to the case, yeah."

"Not really. He thought he was hot stuff then. He thought he was hot stuff when I moved back. He probably thought he was hot stuff right up until he got hit with a bullet. And the recall petition."

The recall petition had hit Wahredua a few weeks into the New Year. After the last murder that Hazard and Somers had solved, disturbing truths about the sheriff had come to light, and those truths had caused an uproar in the community. The petition had drawn ugly lines in local politics, and it had left the sheriff scrambling to solidify his position before the petition reached the requisite number of signatures. The fight would go on for another month at least—or until the petition was successful. Would have gone on. "Guess that's not really his problem anymore," Somers said.

"They say how it happened?"

"Shot in the back of the head."

Hazard was silent for a moment. "Murder?"

"I guess we'll see. I asked what you knew because—well, he's kind of gotten a history over the last few years."

"What kind of history?"

"The *Wahredua Courier*, you ever read it?"

"It's about three pages thick, and they're mostly used car ads."

"Snob."

"Hick."

Somers grinned. "It's not the New York *Times*, I'll admit, but they've got a reporter, Amy Ann Tilden, and she's trying to make a name for herself. She's done some good work. Gotten a lot of pushback, too, but so far she's stuck to her guns. At least, that's what it seems."

"And she writes about the sheriff."

"He's just about the only thing paying her salary." Somers turned at the next road; the sheriff's property lay a few hundred yards ahead, and parked at the drive was a black-and-white with its lights flashing. "Somehow, she got a source at the county jail. I don't know who. I definitely don't know how. But she started printing stories about people being beaten, raped, strangled, suffocated. Not killed. But tortured. She even got a few pictures—nobody you could identify, nobody you could point a finger at, but it really got things going. Some of the local papers picked it up too. And she laid all of it at the sheriff's feet."

"He must have been really happy about that."

"He just about burned down the *Courier*. Every threat you can imagine, that's what he threw at her. Libel, of course, but plenty of other shit. And his deputies have made sure her life is a living hell. That woman's probably had more speeding tickets than anyone you know. She showed me one. It was for going thirty-one in a zone thirty."

"But he hasn't sued."

"That's what's so weird about the whole thing. Well, not weird at all, really. He hasn't sued."

"Because he's afraid she has proof."

"Probably. But it could be that he's just afraid of fanning the flames."

"Why didn't I know about this?"

"Most of it, the big stuff, happened a few years ago. She's printed a few pieces since—last year she had something on his finances, whatever she could get by public record, his pay, all that. But she's quieted down. And things have been better at the jail—at least, that's the word."

"So the fourth estate, having accomplished its objective, quietly retires."

"God, you're weird sometimes. But yeah, I guess so."

"That's bull."

"No, honest. You really are weird."

Hazard flipped the bird. "You know what I meant."

"Sure. But it's a lot more fun to be an asshole."

As they reached the black-and-white, Somers slowed. A crowd pressed against an invisible barrier. Men and women of all ages and races held signs, chanted slogans, and shouted defiance at the sheriff's land. One of the signs said, *Recall Bingham*. Another said, *Give Us A Choice*. A third said, *Racist, Embezzler, Murderer*. And a fourth, quite simply, *Killer*.

The crowd parted reluctantly for the Interceptor, and angry faces stared through the glass. Hazard recognized more than he had expected. Men and women he had seen in the grocery store, men and women who had lived here when he was growing up, men and women who jogged along the Grand Rivere. And a surprising number of men Hazard had seen in the Pretty Pretty. A few of the bolder protesters hammered on the glass with their fists. One red-faced woman fanned them with her sign as though she could blow them away.

Somers swung around the patrol car, waved to the officer inside—it looked like big, red-headed Patrick Foley, a very miserable Foley—and headed up the gravel drive. The sheriff's property butted up against the edge of the city limits. A good stretch of the Grand Rivere curled through the sheriff's land, and the sheriff was also the proud owner of several hundred acres of old timber. It was what, in another time, might have been called an estate or a country house.

And the house itself fit the description: although not as old and grand as the Somerset home, Sheriff Bingham's house was a sprawling brick monstrosity, something a railroad baron had built towards the end of the nineteenth century. It lacked the symmetry and simplicity of the Somerset home; in contrast, the sheriff's house bristled with turrets, with gabled roofs, with wrought iron ornaments. There were faces among those ornaments. Somers remembered, as a boy, those faces. They were watching him now, and he was a grown-ass man, but they were watching him, and he still shivered.

A second black-and-white was parked where the gravel drive looped in front of the brick monstrosity. Somers parked, but before he and Hazard had finished climbing out of the car, Miranda Carmichael barrelled out of the house. She was a petite woman, muscled like a gymnast, with a shock of brown hair that was graying early. Carmichael was known in the department for two things: single-handedly issuing about half of the department's speeding tickets every month, and her tomato-cucumber-and-onion sandwiches that left the refrigerator smelling like sweaty feet. Right then, she looked like she was about to spill her last tomato-cucumber-and-onion sandwich all over the driveway.

She hit the gravel with both feet—perfect dismount, a ten—and streaked towards them, already talking. "I've got them split up and in separate rooms, and Peterson's standing in the hallway where he can keep an eye on them. Jesus, God, did you see anybody else? The chief? The ME?" Here she paused, but mostly because, it seemed, she had run out of breath.

"Where's the body?"

Still sucking air, Carmichael jerked a thumb over her shoulder.

"Where? Living room? Bedroom?"

"By the river."

"Yeah?"

Carmichael nodded.

"How long have they been here?"

"The protesters? Days."

"Non-stop?"

"No. I mean, I don't know. You'll have to ask Foley when they got here, but I'd guess hours."

Somers didn't bother to reply. He glanced at Hazard, and Hazard shrugged.

"Tell Cravens we're checking it out."

"Wait," Carmichael called after them, a note of desperation in her voice. "You can't leave me here. Not with that woman."

Hazard raised an eyebrow to Somers.

Somers shrugged as they left Carmichael behind. "Turns out we can leave her."

"Who's she talking about?"

"I'm sure we'll find out. Whoever she is, you can talk to her."

Hazard frowned. "I don't think that's a good idea. You like to point out how rude I am—oh."

"See? I told you it's more fun to be an asshole."

Somers barely dodged the swat that Hazard directed at the back of his head.

In silence, they rounded the house and found a path that led down the sloping land and towards the river. While the front of the house enjoyed a lawn—dormant for the winter but obviously well kept—the back of the house surrendered to the native prairie. February wind stirred grass that came to Somers's waist. The grass whispered against Somers's coat. Bright sunlight gave each blade its own shadow, and the sky was ultramarine, so blue Somers thought he could kick off and go swimming. And God, he thought as he shivered, wouldn't that be cold.

The trail led them down to a sandy stretch of shore along the Grand Rivere, and at the water's edge, Sheriff Morris Bingham, senior, lay dead. Somers and Hazard paused together at the edge of the sand. Footprints—frantic footprints, left by terrified witnesses—had churned the sand, and it was obvious that no useful prints could be recovered. With a sigh, Somers started towards the body, followed by Hazard a moment later. They passed a folding camp table that was set with clay pigeons. Two rifles lay across the table, and another two had fallen.

"They were shooting for fun?" Hazard asked.

By then, Somers had reached the sheriff. He knelt down. By the end of his life, the sheriff's good looks had thinned and hardened into what some might call dignified but nobody would call handsome. He was a lean, whipcord man. It was in the eyes and nose that the resemblance with his son was strongest. The hair, too, although the sheriff's was salted heavily. Those features were ruined in death; the bullet had ripped away the forehead and nose and one eye. Sand crusted the wound, darkened by blood to the color of rust.

"Somebody moved him."

"Obviously."

Hazard squatted next to Somers. They studied the corpse together.

"He must have had his arms up," Somers said. He glanced around. "There, that's the fifth rifle, in the water there. He must have dropped it when he was shot. So he was taking aim. Maybe he had just fired. His attention was completely focused out there, and he wasn't paying any attention to what was behind him."

With the tip of a pen, Hazard pointed to specks of dried blood and sand on the sheriff's sleeves. He nodded. Then he pointed to the dead man's hand.

"But he didn't get any on his hands," Somers said. "That's odd."

"Murder," Hazard said.

"Maybe a gun went off accidentally. Maybe that's why Carmichael was so worked up—she's got somebody in hysterics because they shot the sheriff."

"Those two rifles," Hazard pointed to the ones in the sand, "fell off the table. The other two are still on the table. And the fifth one is in the river because the sheriff was holding it when he was killed. You got that much right."

"Gee, thanks."

"So what happened?"

"They freaked out. Look at the ground. They were running all over the place."

Hazard nodded.

"And the bullet?"

"Let's hope it's buried in the sand. We'll have to get the metal detectors." Somers considered the Grand Rivere's flow; ice skimmed the surface, and he shivered. "I fucking hate winter."

Standing, Hazard rotated, studying the landscape. Somers gave the body one last glance. The khaki uniform was the same. The brass star was the same.

"His hat."

"What?"

"He's missing his hat. That cattleman hat he always wore."

"Probably got knocked off and fell into the river. Look at this."

Somers glanced around for the hat and then gave his attention to Hazard.

"Up there," Hazard said, pointing to where a wooded bluff overlooked the river. "That's where they shot him from."

"I know you don't think it was an accident, but that doesn't mean it wasn't one of the people down here with him. Somebody could have put the gun to the back of his head and pulled the trigger. They don't need to be up in a tree."

"No."

"What do you mean?"

"I mean you're wrong." Hazard starting walking towards the bluff.

"Son of a bitch," Somers muttered, taking off after him. "Is it too much trouble to ask for an explanation? Or do I just have to take the great Emery Hazard at his word?"

"You have to take me at my word."

"Screw you."

A moment passed, and the only sound was the grass rushing against them. On Hazard's face, a reflective look flickered. "Well, you might be right."

"See?" In spite of himself, in spite of his best efforts, Somers puffed out his chest. Just a little. "We won't know until we get forensics."

"What? Oh, that? No, you're dead wrong about that. I meant you were right that it's more fun being an asshole."

"Was that a joke?"

Hazard lifted his chin and ignored him.

"No, seriously. Was that a genuine, Emery Hazard, no shitting around, joke?"

"The whole point of a joke is that you are shitting around."

"Stop the clock. Stop everything. Emery Hazard just made a joke."

Grimly, Hazard shook his head and kept walking. Somers, grinning, danced in front of him. "Hold on. Hold on. Just hold on for a second, all right. I want to savor this moment. I mean, it's the first time in the history of the world—"

Hazard, without breaking stride, planted a hand on Somers's chest and shoved. Somers stumbled into the waist-high grass. He fell backward, cushioned by the semi-frozen stalks, and burst out laughing. Picking himself up, Somers freed himself from the tangled grass and found the path again. Hazard had gone another ten yards without looking back.

"No blood spatter on the guns," Somers said as he caught up. "If they'd shot him from that close, there would have been blood on the barrel. Bone, hair, maybe more."

"See? You noticed it too."

"God, no. I guessed because you were so certain. Besides, the angle was all wrong"

Hazard kept walking.

"They could have wiped the gun clean."

Hazard grunted, but his eyes flickered as he processed this thought.

"You're enjoying this," Somers said, laughing again and plucking bits of grass from his hair.

"You're the one who's laughing."

"You are. You're practically smiling. Or as close as you ever get."

"It's a murder, Somers. Have some goddamn respect."

"See? Right there. The corner of your mouth always does that when you're in a good mood." Somers spun around so that he was face to face with Hazard and walking backward. He poked a finger into Hazard's chest. "You can't even help it. Look at you. You're trying to be grumpy. You're trying to mope. And you can't."

"What's your point? And get your finger off me before I break it."

What was Somers's point? His point was that he liked seeing Hazard like this. He liked the energy in Hazard's brutishly handsome face. He liked the way those scarecrow eyes sparked like hot metal. He liked everything about this man, every goddamn thing, and he liked seeing him happy. And that, Somers knew, anything close to that, would probably get him a sock on the jaw if he tried saying it.

So he settled for: "You like solving murders."

"I'm a detective. Now," Hazard planted a hand, shoved, and again Somers found himself tumbling into the grass. "Get out of my way."

The morning's frost, half-melted, soaked Somers's hair and face and hands, but he was laughing again. It was a good day. Well, for everybody but the sheriff. It was a great day.

Not because Nico was gone.

Damn, where had that come from?

Not wanting an answer, Somers scrambled after Hazard.

The stand of trees was old: big oaks, mostly, the ground growth sparse because the thick branches overhead swallowed most of the sunlight. Acorns littered the dirt, interspersed with patchy weeds that struggled to survive. Carefully, wordlessly, the two detectives separated and surveyed the area.

"Over here," Somers said. Ahead, at the line of trees, two cigarette butts lay at the base of an oak. They'd been smoked down to the filters, and they looked fresh—untouched by rain or snow. Stepping carefully, Somers moved closer, and then he stopped. "Prints."

Hazard joined him, equally careful to watch where he stepped until they stood shoulder to shoulder. The heat off Hazard was nice, especially today, with the February chill biting into Somers's lungs. They'd shared a bed once. Twice, actually. No monkey business, but—

—the heat of his skin, the bristled texture of his chest under Somers's hand, the way he smelled—

"What are you thinking?" Hazard asked.

Somers wanted to groan.

"Look," Hazard said, pointing down to the riverbank. On the slim strip of sand, the sheriff lay like a tiny khaki doll. "This would be a good place. Straight shot down there."

"Awfully nice of him to leave us some evidence." Somers studied the ocean of grass that flowed down the bluff. "He didn't come that way. So how'd he get here? And how'd he leave?"

"Let's find out."

The semi-frozen dirt beneath the trees had captured partial impressions of what looked like the same pair of shoes. The tread marks all matched, and they looked to be the same size. After a few more minutes of examination, Somers and Hazard agreed that they could move into the treeline. It only took a few more minutes before Hazard hallooed, and Somers picked a path over to him.

A break in the branches overhead allowed sunlight through the canopy, and that sunlight had warmed the ground here, turning the frozen dirt to mud. Tracks led in both directions.

"He came and went this way."

Nodding, Hazard followed the trajectory of the prints.

As they moved through the trees, the stand began to thin, and patches of blue and slate-gray emerged ahead of them. The bluff began to drop, and soon Somers could see that a bend in the Grand Rivere hugged the bluff. As the ground rolled down and the trees thinned, the icy expanse of the Grand Rivere came into view.

Here, instead of the sandy bank where the sheriff had fallen, the ground dropped abruptly into the river. A patch of grass along the bank had been torn away, and fresh mud stared up at them.

"Did you see anything else?" Hazard asked.

Somers shook his head. "Looks like he slipped."

"Looks like."

"Maybe a fishing boat with a small motor. But even something small, they might have heard."

"If they weren't too busy screaming their heads off."

"A canoe. Kayak."

Hazard hunkered down, examined the gouged earth, and said, "He slipped when he was leaving. It's deeper here, where his heel dug into the ground."

"Hope he broke his fucking ankle."

"Let's take pictures and bag the cigarettes. We'll have Cravens get casts of the prints."

Somers offered a mock salute. "You're smiling."

Hazard pushed past him without a word.

But he was. Not outright. But it was that perfectly controlled, perfectly hidden Emery Hazard smile that made Somers light up like a goddamn pinball machine.

Yep, things were perfect. Now all Somers had to do was help Hazard get his boyfriend back.

Trailing after his partner, Somers allowed himself a groan.

"There's that noise again," Hazard called back. "The one from the car. Do you hear it?"

CHAPTER FIVE

**FEBRUARY 11
SUNDAY
1:15 PM**

SOMERS RAISED AN EYEBROW as he stepped into the sheriff's home. Things had changed since he'd been here as a child. Things had definitely changed. What he remembered from his boyhood, when he had occasionally visited with his parents, and from his teenage years when he had come to hang out with the sheriff's son, was darkness. Not that the house had been poorly lit, but simply the abundance of dark wood, dark textiles, and dark furnishings that had turned the old house into a warren of cramped rooms.

Now, the whole place seemed to have opened up. The dark stains had been stripped, the bare wood lightly varnished, and plaster ceilings ripped out to give height to the rooms. Walls that Somers remembered were gone, and in their place, rooms flowed together, giving the space a harmonious, unified ambiance.

It must have cost a fortune.

Carmichael fiddled with her belt as she stood in the center of the living room. When she saw them, she took a nervous half-step. "Is the chief here?"

"On her way, I think," Somers said. "Lloyd and Hoffmeister are down with the sheriff now, and Gross and Norman are on forensics."

Wahredua, too small to support its own forensic unit, relied on its well-trained detectives and officers to collect evidence. Hazard and Somerset had documented what they could until the first uniformed officers had arrived, and then they'd left instructions for the men to continue the work. Somers, for his own part, trusted his fellow cops to do their job. He'd worked with most of them for years. Hazard, on the other hand, still looked like he was sucking on a lemon.

A high-pitched wail came from somewhere upstairs, and Somers raised an eyebrow.

"You guys caught this one, right?" Carmichael asked.

"Yeah, I mean, Cravens—"

"All right. All right. Then you can handle her. I'll stay here. I'll keep an eye on the ones who are down here. But I'm not saying another word to her."

"Who?"

The scream gained in pitch and intensity. Hazard worked a finger in his ear, and Somers waited for something—the wine glasses in the hutch, those would be nice—to shatter.

"Moody," Carmichael said.

"Oh," Somers said.

"Oh," Hazard said.

They exchanged a look. Hazard, as far as Somers knew, had only met Eunice Moody on his return to Wahredua—through Nico and Nico's involvement with Wahredua's burgeoning art community, if Somers understood correctly. Somers, on the other hand, had known Moody for as long as he could remember. She was a fixture on all of Wahredua's ladies organizations: the Methodist Ladies' Quilt and Supper Circle, the Dore Country Club etiquette board, the Welsh Hotel's monthly *fromage* tribute, and the Spring Promenade. In her own way, Moody was as intricately tied into high society as Somers's own mother, and like Grace Elaine Somerset, Moody was much more dangerous—and much more intelligent—than she seemed.

"I guess we'll start with her," Somers said.

Somers led the way towards the noise, and Hazard followed him up the stairs. Hazard looked deep in thought, and twice he missed a step.

"You all right?"

"What?"

"Are you all right?"

"Yeah. You're taking the lead on this, right?"

"I mean, I guess, but—"

"Yeah, perfect."

But that didn't seem to solve anything because Hazard clunked into another step before they reached the landing.

Roy Peterson, the skinniest black man Somers had ever known, stood at the end of a hallway, in perfect position to keep watch on three doors that stood closed. Slumped against the wall, Peterson made a half-hearted effort to straighten when he saw them. Peterson, a veteran on the force, had climbed as far as he wanted to climb. Impressing a pair of young detectives—or anyone else, for that matter—had dropped off his list.

"Like God gave a hurricane lungs," Peterson said, nodding at the closest door. The noise, if anything, seemed even shriller than before.

"Carmichael was pretty rattled."

"Miss Moody took out a clump of her hair," Peterson said, and he mimed ripping the hair out by the roots while he made a popping noise. "Carmichael's fault, I guess. She told Miss Moody that she had to shut up, and then she took a step towards her with her nightstick. Just trying to scare her, I guess. Well, Carmichael got more than she bargained for. Another minute and she'd have been an eggshell."

"Carmichael going to do something about it?"

"Nah. She's tough, but she's not dumb. She knows she made a mistake, and she's not going to double down on it."

Hazard interrupted, his voice harder than usual. "Who else do you have?"

"That room's got Beverly Flinn, the sheriff's administrative assistant. We used to call them secretaries, but that's gone. Nobody's a secretary anymore. Nobody's anything like a lowly secretary anymore." Peterson paused, as though chewing over his last words and savoring them. "The other's got Grant McAtee." Something moved in his dark eyes. "You know McAtee?"

"He's a deputy," Somers said. "Right?"

Peterson nodded. That knowing look lingered in his eyes, though.

"All right," Somers said slowly, glancing at the door. He'd save his questions for later.

"That's all?" Hazard asked.

"Downstairs, Carmichael's got the doctor in the kitchen. Oh, and she's keeping an eye on Randy Scott and Lionel Arras."

Somers whistled.

"Who are they?" Hazard asked.

"Rich men. Very rich. Sheriff had some powerful friends."

Peterson nodded, easing himself back into a slump.

"Let's see what they can tell us," Somers said.

Hazard looked grim, but he pulled out a digital recorder and nodded.

Moody's screams didn't stop when they opened the door. Instead, the noise hit Somers full force—a hurricane, that's what Peterson had said, and it felt like that. Eunice Moody was a large woman, large but proportionate, and she wore—as she always did—a combination of skirt and blouse and cardigan that managed to present her ample breasts like hens on a serving platter. She was at least as old as Somers's mother, he knew, but Moody's face was seamless under a snowfall of face powder.

Tears had tracked through the powder, leaving rivulets and white clumps, and Moody's eyes were huge and red. She surged towards Somers, wrapping her arms around him and crushing him to her bosom, where for what felt like an eternity Somers was lost in an expanse of sagging, lavender-scented flesh.

"John-Henry, sweetheart," she managed before breaking into tears again. "You don't know how horrible today has been, I can't—" She paused, releasing Somers—he sucked in a grateful breath—and eying Hazard. "Oh."

"Moody," Hazard said, jerking his chin in a nod.

"You brought him?" she said to Somers.

"He's my partner, Miss Moody," Somers said.

Moody said nothing. She seemed to have forgotten her former grief, and now she watched Hazard, her lips pursed, her eyes narrowed, her hands pinching Somers's shoulders.

"Miss Moody, we'd like to talk to you about what happened today."

Moody surged away from Somers, as though floating away on a strong current, and settled into a chair. The room—it was a bedroom, impersonal and spare—didn't offer anywhere else to sit except the bed, and so Somers stayed standing. Moody, for her part, had gone back to sobbing, although the wailing, thankfully, had ceased. It was like someone had pressed play, and the tape was rolling again: Miss Moody, grief-stricken, A-side.

"Miss Moody—"

"Oh, it was terrible. Terrible, John-Henry. You can't even imagine. We were having the most wonderful time. Really, we were. Even with those horrible people out in front, we were enjoying ourselves." She dabbed at her eyes. "Do you know how rare that is, how genuinely rare? For people like us, everything is work. You know how it is. Your dear mother carries the same cross."

"Good Lord," Hazard muttered under his breath.

Moody heard him—she scuttled on her seat like she'd taken an arrow to the ass—but she didn't acknowledge him. "Your dear mother, yes. So you know how it is to have a moment, to breathe free of the masks we all wear," long, pink nails rested at the corners of her eyes, "to speak among friends," the nails shifted to the corners of her mouth, lipstick and nail polish matching perfectly, "to throw off the strictures and conventions that bind our breasts," and the nails clutched at her plunging neckline, dimpling an ocean of creamy skin.

"You were fucking," Hazard said. "You can just say you were fucking."

This time, it wasn't an arrow to the ass. It was a flaming arrow to the ass.

"I absolutely will not hear that kind of speech," Moody said, struggling to pull herself to her feet. "I'm a decent, law-abiding woman, a God-fearing woman, a respectable woman, and I won't be talked to that way by a—by a—"

"By a faggot?"

"Come on," Somers said.

"By a degenerate," Moody said. "By a cruel, heartless beast who's never known human kindness, who took a lovely, beautiful boy and shattered him, by a Vandal, by a Visigoth, striking down in Rome the flower of youth—"

"I'm confused," Hazard said. "You were the one freeing your breasts of strictures, pulling off masks, all of that, which sounds a hell of a lot like fucking, but I'm the moral degenerate. Is that right? Because if I didn't get that right, you should go ahead and explain it again for me. At length."

"All right," Somers said. "That's enough. From both of you. Miss Moody, the arts council has more gay people on it than straight. You get along fine with all of them, and you're just trying to bait Detective Hazard because you're angry about Nico. Is that right?"

Moody sniffed, turning in her chair to present her profile, and didn't answer.

"And you're dead set on being a dick as usual."

Hazard glared, and his mouth compressed into a line.

"So let's hear it, Miss Moody. What happened?"

"I won't talk if he's in here."

"You absolutely will talk while Detective Hazard is here. Either now or in two hours, or six hours, or eight hours, or in a month if we have to keep you here that long. No makeup. No mirrors. No hairspray."

"You beast," Moody hissed, her long pink nails moving to her jawline. "You wouldn't dare."

"Out with it. What happened?"

"Fine. Since you've resorted to threats and brutality, I'll cooperate."

"That would be lovely."

"We were here for a meeting." She drew out the word, pinning Hazard with an icy gaze. "Away from the hoi polloi. A meeting where we could talk frankly, which is what I was trying to express to you earlier when I mentioned the unbinding of my breast, and which is, in its own way, allegorical for a reintroduction of the nurturing, maternal milk for—"

"Yes, yes, allegorical. Exactly. What were you meeting about?"

"I was trying to tell you. We were meeting to discuss the recall petition."

Somers's mind moved quickly. Sheriff Bingham's administrative assistant, a deputy, Moody, and two of the richest men in Dore County. It was easy to reach the conclusion: this was Bingham's inner circle as he fought the recall petition. These were the people he had called together to help him in his hour of need.

"You're helping him with the recall petition?" Hazard said. "Why?"

Moody flushed; it was a blotchy, ugly color, and she snaked sideways in her seat to avoid looking at Hazard.

"You're not his type," Hazard said. "You're wealthy, and you're old blood in these parts, so that might mean you'd back Bingham. But you're on the arts council, too, so you're too liberal for the sheriff's platform. You don't have any connection to Bingham by blood or marriage, not that I know, and you're not young enough or thin enough for him to be sleeping with you."

Blotches spread across Moody's face.

For hell's sake, Somers thought. For hell's sake, couldn't that man keep his mouth shut for one minute?

But to Somers's surprise, Moody responded, although she directed her words to Somers. "It's true. I'm not fanatical about Sheriff Bingham. Lukewarm might be the best way to describe my feelings for that man, God rest him. But at the moment, every decent citizen in Warhedua has a vested interest in keeping Sheriff Bingham in office."

"Really?" Somers said. "Why?"

"I'm not an idiot, John-Henry. I know where you and your . . . partner stand. I'm well aware of your involvement in that horrible murder and where your loyalty lies."

"Only one loyalty, Miss Moody: law. That's all."

She sniffed; some of her color had come down, but her nails had gone back to the blouse and the plunging neckline, and they rose and fell restlessly. "Do you know who Dennis Rutter is?"

"The Rutter clan?"

Moody nodded sharply.

The Rutter clan were one of the more prominent white trash families in Dore County—at least, that's how Somers's father had once described them. They numbered, at best guess, well over a hundred, and that didn't count the half- and step- and bastard children spawned in the sprawling Rutter compound. Almost a decade before, just before Somers had joined the force, the Dore County Sheriff's Department had tried to breach the Rutter compound after the Rutter family turned away the Department of Social

Services. Turned away being a very generous euphemism, since what Somers understood was that Pappy Rutter had tried to blow off the poor woman's head and had, instead, shredded his own tin mailbox.

Breaching the compound, though, had been a hollow victory because the Rutter clan had vanished. They'd retreated somewhere into the hills on their property, and they'd stayed hidden until the sheriff's department had finally thrown in the towel and slunk back to Wahredua. It had been a decisive victory for the Rutter clan, and since then, they'd grown bolder and more flagrant in their disregard for the sheriff—or for any authority.

A dark chord thrummed inside Somers. Hadn't he read something about one of the Rutter boys? Hadn't he already seen that name somewhere in connection with the sheriff?

"Dennis," Somers said. "Which one is he?"

"One of the few," Moody said, her mouth quirking and threatening an avalanche of face powder, "who doesn't look like he crawled out of a goat. And, for that matter, doesn't smell like he was raised by a goat. By all reports, he might even pass for human—that is, until he opens his mouth and starts spouting all the Ozark Volunteer nonsense. Oh, yes," she said, when Somers's eyebrows shot up, "the whole Rutter clan is tangled with that nest of vipers, and Dennis more than most. He's their candidate."

"Candidate?" Hazard asked. The hatred in his voice was raw; Somers felt the same. The Supreme Justification of God in the Ozark Citizen Volunteers—which everybody just called the Ozark Volunteers—was an inbred neo-Nazi knock-off: white power, homophobia, anti-government, the whole bag.

Eunice Moody's eyes didn't leave Somers's face. "You haven't heard? He's their candidate for sheriff. I'm surprised you haven't seen the signs."

"There's no election for sheriff," Somers said, but his mouth had gone strangely dry, and he had the vague sense of ionized air, of ozone, like lightning was about to strike the tip of his tongue.

"There will be now. There may well have been one anyway if the recall petition had been successful."

"But they already had signs up," Hazard said. "Before the petition was submitted."

"They're very confident. And they're the reason I decided to help the sheriff. The lesser of two evils, you understand." Her eyes narrowed. Fine lines spiderwebbed through the face powder. "My dear, I really thought you'd heard."

"What?" Somers said, and goddamn it, that lightning was about to strike, was about to fry him. "What's the punchline?"

"His campaign manager. It's Naomi."

CHAPTER SIX

**FEBRUARY 11
SUNDAY
1:36 PM**

NAOMI. THE NAME HIT like Zeus throwing sidearm.

Naomi Malsho.

Hazard felt a tingle, like he'd been singed, but the name had hit Somers dead-on. Somers stood there, his mouth slightly agape, as though trying to keep his tongue from falling out of his mouth. Then he roused himself, his jaw snapped shut, and he swore under his breath.

Naomi Malsho was Somers's sister-in-law. She was also, in Hazard's opinion, a cold, calculating bitch. Grade A bitch. Top of the class bitch. She'd gone off to law school somewhere prestigious. She'd gotten a first-class education. She'd come back, and she'd put those abilities to work for the Ozark Volunteers. She was rabid; that was the only word Hazard could come up with, rabid, because if she was rabid, there was an explanation that might justify her behavior. She was sick. She was diseased. She wasn't sound of mind. Otherwise, if she wasn't rabid, she was just evil.

A thought floated at the bottom of Hazard's brain. A distant worry. Naomi had arranged for Somers to be caught cheating on his wife. Hazard had blackmailed her into revealing the truth. That had facilitated the first steps of Somers's reconciliation with Cora—and Hazard ignored the sudden clench of jealousy, like a fist tightening around his heart. For months, Naomi had disappeared. Now she was back. And Hazard's first, brightest thought was, what if she told Somers?

It took Hazard a moment to realize that Moody was talking.

"—for us to help him."

"The sheriff?" Somers queried.

"Yes, of course. Who else?"

"Not his assistant?"

"No, Sheriff Bingham invited me personally. I don't know about the others. As I was saying, normally I wouldn't have supported the sheriff, but he made his case quite plainly: if the petition was successful, the Ozark Volunteers would pin the sheriff's badge on Rutter, and the rest of us be damned. That was enough for me to put aside old prejudices."

"Can you walk us through today's events?" Somers said.

"Events." Moody's lips pinched together. "That's a very polite word. Brunch at ten. Clay pigeons at eleven. Murder at twelve. Little bullets on the program, something like that."

"Is that what you did today?"

Moody pressed pink nails to her temples. "Yes, John-Henry. That's what we did."

"Do you normally shoot clay pigeons?" Hazard asked, ignoring Somers flash of anger.

"Don't be ridiculous."

"But you did today?"

"I didn't. I refuse even to touch a gun. I hate them. Monstrous things. Monstrous. But the sheriff insisted on talking strategy, and he couldn't stand being in the house. Those were his words. He couldn't stand it."

"Why?"

"Those people out there, of course."

"They bothered him?"

"He never said so, but isn't it obvious?"

Hazard ignored the question; very few things were obvious just because someone assumed they were, and he'd trained himself to avoid that trap as much as possible. "Did the sheriff often shoot guns while planning?"

"I don't know."

"So you stood down there while they fired guns and did—what? Nothing? Stand there?"

"John-Henry, this is ridiculous. He's talking to me like I'm—well, I just don't know exactly."

"Answer the question," Hazard said. "What were you doing?"

"What does one do at a river? I don't know. I walked. I talked. The sheriff wanted me to load those clay things in the launcher but I absolutely refused." She pulled her nails away from her head long enough to waggle them, displaying her reason for refusing.

"And when we fingerprint those guns, we won't find your prints on any of them?"

"This is unacceptable, John-Henry. It's absolutely unacceptable. I won't sit here and be treated like this."

"Are we going to find your prints? Because if you tried to wipe them down, if you think you got them all, trust me: you missed something. And when we find them, we'll drag you down to the station, and then we'll really get going. So let me ask you again, which rifle did you touch? Which one did you pick up? Which one did you—"

"None of them," Moody shrieked, her hands flying away from her temples, her fingers splayed with rage. "I didn't touch any of those damn things, and you can—you can—you can just shove it." She sank back, trembling, her eyes liquid. Where the tears touched the corners of her eyes, they clotted the thick powder.

Hazard took a breath. There. He'd finally gotten something honest out of her.

"We'll go back to the beginning," Somers said, shooting Hazard a glare. "Take a deep breath, Miss Moody. Detective Hazard won't be asking any more questions, I can promise you. Just take a deep breath. Here." Somers produced, of all things, a handkerchief and passed it to the woman. She touched each eye once and then clutched it to her massive, heaving chest.

"I don't have to put up with this, John-Henry."

"I know."

"I'm a good citizen, John-Henry."

"I know, Miss Moody."

"I do my duty, John-Henry. I do my duty. But this man—this man—"

"We're very grateful, Miss Moody. I'm very grateful. Why don't you start at the beginning of the day? Just tell us what you remember. Anything strange? Anything unusual?"

But there hadn't been anything strange or unusual, or at least nothing Moody could remember. Hazard listened, parsing her words, processing her account, but he couldn't find anything to poke a hole in.

Moody's account gave them nothing. Absolutely nothing. She went on in detail about the fruit served at brunch. She raved about a shrimp crepe that had been recommended by Lionel Arras. She tried, until Hazard cut her off, to gossip about Beverly Flinn's choice in wardrobe. And as she droned on, Hazard found himself thinking about Nico. Nico had always said that Moody was fun. That Moody was wickedly clever. That Moody was the life of the party. Sitting there, listening to the catty old woman, Hazard started to wonder. Had he been right all along? Would it be better if he and Nico split up? If they stayed together, was this where Hazard would end up, moving in the same circles as Eunice Moody? For hell's sake, Hazard would rather slit his own wrists.

"That was when we got down to the river," Moody said, and her words drew Hazard back into the conversation. "The men set up everything, while we ladies stayed back and enjoyed the view." Thick eyebrows waggled suggestively.

"What were they setting up?"

"All of it. The table, the guns, that machine that throws the clay discs. Everything. They brought it down from the house."

"All right."

"Well, it didn't take that long, and then we had to put on those horrible earmuffs that are supposed to protect your hearing. As far as I'm concerned, it didn't make any difference. I still jumped a mile every time one of them took a shot."

"How did they do?" Hazard asked.

"They're old men. They're none of them what they used to be. Except Grant, I suppose. He's not so old. And not too hard on the eyes, is he?" For the first time, Moody seemed to fully acknowledge Hazard, and a razor of a smirk crossed her mouth. "Anyway, they missed more than they hit. They drank. They laughed. Well, Lionel and Grant laughed. Randy and the sheriff laughed too, but they didn't mean it, and the more they missed, the less they laughed."

"Were they competing with each other?" Somers said.

"Of course. You can't put two men in the same room for five minutes without them trying to figure out which one is top dog."

"And who was the top dog?"

The question seemed to take Moody by surprise, and for a moment, her voice dropped out of airy playfulness. "The sheriff, of course. He never let anyone forget he was top dog." And then, like a woman dragging rocks up a mountain, Moody tried to lift her voice. "Anyway, we mustn't speak ill of the dead."

"Who else felt that way about the sheriff?"

"What way?"

"That he always had to be top dog."

"You know Morris Bingham. Everybody who ever stepped on his shadow knew the way he was. And I'll tell you something, it wasn't all bad. Sure, he liked to throw his weight around. And I know there have been complaints. I'm not saying he walks on water, no sir, but sometimes you need a man who's not afraid to have a backbone. Say what you like about

Morris, he had a backbone of steel, and that's what we were going to need, especially with that Rutter boy trying to slither into the job."

"Go on," Somers said. "What else happened?"

"Well, nothing. Oh," Moody broke off, tittering with nerves, and her pink nails fluttered. "I mean, except for the shooting."

"Can you describe that?"

"Well, I wasn't looking at the sheriff when it happened. Thank God, John-Henry. Thank the Lord Jesus because I'm going to have nightmares as it is. Nightmares to last a body a lifetime."

"Where were you looking?" Hazard said.

"Randy had just blasted one of those clay pigeons out of the air. He was pretty proud of himself, strutting around like a peacock, just a boy again."

"And then?" Somers said.

"I heard—" Moody paused. The pink nails rimmed her mouth like gaudy, horrible teeth. "I heard it. When it—I heard it. Like dropping a cantaloupe. And I looked over, and he was already falling. I could see the back of his head. I could see it, where it—And I started screaming." She paused. Her fingers flexed fractionally. The tips of those pink nails left white half-moons around her lips as she pulled her hands away. "There was so much blood," she said, obviously fighting for a normal tone. "I'm sorry, I really can't say anything else."

"Did you touch the body?" Hazard said.

"Touch him?" Moody recoiled in her seat.

"Someone moved the sheriff's body after he was shot. Was it you?"

"No, I couldn't—" Her eyes dropped, her shoulders curved in, and her face suddenly seemed hollow. She barely seemed to register their presence. "I couldn't even look."

"Do you know who did move him?"

"Beverly," she licked her lips, and the tip of her tongue came away white with the powder on her face. "Beverly was frantic. She thought maybe that there was a chance."

"What happened next?"

"June—Dr. Hayashi—ran to the house."

"She didn't stay to help?"

Moody snorted, and she dabbed at her eyes again with Somers's handkerchief. "Help? There wasn't anything to do for him."

"Nobody had a phone?"

"I did." Moody produced a clutch, opened it, and withdrew a plastic brick. The phone might have been from the 1990s. "I called 911, of course, but June didn't know that. She ran inside. To call."

"What time did this all happen?"

"I don't know." Moody frowned. Crevasses appeared in the glacial face powder. "Close to noon, I think. No one wanted luncheon because we'd eaten so late, but I remember wishing I'd brought something to drink and checking my watch. That was before—" She swallowed; the crevasses deepened. "Just a few minutes before it all happened."

"All right. Did you see who shot the sheriff?"

"No."

"Nothing?"

"Nothing. I don't even remember looking around, although I'm sure I must have. I was in something of a state." As though reminded of her earlier performance, Moody gave a warbling cry of despair. Hazard cringed; it sounded like the hurricane was about to get its lungs back.

"Anything else you remember? What did the deputy and Mr. Scott and Mr. Arras do?"

"They stayed with us. Grant, sweet boy, was so worried about me. He tried to carry me inside. Did you know that poor young man has a bad back? Such a shame. And at his age."

"Just about anybody would have a bad back if they—" Hazard was forced to stop when Somers's elbow dug into his gut.

"Thank you, Miss Moody," Somers said. "Once we've finished talking to everyone else, we'll make sure you get home safely."

They hadn't made it out of the room before the wailing started in earnest. Hazard, rubbing his bruised ribs, made sure to shut the door on his way out. Moody only screamed louder.

CHAPTER SEVEN

**FEBRUARY 11
SUNDAY
2:02 PM**

WITH A NOD FOR PETERSON, Hazard bumped open the next door and stepped into a smaller bedroom that doubled, to judge by the look of it, as a craft room. Someone had squeezed a sewing machine between the bed and the wall, and plastic storage totes stood four high on the bed, filled with ribbons and fabric and thread. More space on the bed was taken up by stuffed animals. Not just bears: there were giraffes, penguins, leopards, even what looked like a meerkat. The mound of animals had a grim, suffocated look, as though the poor things were trying to escape their own mass.

Seated at the edge of the mountain of plush toys was a small woman. She had bleached hair cut short, jangling earrings, and a stretchy, synthetic top that looked a few sizes too small. Although her face was smooth, her hands gave away her age: they were wrinkled, with the first age spots beginning to appear. Both fists were balled and rested on her knees. She looked like she wanted all those stuffed animals to dogpile on top of her, like she wouldn't mind just staying there, buried under all the plush.

"Miss Flinn?" Somers said, squeezing past Hazard, close enough that Hazard caught a whiff of him, of whatever the hell it was that Somers wore, that smell of sea-salt drying on bronzed skin, of pungent, crushed amber. Close enough that the smooth, golden skin of Somers's neck was at the perfect height, where Hazard could bend down, where he could press his lips against it, draw the skin between his teeth, where he could bite until he heard Somers moan.

What was wrong, Hazard thought. What was wrong with him, that he would think something like that, right now? He was on a case. He had a job to do. He should be thinking about—

—Nico—

—the murder, about the witnesses, about anything except how Somers would taste, anything except that. Jesus, Hazard told himself. Just Jesus. You're sick. A real sicko.

"Mrs. Flinn," Beverly said, interrupting his thoughts. "My husband is deceased."

"I'm sorry," Somers said.

"It's ok. No, really, it is. The sheriff was so sweet when it happened. It was a terrible accident, and the sheriff—he made sure I was taken care of. I could have ended up on the street, you know? I didn't have any skills. Not even typing. But he made sure I was taken care of."

"Mrs. Flinn—"

"Please," she said, bouncing to her feet, extending a hand, staring at her fists, and suddenly flummoxed. She dropped her hands slowly. "Call me Beverly."

Somers smiled. That smile, that goddamn smile. He could smile at a nun, Hazard thought, and her bra would probably explode. That was the kind of smile it was. And it worked. It always worked. Beverly Flinn was smiling back.

"Beverly, I understand you're the sheriff's administrative assistant."

Beverly's smile turned down at the corners. "That's a mouthful. Sheriff Bingham calls me—called me his secretary. He was old-fashioned that way."

"Do you normally work weekends?"

"No, I'm not—this isn't work."

"You and the sheriff were friends?"

"I hope he'd say so. Friendly, at least. He asked me to help him. With the petition, I mean."

"What kind of boss was the sheriff?"

"Old-fashioned," she repeated, her smile strengthening. "I mean, he wanted everything done as efficiently as possible. That never changes, no matter who you work for. But he liked me to wear a skirt and heels. And he had expectations."

"Sexually?" Hazard said. As soon as the word was out of his mouth, he regretted it. Somers's shoulders slumped.

"No," Beverly said, her face pinking. "He—we were always very professional."

"What do you mean, expectations?" Somers asked.

"Little things. Old-fashioned things. I don't know, it's hard to think of examples. He liked me to make him lunch. I'd bring him a sandwich and chips, or I'd make a casserole. Something like that. And he liked things on a routine, you know."

It sounded to Hazard like Sheriff Bingham had been a general asshole, inside and out of the office.

"You didn't mind those things?" Somers asked.

"What? Oh. No. It was all pretty familiar, I'm afraid."

"Where were you working before?"

"Oh, I wasn't working. My husband, I mean. Now there was a man who liked a schedule. Whiskey and soda at 5:30, right when he came in the door. Dinner at 6:30. Dishes done by 7:00." Beverly raised her fists again, seemingly unaware of her movement, and shrugged. "Trust me, if I could handle Michael Flinn, I could handle the sheriff."

"And you didn't mind working overtime?"

"It wasn't work," Beverly said patiently. "I was volunteering."

"To help the sheriff fight the petition?"

"Yes."

"Why?"

For the first time, Beverly blinked. She suddenly seemed to realize that her fists were floating above her legs, and she brought them down so quickly that they thudded against her knees. "What do you mean?"

"I mean, why would you help him?"

"Because—well, I suppose because I thought he was a good man."

Even Hazard, with his limited skills at reading people, could tell that Beverly was scrambling for an answer. Somers didn't show anything on his face. His voice was as smooth as ever. His smile, if anything, only grew warmer. That poor nun's panties would have been incinerated in front of that smile, and fuck Somers for smiling like that.

"Is that true?" Somers said.

Beverly's expression crumpled, and she shook her head.

"Why were you here on the weekend helping the sheriff?"

"Because—because I couldn't tell him no." Her eyes came up, darting between their faces before she dropped her head. "I need this job."

"Did he threaten you?"

"Oh God, no."

"Did he imply that you'd lose your job if you didn't volunteer to help with the petition?"

"No, no. You don't understand. It's not—it's nothing like that. It's just the way he was. I couldn't say no, I just couldn't. I'm terrible at things like that. I know—" She laughed, but it sounded more like a sob, and she brought one fist up to the corner of her eye. "Michael said I was a coward.

He knew I was a coward. And I am. He was right. I could never say no to the sheriff because I'm such a spineless coward." She doubled over, resting her face on her fists, and let out a long, watery breath. "Oh my gosh, I told myself I wouldn't cry. I told myself."

"That's all right," Somers said. "Really, it's all right. You can cry. You can scream. Hey, if you can scream louder than Moody, everybody'll chip in and buy you a trophy."

That made Beverly laugh, and she lifted her head, wiping at her cheeks with her fists. As she straightened, a necklace slipped out from under her collar. Awkwardly, without uncurling her fingers, Beverly jammed it back into her shirt.

"What's that?" Somers said.

"Nothing."

"Those are the masks, right?" He gestured at the hidden necklace. "Like at a theater."

Beverly flushed. "It's not anything, really." Flushing deeper, Beverly struggled to hold back words, and then they burst out. "Yes. I mean, it's what you said. The theater masks. It's just—I liked theater. In high school, you know, and I still do a show now and then. Community theater." She laughed, some of the color leaving her face. "We do our shows out of the community center, so I guess I haven't come very far. That's what Michael said, anyway."

"He didn't like you doing theater?"

"He didn't like me doing anything."

When Somers spoke again, he seemed to be choosing his words carefully.

"And the sheriff?"

"Oh, yes. He was nice about it. He didn't like theater, I don't think, but he came to a few of my shows. I even caught him tapping his foot once. *Annie.*" She covered a smile with one hand. "He had the soundtrack locked in his desk."

Hazard fought and lost to keep an eyebrow from shooting up. Morris Bingham, who looked like a dried piece of leather and had just about as much goodness and grace, had liked Little Orphan Annie. It was like finding out Hitler loved dogs, and through the pounding headache, Hazard felt a wave of vertigo. Had Hitler loved dogs? He'd read something like that once. He thought, at least, he'd read that.

"Can you walk us through what happened today?" Somers asked.

Her story matched, in all the important places, Moody's, and as Beverly recounted the series of events, Hazard's brain whirred, assembling, processing, analyzing, disassembling, and then all over again. The morning had started with brunch, followed by moving their gathering down to the river, where they had taken turns shooting. Beverly promised them she hadn't touched a gun. Like Moody, she had been distracted by Randall Scott's victory dance and hadn't seen who had shot the sheriff. As she reached this portion of the story, Beverly collapsed into dry, wracking sobs.

"Do you remember what time this happened?"

"Just—just around noon," she hiccuped.

"You're sure?"

Beverly nodded. "Lionel kept making jokes about drinking. He said that he only drank after noon, and he had just checked his watch and made a point of saying that he was heading up to the house when it—when it happened."

"No mimosas at brunch?" Somers asked with a gentle smile.

"No, nothing like that. We had to plan, you see. We had to keep things sharp."

"But the sheriff insisted on going down to the river to shoot."

"I don't know," Beverly said, shrugging, her closed fists bouncing. "Honestly. He said he wanted to have fun. He said we didn't have to be boring just because the work was boring."

"He thought the work was boring? When he was fighting to keep his job?"

"I don't think—" Beverly cut off, her eyes hazy as she considered something. "I don't think he ever believed it would really happen. For the sheriff, sometimes the rest of the world didn't matter."

"How do you mean?"

"Take today. He made all of us come over to help fight the petition, and then he drags us out into the cold to shoot. Miss Moody and Dr. Hayashi and I didn't want to shoot. I don't think Lionel did either, although he wouldn't say that in front of Randy and Grant and the sheriff. But that didn't stop the sheriff from marching us all down there. Thank goodness I brought a heavy coat."

"We noticed that the body had been moved."

Nodding, Beverly raised her fists to her cheeks as more tears slipped out. "I couldn't believe it. Even seeing him. Even seeing that hole—even seeing the back of his head, I couldn't believe it. I thought maybe I could do something. I don't know what I thought. And now, sitting here, I know how stupid that was. But I was honestly out of my mind. And anyway, he was dead. There was nothing I could do. There was nothing anyone could do.

Dr. Hayashi ran all the way back to the house to get her bag, but it didn't matter."

"I'm sorry, did you say Dr. Hayashi came back to the house for her medical bag?"

"Yes. Isn't that what she told you?"

"We haven't talked to her yet. Why did she come back to the house?"

"I told you: her bag. She was going to try to help the sheriff."

Hazard resisted the urge to look at Somers. Any doctor—anybody with two eyes—would have known that Sheriff Bingham was beyond the reach of mortal help. Moody had said that the doctor had gone back to the house to call for help. So why had Beverly assumed it was to get her medical kit?

"Is there anything else you can tell us?" Somers asked. "Anything strange you noticed, however small?"

Beverly spread her arms; her earrings jangled as she shook her head.

"I think we'll just—" Somers began.

"Was the sheriff wearing gloves?" Hazard asked.

"What?" Beverly asked.

"Gloves. On his hands." Hazard held up his own hand to demonstrate.

"No. I don't think so."

"What about his hat? That big cattleman hat he always wore."

"I don't know." Beverly screwed up her face. "I thought he was wearing it. He always wore it, just like you said. Why? What's happened to it?"

Hazard didn't answer. Somers glanced at him, as though waiting for more, and then he started again, "We'll just be a little longer, Beverly. Once we've finished taking statements, we'll see if we can't get you all home."

Beverly nodded. She slumped back, almost disappearing into the plush mound of giraffes and elephants and lions. As the tension began to drain from her body, Hazard snapped out a final question.

"What's in your hands?"

Beverly jerked upright. Her eyelids shot up like shades on a broken cord, and her gaze was riveted to Hazard.

"Open your hands," Hazard said.

Wordlessly, she released her fists. Her fingers uncurled slowly, stiffly, as though she suffered from long and crippling arthritis. And when her hands lay open, a piece of bloodstained cotton sat on one palm.

"It's my handkerchief," she said, her voice so thin you could have folded it up in a piece of paper. "I just—his face, there was so much blood, and I—"

Somers sighed, and for some reason Hazard couldn't understand, he shot Hazard a dirty look. "We'll have to take that, Mrs. Flinn." And he produced a plastic evidence envelope and had her drop the cloth inside.

The last thing Hazard saw as they closed the door was Beverly Flinn staring at empty hands, still looking like she wanted those stuffed animals to topple over and bury her alive.

CHAPTER EIGHT

FEBRUARY 11
SUNDAY
2:30 PM

YOU'RE LUCKY HE'S HERE."

"Who? Peterson?"

"Yes, Peterson."

"Because he's standing watch?"

"Because, you big idiot, if he weren't here I'd be kicking your ass."

Hazard's eyes narrowed. "You're angry."

For a moment, Somers looked incapable of speech. Then he pitched the evidence bag at Peterson and said, his voice mangled with some emotion Hazard couldn't quite pin down, "I'm not angry, all right?"

"What are you talking about? You're definitely angry"

Blowing out a breath, Somers shook his head. "I'm not angry."

"You're angry. I know when you're angry."

"Ree, you couldn't tell which way the wind was blowing if it spit in your face. I'm telling you I'm not angry at you. I'm angry at me for not seeing that. Her hands. I should have seen it."

Neither man spoke. Peterson, tucking away the evidence bag, watched them with hooded eyes—interested, but a man with no horse in the race.

"So you are angry."

The red faded from Somers's cheeks, and he laughed and started toward the final door.

"You said it," Hazard said. "You said you were angry."

"Yeah, Ree."

"If you don't like how I do my job—"

"Oh, sweet Jesus." Somers drilled a finger into Hazard's shoulder. "Really?"

"I just think that if you're angry because I saw something that was obvious, even to most untrained observers, and you—"

"Do you want to kiss?"

Hazard tried to swallow, but someone had filled his throat with rocks. He managed to say, "What?"

"Kiss and make up. Is that what this is about? Peterson, is that what this is about?"

Peterson had the wisdom of years; he raised both hands in surrender and didn't answer.

Hazard's jaw was working, but no noise was coming out.

"Is that a yes?"

"You're an idiot."

"So, that's a no?"

Hazard's face was heating. He refused to answer.

"I'm going to take that as a no. Now, can we interview the sheriff's deputy who's eavesdropping behind the door?"

Without waiting for a reply, Somers twisted the doorknob and kicked inwards. The door opened an inch, cracked against something, and bounced back. It stuttered backward. Pushing it open, Somers made his way into the room.

Standing in front of them, a hand to his nose, was a man in a khaki deputy uniform. Hazard had seen Grant McAtee around town; they'd missed each other in school because McAtee was several years younger, but the McAtee family was large, and Hazard had known two of Grant's older brothers. They had been, both of them, quintessential high school jocks: gelled hair, rugby shirts, and their pants falling halfway past their asses. Jeremy McAtee had broken Hazard's nose intentionally during sophomore year. Braxton, two years younger than Hazard, had pulled down Hazard's Levis in the middle of the high school commons. Neither boy, it went without saying, had faced any punishment.

Grant McAtee looked like he was cut from the same cloth. Handsome in that American farmboy way, with dark hair kept short, he was built to pop out of his uniform—more like a stripper than a deputy.

"You stupid fucker," McAtee said, and the words were nasal and muffled as he pinched his nose. "What the fuck were you—"

"Come on, Grant," Somers said. "I could see your shoes under the door. You keep those things polished to a shine; you might as well have passed a flashlight down there." A smirk crossed Somers's mouth. "Eavesdropping's a dirty habit."

"Where's Lender? Where's Swinney? I want to talk to one of them."

"Oh yeah? You got something for them?"

"I want to talk to one of them," McAtee said, but the nasal pitch to his words robbed them of their force. "I don't want to deal with a—"

The silence was so sudden that Hazard's skin prickled. He remembered, to this day, how his nose had felt as Jeremy's fist had smashed into it. He remembered the rubbery folding of the cartilage, then the snap. He thought he'd like to feel that again—this time, from the other side. His knuckles popped, and it wasn't until then that he realized he'd made a fist.

"Easy," Somers said, laughing as he put a hand on Hazard's arm. "Grant, you weren't going to say what I think you were going to say. Were you? You weren't going to say something about Detective Hazard's sexuality. Or my own."

Grant didn't answer.

"It's the twenty-first century, Grant," Somers continued. "The old days are long past. It's ok to be gay. Big news. Don't know if you'd heard. And you wouldn't like to be brought up for a hate crime, would you? Even if you skate past, it'd be a blot on that perfect record."

Still no answer; a trickle of crimson ran under McAtee's hand and curled around his thick lips.

"And," Somers said, leaning closer, his voice dropping into a stage whisper. "If you have any doubts about my sexuality, you can ask your sister about that time I took her to the Supersonic Drive-in. I don't remember five minutes of whatever movie we saw. It might have been *Star Wars*. I know I saw stars."

McAtee's hands turned into fists.

"Go on," Hazard said. "Take a swing."

For a moment, McAtee hovered on the edge. Then, spitting at their feet, he dropped his hands. "You're a pair of fucking assholes."

"That's all public record," Somers said, his smirk lingering a moment before it faded. "Let's get this over with."

McAtee seemed like he might refuse, then he grudgingly gave ground, allowing them into the room. It was a third bedroom, but aside from a twin bed, there was no furniture. No lamps. No light fixture. No chairs. Bleak, February light slipped through a single window. On the far wall, a poster of a 1996 Lamborghini Diablo showed its age, the paper split, the corners curling. Hazard knew without being told that this had been Morris Bingham, Junior's room. The sheriff's son had grown up in this room. Had it always been this empty?

McAtee stopped on the far side of the room, keeping distance between himself and the detectives. His nose, puffy and red, had stopped bleeding, but he still cupped a hand over it. "What do you want?"

"Let's start from the top," Somers said. "What happened today?"

"What happened? The sheriff got his head blown off, you fucking moron. What do you think happened?"

"Why don't you tell us?"

"This is the kind of work you do?" McAtee snorted, and then he winced. "City cops can't even see what's under their noses. Just watch: the mayor will get here, and he'll tell that fat-assed bitch Cravens what's what, and then this'll be back in the county's lap."

"You think you're going to get this case? You're out of your mind."

"Watch."

"I could break his nose," Hazard said. He kept his voice low and even; he'd found that was the best way to get results. "His brother broke mine. I'm pretty sure I remember how he did it."

"You're not going to lay a finger on me."

Somers stepped between them. "Don't be stupid, McAtee. Nobody's touching this case except Hazard and me. That's all. So if you've got something to say, let's hear it."

"I'll wait."

"That's an interesting choice. Deputy gets out here with the sheriff, really cozy on a weekend, and the sheriff gets shot in the back of the head. Detective Hazard, what do you think? Out of all the people here, who do you like the most for that?"

"You're not pinning this on me."

Hazard cleared his throat. "Wasn't it a deputy that leaked all that information to the reporter?"

"Forget that," McAtee said. "I'm not the only one that knew how to handle a gun. Randy, you know he can shoot. Lionel. All those men carried."

"You know what?" Somers said. "I think you're right. It was a deputy. An anonymous source inside the sheriff's office. Somebody who wasn't very happy with how things were being run. Maybe somebody who thought he could do a better job. And now, here we are: the sheriff's dead, and we've got an angry deputy."

"Fuck that. Fuck you. Fuck both of you. I never said I was angry. I know what you're doing, and you can't make that shit stick."

"So you came out here, why? Because you couldn't stand working for an asshole like Morris Bingham anymore? You wanted to take care of things permanently?"

McAtee forgot about his nose long enough to run both hands through his hair. "I came out here because he asked me to. I came out here because of that stupid petition."

"What are you? Some kind of strategic genius? You're going to mastermind the sheriff's comeback?"

McAtee grunted, and it took Hazard a moment to realize that the sound was a laugh. "You know what? I'm glad I'm not. I like my job. You like your job?"

"It pays the bills," Somers said.

"I like my job a lot. People respect the job. People respect me. That's pretty simple, right? I'm doing something I'm good at. I get a badge, a gun, a car. You know what I get because of this job?"

"An ego," Somers said.

A grin split McAtee's face. "I get pussy. Now I know that's nothing to a couple like you, but for a single guy, that's pretty sweet."

"That's two," Hazard said.

"What?"

"I'm counting. That's two." He held up two fingers.

For a moment, McAtee tried to stare Hazard down. Hazard held his position, fingers up, gaze fixed. McAtee, sweating now, glanced away first.

"I don't want to be a strategic whatever. I just want to do my job. The sheriff says come over, I come over. That's all I got to do."

"Even on a weekend?"

"You're a cop. There isn't such a thing as weekends, not in this job. You two are out here, right?"

"So this was work?"

"Call it whatever you want. My boss tells me to jump, I jump. Doesn't matter if it's Easter Sunday."

"And what did Sheriff Bingham want you to do? Besides jump, of course."

"Run errands. He had all those other folk over here. I just did whatever he told me to. Carried all those guns down to the river. Carried that table too, and it damn near broke my back. That kind of stuff."

"You were his butler?"

"You know what? Fuck you."

"So you supported Sheriff Bingham? You weren't going to sign the recall?"

"Course not."

"You weren't the leak to the newspaper?"

"City cops are about as stupid as they come, aren't they? There isn't any more leak."

"You didn't think that Dennis Rutter would make a better sheriff?"

McAtee's handsome, all-American face twisted into a mocking smile. "Oh sure, the Rutters, they're just fine. Bunch of hillbillies going blind drinking their own corn mash and antifreeze and fucking their sisters out in the chicken coop. That's a sheriff right there, Dennis Rutter, just as soon as he can get all that chicken shit off his knees."

"You know Dennis?"

"I know him. I know he doesn't look like his mom and dad were brother and sister, which makes him the best-looking Rutter out there, but that doesn't mean he doesn't have a goat's ass for a face. I should know; I've spent more time looking at that goat's ass than I'd like. On account of his brother—you wouldn't remember that, but the sheriff had me watching him for a while to make sure nothing happened. You know how stupid that motherfucker is? I stopped Dennis last week. He was going about seventy out on Route 17. Middle of the night. That dumb son of a bitch didn't have either headlight working. You know what he'd done? Strapped a couple of flashlights to the side windows." McAtee mimed adjusting the lights. "Like he could see past the hood of that old Chevy. That's our new sheriff, ladies."

"That's three," Hazard said.

McAtee smirked and shook his head.

"You come find me when I'm not working," Hazard said. "You bring Jeremy. Bring Braxton. Bring anybody you want."

"Drop it," Somers said.

"You're big," McAtee said, his smile growing slowly. "You got real big when you left here."

"That's enough," Somers said, stretching out his hands between them as though anticipating a rush. "Both of you just shut up."

"Think you're the big man, too," McAtee said, his eyes shining like steel. "I know a cocksucker when I see one. I know a cocksucker loves to be on his knees when I see one."

"Fuck, man," Somers said, dropping his hands. "Why'd you have to go and say something like that?"

McAtee's grin was a hard, savage slice of teeth. "He knows what he is—"

Before he could finish, Somers had driven a fist into his face. McAtee's head rocked backward, and he stumbled into the wall. Swearing, McAtee clapped a hand over his nose. His other hand swung out in a tight fist, but he caught only air.

"Let's stop it right here," Somers said, but his breathing was rapid, his face flushed, his eyes like moonlight skating tropical blue water. "Or you take another swing and we really get into it."

Hazard calculated the distance between the men, his own average speed, and how hard he'd need to hit McAtee to put him down—maybe permanently. The ache in his head had vanished. His pulse sang in his ears, and he felt a thrumming, pleasant, like everything had snapped taut inside him. He could do it. Before McAtee got to Somers, he could put him down.

The door opened, and Peterson stuck his head into the room. "Everything all right?"

All three men in the room turned towards Peterson and then to each other.

"Fine," McAtee snapped.

Peterson lingered a moment longer, but Somers gave him a nod, and then he withdrew.

Silence pooled in the grimly empty bedroom. Hazard waited. McAtee, he expected, was the kind of guy who would explode into threats. Any minute. Any minute now.

But it didn't happen.

"Why don't you tell us about today?" Somers said, his hand—the one he'd thrown the punch with—in a loose fist, as though he couldn't quite bring himself to shake out the sting.

And McAtee did. He told them everything, and he did it in a flat monotone, one hand still clapped over his nose, his attention fixed on the floor. His story matched, in every significant way, what Moody and Beverly had described. Like them, McAtee had not seen the shooter or any sign of him. He corroborated Beverly's story of turning the sheriff onto his side, and he vouched for the doctor's speedy retreat to the house.

"Why did she go to the house?" Somers asked.

"I don't know."

"No idea?"

"She came back with her bag."

"Why did she do that?"

"I don't know."

Hazard waited, but nothing more came. He glanced at Somers, and Somers arched an eyebrow.

"Did the sheriff wear gloves?" Hazard asked.

"I don't think so."

"You don't remember?"

"He wasn't wearing gloves."

"What about his hat?"

"He had it on."

"What happened to his hat?"

McAtee shrugged; it was the closest he'd come to an emotion since Somers had plugged him.

"Anything else you need to tell us?" Somers said.

For the first time since Peterson had left, McAtee looked up. He still had his nose covered; the gesture seemed unconscious now. He fixed Somers with a flat, empty look. It was the look of a man who had his mind full of killing. Then he shook his head.

"Stay here," Somers said. "Officer Peterson will let you know when you can go."

Hazard followed Somers out into the hallway, and when he glanced back, McAtee was still watching them. He had dropped his hand, and he was staring at them over a puffed-up nose. Murder. It was murder in his face, bright and simple as a knife.

CHAPTER NINE

**FEBRUARY 11
SUNDAY
2:46 PM**

PETERSON DIDN'T ACKNOWLEDGE THEM as they left the landing; somewhere, the patrol officer had found a folding metal chair, and he sat with his legs spread, tapping out a rhythm on the steel. The notes all sounded the same, but something in the tune made Somers think of a death march.

It had happened again. That was the thought, plain and simple, as he shook out his hand. It had happened again, and he wasn't sorry. Not for hitting McAtee, definitely not sorry for that. And not sorry for the rest of it. Not sorry that it exposed how much Somers cared. No, he wasn't sorry for that, not at all. But it sure left him feeling vulnerable. And feeling vulnerable, well, it felt like shit.

On the stairs, Hazard dropped one of his huge paws onto Somers's shoulder.

"What?"

"I was handling that."

Somers stared at him, at the crinkling around Hazard's eyes, at the way his jaw tightened when he was angry, at his hair that was always trying to work free of the carefully combed part and spill over his forehead. He didn't know. He didn't have any idea, not even a clue. And why would he? John-Henry Somerset had been his teenage bully. John-Henry Somerset had made his boyhood a living hell. And nothing changed, that was what life was all about, nothing ever fucking changed, and that's why Hazard would always see him that way: a bully, an unpleasant reminder of his past. Somers had been close. At New Year's, he had been so goddamn close. If he'd just opened his mouth, if he'd just tried. And then Hazard had said partners.

Sure, partners. We'll be partners. When what Somers really wanted, what he had started to dream about, what followed him, what he saw when he turned around too fast and forgot to protect himself, was anything but partners. Forget partners. Fuck partners.

"Partners," Somers said, surprised at how his voice sounded, rough, like he'd been dry for—

—twenty years—

—a week. "That's what that was about."

"I don't need anyone taking care of me. I don't need you fighting my fights."

"That's the whole point of partners, Ree. If you slug him, you're just an oversensitive fag, pardon my language. If I hit him, I'm a stand-up partner."

"That doesn't make any sense. He said what he said. Regardless—"

"Ree, it doesn't matter if it makes any sense. That's how it is."

Hazard's jaw was still tight. His skin—so fair it was practically translucent—showed the pulse in his neck.

"You don't have to like it," Somers said, and holy God, he even managed to work up a smile. "But you do have to say thank you."

"You're an idiot," Hazard said, shoving past him and tromping down the stairs.

Somers caught up to him by the time they'd reached the ground floor, and if he'd meant to say anything more, if he thought maybe he'd try to squeeze that thank you out of Hazard because he knew it would get Hazard all bothered and red in the face, Somers forgot those ideas when he saw Chief Cravens.

Cravens, an older woman with an hourglass shape, stood deep in conversation with Carmichael, turning Carmichael's head and parting the hair to examine the scalp. The spot, Somers guessed, where Moody had ripped out a chunk of hair. The image of Cravens as she tended to Carmichael reinforced Cravens's natural appearance as somewhat grandmotherly, although her face was relatively smooth and her long, graying hair showed careful maintenance. Grandmotherly, though, didn't come close to describing Cravens. She'd been the first—and, for a long time, the only—female cop on Wahredua's force for a long time. She'd climbed to the top, and Somers didn't doubt that she stood on a pile of all the people who'd underestimated her.

"You want to see one of the paramedics?"

"No, Chief," Carmichael said.

"You want to file a report?"

"No, Chief."

"You think about it. I'll back you if it comes to that. Nobody treats a cop like that, not while I'm on the job."

Carmichael's petite features weren't particularly expressive, but Somers could read the mixture of emotions there. Cravens was telling the truth: Somers knew from experience that the chief would back her officers as long as she believed they were right. But Cravens was also ignoring—intentionally, as both Somers and Carmichael knew—the complicated reality of being a cop in a small town. In Wahredua, you couldn't wipe your ass without elbowing the guy behind you. Carmichael might get Cravens's backing, but it wouldn't matter. Moody would hit back with things that cops couldn't touch, with gossip, with slander, with a cold shoulder that would have Carmichael missing party invitations for the next twenty years. Somers knew; it had happened to him when Cora had kicked him to the curb. And it had happened again, in its own way, since Hazard had returned.

Somers stomped the thought down. He didn't like that thought, didn't like what it said about him. He didn't miss the invitations to Saint Taffy's, the local cop bar, after work. He didn't miss the ribbings from the other guys. He didn't miss the easy camaraderie that had marked his relationships on the force until a few months before. He didn't miss any of it. He didn't.

"Detectives," Cravens said, her attention turning away from Carmichael, who retreated with a relieved expression. "What have you got?"

"Not much," Somers said. He laid out what they'd learned in short, declarative sentences, omitting most of the inferences he'd drawn because he knew that, for the moment, Cravens just wanted the lay of the land.

When he'd finished, Cravens put hands on ample hips and nodded. "You're going to finish taking statements?"

"Why wouldn't we?" Hazard asked.

"Right now," Somers said. "We're going to wrap up with the last three right now."

"Maybe you ought to hurry," Cravens said.

"Why?" Hazard said.

Annoyance flickered in Cravens's eyes. Somers wasn't sure how the chief felt about Hazard, not really. She had hired him for her own reasons, reasons that hadn't been fully clear to Somers, although Somers had worked hard to convince her that Hazard was the right choice. And Hazard had borne out Somers's conviction, helping to solve some of the most challenging cases that Wahredua had ever seen. But Cravens had never warmed to him, and Hazard's inability to play all the polite games that kept the world turning made him a thorn in the chief's side.

"I think my partner meant to say we'll do that," Somers said.

"No," Hazard said. "I meant to say what I said: why should we hurry?"

"Because it's a murder investigation, Detective Hazard, and because it's your job." Cravens paused. She drew a breath. "I'm just saying there's been a lot of talk already. The mayor's had me on the phone half a dozen times already. Twice he's had the county prosecutor on the line too, and the two of them talked to each other more than they talked to me. I'd like you two to get whatever you can and get it fast so the next time they call, I have something to put in front of them."

"It's a murder," Hazard said, his jaw set. "Like you said, it's our job. It's our case; we caught it. What does it matter what the mayor says?"

"It matters a lot, Detective Hazard. That might surprise you, but it matters a hell of a lot. And if you don't want to spend the next six months catching pickpockets on Market Street and corralling the hobos in Truant Park, you'll get your ass in gear and take those statements as fast as you can."

Hazard opened his mouth; his eyes—scarecrow eyes, Somers always thought, because they looked like corn at the end of summer, burnt gold—were those of a man who wouldn't mind pulling on the gloves and taking a few swings, but Somers shoved him towards the back of the house.

"Right now, Chief," he called over his shoulder.

"Don't push me," Hazard muttered as Somers hustled him into the next room and towards the kitchen.

"Keep walking."

"I am walking. Stop it. I'm goddamn walking, all right? Will you stop it already?"

"I don't know. Maybe. Maybe not."

"What do you mean—Somers, I swear to God, you're going to have to hire somebody to wipe your ass because I'm going to break your—Jesus." Hazard jumped like a cartoon character; Somers was surprised his head didn't get stuck in the ceiling.

Somers stopped and stared. "You're ticklish."

Red slashes marred Hazard's pale cheeks. "I am not."

"You are, you're—" Somers reached out, but before he could make contact, Hazard stepped out of reach.

"You do that," Hazard said, the red in his cheeks so dark that it was almost purple, "you do that, and I really will break your hand."

"How did I not know this about you?"

"Drop it."

"We've known each other for a long time."

"I said drop it."

"I've touched your—"

"One more word."

Somers scanned Hazard's face and saw disaster, dinosaur-ending-disaster, that level of disaster, and said, "Yeah. Ok. Right."

Hazard didn't say anything more. He crossed his arms, as though warding off another attempt by Somers, and the pose made him look strangely vulnerable.

"Just one last thing."

Hazard looked ready to bolt. Or maybe ready to pull his .38 and shoot.

With a smirk, Somers said, "That thing you said. About hiring someone to wipe my ass. I'm a little hurt. We're partners. And roommates."

"We're not roommates."

"And I thought maybe you'd be willing to help me out."

Through gritted teeth, Hazard said, "Not even with sandpaper. Not with a sandblaster, for that matter."

"That hurts."

Silence.

"That really hurts."

"It would hurt a hell of a lot more with a sandblaster."

Somers burst into laughter, and he saw some of the—

—fear, holy God, Hazard was afraid, afraid Somers would touch him—

—tension in Hazard's shoulders ease. Hazard didn't smile; he didn't even come close. But the hard slice of his mouth softened.

"You want to take a few statements?" Somers asked.

Hazard's nod was a fractional inclination of his chin.

"If that's not too much trouble, I mean."

Hazard's eyes narrowed.

"Seeing as it's your job and all."

Hazard's face set in a scowl.

"And the chief did make a special request."

Hazard's middle finger flipped up.

Somers laughed. "Why couldn't you be this charming when you were talking to Cravens?"

Stiffly—his arms still protecting his ribs—Hazard stalked towards the kitchen.

Whatever Somers had been expecting of Dr. Hayashi, it wasn't what he found in the kitchen. A tall, large-boned woman stood on a kitchen chair, one hand gripping a cabinet door while she fished for something on the uppermost shelf. She had long, dark hair. Beautiful hair. And that was where the beauty ended.

"Dr. Hayashi?" Somers said.

Jerking backward in surprise, she barely caught herself from falling. It took her almost a full minute to recover, and during that time she inched slowly and awkwardly in a circle until she was facing them.

"Oh—um—I—"

The acne scars were deep. Her eyes were buried somewhere near the back of her skull. A smile might have helped, but she looked so lost, so confused, that Somers had the impression she'd set her smile down somewhere once—while riding the bus, maybe—and had forgotten it.

"Um—I—uh—yes?"

"My name is Detective Somerset. This is Detective Hazard. We'd like to talk to you about what happened today."

"Oh. Yes. All right." In one hand, she held a bottle of cooking sherry she'd retrieved from the cabinet, and she glanced at it absentmindedly as she climbed down from the chair.

"Would you like to sit down?"

"Oh. No. No, thank you." She looked at the bottle again.

"I don't think that'll be very good to drink," Somers said, with his best smile to soften the words.

"Oh. Oh. Really?"

"No, I don't think so."

"Oh."

"Dr. Hayashi, could you tell us why you were here today?"

"Oh. Yes. I was here to help the sheriff."

"Help him how?"

"Hm. Um." She seemed at a loss. "With the petition?"

"Is that right? How were you going to help him with that?"

"I don't, um, know. He asked me to come."

"Are you close with the sheriff?"

"Oh. No."

"Was it strange that he invited you to help with the petition?"

"Oh. No. No, I don't think so." Dr. Hayashi seemed to realize that more was expected and added, "I contributed to his last campaign."

"Are you from Wahredua?"

"Oh. No. No, I moved here about ten years ago."

"What brought you here?"

"The university."

Somers frowned. "Wroxall doesn't have a medical school."

"No, I—I wanted a quiet town, but I wanted it to have some life. You know. The college."

"How do you like it?"

"Oh, yes, it's fine."

"Were you the sheriff's physician?"

Dr. Hayashi blinked. It seemed to take an extra second, her eyes were so far back. "Yes, uh huh, yes."

"And you contributed to his campaign?"

"Yes, that's right."

"Why?"

For a moment, the doctor didn't seem to understand. "Excuse me?"

"Why did you donate to his campaign? Did you agree with his politics? Did you think he was a great candidate? Were you impressed by his record?"

"Yes."

"Yes?"

"Yes, all of that."

Somers cast a sidelong glance at Hazard, but the big brute was studying Dr. Hayashi from under his neanderthal forehead. "You weren't troubled by stories about corruption?"

"No."

"Was the contribution sizeable?" Somers smiled again, trying to smooth out the question. "I'm just trying to understand why the sheriff would invite a physician who at one point contributed to a re-election campaign to help him strategize for the recall petition."

"I, uh, I have connections."

"Really? Your practice, other doctors—"

"No. Well, yes, but, no. That's not—" Dr. Hayashi hemmed for a moment. Her eyes were glued to the cooking sherry. "I'm the former president of the AACC in Warhedua."

"AACC?"

"Asian American Chamber of Commerce," Hazard said in his gravelly voice.

"All right," Somers said. "So it was just politics?"

For the first time in their conversation, a little light went on in those cavernous eyes, and Dr. Hayashi looked like she might have remembered where she'd dropped that smile. "Right. Exactly right. Just politics."

As they questioned her about the day's events, her account corroborated what they'd heard in the first three statements. Dr. Hayashi, however, had one startling announcement.

She had seen the shooter.

"Excuse me?" Somers said.

"I saw him."

"Can you describe him?"

Dr. Hayashi clutched the cooking sherry in both hands. "He was on the hill. Up from the river." She released the bottle long enough to gesture with her right hand. "Right at the edge of the trees."

"All right."

"That's really all I can say." Her eyes flicked to the counter, where a smartphone sat. And then her gaze was fixed on them again.

"Can you remember anything else?"

"Oh. No. Not really. He was a long way off. I couldn't really make out any details."

"Height? Weight? Clothing?"

She froze as though Somers had turned a spotlight on her.

"That's a good distance from where you were standing," Hazard said. "How did you see him?"

"He moved." She hunched in the chair. "That's all, I saw the movement, and then he was gone. And then I realized what had happened, and I saw the sheriff, and I—I don't know." She stared at them with those dark, hollow eyes. "Should I have gone after him? I don't know. I didn't—I wasn't thinking clearly." Her eyes darted towards the phone again.

"No," Somers said. "You would have been putting yourself in danger."

"What did you do?" Hazard asked, the words hard and cold and measured.

For a moment, Dr. Hayashi seemed to forget the bottle, and she spread her arms. "He was dead. The sheriff, I mean. I couldn't do anything. I saw the wound, and I knew I couldn't do anything. That kind of trauma to the head—he didn't have a chance."

"So what did you do?" Hazard said.

"Oh. Yes, I see. I came back to the house."

"Why?"

"To get my bag." She pointed to the kitchen table, where a heavy leather satchel sat. It didn't look like the traditional black doctor's bag. It looked like something a combat medic might carry.

"But you just said that you knew the sheriff was beyond helping," Somers said.

"Oh. Oh, yes. I knew that. But I thought, maybe the others. Maybe they were hurt. Or maybe they needed a sedative."

"Did you administer a sedative to anyone?"

"No, no. I didn't." Again, her eyes flashed to the granite counter and the phone.

Too bad, Somers thought. Really too bad. Miranda Carmichael might have kept all her hair.

Somers probed for more, but the doctor had nothing else to offer. With a sigh, Somers nodded at Hazard, who perched on the edge of his seat.

"Was the sheriff wearing gloves?" Hazard asked.

"Oh. No. I don't think so. Why?"

"What about a hat?"

"Hm. Oh. Yes. Yes, he was wearing a hat. Why?"

"What happened to his hat?"

"I don't know."

"What about your phone?" Somers said.

"My—my phone?"

"Could we look at it?"

"I don't think—don't you need a warrant?"

"Only if you say no." Somers gave her his best smile. "There's no reason you'd say no, is there, Doctor?"

"I don't think—"

"I don't know. I—" She chewed her lip. "There's nothing relevant."

"Perfect. It won't take us long to glance at it."

Despair darkened her eyes, and she swiped at the phone's screen and passed it to them.

It didn't take Somers long to find something interesting. "This picture. Who took it?"

"The sheriff."

"Why?"

"I—I asked him to."

The photograph showed the people that Somers had already spoken to—Deputy McAtee, Eunice Moody, Beverly Flinn, Dr. Hayashi—and two men that Somers knew by sight but whom he still hadn't talked to: Randall Scott and Lionel Arras. Arras was dressed in chaps, a leather vest, and a cowboy hat. He looked like a cross between an asshole with money and a downright moron.

Somers skimmed the rest of the pictures, the texts, and the calls, but he saw nothing out of the ordinary. The first picture had been interesting, but that had been the only one.

Neither detective had additional questions, but Somers did send Dr. Hayashi's picture to his own phone. He wrapped up the interview and followed Hazard back into the main part of the house. They had two more statements to take, and Somers had the sinking feeling that they weren't going to be any more help than the others.

Still, Somers thought, consoling himself, he had learned one important thing. One fact that might turn out to be critical. It could change everything about how everything else played out. Everything.

Emery Hazard was ticklish.

CHAPTER TEN

FEBRUARY 11
SUNDAY
3:15 PM

WHEN SOMERS PASSED THROUGH the front room again, Cravens was on the phone, her chin tucked against her chest, her posture rigid. Through the picture window, Somers saw Carmichael standing on the driveway. She had buried her hands in her pocket, and she had popped the collar on her heavy uniform jacket, and she looked very small against the enormous blue sky.

At the end of the hallway, three doors stood closed. Picking one at random, Somers opened it. On the other side, he found a home office, but there was nobody waiting. He tried the next door. This time, he found what might have been called, a hundred years ago, a sitting room or a sewing room or a drawing room. The sheriff's wife, while Somers had been growing up, had always called it the coat closet, but it wasn't anything like a closet aside from the coat stand in the corner.

A string-bean of a man sat in the room. He had on jeans and a flannel shirt and work boots, but he didn't look like he'd ever used the boots for working—or the jeans or the shirt, for that matter. His big, gnarled hands he clasped between his knees, and he'd plastered his iron-grey hair to his scalp with Vitalis—the room stank of hair tonic. He looked like a man who had worked hard his whole life, come into money late, and hadn't the faintest idea what to do about it. His shirt and his jeans were soaking wet, and a damp outline marked where he had been sitting.

Somers placed him immediately: Randall Scott, whom the other guests had referred to as Randy. Scott was a rich man. One of the richest in the county. He had quilted together an enormous agriculture business, and his farm—as he casually referred to it—employed hundreds of people in the area, not to mention seasonal workers, often migrants. Somers didn't know Scott personally; Scott had never ascended to the heights of Wahredua's society. But Somers did remember something his father had once said: some people knew how to turn lemons into lemonade, but Randall Scott knew how to turn shit into gold.

As the detectives entered, Scott rose and shook their hands. His grip, callused and firm, spoke of a lifetime of manual labor. Somers introduced himself and Hazard, and Scott nodded.

"I've heard all about you boys. What you've done around here."

"We'd like to take your statement about what you saw."

Scott nodded again and gestured to his wet clothes. Red came into his cheeks. "Fell in the river. When I saw what happened to the sheriff, I stumbled. Damn embarrassing. McAtee—he's that young pup in a deputy's uniform—McAtee went around telling the whole world I fainted. Officers, I did not faint. I can tell you that much."

"Let's come back to that. Could you start by telling us why you were out here?"

"What's an old fart like me doing in mixed company, is that what you mean?" Scott flashed a smile of huge, yellow teeth.

"It's an odd mix," Somers said. "I don't imagine you and Miss Moody get together to play bridge."

"No, sir. We don't."

"What brought you out here?"

"The sheriff invited me."

"To what end?"

Again, Scott flashed his yellow smile. "Same as always. Shoot skeet, drink, talk."

"Is that all?"

"You mean about the petition."

"What about the petition?"

"Well, I was going to help him, that's for damn sure. But mostly I came because the sheriff keeps some damn good whiskey in the house."

"So you supported the sheriff politically?"

"Yes, sir."

"What do you make of the protestors?" Hazard asked, the question breaking the flow of Somers's thoughts.

Scott's craggy features firmed. "Your father was Frank Hazard, that right?"

"I'm asking you about those people out front. What'd you think of all that?"

"I knew Frank. Not well, I'm not saying that. But I knew him. Your mother too. She was a beauty, and the rest of us, we all thought she'd lost her mind when she went running after your father. I'm not saying a word against him, you understand. I'm just saying what was said. They turned out fine, didn't they?"

Hazard didn't answer. His face had gone pale and rigid like porcelain, like it might shatter if anything moved too fast.

"They moved away, didn't they?"

"Yes."

"They doing fine?"

"Yes."

"You came back here, and that was some talk, wasn't it?"

Again, Hazard remained silent.

"What a fellow wants to do on his own time, as long he's not harming anyone, that's his business. I don't have any objection to that. I wanted to say that to you. I wanted you to know you've done respectable work here. You made your father proud. Mother too, I expect."

"We're not talking about my family," Hazard said, the words brittle. "I'm asking you about those protestors."

Scott hesitated. Something in his old, lined face looked suddenly weary, as though some great disappointment had just been realized—not Hazard, not particularly, but something larger. Something that you had to be older to see fully, to understand.

"They've got their rights, don't they?"

"They do," Somers said, intervening because Hazard still looked like if you breathed on him, a really good lungful, he might crack down the middle. "But what they're saying about the sheriff, that didn't change your mind?"

"Hard to change an old man's mind. I know what they're saying. I've heard about all that, about the county lock-up, about the work camps, about what the sheriff's handled wrong—just about everything if you read the paper. Some of it is true, I judge. Some is not. But the thing is, I think Sheriff Bingham, he did a good job. Law and order, that's a thing everybody talks really pretty about. Then you get in there. Then you see how it's done. Then it's not so pretty, but nobody wants to say that, so they point the finger, and then everybody's pointing the finger, and that still doesn't get to the truth of it." His enormous yellow smile emerged again. "You know what I think? I think those people out there, I think they feel helpless. Nothing in the world makes a man angrier than feeling helpless, isn't that right?"

Somers left the question unanswered and proceeded to walk Scott through the day's events. Scott remembered nothing unusual about the sheriff's behavior, nothing unusual about the other guests, nothing unusual about the unfolding of the day's events. It wasn't until they came to the moment of the murder that Scott's answers began to differ.

"Can you tell me what happened," Somers said, "when the sheriff was killed?"

Nodding slowly, Scott said. "Some of it, I suppose. What I saw."

"Go ahead."

"I'd just made a shot. Really tricky one, the damn thing low, lower than I expected, and moving against the water. I'm not a young man. Don't have the eyes, not what a young man does. But I made it. Haven't made a shot like that in fifty years, that's what I'd say." Scott's wrinkled face reddened. "And I may not be a young man, but I'm still a damn fool. Age doesn't take that out of you. If anything, it just packs it in deeper if you take my meaning."

Somers smiled and nodded.

"Anyway, I turned around and kicked up my heels, just like a damn fool will do, and—and I seen him." The slip into ungrammatical speech was marked by a hoarsening of Scott's voice.

"Who?"

"The man. That fellow with the gun. He was up on that rise of land, right where the oaks pick up. He had the gun on his shoulder, and I had this fool thought—" Scott cut off. His next words sounded distant, as though he were lost in the memory. "I thought we must look so small to him. So small from up there. Like we was nothing but ants." He stilled. Then, rousing himself, he spoke with some of his former vigor. "The bastard took the shot, and that's when I realized."

"Realized what?"

Scott's mouth quirked as he searched for words. Spreading his hands, he shrugged.

"Can you describe the shooter?" Somers asked.

"I thought he was a hunter. Now, looking back, that's all wrong. He didn't have on the right colors. Blaze, you know. I thought maybe geese, and I thought, what a fool, the week after the season closes and he's out on the sheriff's land."

"So you can't describe him," Hazard said.

Somers fought the urge to throw an elbow.

Scott, however, chuckled. "Just like Frank, just something he'd say. I said hunter because he was all in a color. One of those heavy, padded things some men wear when they hunt. Might have been camo. Might have been olive. Might have been brown. I'm not a young man. Don't have the eyes, you understand."

"How did you know it was a man?" Hazard pressed.

"I'm not a young man, but I still got eyes."

"What you've described, a figure seen from a distance and wearing thick, padded garments, that could describe anyone, male or female. You can't tell us height or weight; why do you think you know the sex?"

"Well, I just knew."

"You just knew."

"I still got eyes, dammit."

"Write that down," Hazard said to Somers, never mind that Somers didn't have pen or paper in hand. "He knows it was a man because he's still got eyes."

"Hell, you are just like Frank. Just as proud. Just as stubborn. Carrying a chip for the whole world."

The words rolled off Hazard, his face expressionless. Somers opened his mouth to say something, but from the hallway came the sound of raised voices.

Stabbing a finger at Hazard, Scott said, "You ever worked cattle? No. You ain't never worked cattle. Not a day in your life."

"I think we're done," Hazard said.

"You get out there, you work cattle, and then you come tell me I can't tell a man from a woman. You look out over the herd and you got any sense, any sense at all, and you know. This is the same."

"Why? Because he had horns like a bull? Because his dick and balls were out swinging?"

"To hell with you, then. You don't believe me, don't believe me."

"My partner," Somers said, "is just trying to verify what you've said. Is that when you fell?"

"I took a bad step, that's all. Went ass-first into the river and dragged myself out. The whole thing couldn't have taken more than fifteen seconds." He paused. "I did not faint."

"We're grateful for your statement, Mr. Scott. You've been a huge help; this is the most useful information we've had all day."

Scott, stiff as cold iron in his chair, didn't answer.

"Anything else you can tell us, Mr. Scott? Anything you think might help us?"

Scott, with a rigid jerk, shook his head.

With a sigh, Somers glanced at his partner.

"Was the sheriff wearing gloves?" Hazard asked.

"No."

"What about his hat?"

"What the hell kind of hat?"

"Was he wearing a hat?"

"Yes, I suppose. And I suppose you're going to ask me how I knew it was a hat and not a mitten or something like that."

"What happened to the hat?"

"What do you mean? He was wearing it, wasn't he?"

"No."

"I'll be damned." Scott paused, reflecting. "Well, I'll be damned."

Somers shook his head. The shouting out in the hall had grown louder, and he recognized Cravens's voice and a man's. Then a door slammed.

"Detectives," Cravens shouted.

Somers threw open the door and sprinted down the hall. Cravens stood near the picture window, hands on her hips, face twisted into a frown.

"What?" Somers said, glancing around. Outside, Carmichael was trotting back towards the house along the driveway, as though she were doing laps. "What happened?"

Cravens pointed out the window, and Somers glimpsed a low-slung sports car sliding around a corner.

"There goes your last witness."

CHAPTER ELEVEN

FEBRUARY 11
SUNDAY
3:39 PM

LIONEL ARRAS HAD FLED. He had run past the chief, ignoring her shouts, and barreled straight into Carmichael. The small woman had been knocked to the ground, and in the intervening time, Arras had gotten into his car and driven away.

"Foley," Cravens snapped into her radio. "Stop him." A burst of static answered, and Cravens glanced at the two detectives. "Took your time, didn't you? Why don't you go down to the shore and see if they've got anything useful?"

Opening his mouth, Hazard prepared to explain that taking statements always required time, and he was pretty sure he had some solid statistics to back it up, but before he could get anything out, Somers had kicked him in the ankle. Hazard's jaw snapped shut, and he followed Somers out of the house.

Hazard and Somers returned to the crime scene, leaving the chief, Carmichael, and Peterson to release the witnesses. Down at the sandy strip of shore along the Grand Rivere, the detectives found four uniformed officers working forensics. Norman and Gross, although not related, looked like they could have been brothers: pot-bellied, balding, always wearing shirts with yellow rings under the arms. Hoffmeister and Lloyd, on the other hand, couldn't have been more different. Hoffmeister, tall and thin and sallow, the color of aged styrofoam, contrasted with Lloyd's stocky build, dark skin, and elfish smile.

When Hazard stopped at the edge of the tape, Norman and Gross were still photographing the scene. The two patrol officers, from what Hazard had seen over the last few months, were generally about as useful as a two-story outhouse, but word was that they did a decent job on forensics. Hazard had his doubts; he couldn't imagine Norman and Gross doing a competent job of wiping their asses.

"Shouldn't have walked there," Hoffmeister said, huffing into his cupped hands to warm them.

"The sand was shit anyway," Hazard said. "Nothing you could get out of it."

Hoffmeister shrugged. "Shouldn't have walked there."

"You already video?" Somers asked.

Nodding, Hoffmeister indicated the handful of markers that had already been placed at the scene: the table, the rifles, the clay target thrower, and so on. "Once they're done, we'll start bagging everything. Lloyd's got the sketch pretty much finished."

"What about up there?" Somers said.

"We'll get there."

"You need somebody up there now. You need to lock that down."

"We'll get there."

"Get up there now," Hazard said. "You're just chafing your ass here."

Blowing on his hands again, Hoffmeister delayed just long enough to make his point. That was the kind of guy he was, Hazard had learned. The kind of guy that had to measure his dick against everything he came across, had to piss on every hydrant he passed. Then, collecting Lloyd, Hoffmeister went up the bluff to secure the scene where the shooter had been.

For another handful of minutes, Hazard and Somers waited, watching as Norman and Gross continued to photograph. The patrol cops weren't fast. They were about a hundred miles away from fast. Hazard hoped that was because they were doing a thorough job, but again, he had his doubts.

"Did you see the bullet?" Hazard, bouncing on his toes in an effort to stay warm, pitched the question towards Norman.

"Uh-huh," Norman grunted.

"That's the most important thing. If you've got to get on your hands and knees and sift every ounce of sand, that's what you've got to do."

"Uh-huh."

"That's the case, you get it? That's the whole goddamn case."

"Yessir."

"That marker, the one over in the grass. Did you already comb the grass over there? It looks like you haven't been in it yet, and I want you to comb it as soon as you're done with the photos."

Acting as one, Norman and Gross both lowered their cameras. They glanced at each other.

"Detective," Gross said, "it's cold out."

"I know it's cold out," Hazard said. "I want to know what you've marked already and what you've still got to mark. If you've got—"

"It's cold out," Gross said again. "Best thing to do would be wait where it's warm."

"I'm not cold. I'd like you to tell me what you've got marked in the grass over there."

Sighing, Somers tapped his arm. "Ree, let's go."

"This is our case. I'm saying they should comb that grass because it doesn't look like they took more than a step into it."

"Sure. That's great. Let's go up to the house, though. Let these guys finish."

"I don't—"

"C'mon." Somers feigned a jab at Hazard's ribs, and Hazard lurched backward. With a mocking grin, Somers turned and started back up towards the house.

Hazard, red in the face, followed. "You find that goddamn bullet," he called over his shoulder. "And comb that grass."

"Ask," Somers said when they were halfway back to the house.

The wind whipped the tall grass against their legs, and the sound of it was an enormous, swelling ocean sound. Hazard's breath had stopped steaming, and his lungs ached with the cold air.

"What?"

"You ask. Next time."

"Who? Norman and Gross?"

"It doesn't cost you anything."

"They hadn't gone into the grass, Somers. They need to go through that whole area. They've got to do it right."

"They are doing it right, Ree. They'll do their job. All you had to do was ask nicely."

Hazard didn't respond.

"So?"

"What?"

"Will you just ask next time?"

"They're not babies."

"Could you just ask? Could you ask nicely?"

"What's this about?"

"Nothing," Somers said.

"What's your take on Arras?"

"Do I think he's guilty because he ran?" Somers stopped walking. He looped a blade of grass around his palm, tugged, and the brittle fibers broke. "Hard to believe that the other five wouldn't have noticed if Arras had walked up the hill, shot the sheriff in the back of the head, and come back down to pick up his hat."

"I never said that's what happened."

"He ran away." Somers shrugged. "It doesn't look good, but that doesn't mean anything."

"He didn't want to talk to us."

"Lots of people don't want to talk to us. You don't want to talk to me sometimes."

Hazard ignored that. "He didn't listen when the chief tried to stop him."

"So he's an asshole."

"Or he's afraid."

"You think he planned this? You think he hired somebody? If that's it, why would he run? That just makes him look guilty."

"Maybe he thought we had something on him. Maybe he thought one of the others did. Maybe his nerve broke. That happens; things get real, and people panic. It's not just a plan anymore."

"Maybe."

"Why do you say maybe? What do you know about him?"

"I'm saying maybe," Somers said. "That means maybe. I'm not saying no. And I don't know anything about him, not really."

"You said maybe like you meant no."

"I said maybe. That's all I meant."

"That's not how you said it."

"If you're going to argue like we're married," Somers said, turning on that vintage, golden-boy smile, "then you've got to do the good parts of marriage too. In fact, you should probably ask me to marry you first."

"You're an asshole."

"That's not a very sweet proposal."

"You're a moronic asshole."

"I know you're trying, and that's what matters. But I have to think about it. I don't want to rush into things. I want this to last forever."

"You're an imbecile." Hazard shoved past Somers and stalked towards the house.

From behind him came Somers's laughter and then, "Next time you ask me, I want you to have a ring. And be on one knee."

Hazard thought about throwing the finger, but he stopped himself. That was what Somers wanted, for some perverse reason. That was always what Somers wanted. And all Hazard wanted was to—

—shut him up, just for one blessed minute of silence, and the best way would be to kiss him, stop him from saying every stupid thing that popped into his head, and the look on his face, that look would be priceless—

—wring his damn neck.

When they reached the house, Cravens was waiting in the front room. As they came inside, she stood straighter and smoothed her hair.

"Detectives."

"What happened?" Somers said. "Is it Arras? What's wrong?"

"He blasted past Foley," Cravens said. "We'll get him for speeding, reckless driving, and I'm half of a mind to lock him up as a material witness, just to teach him a lesson. First we've got to find him, though, and I've got Moraes headed over to his apartment."

"What happened?" Somers asked again.

"I want you to know I didn't roll over on this. I said you can handle it. I know you'd do it right."

"What happened, Chief?"

"The mayor's convinced that, given your history with the sheriff and his family, you're not best suited to this case."

"You're giving it to Lender and Swinney?" Hazard asked. "Because—what? Because the mayor knows we won't let him pull our strings? This is a mistake, Chief."

"Swinney and Lender aren't catching it either. I tried that. The mayor wouldn't have it. He talked to the county attorney, and Daley agreed that this case is serious enough—"

"What the hell does that mean?" Hazard demanded. "Serious? Like the rest of the cases we handled aren't serious? Like Windsor wasn't serious? Like Somers's father being shot, like that wasn't serious?"

"That's enough, Detective. I didn't make this decision. I don't like this decision. But this is above you, and it's above me, and there's nothing we can do but roll with it."

"This is bullshit."

"What'd he do?" Somers asked. "Call up the Ozark Major Case Squad?"

"They're coming," Cravens said with a nod. "Detectives from five counties. Most of them will be here tonight, and they'll run down leads until it's within our manpower."

"This is bullshit," Hazard said again, louder, and he kicked a chair hard enough to topple it.

"Get yourself under control, Detective Hazard, or I'll have you on desk duty. Do you understand me?"

Hazard fought the urge to kick the chair again, kick and stomp until it was nothing but slivers.

"Do you understand me?"

"Yes."

"What else?" Somers said. "There's more. You wouldn't look like this if there weren't more."

"He's asked the state to appoint a special prosecutor. From the Attorney General's Office. He'll take charge of the investigation." Cravens let out a breath. "If we're lucky, we'll get to keep a hand in and maybe scrape by. If not, well, get ready to be ridden hard, boys, and still come out looking bad."

"Who?" Hazard demanded.

"From what I heard, he's a real hotshot. An up-and-comer. He's made a name for himself. He wants to make a bigger name."

"He's a politician," Somers said like a man spotting a cockroach.

"He's got juice inside the AG's Office. Lots of it, I hear. And that means he's going to want to blow this up, put his fingerprints all over it. I think we should see this as a good thing: he wants this case solved, and he also wants to do it right."

"Or he wants it solved, and he's willing to hang it on the first person he can find."

"Did you get a name?" Hazard said. "Who is this brain-dead ass-kisser that's going to be running the show?"

"Hazard," Somers said, his face red, jerking his head to silence his partner.

"No, I want to know. I ought to know the name of this Jeff City boy who wouldn't know a real investigation if it chewed his balls off."

"Ree—"

"Come on, Chief. What's this motherfucker's name?"

"This motherfucker's name," a pleasant voice said behind him, "is Sal Cassella. And I'm guessing you're Detective Hazard."

Hazard remembered once, in elementary school, he'd had to sing. Everyone had to sing in elementary school. There weren't electives in elementary school. There weren't choices. The class sang; everybody sang. And somehow, Emery Hazard had found himself at the front of the stage, and he'd had to sing about Mother Goose, some ridiculous song about nursery rhymes, and even then, even in elementary school he'd known that the song was banal, that the content was trite, that the music pandered to sentimentalism, that it was the relish of irrational, mindless emotion.

But it didn't matter; knowing all of that, despising the trivial song that, even as a boy, he'd known had been foolish, none of that mattered because he forgot the words. And when it was his turn to sing, when every eye spun towards him, when it felt like the stage lights had cranked up to a thousand degrees and he might burst into flame, he'd forgotten the words, forgotten those goddamn trite words. He remembered the heat of those stage lights and remembered sweating so much that he thought he could just melt down into his shoes and disappear, and he hoped it would happen because it would have been better than standing there, mute, until Miss Evangeline motioned for the next boy to sing his part.

And now Hazard found himself wondering if he could melt again. Sweat. He'd never known he could sweat so much, like his body had saved it up and had just decided to blast down the dam, sweat like a river.

When he turned around, though, he forgot about all of that. He forgot about the damp cotton bunched under his arms, about the heat in his cheeks, about the pinpricks in his bowels.

Hazard had seen Sal Cassella before. He'd talked to him before. Sal Cassella, their new special prosecutor, was the very handsome man, the Kennedy-handsome man, whom Hazard had met the night before in the Pretty Pretty.

CHAPTER TWELVE

**FEBRUARY 11
SUNDAY
4:15 PM**

"I'M SORRY I KEPT YOU WAITING," Cassella said, moving into the sheriff's house and shutting the door behind him. "Jeff City isn't far, but I had to settle a few things before I left."

Shock whited out Hazard's brain, falling over it like static. Sal Cassella had been in a gay bar last night. He had flirted with Hazard last night. He had watched Hazard punch out a frat boy last night.

And God, Cassella was hot. Even in the dim lighting of the Pretty Pretty, Cassella had clearly been an attractive man: dressed in a sports coat and tie, but managing to look at ease in the clothes; tall, broad across the chest, and with a jaw like something that had been chiseled—and chiseled by someone who knew what he was doing. Hazard remembered his thought from the previous evening: this man had the good looks of a politician. Then Hazard had to fight back a groan. Of course he did. Because he was a politician. Hazard waited for the acknowledgment and recognition.

A single, panicked thought ran through his mind: what would Somers say?

Cassella's attention, though, moved past Hazard and stopped on the chief. "Can you fill me in on what's happened so far?"

That was it. That was all. Hazard took a breath and tried to force the heat from his cheeks. So that was how Cassella wanted to play it. All right. All right, that was all right. At least Somers wouldn't have to know.

And, Hazard realized with a flash of insight, this gave him leverage. Cassella implied he had just come from Jeff City, but that wasn't exactly true. He'd been in Wahredua last night. The lie was an omission, but it was still a lie. Was Cassella still closeted? Or was there another reason for his misdirection?

Cravens was explaining what had happened so far in the investigation. As she did, Cassella nodded, occasionally stopping her to ask a question for clarification, thumb tracing the cleft in his chin like a goddamn Disney prince.

When Cravens had finished, Cassella said, "It sounds like things are pretty well in order."

"What's next?" Cravens asked.

"Chief, I'm here as the state's special prosecuting attorney. I know my job. I'm good at my job. And I'm also smart enough to know when other people are good at their jobs, and it's obvious that you run a strong department. I recognize those two—they've been in every state paper from KC to St. Louis—and I know their reputation. About the best detectives this side of the Mississippi, from what I've read."

"We've worked hard," Somers said with an easy-going smile. "And we've had some luck. That's every investigation, though. There's always that question of luck."

"Looks to me like you and your partner have made your own luck. That's the kind of men I want to work with on this case. And I can promise you this much: I'll work just as hard as you do. This kind of thing, this kind of killing, it goes to the heart of what makes us a nation. It goes to the heart of law and order, of justice, of a man's right to be safe and peaceful in his own home. If we let this slide, we might as well throw open our doors and welcome chaos into our homes. What we've got here, what we're fighting, we're talking about a way of life."

"That's great. That's true, isn't it, Hazard? That's really true. You hit the nail on the head."

"Thank you, Detective," Cassella said, pumping Somers's hand. "Thank you for all that you do."

"We've got some leads we want to follow up on," Somers said, and Cassella was still holding his hand, just a moment too long, and Hazard felt a ping inside. "We're going to get on that right now. We won't let you down."

Cassella, still smiling, still holding Somers's hand—still, and what did he think it was, the motherfucking Olympics of handshaking?—nodded, but he said, "I like that energy, Detective. I like that hustle. But listen, we've got to strategize about this. We've got resources coming. I'm talking the Ozark Major Case Squad. I'm talking forensic support from the state highway patrol. That's some heavy firepower, Detective, and we don't want to waste any of it."

"I was thinking," Somers began.

"That's right. That's right, that's what I want. I want you to keep doing what you do best. You keep thinking. Until we've got boots on the ground, though, we're in a holding pattern. That's the best thing you can do, Detective. Put that brain to work."

"Detective Hazard and I, we've got a good partnership, and we like to do things—"

"I don't doubt that. I don't, Detective. Not at all. But you're part of a team now. Teams play differently. You've got to play differently if you want to win. Tell you what. You're up and ready to go. Blood's hot. I get it. You want to do something. Am I right?"

"Yeah, that's it. We've got our own way of—"

"So this is what I'm going to do. I'm going to cut you in on the action early because I know you two—God, I feel like I do, anyway. And I want you on the most important part of this. Let me just follow up on a few points with the chief, and I'll give you your marching orders. All right? All right. Why don't you and your partner wait on the porch for me? I'll just be a minute, and then we'll get you on your way."

"I—"

"That's right, Detective. Right outside. Just give me a minute."

The look on Somers's face made Hazard fight a smile. Somers looked like he'd been hit by a truck.

"Come on," Hazard said, nodding at the door and leading the way out to the porch. They stood there in silence. Already, the sky was darkening. The pale, brittle blue of day deepened, the color richer now. Sunset was still so goddamn early. Blue, then violet, then black. Hazard's breath steamed. The cold stung his eyes.

"What the hell just happened?" Somers said.

"You—"

"Don't. Whatever you're going to say, don't say it."

Hazard was silent.

"It's like he wasn't even listening. Like he didn't hear a word I said."

"He heard you."

"I know. That's the worst part, Ree. I know he heard me. And he—he ignored me. He twisted my words around. I never even got to finish what I was saying."

"A couple of times you did."

"Whose side are you on?"

"He's a politician."

"Did I not speak loud enough? Do you think he was distracted?"

Blowing out a thin line of white, Hazard glanced through the picture window. Cassella and Cravens were talking now. Cravens had hands on hips, and her jaw was set, but she was nodding.

Somers was still ranting. "To treat detectives like that, especially with our reputation for solving—"

"He doesn't care about any of that. Politicians care about one thing, Somers: lining the world up so they can fuck it just right. And before you get going again, I've got to tell you: he lied."

"What?"

"He lied about just getting to Wahredua today."

"What are you talking about?"

"Last night, Cassella was here. In town. And then the next day, the sheriff gets shot, and he happens to be called in as the special prosecutor. Doesn't that seem strange to you?"

"How do you know he was here?"

"Just trust me, all right. Doesn't that seem strange?"

"Did you see him?"

"Somers, will you drop it already? In a couple of minutes he's going to be out here, and I want to know how we're going to play this."

"Ok. So you saw him last night. Where? I thought you were out with Nico. Where'd you go to dinner?"

"What the fuck does it matter where we went to dinner? I saw him. That's all that matters. The first thing we've got to do is put in a few calls and try to figure out how he caught this case. Did he pull strings? Did he—"

"You didn't see him at dinner." Somers chewed his lip. Then his whole face brightened with realization. "You saw him at the club."

"If he pulled strings," Hazard said, sensing an edge of desperation in his own voice, "then we need to know which strings. We need to know what kind of leverage he has. If he's got somebody high up, somebody who could get him this case, then the next question is why he wants to be here. It could just be that he wants to make a name for himself. You heard him in there—he's already got the speech written, and he'll give a dozen different versions of it tomorrow. But what if it's something else? He was here last night; that's got to mean something."

"You didn't want me to know where you saw him. And you definitely didn't want me to connect you—or him—back to the club."

"Drop it, Somers."

"Because he's gay? Who cares? You know I don't give a damn about that. So it's something else. Did you kiss him? Grind on him? Dance up on him?"

"You're quite possibly the stupidest man I've ever met."

"No, you're not the cheating type. You get cheated on."

"What the fuck does that mean?"

"It's something else. Something you don't want me to know." Somers's tide-pool eyes widened. "He hit on you."

"He didn't hit on me. He bought me a drink. One goddamn drink, and I said two words to him. That's it. And if you ever bring this up again—"

At that moment, the door opened, and Cassella stepped out onto the porch. He made a show of rubbing his arms against the cold, and he beamed a smile that looked like it had been bleached in a few gallons of peroxide. "Boys," he said. "Sorry about that," and he jerked his head towards the house. "She kind of goes on, doesn't she?"

"If that's a complaint about our chief," Hazard said, "you can stick it up your fucking asshole."

"Oh, man. No. No, that's not what I meant at all. Sorry, I didn't even think about what I was saying."

"Mr. Cassella," Somers began.

"Just Sal."

"Sal, we've got a case to work. Standing out here in the cold isn't getting us any closer to finding the sheriff's killer. I know you've got a plan. I know you're putting troops on the ground. While you get them mobilized, can't we be your—you know, like a strike force? Send us in first to soften them up."

Cassella appraised Somers; his attention was hard to read, but Hazard had seen plenty of guys check Somers out before, and it was clear that Cassella liked what he saw. All Cassella did, though, was chafe his arms again and beam that spotlight smile.

"Detectives, I told you, I need you on the most important part of this case. That's where I'm going to put you. Can I trust you with that?"

Somers nodded, his easy-going grin slipping back onto his face. "Yeah, Sal. Yeah, we've got it. We've already got a few leads. A couple of our witnesses—" Somers cut off because Sal was already shaking his head.

"No, no. You didn't understand me. I'm putting you guys where I need you the most. Backgrounds."

Neither Hazard nor Somers spoke for a moment.

"Excuse me?" Somers said.

"This is bullshit," Hazard said.

"Detectives, I need your investigative skills turned on anybody that comes up in this case. This is your town; you know these people. I want info on the victim. I want info on our witnesses. When the major case squad brings us leads, I want info on them."

"This is bullshit," Hazard said again, spitting into the snow.

"Sal, you're making a mistake," Somers said.

"Detectives, I'm going to make something perfectly clear. I'm a straight shooter. I say what I'm thinking, and I'm going to tell you what I'm thinking. I think you're upset. I think you feel like you're having this investigation ripped out of your hands. I think you feel like you're not being treated fairly, and maybe, you're feeling a little bit sorry for yourselves.

"But let me make something perfectly clear to you: I respect you, and I value your contributions to this case, but it's my case. I'm going to work it the way it needs to be worked. If you don't like that, I'll drag some of the boys from the Attorney General's office down here and we'll do the investigation that way." Cassella drew in a breath, as though about to say more, and then let it out slowly. The tension in his face eased. "We're all worked up. This is a big case for you; it's a big case for me. So let's do it right. Take the night; go home, crack open a beer, talk shit about me, get it off your chest. Come back tomorrow morning. If you want to do your job, you get to work on those backgrounds. If you don't—" Cassella shrugged.

"That's another bullshit move," Hazard said. "Turning this on us, making it sound like it's our choice."

"It is your choice, Detective Hazard. And that wasn't a request. That was an order: go home. Until you've made up your mind about this, I don't want you anywhere near my case. I've got plenty of cops who will do what I ask them to do."

"Let's go," Somers said, catching Hazard's sleeve.

Hazard shook him off. "I'll catch up."

Raising an eyebrow, Somers nodded and took the stairs two at a time. He trotted towards the Interceptor.

Cassella rubbed his arms, as though suddenly reminded of the cold, but he met Hazard's gaze steadily. "Something else, Detective?"

"You tell me."

Both men were silent a long moment. Then Cassella shook his head. "Go home, Detective. Think about this real carefully. And make the right decision."

Hazard took the stairs and caught up with Somers. As Somers guided the Interceptor away from the sheriff's house, Hazard repeated his terse conversation with Cassella.

When Hazard had finished, Somers thumped his thumbs on the steering wheel. "He's calling your bluff."

"I know."

"He thinks you won't press it."

"I know."

"So what are you going to do?"

"I already told you: we're going to ask around."

Somers sighed, but a smile tugged at the corners of his mouth. "You always get me into trouble."

"Trouble's about the only thing you're good for."

Somers's smile widened for a moment, and then it faded. "You know what he did, right?"

"Cassella?"

Nodding, Somers turned the Interceptor towards the blackness along the horizon. "He sidelined us. Took us out of the game. Got us out of the way completely."

Hazard nodded. And that was one more reason he was going to take a closer look at Sal Cassella.

CHAPTER THIRTEEN

**FEBRUARY 11
SUNDAY
5:00 PM**

SOMERS COASTED THE LAST FEW YARDS, letting the Interceptor settle against the curb, and killed the engine.

"This is strange. Dropping you off here."

"You keep saying that. You've said it every time."

"You want to stay at our place?"

"I haven't stayed there in a month, Somers. As soon as the lease is up—"

"I know, I know. But I thought tonight, after everything that happened."

Darkness was creeping in. The glass showed their watery reflections.

"Do you want me to come up with you?"

"God, no."

"I'll come up."

"If Nico's home—"

"I'll hang back. If he's home, you give me the signal and I'll bolt. All right?"

Hazard grunted and swung open the door.

Somers took that as acceptance. He did as he'd promised, keeping a few feet back as he followed Hazard into the trendy apartment building in the trendy part of town. The only sound on the stairs were their footsteps. Nico's apartment was on the fourth floor, and by the time they reached it, Somers's heart was beating fast. It didn't have anything to do with the four flights of stairs, though.

Hazard jimmied the key, opened the door, and was silent. The darkness inside was a statement. The silence inside was a statement. The emptiness — Somers watched that emptiness catch Hazard like a slap in the face.

"Nico," he called.

Somers watched, hurting. That took guts, to call out for him like that. It took guts to hope, maybe, that the lights were off, that the apartment was silent, and that somehow it was just a misunderstanding. It took guts to hope that Nico might walk out of the bedroom and things might still be all right. God, it took guts, and Somers didn't know if he could watch anymore.

"Ree, maybe I should—"

"Why? What the fuck does it matter? He's not here, is he?"

"I know, but you're upset."

"Yeah. So?"

"Maybe you want to be alone."

The door had started to swing shut, and Hazard kicked it open. The crack echoed up and down the hallway. He walked into the darkness, and his voice came back ghostlike. "You invited yourself up here, Somers. Since when has it ever mattered what I want?"

And that hurt, too.

Somers had to turn on the lights when he went inside; Hazard was moving through the darkness, kicking things out of his way without any concern for what he might run into. The apartment looked like shit; it always looked like shit, but now it looked worse. It was obvious that Nico had come through the place like a marauder: he had overturned the laundry baskets, scattered clothes across the sofa and table and chairs and floor, knocked down half a dozen coats and jackets in the closet, dragged a roller suitcase halfway across the room, turned it on its side, and abandoned it. He had done everything possible to make it clear that he'd been there. And he'd done it to annoy Hazard.

"This is nice," Somers said, hooking a turquoise jockstrap by the band and displaying it. "Yours?"

Hazard didn't look back. He just kept kicking. He kicked a pile of t-shirts. He kicked the roller suitcase, and it crashed into the wall and left a dent. He kicked the sofa, and his foot bounced back, and he swore.

"Break a toe?"

"What the fuck do you want?"

"You're really going to stay here tonight."

"I sleep here, don't I?"

"After—" Somers swallowed what he'd been about to say. "After Nico came through here and did this?"

"Doesn't look any worse than it usually does."

"You're pretending it doesn't bother you."

"I'm pretending I still have a fucking boyfriend, Somers, and it's not easy when you're here."

Now, Somers thought. Now, now, now. What exactly did that mean?

Hazard was favoring his foot.

"Want me to kiss it and make it better?"

"Fuck you."

"Take off your shoe and let me look at it. Come on, I'm serious."

"It's fine."

"I'll order takeout."

"I'm not really hungry."

"You're going to eat something. The only question is, will it be something you like?" Somers moved to the fridge, where Nico had hung a half-dozen different takeout menus: Chinese, Indian, pizza, Thai, a second Indian, and Ethiopian. "What do you want?"

"I told you I'm not hungry."

"Yeah, but you're not telling the truth. I'm going to count to five. And if you don't tell me what you want, I'm going to order—" Somers hummed and scanned the menus. All of them except the Ethiopian were wrinkled and stained, obviously well-used. "Ethiopian. One."

"I told you I don't want you to order food."

"Two."

"I've got shit in the fridge."

"I don't eat shit. Three."

"Look, I'm not hungry. You order something you want. Order whatever you want. But I'm not eating."

"Four."

"Jesus Christ. Jesus fucking Christ. Order a fucking pizza."

"What do you want on it?"

"I don't care, Somers."

"One."

Hazard was growling now, the noise so primitive and fierce that it raised the hairs on Somers's neck. "Sausage. All right?"

"I could make a joke about that."

Dropping onto the sofa, Hazard covered his face with his hands.

"I could. I've got a lot of jokes for it, really."

"Please God," Hazard muttered.

"But I won't. Because you're having a hard day."

Somers called in the order, nudged a chair towards the sofa, and sat by Hazard. Close. They made two points of a triangle, and if Hazard stretched, if he scooted, if he so much as wiggled, their knees would touch.

"Let's start by texting him," Somers said.

Hazard dropped his hands. "Are you insane?"

"Just a short text."

"You're out of your goddamn mind."

"Ree, I told you we were going to get him back. I meant it. Now get out your phone."

"I don't have anything to say to him."

"Excuse me?"

"You heard me. I didn't do anything wrong."

"You beat up a guy because you saw him kiss Nico."

"Yeah."

"You were jealous."

"He's my boyfriend. What am I supposed to do, let some frat boy—"

"And we already established that Nico isn't the kind of guy who gets off on jealousy." Somers paused. "I am, by the way. Well, within reason. In case it ever comes up."

Hazard spit out two words. "It. Won't."

"As far as Nico's concerned, you don't trust him, you don't respect him, and you're controlling, obsessive, and maybe a little psychotic."

For a moment, Hazard seemed to absorb that. Then, swearing, he threw a pile of clothes off the couch.

"Maybe a lot psychotic."

"I'm not psychotic. I'm not controlling. I'm not obsessive."

"Yeah, I know. And here's the thing, dummy: Nico probably knows too. But you freaked him out, and he's got that guy, whoever he's staying with—"

"Marcus."

"He's got Marcus whispering in his ear." Somers frowned. "Is he the one you told me about? The one Nico keeps waiting in the wings?"

"That's not how it is. He likes Nico. He'd do just about anything to break us up. But Nico's not keeping him in the wings."

"Ree."

"He's not. He's not, Somers, so wipe that look off your face."

"All right. If you say so. Anyway, he's got that guy whispering in his ear, and it's messing with his head. He's going to be thinking about every bad thing that's ever happened between the two of you. We've got to change that."

A full minute passed. Hazard, with the blue-black stubble bruising his jawline, with his long, dark hair tumbling over his forehead, with his chest and arms just about popping his shirt, Hazard looked like a sculpture. Not *The Thinker*, but maybe *The Worrier*.

"We'll start with the text," Somers said. "Then flowers. A card. Maybe chocolates. Dinner at the Moulin Vert. Just like I told you."

"That's cheesy. He's never going to fall for it."

Letting out a sigh, Somers shook his head. "People don't fall for romance, Ree. It's not a trick. You're trying to show him you're sorry. You're trying to show him how much you value him."

"It feels like a trick. Why can't I just tell him that stuff, and he can move back in?"

"You're joking, right?"

"It makes sense."

"Oh my God. You're not joking."

"We had a fight. I apologize. He comes back. I don't see why that's so crazy."

"You're not joking. You know what you are? You're hopeless."

"Quit looking so happy with yourself," Hazard grumbled, dragging his phone out of his pocket, "and tell me what I'm supposed to say."

"Hey," Somers started. "I'm really sorry about last night. And about today." He paused. "I'm going to give you some options, and then you put in what you want, ok?"

Hazard nodded.

"I love you. You're the most important person in my life. I've never been happier than when we're together. You're a part of me that I didn't even know I was missing. Even when we're fighting, even when you're giving me shit, I know you care about me more than anyone else in the whole world. I know you put up with a lot from me. I love you for that. I love you for the amazing man that you are." Somers's throat was thick. His eyes misted, and he blinked rapidly.

Still texting, Hazard nodded. "Damn, Somers. That's amazing. Where'd you come up with that?" And he looked up then, the long, dark hair wavy across his forehead, those scarecrow eyes full of gold fire, a pink glow along his cheekbones. So beautiful. And so goddamn oblivious.

"Just rolls off the tongue. You've got what you want?"

"How do I end it?"

"I'd really like to see you again and talk about this. I value what we have too much to let it slip away because I made a stupid mistake. I hope you'll forgive me."

As Hazard finished swiping at his phone, he said, "This is the longest message I've ever sent."

Somers couldn't summon up an answer; he was still blinking furiously.

"You got something in your eye?"

"No."

Hazard looked like he might ask again, but then the phone buzzed.

"What's he say?"

"'Is this Somers?' Damn it. I knew I shouldn't have asked you for help."

"Let me see."

"No. Damn it."

"Ree, let me see."

Thrusting out the phone, Hazard dropped back into the sofa cushions.

But there wasn't really anything for Somers to see; that was all Nico had sent: *Is this Somers?* The little bitch.

"Tell him it's not me," Somers said, pitching the phone into Hazard's lap.

"He's going to know, Somers. He always knows. For all I know, he saw the Interceptor outside, and as soon as I lie, he's going to show up and confront us. Damn it. Damn it, damn it, damn it."

"Has he done that before?"

"What?"

"Shown up out of the blue to try to catch us?"

Hazard closed his eyes.

"He did. At Christmas, holy shit, he did. That's why he showed up at our place? Because he thought we were banging? And that's the guy you want to be with?"

Hazard's eyes opened to slits. "What?"

"Nothing."

"What did that question mean?"

"It didn't mean anything. I said something. I'm stupid like that sometimes. Just let it go."

"No. You did that this morning. Go ahead, Somers. What do you want to say so badly about Nico?"

"I don't want to say anything."

"Bullshit. You want to say he's a baby. You want to say he's immature. You want to joke about his age, about how he isn't a good fit for me, about how stupid I am for dating him."

"That's not what—"

"Come on, you've been saying it for months. Say it now."

The doorbell rang. The two men stared at each other.

"I want you to be happy," Somers said.

"Answer the door. That's your damn pizza."

"Ree, I'm sorry I've been a shit about Nico. I am. I'm trying to help now, though."

"Get the goddamn door."

It was pizza, and Somers tipped the guy and cleared the table. Steam was still rising from the golden-brown cheese.

"Sausage."

"I can see what it is." Hazard stormed to the fridge and stormed back with two bottles of beer.

"It's just a little on the nose, don't you think?"

"Eat. Drink. No talking."

Somers ate. And he drank. Hazard had a slice of pizza. He had a beer. And then another. And then another.

"You might want to pace yourself."

In answer, Hazard got another beer.

"You need to take those pills, right? For your head?"

"I'm fine."

"Is it hurting?"

"I said I'm fine."

Somers brought the pills, and Hazard swallowed them with another beer. After that, Somers had a second beer. And when Hazard brought him a third, he had a third.

Hazard's phone buzzed again, and this time, Somers snatched it. *I guess that's my answer.*

"What's it say?" Hazard sounded drunk. His eyes were glassy, and at some point during the drinking, he'd undone the top three buttons on his shirt. Ivory skin showed in the gap, and a scattering of dark, straight hair. The pills might not have been a good idea with the beer, Somers realized.

"Nothing. He's being bitchy."

"Let me see what he said."

"Just leave it until tomorrow, all right?"

Hazard made a lunge, but his coordination was off, and he was slow.

"Give me the damn phone."

"Just let it go for tonight."

With an obvious effort, Hazard pulled himself upright. "Give me that phone."

"How many have you had?"

"I'm going to call him."

"You're loaded."

"I'm going to get that phone if I have to pin you down and take it."

The words were like a hot breath on the back of Somers's neck, and he flushed. He must have been distracted—he definitely wasn't thinking about what it would feel like to be pinned under Hazard—because the next thing he knew, Hazard had snagged the phone.

"I am. I'm going to call him."

"You're being stupid. Don't fuck this up."

"You don't know." Hazard paused, peering at the phone's screen. "You don't know what you're talking about."

"I don't know what I'm talking about?"

"You fucked up your marriage. You don't have any idea what you're talking about."

"Oh yeah? Well fuck you. Fuck you, Ree. And you know what? That's my whole point. I know how to mess things up. I'm telling you not to do this."

"You don't know." Hazard mumbled as he punched at the phone. Then he held it up to his ear.

Somers gave up. He moved into the kitchen and started opening cabinets. Not a whole lot; college boy stuff, bachelor stuff. Ramen. Mac and cheese. A few cans of soup. He tried the freezer. There, in the back, vodka, ice cold.

He poured the first drink as Hazard started talking.

"Yeah, it's me. Who the fuck else is it going to be? Yeah. Yeah, he's here. Yeah, he's—no. No, Nico. You listen to me. You listen to me for once. Yeah, you're goddamn right I'm yelling at you. Yeah—no. No, I'm not drunk. I'm not. You need to listen to me. Yeah. Somers is here. Yeah, I know you think that's un-fucking believable. I know. I know exactly what you think. You're always telling me what you think. I—no. No, you listen to me. He's my partner, Nico. My partner. Fuck that, I'll yell as loud as I want. You want to hang up on me? Fine. Hang up on me. But he'll still be here. He's here because he's my friend. I don't care if you don't like that. He's. My. Friend. He's—" Hazard wobbled, pulled the phone from his ear, and stared at the screen. With an inarticulate shout, he hurled the phone at the wall.

Somers threw back the second shot of vodka. "That went well."

Slumped on the sofa, Hazard didn't respond.

"Ree."

Silence.

"Ree."

Silence.

"Hey, Ree."

"God, what?"

"That went well."

Hazard looked like he was trying to melt into the sofa.

Bringing the bottle of vodka and a small tumbler, Somers went to the far side of the sofa and stretched out, kicking off his shoes and settling his feet across Hazard's lap.

"Get off me," Hazard growled, shoving Somers's feet away.

"Come on." Somers slid his feet back into place.

"I said get off."

"Remember when you said I was your friend?"

Hazard spun to look at him, eyes wide, his jaw set like he was planning on biting a dinner plate in half. But he didn't shove Somers's feet off him this time. And after a moment, one of his big paws came to rest on Somers's calf.

"Hey, Ree."

That big, callused paw skated up Somers's calf, hesitated at the knee, and reversed course.

"Ree."

"What?"

Somers's fought a giggle. "That went well."

This time, Hazard gave Somers's feet a mock shove, and then he started to laugh. The laughter built in volume and intensity until Hazard was shaking and he buried his face in the sofa. Somers fought the urge to reach out and run a hand through that silken hair.

"You're an asshole," Hazard gasped when he finally caught his breath.

"I know."

"I'm an asshole."

"I know."

"Why did you let me call him?"

"It's going to be ok. You'll get him back. Maybe not tonight, but you will."

Neither of them spoke for a long time after that. Hazard's hand slid up Somers's leg again, the touch firmer this time—still tentative, still exploratory, but slightly more confident. Somers shifted his weight, spread his knees. God, he thought. Just a little higher. Please, tonight, let it be tonight, and all the rest of this mess will be over.

But Hazard's dumb mitt stopped at his knee every time. And he poured himself a shot of vodka and tossed it back.

"That's enough," Somers said.

This time, Hazard poured one for him.

Tonight, Somers was thinking, the word vibrating in time with his heartbeat. Let it be tonight. And he pounded the shot.

And then Hazard poured himself one.

"No," Somers said, touching Hazard's wrist when the glass came back towards him. "No, I'm—"

But he forgot what he was going to say, and he did the shot.

And at some point, it became easy to talk.

"Can I ask you something?"

"You can ask me anything." Hazard leaned towards him, his dark hair spilling into his eyes. "You're my best friend. You know that? My best friend."

"Can I ask you about Nico?"

"You can—you can ask me about fucking anything."

"Why do you want to be with him? I'm not trying to be an asshole. I just want to know. What is it about him?"

Hazard was silent for a long time. His hand stalled on Somers's calf. His breathing deepened.

"He's nice to me."

"A lot of guys would be nice to you?"

Hazard didn't answer. He'd gone stock-still. His eyes, Somers realized, had flooded, and he plunged his face back into the cushions for a moment and drew a ragged breath.

"Ree, what—"

"Oh my God, I'm so fucking drunk."

"What's wrong?"

"Nothing."

"Ree."

"You know the first guy I dated? His name was Alec. Alec," Hazard pronounced the name again, as though he wasn't sure of the sound. "First guy I ever really went with. He was blond." Hazard paused, blushing, and then blurted, "Like you. And I don't know why I stayed, John."

The name, that shortened name that Hazard had never used before, turned in Somers's chest like a key, and sweat broke out across his chest, under his arms, on his forehead, sweat like he was standing in front of a bonfire.

"I don't have any clue why I stayed. I should have left. I could have left. I could have stopped him."

"He—what? He hurt you?"

"At first, he just used his hand. He liked it. He told me I liked it too, and I wasn't sure, I thought maybe I did. And then the belt. And I knew I didn't like that, but I didn't—I didn't fucking stop him. He'd chase me around the apartment. He'd laugh." Hazard peeled his touch away from Somers's leg and covered his face with both hands. "Aw, fuck. I'm so fucking fucked up."

"Ree, nobody should have done that to you." And that invisible bonfire was still roaring, and Somers was still sweating, and his stomach flopped because he thought that he had been the first one, the first one who had hurt Hazard, the one who had made it possible for all the rest to hurt him. "You don't deserve—"

"And you know about Billy, right? I mean, you've heard enough. You're not stupid. You're not. You're really not, even though you let people think you are. You're smart."

"Ree, you don't have to talk—"

"I mean, you know he was cheating on me. I didn't know. Or maybe I did, deep down. And the way he talked to me like I was small. Like he could step on me and scrub me out with his shoe, like that. And you know what the fucker is? I met him the night I left Alec. I walked down the stairs, and there he was, and then—and that's all, I guess." Hazard lifted his hands from his face. "You want to know why I like Nico? Because he's nice to me. Because he cares about me."

That heat was still burning inside Somers. He was still sweating, so much sweat that his shirt clung to his chest. Between the two men, the air had drawn taut with the spillover of emotion and desire. Somers cleared his throat to talk and he wasn't even sure what he was going to say.

"I'm glad, Ree. I really am. But do you love him?"

Hazard's head rolled backward until it was resting on the sofa, and he didn't answer. Ten minutes might have passed that way. Twenty. Somers never knew. When Hazard spoke again, his voice had gone flat, stripped down to a careful neutrality. "I screwed up your whole evening. You probably had plans."

Somers thought of Cora. He thought of the times she still didn't answer his calls. He thought about the nights she had plans, the nights she asked him not to stop by the house. He thought about the night the week before when he had driven past Cucina Familia and seen her coming out, seen her very well dressed, seen her cheeks flushed and a smile on her lips.

"I need to barf."

Hazard helped him stand, and Somers slipped and fell against him.

"You're wasted," Hazard said.

"I'm fucked, Ree," Somers heard himself saying.

Hazard, looping an arm around Somers's waist, drew him towards the bathroom. "You shouldn't have gotten the vodka."

"No, I'm fucked." Somers was speaking, and the words were pouring out, but he heard them as though someone else were speaking. "I'm fucked with Cora. I fucked everything up and it's never going to be right again. Just like I fucked everything with you."

Hazard paused, and the sudden stop jolted Somers. "Come on."

"No. I'm so fucked."

"You should have left the vodka."

They barely made it to the toilet in time. And when Somers had finished, Hazard helped him up and wiped his mouth and carried him—goddamn carried him, just like a baby—to the bedroom, and he pulled back the sheets and slid Somers in.

And the last thing Somers remembered as Hazard pulled away was leaning up to kiss the side of his neck, and Hazard's muffled laugh, and his deep voice saying, "Next time, I'll brush your teeth."

CHAPTER FOURTEEN

FEBRUARY 13
TUESDAY
11:27 AM

THEY HADN'T SPOKEN ABOUT THAT NIGHT. Even now, under the fluorescent lighting of the station's bullpen, Hazard hunched lower over his computer and felt his face flush as the memory crashed forward into his consciousness. They hadn't talked about it, thank God. Hazard didn't remember most of it, he was sure, and thank God for that too. But he remembered running his hand up Somers's leg. He remembered throwing a boner like he was sixteen again. He remembered saying too much, and even now, days later, he had to stifle a groan as he tried to squash the memory.

"You all right?" Somers asked from the opposite desk.

Hazard ignored him.

The last two days had been spent in a frenzy of activity. Sal Cassella's command of the Ozark Major Crimes Unit had been absolute, and he had been serious about his plans: while detectives from the five surrounding counties tracked down leads from the sheriff's shooting, Hazard and Somers had been glued to their desks, digging up every scrap of information they could find about the witnesses—in other words, shuffling their feet.

Sure, they'd sat in on the daily briefings. They'd heard updates. But without context, without all the information, it hadn't mattered. They hadn't even been allowed to conduct the interview with Lionel Arras, the witness who had fled the sheriff's house, when the uniformed officers finally caught up with him. Instead, Hazard and Somers had spent that time typing up the statements they had taken from the witnesses they had managed to speak with.

With every day—with every hour—their chances of solving this case grew smaller, and Hazard felt mounting frustration. He couldn't put together a puzzle if he didn't know what the pieces looked like. For hell's sake, he didn't even know if there were any pieces. For all Hazard knew, they were just spinning their wheels.

"This is stupid," Somers said. "We're spinning our wheels."

Hazard punched at the keyboard hammering out another sentence about Lionel Arras; he'd stumbled onto paperwork Arras had filed when he incorporated his financial advisement firm, and now Hazard had to update the dossier. Not that it mattered. Nobody was going to care what Arras had listed as the mission statement for his business—*Semper Fidelis*, which was both unoriginal and offensive since Arras had never served with the Marines.

"We should be doing something."

Hazard ignored him.

"There was a car wreck on Route 133. We could go work that. Just direct traffic, stuff like that."

"Automobile accidents are a nightmare."

"It'd be better than pushing paper."

"The driver was a lawyer. I'm not pulling traffic duty because some small-town lawyer got loaded and plowed into a tree. Anyway, it's out by Honey Creek. Not even our jurisdiction."

For a minute—not even a minute—Somers was silent. Then: "Hey, Ree."

Hazard pecked out another phrase and then backspaced because he'd mashed two keys. The keyboard was just too damn small.

"Ree, did you hear what I said?"

"Don't you have work to do?"

"Here's my work," Somers said, kicking his legs up onto the desk and fanning open a file. "Eunice Moody, age sixty-five, born in Wahredua, died in Wahredua—"

"She's not dead yet."

"I'm imagining a better world." He cleared his throat. "Died in Wahredua. Daughter of rail transport baron Wilfred Moody, also deceased. Among Wilfred Moody's investments were the original Wahredua Power Plant, a portion of the now-Missouri Pacific lines, warehouses along the Grand Rivere, and a shipping concern that ran freight up and down from New Orleans." He snapped the file shut. "What do you think?"

"Nobody's going to care about her father."

"But it's interesting, right?"

"No."

"You do one."

"I'm working."

"Come on, your best one."

"I'm typing a report."

"Ree, just tell me one thing that was interesting. One thing. I'm falling asleep over here. I'm dying."

"I'm imagining a better world."

"Ouch."

Hazard picked out another word and swore. He'd mashed half the damn keyboard that time.

"I said ouch."

"I'm trying to finish this damn report."

"Your fingers are too big."

Hazard ignored him.

"I'll do another," Somers said graciously, "while you think of one. Randall Scott. Fifty-seven. Gallbladder removed in 2002 — the *Courier* wrote a piece on that, did you know? Big news in small town. He's in the *Courier* a lot. I did research."

"I might have a heart attack."

"Pretty impressive, right?"

"You've got to break that news slowly, Somers. That kind of shock could kill a guy."

Somers fanned himself with the file and settled into the seat. "His father bought up a lot of the land they currently own in the late 1930s. Lots of people were willing to sell back then. And our friend Randy was the talk of the town in 1977 when he was named Mr. 4-H. Even got a picture." Somers flipped the file around to display a young Randy Scott, still thin as a beanpole. "A son who's dead. Pretty ugly — we were at college when it happened, but a lot of nasty rumors were going around, and then he ended up dead."

"This is hell."

"No, it's Wahredua."

"This is my hell. Sitting here with a keyboard that doesn't work —"

"It works fine. You've just got fat hands."

"With a keyboard that doesn't work," Hazard emphasized, "listening to you gossip like an old fishwife, and I can't leave, I can't go anywhere, I can't shut you up."

"Sorry, I didn't know you felt that way. I'll be quiet."

"Thank you."

"If you'll tell me something interesting you found."

Hazard groaned.

"Come on," Somers said. "I know you found something juicy."

"Something juicy like Randall Scott being named Mr. 4-H?"

"Or like—" Somers scanned a page. "Dr. June Hayashi graduated from Stanford Medical School. Anything. Just give me something, Ree. We've been doing this for two days. I'm stir crazy. If you tell me, I'll—"

"Please don't."

"I'll buy the next round of flowers."

Fighting another groan, Hazard dug through the folders on his desk. He'd sent flowers to Nico. Twice yesterday. Once already today. He was a public servant, and he had a very angry boyfriend, and if things kept up this way, he was going to be broke in a very short time.

"Beverly Flinn," Hazard snapped the file open so hard that the manila folder tore along the edge. "She was born in Wahredua."

"More than that."

A growl was building in Hazard's throat. "She does community theater."

"We know that. And would it kill you to do this with a little showmanship?"

"She won the Dore County Actors Guild Award for Best Actress in *Macbeth*. She played Lady Macbeth." He slapped the file onto the desk. "Is that enough?"

Somers frowned and squinted. "Could you undo the top button of your shirt? I'm not asking for myself, but I think the people would really like it."

This time, the growl broke free as Hazard turned back to his work.

"Wait, wait. I've got a good one. You'll be interested in this one. I promise."

Hazard hated himself for hesitating.

"Grant McAtee," Somers said, dragging another file out of a stack. "Our favorite deputy."

"What?"

"Born with a silver spoon in his mouth."

Shaking his head, Hazard lifted his hands over the keyboard.

"I'm not just talking a nice home, Ree. I'm talking a silver spoon in his mouth and a silver stick up his butt. I'm talking money. Serious money."

"And he's working as a deputy? Why? He doesn't seem like he has a particular love for law and justice."

"See? I told you you'd be interested."

"I'm not interested. I'm curious."

"They're the same thing. And he can't touch it. Not a penny of it, it turns out."

"What? How in the world could you know that?"

Paging through the file, Somers stabbed at a document towards the back. "Dear old mommy's will. She specifies in the will and in the trust documents—I've got those too—that the money is to be held in trust until all of the trustees agree that McAtee is of sound judgment."

"Who were the trustees?"

"Who do you think?"

"Bingham."

"That would be a pretty good motive."

Hazard felt a thrill of excitement. This was the closest they'd come to a break in the case. They finally had a thread they could follow. They finally had—

Breaking out into laughter, Somers waved the file dismissively. "Sorry, I couldn't help it. The sheriff's not mentioned anywhere in the paperwork. Just a couple of snowbirds that shuttle between Phoenix and Milwaukee, and an old guy in the Florida Keys."

Hammering at the keyboard, Hazard typed a sentence that rocked the whole desk. This sentence was about—Hazard tried to repress a shudder—the differences between Arras's original and revised ten-year business plans.

"Now you give me one."

It was better than typing. That treacherous thought wormed its way through Hazard's head. Anything was better than trying to type one more sentence about Lionel Arras's business.

"I got a copy of Sheriff Bingham's transactions over the last year," Hazard said, dropping his voice.

"What?"

"While I was working on Arras's file."

"How?"

"I asked for them."

"And Cassella showed them to you? He wouldn't show us a TV Guide if he thought it had something to do with this case."

"Cassella didn't show me. I called Arras's office and told them we'd lost the first copy. I asked for another copy and gave them the fax number for the bullpen."

"You're devious."

"I am not."

"You're sneaky."

109

"It was a simple request, Somers."

"What else have you lied about?"

"I don't lie." But Hazard squirmed and added, "Normally."

"What'd you find?"

"He's been liquidating a lot of assets. He pulled money out of the state pension early—big penalties on that—and he'd sold off some stocks. Did you know he had a mortgage on that house?"

"His family has had that house forever. There's no way he owed money on it."

"A lot of money, it turns out. A few hundred grand."

Somers was silent for a moment. "I know I just pulled your leg about McAtee. Is that what this is? Are you getting me back?"

"No."

"I know you're a liar now."

"I'm not lying."

"Well, what does that mean? We're combing through stuff about witnesses. That's fine. Cassella wants to cross them off his list in permanent marker, I get it. It's a waste of our time, but I get it. But what you just dug up—Jesus, Hazard, did you tell them?"

"It's not like you have to be a genius to see it. If I saw it, anybody can. The question is what they're doing with it."

"That much money—what is it? Drugs? Prostitution? Extortion?"

"According to that reporter for the *Courier*, he's done a lot of bad stuff. Maybe some of it caught up to him."

"We're talking how much?"

"Half a million. Maybe a little more."

"If he spent it on drugs, he'd be dead by now."

"He is dead by now."

Somers shook his head. "We've been sitting here for two days, shoveling this shit, and the whole time you had a serious lead on why somebody might have killed him? Why didn't you say something?"

"I was finishing my reports."

For a moment, Somers seemed speechless. He made a strangled noise in his throat, and Hazard hid a smile.

"We've got to follow up on this," Somers finally managed to say. "This could be our break. Tonight, once we're off duty, we'll get out there and do some digging."

"Sure."

"Finally."

"If I finish my reports."

"I could kill you."

Hazard shrugged.

"You're bigger than me, but I could still shoot you."

Before Hazard had to answer, the door to Chief Cravens's office crashed open.

"Detective Somers," Cravens shouted. "Detective Hazard. Get in here."

CHAPTER FIFTEEN

FEBRUARY 13
TUESDAY
11:45 AM

CRAVENS, SEATED BEHIND HER DESK, fixed the detectives with a glower as they entered the office. Cassella lounged in a chair, legs kicked out like he was poolside.

"Sit down," Cravens said.

"Something wrong?" Somers asked, glancing at Cassella and Cravens as he lowered himself into a chair.

"Besides the fact that you've whined and puled and moaned for two days straight? No. Nothing's wrong."

Cassella cleared his throat. "I would have said bitched."

Somers didn't take the bait; he just offered Cassella a smile. Smiles were free, they were nice, and they were pretty damn useful. Hazard didn't look like he'd know a smile from a kick in the ass. The big lug was staring at Cassella like he wanted to knock a hole in him.

"The Ozark Major Crimes Unit is done," Cravens said. She picked up a file on the desk and toyed with the edges. "They headed home this morning."

"You caught someone?" Hazard said. "That's impossible."

"Thank you for that vote of confidence," Cassella said.

"We can't keep detectives from five counties doing our jobs," Cravens said. "What's more, we can't afford them even if we wanted to. They did what they were supposed to do." She fiddled with the file again. "They ran down every lead that came in and they left us with the solid ones."

"While we sat on our asses," Hazard said.

"I explained that," Cassella said in his best speech-giving voice. "I wanted you two working the local angle."

"Mr. Cassella was also worried that we might be . . . parochial," Cravens said, the word so sour it could have curdled a dairy farm. "He worried that you two might let your local knowledge bias your initial investigation."

"Because we're not professionals," Hazard said. "Because we're bumpkins with our heads up our asses."

"Nobody said anything like that," Cassella said. "Nobody thought anything like it either. I told you both: I respect you. I respect the fine work you've done here. You're some of the best detectives our state has, and that's why I'm turning this back over to you."

"You are?" Somers said.

"Now that we've got a direction to take this case, I want you two to run it into the ground. Find the son of a bitch who did this and put a bow on him. Do what you do best."

Cravens, sighing, slid the file towards Somers.

The first packet of papers was prefaced by a typed report and—Somers sighed—chicken-scratch. He recognized the handwriting. And, for that matter, the report.

"Look familiar?"

"That's my file on Lynn Fukuma," Hazard said. "What's it doing in there?"

Somers flicked a photograph, dated to the day of the murder, clipped to the corner of the file. Someone had taken the picture outside the sheriff's home, from a position on the opposite side of the road. It showed the protesters and their signs framed against the ancient monstrosity of the Bingham house. A second photograph, larger, had been paperclipped underneath this, and Somers worked it free and studied it. It was clearly an enlargement of the first. Although the resolution was slightly worse, the original must have been fairly high quality because the photograph had fared surprisingly well. Beyond the crowd of protesters, on a crest of the Bingham land, a figure was moving towards a wooded hilltop. The figure was small, slight, and dark. It could have been Lynn Fukuma. It could have been any of a thousand different people in Wahredua.

But it might have been Fukuma. In Hazard and Somers's first joint investigation in Wahredua, the college professor had been an important suspect. With a history of violence and a vicious hatred of almost everything, Fukuma had made plenty of enemies, and Somers wouldn't have been surprised if the sheriff were one of them.

"Who took this?" Somers asked.

"The shirt," Hazard said, tapping the enhancement and then slipping a third photograph free from the file. In the enhancement the figure who was trespassing on the Binghams' land—and who was heading in the general direction of the bluff where someone had shot and killed Morris Bingham—wore a coat with three white stripes. Hazard turned the third photograph in his hand and then juxtaposed it to the enlargement.

The third photograph showed Fukuma at a rally: up close, her pageboy haircut blown back by wind, her mouth open in a scream. Her sign read: *Die American Pigs!* She was wearing a black coat with three white slashes along the sleeve.

"She's missing a comma," Hazard said.

Somers ignored him. "Who took this?"

"A local news crew showed up for the protest," Cassella said. "We managed to get a copy of their photographs."

"There wasn't a news crew when we arrived," Hazard said.

"This isn't the United Nations. They snapped a few pictures, got a few sound bites, that's all."

Somers frowned and studied the photographs again. "And a picture of someone who might be Lynn Fukuma headed into the sheriff's woods."

"It's Lynk," Hazard said. "She presents as male, remember?"

"She doesn't present as male. Not exactly. God, her last big idea was anything but pro-male."

Cassella raised an eyebrow.

"Legislating mandatory castration," Hazard said.

Wincing, Cassella said, "The Major Crimes Unit wasn't able to track her down, but the chief put some patrol boys on her door. When she comes home, we'll find her."

"If she comes home," Somers said, sliding the paperclip over the photographs again and turning to the next bundle of documents. "For all we know, she's in Venezuela by now."

"Chavez better keep an eye on his balls," Cassella said, and Somers grinned in spite of himself.

"Chavez is dead," Hazard said.

"Just a joke," Cassella said.

"He died five years ago."

Somers, sighing, examined the next packet. This one was much slimmer: several photographs, all enhancements and enlargements of a single shot; and a brief, typed report.

"You didn't write this," Somers said, dropping the report in Hazard's lap. "Not near enough damn semicolons. So this," he tapped the glossy photographic paper. "This is where you're pushing."

"We're not pushing anywhere," Cravens said. "This is a legitimate lead."

"And you happened to have a report ready to go? And don't tell me you just did it; Hazard and I have been doing all the background checks. You had this sitting in a drawer."

"I don't like your tone. I don't like what you're implying."

"Is this why Mayor Newton called you in?" Somers said to Cassella. He angled the photos towards Hazard. "If I'm not mistaken, that's Dennis Rutter. Isn't that who the Ozark Volunteers are putting up for sheriff?"

Cassella maintained his casual, almost lounging posture, but Somers hadn't missed the thousand different micro-adjustments: the new tension around his eyes, the change in his breathing, the tendons on the inside of his wrist, more. All of them said the same thing: Cassella was on high alert.

"You're suggesting that your mayor—with the cooperation of the police chief—is taking advantage of this situation and trying to frame a political rival?"

"No."

"Oh. So you're suggesting that he killed the sheriff and then framed Mr. Rutter?"

"No."

"What exactly are you saying, Detective Somerset?"

"I'm asking why you have a file on Rutter that I didn't write and that Hazard didn't write."

"You aren't aware of every investigation inside this department," Cravens said. A flush had moved into her cheeks, and she slapped both hands onto the desk. "And if I get a whiff that you're spouting anything like what I thought I just heard, I'll find new detectives who can do this job."

Somers met her stare for a moment—not too long, not the way Hazard was glaring at her, but enough to remind her that he wasn't a pushover. Then he shrugged and looked away.

"That picture," Cassella said, "was taken by a speed camera on Route 17. Right by the pullout on the Savoy branch of the Grand Rivere. That's— oh, a mile or so downriver of where the Grand Rivere runs through the sheriff's land. Those speed cameras, they're experimental. The Highway Patrol is just trying them out. Pretty lucky, right? That's Dennis Rutter—" He indicated the man behind the wheel of the truck. "And that's a kayak."

"We goddamn know what a kayak is," Hazard said. "When was this taken?"

"Sunday. About 12:30pm."

The implications were clear. The timing was right. The distances were right. And Somers had seen, for himself, the footprints that led down to the water. He had seen the patch of earth torn away where someone had slipped while going down the bank. Into a kayak, for example. At 12:30pm, the Wahredua PD were still scrambling to get the crime scene locked down. Nobody was looking a mile downriver for a man with a kayak. Not yet.

"We want all the footage from the camera. All of it. This is just too damn convenient."

"You'll get it."

"So what'd Rutter say?"

Cassella's eyebrows knit together.

"He rabbited," Cravens said. "Judge Platter wouldn't sign a warrant until we'd gone down there and knocked on the gate and played nice first."

"And they wouldn't let you an inch inside that compound," Somers said.

"By the time the judge signed a warrant, Rutter was gone. We went through that whole stinking heap, and he was gone."

"Nobody knew where he was," Cassella said with a smile. "I asked."

"Big surprise," Hazard muttered.

"So we're supposed to run him down?" Somers said. "When the Ozark Major Crimes Unit couldn't do it?"

"It's not that we couldn't," Cassella said. "This is a question of time, resources, priorities—"

"You couldn't do it," Hazard said. "And you want us to do it. That's how it is."

"That's enough, Detective Hazard," Cravens said. "Detective Somerset, you have resources. You have a connection to the Ozark Volunteers that has provided reliable information in the past."

"No way," Hazard said. "No fucking way."

"She's not talking to you," Cassella said.

"I don't care. I'm telling you no fucking way."

Somers grimaced. "You want me to talk to Naomi, I'll talk to Naomi."

"Why?" Hazard said. "She only talks when she wants to play us. We can't trust her. Talking to her is a mistake."

"Drop it, all right? I'll talk to her."

"This is a mistake. This is a huge mistake."

"That's enough, Detective," Cravens said.

"So we've got two people in the wind," Somers said. "Hell of a job your guys did."

"Three, actually," Cassella said, holding up three fingers with an apologetic smile. "Keep going."

Somers slid out the last packet. The photograph on the front was in color, and it had clearly been taken for official identification. The woman had dark hair pulled into a ponytail and a flat-featured face. Wide-hipped and stout, she looked like she'd have been better suited to waitressing or bartending in one of those cheap, roadside dives. Instead, she wore the khaki uniform of a sheriff's deputy.

Behind the photograph, an employment record detailed a mediocre career. Lisa Dudley had been employed by the Dore County Sheriff's Office for almost four years. She had no commendations, no endorsements, no recognition. For the first two years she had ridden a desk in the sheriff's office, a boring but comfortable day job. Then, early in her third year, she had been transferred to the third shift at the county jail. Shortly thereafter, she had resigned, although the file had no explanation of why.

"Who'd she piss off?" Hazard said, reading over Somers's shoulder.

"Take a guess," Somers said as he turned to the next page. This was separate from her employment history, and the paper was wrinkled, as though it had been wadded up and thrown away and then recovered. It was a civil complaint that had been filed by Lisa Dudley against Morris Bingham, senior. It alleged assault, battery, and intentional infliction of emotional distress. The documents had been served to Bingham on Friday.

"Was there anybody who didn't want to kill him?" Hazard said.

"Sounds like you've got something in common." Somers tapped the folder. "She's missing too?"

"We talked to her mother and father—they live about halfway between here and St. Elizabeth. They say this is Dudley's routine, now. She works odd jobs, saves up cash, and is wired like a ticking time bomb. Then she blows, and she's gone for four, five days."

"When did she start her last binge?"

Cassella's lips parted over perfectly even, perfectly white teeth.

"You're fucking kidding me," Hazard said.

"Sunday morning," Cassella said, his smile broadening. "And she took her dad's rifle with her."

"Three of them," Somers said. "Three, and they're all in the wind."

"There's one more thing," Cravens said. From her desk, she withdrew a piece of paper. It was obviously a photocopy, and it was even more obviously something that Cravens wished she could hide. She hesitated for a moment, as though considering calling off the whole thing, and then, with a sigh, she passed it to Somers.

The photocopy robbed the letter of some of its effect. Somers could tell that the original would have been textured, layered. Letters were cut and pasted onto the page. Some of them looked like newsprint. Others might have been glossier—magazines, maybe. A few were obviously cloth. And one—the first O that appeared in the message—was an antique button the size of a silver dollar.

"That doesn't leave this room. Not the copy, and not any word about it either. Am I making myself clear?"

"Where's the original?" Hazard asked.

"With Highway Patrol forensics," Cravens said. "Swinney's at their lab; she'll be there until we've closed this thing or they've got nothing left to tell us."

Somers studied the note a moment longer before passing it to Hazard. "Where was it?"

"In his desk. At home, not at work." Frustration crackled in Craven's voice. "Why the fool didn't say anything, I'll never know."

The message was simple. The letters were easy to read, even in photocopy.

Sheriff, you're going to die.

CHAPTER SIXTEEN

**FEBRUARY 13
TUESDAY
12:07 PM**

SOMERS BARELY HEARD THE REST of the conversation between Cassella and Cravens. He knew that they were arranging administrative details — who would report to whom, when reports would be filed, all the rest of it. Somers didn't care; the power dynamics in that room were obvious. Cassella — at least figuratively — had the biggest swinging dick, and Cravens wasn't going to go up against him because the mayor had thrown his weight behind Cassella.

That was suspicious, and Somers turned over the thought in his mind as he and Hazard left the chief's office with the folder. With the folder, but without that last, most interesting piece of evidence: the photocopied death threat. Cravens, true to her word, had hidden the copy away in her desk as soon as they had finished looking at it.

Too many things were strange about this case. Too many things were off. Somers didn't like the feeling, and to judge by the way Hazard crashed out of the office, neither did he.

When they reached their desks, Somers picked up the phone. Hazard looked at him.

"Swinney. Let's see what Highway Patrol forensics can do."

Hazard hesitated and then made a slicing motion with his hand. "Not here."

"What?"

"Come on."

Still carrying the folder under his arm, Hazard led the way out of the station. Eyes followed them; the department was small, and the tension had thickened over the days with Major Crimes in the building. Somers ignored the questioning glances.

Outside, Hazard jogged across the street, down half a block, and into a park. Somers followed, huffing in the frigid air. The day was blue, bright, and bitterly cold. In the park, everything had yellowed. When Hazard finally stopped, they stood beside a fountain that burbled a trickle of water in spite of the February weather.

"Why didn't you tell me to get my coat?" Somers asked, blowing on his hands.

"It's not that cold."

"That's because you're fat."

"I'm not fat."

"You are. This winter, living with Nico, you've gotten fat. You've got a fat ass. That's why you're not cold."

Hazard's eyes narrowed. "I'm not fat."

With a shrug, Somers dialed Swinney. As it rang, he said, "Your pants don't fit. Not the way they used to."

Hazard opened his mouth to respond, but Swinney came on the line. "Somers?"

"Yeah."

Swinney was silent a moment. "Am I on speaker?"

"Yeah. Just Hazard and me."

"You sure?"

Cocking an eyebrow at Hazard, Somers said, "Pretty sure. Hazard dragged me to that tiny park across from the station. I'm liable to freeze my ass off."

"All right. What's up?"

"That's what we're calling about. Major Crimes is finally out of here, and they kicked it to us. What's it like having the unlimited resources of the Missouri State Highway Patrol on our side?"

With a snort, Swinney said, "Not quite unlimited. Everything's triage. They fast-tracked a few things, but the rest of it's bogged down. Let's see. They won't touch the DNA testing on the cigarette butts you found."

"What?"

"Sorry. They're overloaded, and until you've got something to match it against—a legitimate suspect, they're saying—they're not going to do it."

"Unsurprising," Hazard said. The big bastard just stood there; he didn't even look chilly. "But unfortunate."

"Lots of unfortunate stuff," Swinney said. "They also bagged the blood splatter, clothing, all of that. We already know what happened: he got shot in the back of the head. They did, however, run some fancy model and they told me that based on the angle that the bullet entered Sheriff Bingham's head, that bluff could be where the shooter was at."

"It couldn't have been somebody down lower?" Hazard said.

"Guess not. They ran ballistics on the bullet they recovered, by the way. And on all those rifles that were down at the beach. No match."

"Unsurprising."

"You're full of good news," Somers said. "Do you have anything we can use?"

"Norman and Gross took casts of the footprints you found. The Highway Patrol tech was pretty impressed; he said they did a good job."

"They've got something?"

"The shoes are most likely a men's size eleven. They're trying to match the tread, but a lot of it had worn away."

Somers sighed. "So we've got a bullet fired from a rifle from the bluff by a man of average height."

"Average weight, too. That's what they said, anyway, based on the depth of the depression."

"Perfect," Hazard said. "Just about anybody in ten counties could have done this."

"Not you," Somers said.

Swinney's voice crackled. "What?"

"I said not Hazard."

"Shut up," Hazard said.

"He's too fat. It couldn't have been him up on the bluff; he would have sunk halfway to his knees in that mud." Somers eyed his partner. "And his pants are splitting down his ass."

"They are not," Hazard said.

"I thought he'd put on a few pounds," Swinney said.

"Both of you shut up."

"Did you ask him if it's because he's been living with Nico?"

"That's exactly what I said." Somers shook the phone triumphantly at Hazard. "Swinney, you're a genius. That's literally what I said."

"You're both imbeciles," Hazard said. "Do you have anything else? Or can we get out of the cold?"

"I thought it wasn't cold out here."

"Swinney?"

Swinney's voice, laced with amusement, came down the line. "Nothing. I'll keep rattling the cage and see if those lab monkeys can—oh, yeah. Here. Those cigarettes? They did identify the brand. I guess they can do that. Fortuna. That's some cheap shit, Detectives."

"So we're looking for an average-sized man who doesn't spend a fortune on cigarettes," Somers said. "I guess that's something."

Swinney laughed. "Glad to make your day."

"Hey, Swinney, if anything changes—if they take another look at those prints, if they realize the guy that made those prints, that he was probably two-fifty, maybe pushing two-sixty, because his live-in boyfriend was serving him junk food all day—"

"Fuck you," Hazard said.

"—you call me direct, all right?"

"Boy," Swinney said. "I'd hate to have to do that. But I will. If they figure out it was a guy who's been packing on pounds because he's finally got a cute piece of ass and doesn't have to keep himself up anymore—"

"Fuck you too, Swinney. Fuck both of you."

With a laugh, Swinney disconnected the call.

Hazard glared at Somers and marched back towards the station.

"Ree," Somers called after him. "Ree, what's the hurry? Ree. Hey, Ree. I thought you weren't cold."

CHAPTER SEVENTEEN

**FEBRUARY 13
TUESDAY
12:29 PM**

INSTEAD OF RETURNING TO THEIR DESKS in the bullpen, Hazard waited at the Interceptor.

"Can we go inside now?" Somers asked. "Please."

"We can't talk in there. You get that, right?"

"Yeah, all right. Cassella. If we're going to turn into human popsicles, can I at least grab my coat?"

"You're going to get in touch with Naomi, right?"

"I'm getting my coat, Ree. I can't feel my nose."

"She won't talk to me."

"I'll just be a minute."

"Somers, I'm serious. You've got to be the one that reaches out."

Shoving his hands into his armpits, Somers gave a vigorous shiver. "Fine."

"Right now."

"I might die of pneumonia. If I do, I'm going to blame you. I'm going to curse you from my death-bed."

"Grab your coat, you big baby, and then call her."

His cheeks already pink from the cold, Somers flushed a deeper, mottled red. "I'll do it tonight."

"Why?"

"She changed her number, Ree. Can you drop it?"

"So call Cora and get her new number. Why are you squirming like that?"

"Because it's so cold out here my balls are about halfway to my stomach. Just drop it, all right? I said I'd do it."

"When?"

The red stained his cheeks even darker. "Tonight, all right? I'm having dinner with Cora tonight. I'll ask her then. And before you say anything, no, I'm not going to call her right now. Things have been rocky enough lately. I'm not going to give her a chance to cancel on me."

Hazard absorbed the words slowly. It was cold; he finally realized how cold it was, like it had dropped another twenty degrees after Somers's last sentence. He knew Somers was still trying to patch things up with—

—the bitch who had dragged him along for almost a year—

—his estranged wife, but he'd thought that things had cooled off again between them. There had been something strange at New Year's, another major blow-up between the two of them, and it had left Somers and Cora walking on eggshells around each other. Hazard had thought maybe things were going to end for good.

No. Damn it. That wasn't the truth, and Hazard hated lying to himself, and he forced himself to look the ugly truth right in its mug. He hadn't thought that things were going to end between Somers and Cora. He had hoped. He had hoped that things would fizzle out, or that they would explode, or that one night Cora would just disappear. That's what he'd hoped. And he knew it made him a jerk. It was selfish. It was childish. It was utterly irrational because Somers might be bi, but he definitely wasn't interested in anything serious with a guy. Even the few pseudo-sexual encounters between Hazard and Somers had always been physical, raw, immediate, without any hint that deeper feelings might lie behind them. Why would there be? Somers liked messing with Hazard's head, sure. He might even want to screw around if he were single. And they were friends, sure. But that was all. Friends. That was all it was ever going to be. That was all, no matter how much Hazard hoped—

"Stop thinking about me."

With a rush, the world came back around Hazard, and he realized he and Somers were standing an inch apart.

"What?"

Grinning, Somers poked Hazard in the chest. "Where'd you go? I've been talking for like five minutes."

"I was listening."

"What'd I say?"

Hazard racked his brains. "Fukuma."

"Fukuma."

"You said we should try Fukuma now. And we'll see what Cora tells you about Naomi." Hazard's heart pounded in his chest. Sweat iced his forehead.

"Lucky guess."

"Can we grab our coats?"

"You're blushing," Somers said as he headed towards the building. "I know you were thinking about me."

"Thinking about what I'd do with a partner who didn't bitch about everything. And I'm not blushing. It's cold outside."

"I thought you weren't cold."

At that point they entered the station, and Hazard let out a breath of relief as they collected their coats. They got into the Interceptor, and Somers started the drive across town. The bulky SUV's suspension was the only noise for the first quarter mile.

"I'm sorry," Somers said.

Hazard ignored him.

"Really. I am. You were thinking about Nico; I know that. I was just messing with you."

Hazard studied the transition outside the car. Old-town Wahredua gave way to the thriving developments around Wroxall College: the storefronts with their fresh brick and plaster, the wide streets, the succession of crosswalks and campus emergency call stations and crowd-share bike rentals that marked the perimeter of the college's influence. Nico had been hammering at Hazard about using those crowd-share bikes. He'd been going on and on about it. Talking about getting out more. Getting fresh air. A sliver of worry worked through Hazard.

Had that been code? Had Nico been saying that Hazard needed to drop a few pounds? Hazard kept the same routine; he still hit the gym regularly. But the last few weeks, going out every weekend, it had been . . . stressful. Stress did strange things to the body. And Hazard had wondered, recently, if a few shirts—and maybe a pair of trousers, just one pair—if they'd shrunk in the wash. And God, now that he thought about it, that sounded like—

"And I forget that some people have issues with body image and their weight, and I—"

"Oh my God," Hazard groaned. "What do I have to do for you to stop talking?"

"Ree, I'm just saying you should think about your health long-term. Carrying that much weight—"

"I could break your jaw, I guess. I could do that."

"I'll be quiet."

125

Somers, however, didn't quite live up to his promise, and before they'd gone another block he said, "What was that all about, going to the park?"

Hazard shook his head.

"I'm not trying to be an asshole, this time. I just want to know. Do you think there's a dirty cop? Or is it just Cassella you're worried about?"

Shrugging, Hazard turned into Wroxall's North Quad. The older buildings here were stained limestone, showing the scars of years. The newer buildings were heavier, darker granite. And the newest buildings were glass and steel. As Wroxall had successfully competed for students and donations, it had become rich. As it became rich, it became powerful. It had come to dominate the rural town in a way that few other forces could. And, Hazard thought as he eyed a monstrous glass-and-steel structure from the 1970s, in places the college looked like a spaceship had exploded on campus.

Inside the Division of Social Sciences, Hazard smelled lemon polish and floor wax. He heard the echo-filled silence of stone and wood as their shoes clicked on the steps. A boy and girl—in their twenties, probably, but Hazard couldn't help thinking of them as boy and girl—passed Hazard and Somers on the stairs, and Hazard fought to keep his eyes from wandering. As a boy himself, he had enjoyed coming to the college to ogle the male students. This boy, the one passing them on the stairs, had long hair and a ratty flannel shirt. The 1990s had been good for the grunge look, and it was back strong again now.

Hazard caught a smirk on Somers's face as he turned his attention away from the boy in the flannel shirt.

"Don't say anything."

"Never."

Under the door to Fukuma's office, a strip of darkness showed. Hazard rapped on the wood anyway, but there was no answer. He knocked again. The noise rattled the door and ran up and down the hall, but no one emerged from their studies. The ivory tower was a hell of a good place, it seemed, for blocking out anything you didn't want to deal with.

The third knock, loud enough that Somers winced, drew a carrot-haired girl from a room farther down the hall.

"Professor Fukuma is gone."

"That's critical thinking," Hazard said to Somers. "Objective analysis of a situation without accepting facile or preconceived solutions. That's what they teach them here."

"Could we talk to you for a moment?" Somers said.

The carrot-haired girl looked behind her, as though they might be talking to someone else, and then disappeared back into the room.

"Can I handle this?" Somers said.

"I'd love that."

"Because you seem like you want to pick a fight."

"I really want you to handle this. I'm really looking forward to it."

Somers eyed him. "I'm not stupid."

Hazard said nothing.

"I went to college."

"I heard. Mizzou, right?"

"You're really being an asshole."

"I thought you were going to handle this."

"Is this because I caught you checking out that boy? Because I know you were just looking. He's not your type."

"You don't know my type."

"Is it because I said you're getting fat?"

"I'm not fat."

"I said getting fat."

"Somers, if you're going to handle this, you'd better do it. Now."

They found the girl in a small lounge. An electric kettle chittered near the window, and an aged, champagne-colored doily covered a coffee table that looked like, at some point in its past, it had been kicked out of a window. The carrot-haired girl sat dunking a tea bag in a mug. At her feet lay a bookbag with a strap torn loose, and next to it, a cascading stack of papers.

"It's a free country. I don't have to talk to you."

Somers nodded. He was smiling, one of his boy-next-door smiles, and it hit the girl like a runaway train. "Of course not. And I'm sorry to take up your time. I know you've got a lot to do. You're preparing for a class, right? Professor—"

The girl blushed a pretty pink that clashed with her hair. "Oh no. I'm not a professor. I'm just a grad student." A frown flickered on her face. "Do you—"

"If you don't mind," Somers said, sinking into a chair. "Just a minute of your time. I'm Detective Somerset. This is Detective Hazard."

She nodded. "I know. I've heard about you. I mean, I remember you too. When you came last time."

"Have we met?"

"No, but I saw you. I'm sorry, I'm not doing any of this right. My name's Theresa."

"Nice to meet you, Theresa. So we haven't met."

"No. I saw you when you came to talk to Professor Fukuma. When—when those murders were happening. She told us you were coming. She told us what you were going to do."

"What?"

Staring at Somers, with his easy good looks and natural charm, the girl grew flustered. "I don't know. I'm sorry, I shouldn't have said that. You were just doing your job, weren't you? Professor Fukuma, she's just had a hard life, you know? I think she expects the worst."

"That makes sense," Somers said, nodding sympathetically. "People who have been treated poorly learn to expect the worst."

Hazard was feeling pretty poorly treated right then. He was feeling, in fact, like he might throw up if he had to listen to the two of them much longer.

"You're looking for her again, aren't you? Professor Fukuma, I mean. Did she—did something happen?"

"Could you tell me how you know Professor Fukuma?"

"She's my adviser."

"What does an adviser do?" Somers's smile brightened. "Besides advise, that is."

"Oh, she reads my thesis. Parts of it, at least, when she has the time. She gives feedback. She's ferocious, you know. My last paper, she ripped it to shreds."

"I had a professor like that. You know what? I think he only did that to the students he respected. That's what he made it seem like, anyway. The ones he didn't care about, the ones he didn't think had anything interesting to say, those were the ones he let skate."

"Yes, exactly. That's exactly how it is. It's so hard to explain to someone who isn't inside academia. They just don't understand, no matter how much you try." Her eyes cut towards Hazard, and he fought the urge to snort.

"You said that Professor Fukuma was expecting us?"

"That was last time. I really shouldn't have said that."

"I'm guessing the professor doesn't care for us very much."

Biting her lip, Theresa tried not to answer.

Somers laughed. "It's ok. What'd she say? I bet she really went after my partner, didn't she? Something about how he's an embarrassment to the LGBTQ community, right? You don't have to answer; she hit him with that stuff pretty hard last time."

But Theresa was already nodding. "Yes, exactly. She blogged all about it—she's got this blog for the LGBTQIA+ Anti-Federalist Union. You—well, she said you would make a nice eunuch." Her nodding grew more vigorous.

"And that's high praise for her. For a man? That's about the nicest thing she's ever said."

This time, the laugh escaped before Hazard could stop it. As quickly as he could, he turned the laugh into a cough, but he was too late. Theresa's face colored, and she crossed her arms.

"Excuse him," Somers said. "He's too busy trying to infiltrate the patriarchy. He claims he's going to bring it down from the inside, but just between us, I think he's got a bad case of straight-man envy."

"What did you say?" Hazard said.

Theresa, however, had relaxed in her chair, and laughter lightened her expression.

"I am not trying to infiltrate—" Hazard said.

"Why don't you take a walk?" Somers said.

Growling, Hazard left the lounge. As he headed towards Fukuma's office, he heard Theresa speak in a low voice.

"Are you here because of the fight? Is Professor Fukuma in trouble?"

Hazard couldn't hear Somers's answer, but he knew that the blond man would handle the rest of the interview without any problems. Meanwhile, Hazard was going to do some exploring. He found Fukuma's office again and reached into his pocket for the set of bump keys he had begun to carry.

Things had been different since his most recent high-profile case. Things had changed inside Hazard, important things, although he wasn't sure he could put his finger on everything that was different. Some of it had to do with Nico, and some of it had to do—in a murky, subterranean way— with Somers. Some of it had to do with Hazard's only real memory of how the case had ended: a fragmented recollection of lying on the ground, unable to move, with gasoline soaking the basement around him. He remembered only the pain in his head, the stench of the gasoline choking him, and the sound of Somers's voice. He had been sure he would die. He had been sure that the voice was a dream. But he had tried anyway. He couldn't talk, not really, so he had tapped on the drywall, hoping the noise might draw Somers, hoping that the voice wasn't a hallucination brought on by the gasoline fumes. He had lain there, staring death in the eye, and he had thought of Somers, had reached out for Somers—and, against all odds, it had been Somers who had saved him.

Things had been different. Hazard shook off the dark memory; his head had begun to pound again. Things had been so different since that day. And one thing that had been different had been how Hazard saw his work. Until that day in the basement, when a mixture of head trauma and chemical poisoning had scrambled Hazard's brain, everything had been black and white in his work. He wasn't oblivious to the shades of gray in between, but he saw himself and his actions in unambiguous terms.

Now, though—well, now everything felt muddled. And Hazard found it hard to toe the lines that had previously seemed so clear. So when he and Somers had been assigned to background work, it hadn't bothered him to call Arras's office and lie to get the records. It hadn't bothered him at all. Just as it hadn't bothered Hazard to knock that frat boy around at the Pretty Pretty. It felt like some new part of him had taken control. No, that wasn't quite it either. It felt like a part of him that had been repressed—chained by devotion to reason and analysis—had shaken itself loose. And it felt dangerously good, even with the damn headaches.

So he reached into his pocket and brought out the set of bump keys that he had recently purchased. With his other hand, he rattled Fukuma's door. It was loose in its frame, and the lock looked ancient. It only took Hazard two tries to find a key that fit, and after that, it took less time than breathing. The door opened, and Hazard was inside Fukuma's office.

It hadn't changed since the last time Hazard was in it. Bookshelves still lined three of the walls, crammed with volumes in expensive bindings. The air smelled of old paper, fading incense, and cigarettes. That made Hazard hesitate. What brand did Fukuma smoke? Fortuna? That would be too much to hope for.

On the fourth wall, a slit of a window allowed gray February light into the room. No shelves marked this wall, but instead, Fukuma had hung a poster. The wording was simple, and Hazard had seen it before, but it gave him new pause: *Death To Our Enemies, Death to the Friends of Our Enemies, and Death to Those Who Are Not Our Friends.* Fukuma's message, at least was clear. He wondered how closely her actions aligned with her words.

He wasn't sure what he was looking for. A neatly signed confession would be nice, of course. Or, if that wasn't available, Hazard would have happily accepted the murder weapon, complete with forensic evidence that Fukuma had used it. Instead, though, he saw what he had seen last time: a barren cell in the ivory tower, Fukuma's tiny kingdom where students groveled and where tenure allowed her to speak and act with impunity.

Fukuma's desk held nothing promising either: two mugs that had obviously been used but that Fukuma hadn't bothered to wash yet; a pamphlet for the LGBTQIA+ Anti-Federalist Union—that sounded like one of Fukuma's wet dreams—a box of tissues, a stack of papers that needed to be graded, and even an old-fashioned music box. Hazard popped the lid with his pen and grimaced. Originally, the box must have contained a wooden figurine that had danced in time to the music. Someone—Fukuma, perhaps—had stripped out the original figurine, though, and replaced it with a headless doll whose sexual organs had been graphically illustrated with a red marker. The contents of the desk, in Hazard's opinion, were just about right for someone as batshit as the professor.

From the hallway, Somers's voice came clearly, and Hazard realized that his partner had finished the interview. Hazard left the office, pulling the door shut a moment before Theresa followed Somers out into the hall.

"Thank you again," Somers said.

Theresa hunched her shoulders; she looked unhappy and frightened, and she took Somers's hand in a limp grip before retreating into the lounge again.

"Please don't tell me you did what I think you were doing," Somers said as they headed down the stairs.

"I didn't find anything."

"Jesus, Ree. We've got to have a warrant for that kind of stuff. We're walking a tightrope with this case anyway."

Hazard shrugged. As they stepped outside, winter blasted them in the face, and Hazard blinked to clear his stinging eyes. "Any luck?"

"Yeah. She gave up Fukuma pretty fast, actually. A cabin south of here." Somers frowned. "You know, professors should really treat their grad students better. All she wanted was someone to listen to her."

"And feed her all that bullshit sympathy." Hazard wrestled, trying to keep from asking the next question, but it came out anyway. "How'd you know all that?"

"What?"

"The stuff about grad students. What she wanted to hear."

"Oh. I was a TA one year for this dinosaur who taught an American history class. All the freshmen took the class, and the professor didn't want to do any work. He lectured, and I graded every damn paper that those kids wrote. It's not the exact same, but . . ."

"You graded papers."

"You don't have to sound so surprised."

"You."

"Jesus, will you stop it with that already? I've got brains. And a killer body. I'm the whole package."

"I think I just threw up in my mouth."

"It's not my fault I'm drop-dead gorgeous and smart."

Hazard gagged.

"So," Somers said, "do we try to catch Fukuma at her vacation rental right now?"

"Yes. If we're lucky, we'll get there before that grad student has second thoughts and decides to warn her."

"Ree?"

They had reached the Interceptor, and Hazard swung up into the seat.

"Ree, you know I was just joking. About you having straight-envy. It was just a joke."

"Can we go, please?"

"There's no way you'd have straight-envy."

"God, Somers."

"No way. I mean look at you: you've got pretty boys dropping at your feet. I mean, Nico, for example. You're hot. That's what I'm saying. Anybody can see it."

Hazard stifled a groan. "You know what? I think Fukuma was right. You'd be a hell of a lot easier to be around if you were a eunuch."

"Damn, Ree. That's not funny. Not even close to funny. You shouldn't joke about that kind of stuff."

"Hits a little too close to home?"

"No, I mean you shouldn't joke about it. You. Personally." Somers raised his eyebrows innocently. "Someday you might have a shot at my junk, and you'd be pretty pissed if it were damaged."

Hazard swung the punch slow and wide, and Somers, laughing, had plenty of time to dodge.

CHAPTER EIGHTEEN

**FEBRUARY 13
TUESDAY
1:57 PM**

THEY DROVE ALONG THE old state highways marked in black and white, passing fields of stubble that sparked with frost in the sun. They drove in silence, and Somers had no desire to fill it. He didn't feel the need to come up with clever jabs. He wasn't searching for funny stories. His jaw wasn't dropping open, the words weren't pouring out, the way they did when he was alone with—

—Cora—

—just about anybody else. And that was dangerous. That was shallow-water diving. Because it was just so comfortable. It was so easy with Hazard, easy in a way that Somers had never expected it could be, had never hoped it could be. So easy that his mind started running forward. This is what it would be like on lazy Saturday mornings, when neither of them wanted to get out of bed and start the day. This is what it would be like on long drives—when they went across state to visit Hazard's parents, when Somers saw them again after all these years, they would drive like this, in perfect silence, and if he got worried about what Hazard's parents would say, if he wondered how well they remembered the past and what Somers had done, Somers knew that Hazard would hold his hand, and he wouldn't say anything because he was Emery Hazard, but he'd hold Somers's hand and they'd drive like this a while longer, just the two of them, just the sunlight and the thrum of the motor and just this silence, this perfect, easy silence between them.

With a start, Somers caught himself reaching over to take Hazard's hand, and he jerked it up and punched at the radio. The Bluetooth picked up the last playlist from his phone, and Emmylou Harris started singing.

"What the hell?"

Somers pretended not to hear.

"Somers, what the hell is this?"

"It's music."

"Like hell." Hazard screwed up his face bulldog-style. "Is that a banjo?"

"It's good music. And that's not a banjo."

"I know a banjo when I hear one." Hazard reached for the radio. "I listened to enough of this redneck shit—"

Somers shoved his hand away.

Hazard hesitated. Then he reached for the radio again.

Somers shoved his hand again.

"It's not a banjo. It's a mandolin."

"Banjo. Mandolin. Who cares? I don't want—"

Again, Somers caught his wrist and knocked his hand away. "I'm driving. I get to pick."

Hazard wrung his wrist, as though it hurt. "Those are the rules?"

"Yeah. Hell yeah. Those are the rules."

Sinking back into his seat, Hazard muttered, "You're always driving."

"I heard that."

The cabin sat at the end of a rutted dirt road, lost in the brittle, grayish-green of the winter foliage. On its own merits, the cabin must have cost quite a bit of money: it looked more like a ski resort than a cabin, with lots of glass and stone mixed into the log frame. It also sat on a stretch of smooth river—not the Grand Rivere, but another waterway that cut towards the Ozarks. That, too, added to the cost of the land, and Somers wondered how much the whole package was worth. Quite a bit, he imagined. And he wondered who Lynn Fukuma knew that had this much money.

"No car," Hazard said.

"You think Theresa called?"

Hazard grunted, and instead of answering, he dropped out of the Interceptor while it was still rolling to a stop. Somers followed, and they took the stairs to the porch. When Hazard knocked, the silence that came after seemed enormous.

"You could have waited."

"What?"

"You could have waited until I stopped the car."

Silence from Hazard.

"I'm just saying, it would have been safer if you'd waited. I know you were angry about the music, but still. If you break both legs, I'm not taking care of you."

"I got out of the car like half a second early."

"Like you said earlier: I'm not wiping your ass."

"Jesus, Somers, if I break my legs I can still wipe my own ass. And I'm not—" Red slashed across Hazard's cheekbones, and he took a deep breath. "She's not here. Let's go."

Somers moved the length of the porch, shading his eyes and studying the windows. His breath fogged the cold glass. "She's still here. Panties, a bra, a beer bottle—no, make that a lot of beer bottles. I can see a travel bag. And shoes. She's still here. Unless she went out barefoot."

"She's not answering the door."

"Well, Ree, she might be a killer. Maybe she has a reason to be hiding. Let's check around back."

They walked around to the back of the house; a deck extended over the dropping hillside, and Somers found the stairs and took them to the top.

Like the rest of the house, the deck showed a great deal of money: a patio furniture set that had probably cost a few thousand dollars, a massive stainless steel grill, and a hot tub. The hot tub was currently in use. It rumbled and sputtered. Splashing in the water were two very naked women. They were wrestling, and the bubbles didn't hide any of their more interesting parts.

Somers was a lot of things. He was, he knew, occasionally annoying. He was, he thought, a loyal friend. He was, he had found out, still a red-blooded man, and he was at that moment having a hard time looking away.

"Pervert," Hazard said, elbowing Somers and marching onto the deck. "Ladies, I'm Detective Hazard—"

With twin screams, the women threw themselves backward. Water sloshed forward, slopping onto the deck, and the women clutched at each other.

Lynn Fukuma, who preferred to be called Lynk, was still very much a woman. And the girl next to her—really, honestly, truly, barely more than a girl, maybe twenty years old at most—was stunning. And Somers realized he was staring at them both, and that they were naked and wet and staring back at him.

"I'm Detective Somerset," he said. "Professor Fukuma, you might remember us."

Fukuma unleashed a string of swears—most detailing exactly how well she remembered Hazard and Somers, what she thought of their anatomy, and how their personal and professional lives could be improved by improvising various sex acts with household objects.

"I've never tried that one," Somers said to Hazard, after one particularly inventive suggestion.

Hazard shrugged. "It's sticky."

And Somers suddenly found that he was blushing.

"Come on out of the hot tub, ladies," Somers said over Fukuma's tirade. "You can grab some clothes and then we'd like to talk."

"And Professor Fukuma," Hazard said, nodding at the far side of the hot tub. Fukuma's eyes jerked guiltily in that direction before she pulled them back to the front. Hazard reached into his jacket and set a hand on the .38 he carried in a shoulder holster. "Stay away from the gun you've got over there."

CHAPTER NINETEEN

**FEBRUARY 13
TUESDAY
2:12 PM**

THE WOMEN GOT OUT OF the hot tub without incident, and the young blonde said they ought to go inside. Somers allowed the two shivering women into the living room. Fukuma ran a towel through her pageboy hair; she wore a pair of board shorts and a loose-fitting camo t-shirt. She sat with her knees spread wide. Somers guessed it was a power pose.

Her companion—the hickeys on the girl's neck made it clear how far their relationship went—was named Cynthia, and she was nineteen and, quite obviously, terrified. Blond, beautiful, and beginning—this, too, was a guess on Somers's part—to explore a new part of her sexuality. Hazard's abrupt end to their playing might have put a damper on further exploration, and Somers thought that was a shame.

By the time the two women huddled next to each other on one of the cabin's large, expensive sofas, Fukuma had already run her gamut of legal defenses, insisting that she wanted nothing to do with them and that they had no right to be on the property, but the blond's invitation had negated that. Fukuma had gone quiet when Hazard asked if the pistol by the hot tub was registered in her name, but again, that wasn't mandatory in the state.

"That's for self-defense," she finally said. "That's why I've got it. Lots of people would like to see me dead."

"I believe it," Hazard said.

"You're one of them. You wouldn't blink an eye at gunning me down. That's what you are: a killer. There's lots of people. Every day I've got someone out there. Because of who I am. Because of the work I do. Because I won't sign on to the heteronormative, cis agenda pushed in our state."

Fukuma talking, in Somers's opinion, was worse than Fukuma yelling.

Hazard set the pistol on the coffee table, the magazine removed, the chamber empty. "We'd like to ask you some questions. If you don't want to talk here, we'll go to the station."

"Talk?" Fukuma's hard, dark eyes were focused on Hazard. "To you? To the Wahredua Police Department's convenient cum-dump? That's what they hired you for, wasn't it? They wanted a nice, trained faggot they could drop a load in when things got stressful. Isn't that right, Detective Somerset? Isn't it nice to have a cock-sucker on his knees right at your very own desk?"

Hazard was silent, but the red slashes had appeared again over his cheekbones.

"Professor Fukuma," Somers said, "I'm going to be your friend. I'm going to tell you that you're in trouble. And I'm going to make it clear that your best bet, at this point, is to cooperate fully and clear yourself as a person of interest in this investigation."

Fukuma arched her back, widened her knees, and sank deeper into the sofa. She looked like she wanted to kick up her feet and watch the game. Somers was half-surprised she didn't slide a hand down the front of her shorts. "You," she said, studying Somers. "You could still be trained. You're still civil enough. I'd recommend that they take your balls, though. Or maybe—yes, maybe chastity. Something to humble you. Something to remind you who owns you. That's all men are, you know. Property. Once you control their cocks, you control the rest of them. A lot of women use pleasure to do it, but that's a waste."

Hazard made a vicious, coughing noise, and Somers glanced at his partner. The red had darkened Hazard's face, and his lips quivered. It took Somers a moment—a painful, unbelievable moment—before he realized what he was seeing.

Emery Hazard was trying not to laugh.

And then the humor of it hit Somers, and he burst out laughing. Hazard threw back his head and roared with laughter. It was so different from his normal composure, from his quiet, restrained chuckles, that Somers found himself laughing harder. The two men laughed until tears streamed down Somers's face.

Fukuma's knees drew together, and she shrank forward, her weight shifting towards Cynthia. "What's so damn funny? What the fuck are you laughing about?"

"Take your balls," Hazard managed to get out. "Jesus, she really did—she really did—" And then he couldn't speak anymore, and the two men burst into laughter again.

When they had settled, Somers wiped his face again and said, "Professor Fukuma, why don't you tell us about the protest on Sunday?"

"What about it?"

"Where were you?"

"At the protest. Are you an idiot? Why are you asking me?"

"Did you know Sheriff Bingham was shot and killed during that protest?"

Fukuma's eyes darted to the gun on the table. Cynthia, beside her, drew in a tiny, shocked breath.

"Would you like to tell us where you were during the protest?" Hazard asked.

"I was there. You know I was there."

"On Sheriff Bingham's property?" Somers said.

"It's nobody's property. Nobody has a right to private property any more than they have a right to wealth or land or status or privilege."

Somers didn't bother retorting; he just glanced around the million-dollar cabin and smiled.

"Where were you?" Somers asked again.

"At the protest. You're a fucking idiot, that's what you are, and this is a waste of my time. I want you to leave. Cynthia, tell them they have to leave."

Cynthia opened her mouth, but before she could speak, Somers slid the photograph of Fukuma out of the folder. "What about this?"

Again, Cynthia drew in a tangled breath, and she wriggled free of Fukuma. "You—"

"Cynthia, don't be stupid, it's not—"

"You told me you went to the bathroom. You told me you went up the road to the bushes." Cynthia's full, red lips tightened. "Officers, I can't—I don't want to be here. Not with her."

"Cynthia," Fukuma snapped. "You're being dramatic. I told you I don't like that. I don't like it when you act like a spoiled, bourgeois princess. I don't like this side of you. It's ugly to me. Is that what you want? Do you want to be ugly to me? Tell them to leave."

Cynthia, her lips pressed shut, shook her head, but she was crying.

"You can sit over there," Somers said, pointing to a chair towards the back of the room. "But you can't leave. Not yet."

Nodding, Cynthia hurried to the chair and curled away from Fukuma.

"You're pigs," Fukuma said. "I thought you were dogs but you're pigs. Typical, male, chauvinist pigs. You're tools of a machine that cares nothing about you, and you know it. Some of those pigs, they don't know it, but you do. You know. And that makes you worse than the rest of them. That makes you the worst type of straight, cis, white male pigs. People like you, you're the ones that should be dragged out and shot in the back of the head."

"That's an interesting statement," Somers said. "That's exactly how the sheriff died. How did you know that, Professor? Those details haven't been released."

Fukuma paled.

"Why don't you tell us what you were doing? Why were you going onto Sheriff Bingham's property?"

"I was going to make my point."

"That's a very ambiguous statement. Do you mean you were going to shoot him?"

"No. That's how it always is with authority figures. That's how it always is with the mechanical forces of the heteronormative patriarchy. You think in terms of hierarchy, binary, linearity. You see a straight line and the first thing you think is that a straight line is the perfect path for a bullet."

"You seemed pretty fond of bullets before," Hazard said. "Back in California, when you were part of the San Andreas Deep Ecologists. When you blew up that construction site. When you instigated the California Queer War. When you shot up that hotel and killed twelve people. When you killed a young mother."

"You don't know anything. You sit there, at the top of the pyramid with your white, male privilege, and you think just because you can see to the horizon that you can see the whole world. You don't know the first thing about me."

"I know a petty, selfish tyrant when I see one. I know a hypocrite. I know a sociopath."

Fukuma opened her mouth, but Somers spoke first. "Professor Fukuma, you're not answering our questions. I think we should move this conversation to the station."

"No." Fukuma shook her head. "I was going to vandalize the house."

Somers raised an eyebrow.

"I had spray paint in my bag. And I had some dog shit. I was going to tag the house and leave him a present. That's all."

"Can anyone confirm that?"

Squirming in her chair, Cynthia gave a short nod. "She had the spray paint. I saw it."

"Were you carrying a weapon?" Somers asked.

Fukuma shook her head.

Somers glanced at Cynthia.

The blond girl shrugged. "I don't know. I didn't see one."

"You didn't have a rifle?" Somers asked.

"I didn't have anything but what I told you."

"Weren't you afraid?" Hazard asked.

"Just because I'm a woman of color doesn't mean I'm afraid of white power."

"I was referring to the guns."

"I heard them shooting. I wasn't afraid. The contrary, actually. I knew they'd be distracted, so I saw my opportunity."

"You weren't worried that one of them would see you? You weren't worried that they might overreact to seeing a stranger on the property?"

"You can't shoot a woman just for walking."

"That's not what I asked."

"I wasn't afraid of them. I'm not afraid of anything a white man can do to me."

"Can you describe what you did?" Somers said.

"I followed the treeline along the bluff. I was going to stay out of sight as long as possible and then cut back towards the house. When I saw them, I stopped."

"Saw who?"

"All of them. All those bourgeois pigs."

"The sheriff and his guests."

"Them."

"You saw them. Why did you stop?"

"Something was wrong. The sheriff was lying on the ground."

"What did you see?"

"I told you: he was already on the ground."

"Anything else?" Hazard said. "All of it. Tell us everything."

Fukuma spread her hands. "Someone, a woman was turning him over. She looked like something out of an old movie. You know, a Western. A woman with a white handkerchief trying to clean up the man she loved."

"You think Beverly Flinn was in love with the sheriff?" Somers said.

"Like I said, it was like something out of a Western. Very machista. Very patriarchal. Even after he was dead, she was still cleaning him, washing his hands and face like he was a child. Men like that, you know. They want to be infantilized. They need it. That's where their obsession with breasts originates. Sex becomes another locus for nourishment. The vagina is the ultimate site of childhood fantasy."

"What else?" Somers said.

"Another woman looked at him for a moment, and then she ran straight back to the house."

"What were the others doing?"

"Pacing, mostly. One guy, he had a hat in his hand, and he kept walking towards the river like he was about to blow his fancy brunch. And that deputy just kept turning in a circle. I think he had a gun in his hand, and he looked so stupid he might as well be standing there holding his cock. Then the woman came back with a big old satchel. She could barely keep it on her shoulder—kept dropping it—and then she got there and couldn't do a damn thing."

Frustration knotted Somers's shoulders. His gut told him that Fukuma was telling the truth, and her account matched what the witnesses at the shooting had told them. "Did you see anyone else?"

Frowning, Fukuma said, "No."

"The guy at the river: go back to him."

"He was just walking towards the river, then he'd turn and walk back."

"Did he fall in?"

"What? No. Why?"

"At any point was he in the water?"

"No. But he could have been wet. Maybe that's why he was walking around so much. I didn't really pay attention."

"All right. Is that all? Anything else significant?"

"You mean, did I see the shooter? No."

"What did you think of the sheriff?"

"Personally? He was a pig."

"Professionally?"

"A big, fat pig."

"So you didn't support him in the recall petition?"

"I had every student in my lecture sign that damn petition. I would have signed it myself except I believe that participation in a homorepressive democracy is a form of complicity."

"For hell's sake," Hazard breathed.

"When was the last time you saw the sheriff?" Somers asked.

"When he was dead on the sand." Fukuma's expression suddenly grew distant, almost closed.

"What about before that Professor Fukuma?"

"Hmm?"

Her eyes were still looking at some other place, some other time. "I don't know. I don't remember. A city council meeting, I would guess. He was usually present."

And suddenly, with a ping deep in his gut, Somers knew she was lying.

"Are you sure about that?"

"Mm-hm."

"Did you see him Saturday night?

Fukuma's gaze sharpened, and she looked at Somers dead-on. "So. I have a Judas. Who was it? Which one of those bitches? Cynthia?" She craned her neck to stare at the blond girl. "Cynthia, you little slut, was it you?"

"Professor Fukuma, would you answer the question?"

"Yes. Yes, you fucking dog. You fucking cum-eating dog. Yes, I saw him Saturday night. You know. My little Judas, my little bitch Judas told you already. You know I saw him."

Cynthia, her knees drawn up to her chest, was crying. "Leave her alone," she called to them. "Just leave her alone."

"Where?" Somers insisted.

"At a dinner. A dinner for fat, white man who have gotten fat eating the food out of other people's hands."

"So you admit that you approached the sheriff at the fundraising dinner he held on Saturday night."

"Yes. I talked to him."

"How would you describe that encounter?"

Fukuma threw back her head and laughed. "So this is what it's like. This is what it feels like when the ones you love, the ones you trust, the ones that have given themselves to something greater than all of you, when they put a knife in your back. This is the ultimate corruption. What did you offer her? Did you plow her? Did she call out your name, pull your hair, ride you? What makes someone turn on the cause? Money? Is this capitalism, or is this patriarchy?" She looked ready to cry, and she put her fists below her wet eyes. "What the fuck is the difference?"

"Why won't you just leave her alone?" Cynthia called to them, wiping her eyes with the heels of her hands.

"Please tell us about that encounter with Sheriff Bingham," Somers said.

"You know what I said. You know. And you'll have it out of me one way or another, won't you? You'll have it out of me the way they twisted the truth out of women for centuries. You'll squeeze it out of me. You'll pile rocks on my chest so that I'll drown when I speak the truth."

"For hell's sake," Hazard snapped, loud enough to startle Fukuma. "Enough. That's just fucking enough already. Answer the question."

Curling over her knees, Fukuma suddenly looked all of her forty-odd years, tired, beaten-down. "You know what I said. I said I'd shoot off his face the next time I saw him. I said it'd be the only justice our county had seen in the last thirty years."

CHAPTER TWENTY

**FEBRUARY 13
TUESDAY
2:27 PM**

HAZARD AND SOMERS STOOD TOGETHER on the far side of the cabin's elegant main room, far enough that they could speak quietly to each other without being overheard while still keeping an eye on Fukuma and Cynthia. The two women looked broken; Fukuma bowed at the waist, her face supported in her hands, while Cynthia had balled herself up in the chair at the back of the room. Hazard didn't feel an ounce of pity for either of them. His mind, instead, whirred as it tried to process Fukuma's words.

"I didn't see that coming," Somers said.

"Theresa didn't tell you."

"No. She just said it had been an ugly conversation. Jesus, shoot off his face? And then the next day . . ."

"It wasn't her."

"I'm not saying it was her. But I'm saying it's a hell of a coincidence. And Ree, she was there. You heard her: she described that scene perfectly."

"I know. But she didn't shoot. The picture."

Somers offered the folder, and Hazard flipped through it. He found the enlargement of the photograph. It showed Fukuma from behind, wearing the coat with the three white stripes. "There you go."

"I know we can't see the face, Ree, but she admitted she was there. And before you tell me we can't arrest her, I know. Everything we've got is circumstantial. But—"

"No, look. The coat. Remember, Randall Scott said the shooter was wearing a dark coverall. Olive-colored, maybe camouflage. That's not what Fukuma was wearing. And she didn't have a gun."

"Who cares? Maybe Scott didn't know what he was seeing. Maybe she planned ahead. She had the coverall and the gun hidden in the trees. She waited for them to go shooting, crept onto the bluff, pulled on the coverall, and took the shot. Then she dumped everything in the river—we saw the tracks, Ree, right down to the water—and she looped back to the protest."

"Yes, we saw the tracks. And the analysts at the lab said those tracks were made by a man of average height and weight."

Somers snapped his mouth shut. After a moment, he said, "All right."

"Excuse me?"

"Don't be an asshole. I see your point. But—" Somers bit his lip, and just seeing that, just seeing how perfect he looked like that, made Hazard think that maybe this was what Somers looked like in the heat of passion, his lip drawn between his teeth, teeth puckering the red flesh, turning it white with pressure. Somers spoke again, interrupting the fantasy. "I don't know, Ree. She's lying about something."

"Yes. She lied about that meeting. She didn't expect us to know about that, and she thought she could hide her most recent encounter with the sheriff. For obvious reasons, since she threatened his life the day before he died."

Somers frowned, but he didn't argue. "So we leave her?"

"I don't see what else we can do."

They left Fukuma and Cynthia; based on the way the interview had gone, Hazard expected that there would be significant fireworks between the two women after the detectives were out of sight. The last thing Hazard saw through the Interceptor's window was Fukuma turning on the blond girl, arms flying up, already shouting.

"Right before Valentine's," Somers said.

And that brought everything crashing back. "Don't remind me."

"Try him again."

Hazard grunted.

"Ree, just try him. You've been sending all those flowers, waiting for him to call. Did you ever think about just picking up the phone and trying to call him?"

"Your advice last time went spectacularly well."

"All right, I screwed up. I should have realized Nico would get mad. But I'm telling you, give him a call. That big baby is waiting for it. I promise."

Hazard let the cornstubble roll past them on either side.

"Ree."

The sun had passed its peak. White smoke from the Tegula plant curlicued against china-blue sky.

"Have you tried calling?"

Around here, the trees were mostly oak, and old-growth, and their spindly upper branches tilted in the wind.

"Not even once?"

"Oh for the love of God, Somers. Fine. Will you pull over?"

"I thought we'd head to the Rutter Compound and see if our boy Dennis has come back home."

"Yeah. Sure. But pull over; I'm not calling Nico while I'm sitting next to you."

"I'll be quiet."

"Just stop the damn car."

Hazard got out; there wasn't a shoulder here, not even a strip of gravel next to the asphalt. Frost-yellow grass crinkled underfoot as he counted twenty paces, which he thought might be far enough to be safe. It was hard to tell. The universe had been a real bitch lately, and Nico had an uncanny sense for when Somers was around.

To Hazard's surprise, Nico picked up. "Hey."

"Hey."

A massive Ford hauling a trailer whipped along the highway; the wind from its passage flattened Hazard's trousers against his legs.

"Are you outside?"

"Yeah. Hey, I'm sorry." Waiting for a response, Hazard adjusted the phone against his ear. "Listen, Nico, I know what I did was shitty. At the club, I mean. And the rest of it, too. I should have listened to you. I should have trusted you. I should have been more respectful."

In the silence that followed, Hazard bounced on his toes, trying to keep his feet warm. The cold cut straight through his leather wingtips.

"Did Somers write that for you?"

"No."

"He's there, though."

Hazard bit back what he normally would have said. "Up the road a little. In the car. Warm."

"You don't have your scarf, do you?"

"No."

"Emery, it's February. It's the middle of winter. I bet you don't even have your coat on, and if you—"

"Will you come home?"

Something in the Interceptor kicked on, the motor suddenly louder.

"Yeah. I mean, I'd like to."

"Well, it's your apartment."

"It's our apartment. And I know I messed up too. Can we—can we just talk tonight?"

Talk. Talk, talk, talk. There was always more talk. Always something else they had to talk about. They were going to talk about Somers, for sure. They were going to talk about work and the long hours. They were going to talk about how Hazard needed to behave in public. About trust. About respect. About Nico's motherfucking rights.

"Yeah."

"So, I'll see you tonight?"

"Yeah."

"Love you, Emery."

"I'll see you tonight." Hazard disconnected, spat into the grass, and double-timed it back to the Interceptor. A semi rattled past, carrying three tractors, a cyclone of steel and rubber. Hazard barely heard it.

Love you.

Wasn't that just perfect?

CHAPTER TWENTY-ONE

FEBRUARY 13
TUESDAY
2:40 PM

SOMERS WATCHED IN THE REARVIEW MIRROR as Hazard marched down the road. The big Neanderthal probably thought if he went twenty yards, Nico wouldn't be able to guess that Somers was nearby. Bundled in his heavy winter coat, Hazard looked even more massive than usual, like someone had put him together out of tree trunks. And that ass. In the rearview mirror, Hazard stomped down the winter grass, and Somers felt himself smiling and thinking it was a trick of the glass, right, objects may be bigger than they actually are, right, because that ass looked like a picnic bench when the wind lifted Hazard's coat. Right. And the smile got a little bigger, and Somers's face was hot like he was fifteen all over again.

His phone vibrated, and Somers didn't recognize the number. Cassella, maybe. He answered.

The voice, however, was a woman's, and it was familiar, and it made his balls pull up like he'd dunked them in ice water. "John-Henry. Long time no see."

"Naomi."

Naomi Malsho was many things: she was beautiful, intelligent, a trained lawyer, and one of the insane masterminds of the white supremacist group known as the Ozark Volunteers. She was also Somers's sister-in-law, Cora's sister. She had engineered Somers's affair—although Somers recognized his own fault—and had immediately taken the information to Cora in an effort to destroy the marriage. She had mostly succeeded until a few months ago, when Cora called out of the blue and wanted to start working things out. Somers had his suspicions about what had prompted the change. Nothing he could put his finger on, nothing definite, but he had thought about it a lot. It had something to do with Hazard; of that much, he was certain.

"I think we should talk."

"That would be good. We've got some questions for Dennis Rutter. It'd be in his best interest if he cooperated."

"Spoken like the mindless drone that you are, John-Henry. It's nice to see that nothing changes with you. Dinner. Tonight."

"No way. I've got plans tonight with Cora."

"Call her and cancel. You'll see her tomorrow. I'm watching Evie."

"You're watching Evie?"

"I'll call you later with a time and place. If you want to talk to Dennis, you'll have to talk to me first. And I'm only talking to you tonight. At dinner."

Naomi didn't wait for an answer; she disconnected.

At that moment, the Interceptor's door opened, and Hazard pulled himself into the SUV. He looked like he'd been dragged behind a horse. A horse with a hell of a lot of go.

"What's wrong with you?" Somers said.

"Nothing. Who was that?"

"Nico didn't answer?"

"He answered. Who were you talking to?"

"Was he still mad?"

"Jesus, Somers, it's fine. It was perfect, all right. Can we go?"

"It's just that you don't look happy."

Hazard, parting his lips in a grimace, said, "How about now? Just drive already."

"We're going to have to work on that. For when you see Nico, I mean. He's not going to like it if you look like that."

To Somers's surprise, though, Hazard didn't rise to the bait, and the big man just stared out the window. A dark thrill ran through Somers before he tamped it down.

"That was Naomi, to answer your question. She wants to meet. Tonight."

"Thank God," Hazard breathed. "I was supposed to see Nico." As Somers eased the Interceptor forward, Hazard added in a low voice, "We were going to talk."

Somers fought to keep an eyebrow from rising. "Ree, you need to see him."

"This is the perfect excuse."

"It's the perfect way to really stick your foot in it. If you cancel now, he'll be furious."

"I'm not letting you meet Naomi alone."

"I can handle her. You're going to see Nico; I'm not taking no for an answer."

The Interceptor's vents hissed hot air, and the tires rumbled along the uneven asphalt.

"Fine," Hazard said.

"You owe me. Big."

"I owe you? I don't even want to see him."

"Yep. You owe me really big. First, for meeting with Naomi. And second, for keeping you from screwing up your last chance. That's big stuff. Like, another double date. That kind of big."

"Not a chance."

"I'm canceling dinner with my estranged wife the day before Valentine's. And I basically saved your relationship. We're doubling again. Next Saturday."

The SUV rocked over a pothole, and Hazard said, "Dinner. That's it. Cheap, too. Not the Moulin Vert again."

"Jesus, you must be fun with all the boys. A cheap dinner and then home to bed before nine."

"Before seven."

"Will the dollar menu at Taco Bell be all right? Or should I just pick up some granola bars at Aldi? We could split them so it doesn't get too pricey."

Hazard threw the bird, and Somers laughed.

The Rutter Compound formed the third point of a triangle between Wahredua proper and the cabin where Fukuma had been hiding. Paved roads ended at least a mile before the gates, and as the Interceptor rumbled over the rutted dirt, Somers was grateful for the dry days preceding their visit. On either side, scrub walled the corridor, and the old growth trees made a bony canopy overhead.

The gates themselves were clearly handmade, with barbed wire strung around raw timber. Every conceivable warning sign had been nailed to the front: Beware of Dog, Residents are Armed and Dangerous, No Trespassing, Trespassers will be Shot, Private Property, No Poachers, Poachers will be Poached, We Assert Our Right to the Second Amendment, One Free Nation Under God, Government Ends Here. Perhaps most articulate was the hand-painted sign tacked near the center of the gate that said, simply, Go the Fuck Away.

Beyond the gates, a few acres of uncleared land rolled towards a cluster of prefabricated homes—mostly double-wide trailers, but Somers spotted the silver bullet shape of an Airstream trailer that was probably from the 1950s, and towards the edge of his vision, he thought he saw a log cabin. Not a fancy luxury retreat like the one where they had found Fukuma, but an old, tumbling-down thing like something Abe Lincoln might have helped build after splitting rails.

Somers laid on the horn. He went at it, on, off, on again, for what might have been five minutes.

"Cut it out," Hazard said. "Let's go."

"They've got to at least come out and tell us no. They've got to at least do that much."

But nobody did come out. Not a soul. And finally Somers had to admit he was stumped.

"They're probably too busy lining up their cousins for the next round of inbreeding."

"Cousins if we're lucky."

"We could take a walk. If we accidentally stumble onto Rutter land, we might find something interesting."

"Not a chance. Not without a warrant and a hell of a lot of backup."

"Pussy."

"Idiot."

Somers grinned and pulled out his phone. He typed a text to Cora: *Please don't be mad. I can't do dinner tonight; work*. There was never a good way to talk about work with Cora; she started seeing red as soon as the word came up. Better to do it short and sweet.

Her text came back in a single word: *Fine*.

Tomorrow?

No reply came, and Somers dropped his phone on the dash. "I'm a dead man."

"She'll understand."

Groaning, Somers shook his head, reversed the Interceptor, and started back towards Wahredua. After a few miles, he said, "I guess we're going to see if Deputy Dudley is back from her bender."

"Ex-deputy Dudley."

"Naomi."

"No, that's not her name."

"No, you big lug. Naomi's doing this. The thing with Rutter."

Hazard raised an eyebrow. "I didn't think the Rutters liked any sort of authority. One of the signs back there said, 'Government is When You Give Ass-Rapists a Salary.' They don't sound like they prize civic duty."

"First of all, I wish you hadn't seen that because I'm buying you that same sign for your birthday."

"Fuck off."

"And second, I'm serious. You heard what Cassella said. He said they went through the compound and Dennis Rutter was gone. Not everybody. Just Dennis. That means people were here. They opened that gate and let them in. They might not have liked it, but they did."

"But now the place is deserted."

"We're on the case now, and Naomi sees a chance to make us dance. She makes a few phone calls, and now our investigation depends on talking to her. She wants something."

"Forget her. We'll get a warrant and tear up every inch of land in that shithole. We'll find them."

"Yeah. You, me, and what army? The other twenty cops? Maybe twenty-five, thirty deputies? You know how much land the Rutters have? We'll be pulling pension checks before we finish. Damn it. She's doing this on purpose."

"Why?"

"That's a hell of a good question."

CHAPTER TWENTY-TWO

FEBRUARY 13
TUESDAY
3:30 PM

STELLA AND ARNOLD DUDLEY owned a small home just off the state highway between Wahredua and St. Elizabeth. The house had probably been peach-colored; now it was almost no color at all, and the gutters peeled away, and grass grew thick in the gravel drive. A single car, a Ford Taurus with rusted wheel wells, sat at a diagonal across the gravel.

When Hazard knocked, an old woman answered almost immediately. She introduced herself as Stella Dudley and, without another word, led the two detectives through the house.

"They're here," she called as she rapped at a door.

The woman who answered looked like a cartoon character who'd been wrung out with the wash. She wasn't fat, but she was big, and she had a stretched-out quality that her sallow complexion and baggy clothes—a t-shirt printed with an enormous Garfield came almost to her knees—exacerbated.

"Lisa Dudley?" Somers said.

She nodded and trudged back into the room. Collapsing on the bed, Dudley covered her eyes with one hand and, with the other, gestured to a pair of straight-backed dining chairs that sat against the wall.

"You were expecting us."

"Somebody came by. Really put hell into Ma."

"Hangover?"

"You know what mouse turds taste like?"

"Can't say I do."

"It's like that. And like I ate the whole mouse on top of it."

"Maybe a little..."

"No. I'd just get started all over again. Ma calls this part the Jesus cure. Like Jesus wants me hungover just to teach me a lesson." Dudley stripped her fingers away from her face. "I've seen you guys. You're the gay, right? Is that what you call yourself?"

"No," Hazard said.

"You're not gay? Or you don't call yourself that? I don't mean anything by it. I'm just curious." She covered her eyes again. "The girls at the office call you the lion. Somerset, I mean, not the other one."

"They do?"

"Because of that hair. Tawny. They've got bets about what you look like under that suit. They've got enough bets they could strip you down and lay you flat and use you for craps. Every one of those girls betting the horn bet on account of, well, you know."

"The lion," Hazard said, studying Somers until his partner blushed.

"Ms. Dudley," Somers said. "We've got to ask you some questions."

"I don't know where I was. I don't know what I did. But hand to God, I didn't shoot that man."

"Who's that?"

"The sheriff. I didn't. I might have wished I did, but I didn't. And you know what Ma says: if wishes was fishes."

"Let's go back a little. How long did you work for the sheriff?"

"A few years. Three, now, I guess."

"What was that like?"

"All right at the beginning. I had that day shift, you know." She peeked between her fingers. "You know all that. You read up on me."

"Tell us anyway."

"I worked a desk. I didn't get into all this because I wanted a shootout at the OK Corral. I wanted a decent salary and benefits and I wanted to come home at the end of the day and not have a damn thing to worry about. So a desk was fine by me. I didn't want to sit in a car six hours a day. I didn't want the OK Corral."

"You said at the beginning."

"That's right. Until Grant McAtee got his pecker all in a twist."

"McAtee?" Hazard said, exchanging a look with Somers.

"If he wasn't the sheriff's pride and pet, I don't know who was. It didn't matter what McAtee did. Didn't matter in the slightest. He could've driven a tank flat through an orphanage and Bingham would have shrugged and sent the rest of us for brooms. And you know what?" Her fingers scissored together again, blocking her face. "Bingham told him things. I know he did.

I walked in one time, and they were—well, they were just talking. But I knew they were talking something serious."

"What kind of things?" Somers said. "What did the sheriff tell him?"

"I don't know. Things about people in the county, I think. You know the sheriff. He had a nose for that kind of thing."

Hazard didn't nod but only because he caught himself. He'd experienced first-hand the sheriff's use of blackmail. The matter hadn't gone any further—Hazard wasn't sure why, although he suspected that the sheriff was simply waiting for a better opportunity—but he knew that Dudley was telling the truth. The mayor and the sheriff had both, in fact, threatened to blackmail him. Hazard had left his job with the St. Louis Police Department after his partner had stolen drugs from evidence and the captain had threatened to pin it on Hazard. In a small town, even a whisper of a dirty secret was a valuable currency.

The thought sent a small thrill through Hazard. Perhaps that was the motive they were looking for. And it meant looking more carefully at their suspects, looking deeper into their past. Just that day, for example, Hazard and Somers had found Fukuma with a very young co-ed. And Fukuma had a dark, bloody past. What about Dennis Rutter? Did the Ozark Volunteer's candidate for sheriff have anything to hide? Or, for that matter, what about a drunken ex-deputy? It was hard to imagine a woman in an XXL Garfield shirt harboring dark secrets, but Hazard was smart enough not to be trapped by his prejudices. His eyes darted to Somers. Well, most of the time.

"Anyone in particular?" Somers said.

Dudley shook her head.

"Anything about you?"

"I knew you'd get to that. Everybody always gets to that. They'll look you straight in the eye, pretend they don't know, and the minute you're down, they're already carving at you."

"Why don't you tell us what happened?"

"I told you: McAtee got his dick all pretzeled up."

"Because you rejected his advances. He approached you sexually."

Dudley snorted and then, rocking her head to the side, winced. "God, no. I mean, look at me. And McAtee, well, even if he's not Mr. Club Fitness, he's still soft on the eyes. And he's got money somewhere. It's all tied up, but that doesn't matter to some girls. They just see it waiting down the road."

"What got McAtee's dick in a knot?" Somers asked.

"There's a pretty little girl down there. Well, she was down there. She moved, I think. Laura Gunderson, only it's Laura Donahoe now on account she got married and moved to one of those little flyspecks in the boot-heel. But she was there, and she wasn't a deputy. She just ran copies, made the coffee, picked up lunches when it was time. She couldn't have weighed a hundred pounds, not even if you dunked her in the Grand Rivere.

"Well, McAtee took a liking to her. Talked to her. Followed her. Honest to God, one time he even tickled her, and I'll tell you this much, I've never seen man or woman or dog or cat as uncomfortable as Laura looked that day. And the whole time she was engaged to Donahoe, only she never said a word to him about it on account of McAtee's temper. I should have been that smart. Would to God I'd been that smart."

"You told him to leave her alone."

"He grabbed her breast. Right there, brassy as you like, in plain day. And I wasn't going to watch that. I grabbed him by the balls, walked him out of the room and two doors down, gave a little twist, and had McAtee doing the two-step just fine by the time I left. Yes, ma'am. No, ma'am. Just peaches. Only that's not where it stopped. I should have realized—" Violently, she rolled to the side and snatched a plastic tub from under the bed. She held her head over the tub for a moment, her jaw working, but nothing came out. Then, sweating and shaking, she tossed the tub and flopped back.

"You threatened McAtee, and he went to the sheriff."

"He went to somebody. I don't know. I just know a couple of weeks later, I was showing up for my shift at eleven at night, and I was taking shoelaces off drunks in the county jail instead of drinking coffee at my desk at a decent hour."

"No one said why?"

"Everybody knew. I knew. I'm not stupid, detectives. I'm big and fat and ugly, but I'm not stupid."

"You no longer work for the Sheriff's Department."

"On account I'm a no-good drunk."

"That's why you were fired?"

"I resigned, I'll have you know. Got a spot of dignity left. And the sheriff pointed out that nobody would want a woman who'd been kicked out for dereliction of duty. That's what they call it, you know. I slept six hours in a ditch, my bare ass in the wind, not a saint or sinner to cover me with so much as a fig leaf, and they call it dereliction of duty because I didn't make my shift. So I resigned. I'll get cleaned up. I'll get another job."

"Have you always been a drunk?" Hazard asked. He saw the flash of irritation in Somers's eyes, but he ignored it.

"No," Dudley said. "I drank a lot when I was a girl. Thirteen, fourteen. They say that's when it starts. It gets in your brain. I saw a cartoon once, and it was all about this robot, and they kept yanking out wires and plugging em back in, and it's like that, I think. Once they've scrambled the wires, you always want a drink. Nothing's going to change that except Jesus.

"But I found him. Jesus, I mean. I tell Ma and Pa that I found him swimming in shit in the Skadsens' outhouse, but I only say that to make them mad. The shit, though, that part's true. I fell right down there. Skunked, totally, and I fell down in all that shit. The smell, that's enough to make you see Jesus."

"You were sober then?" Somers said. "When you began work at the Sheriff's Department?"

"Dry as a minister's wife. I hadn't touched a drop in five years." Again, Dudley curled her fingers away from her face, exposing her broad, swollen features. "You want to know why I'm in the bottle again. You think it was McAtee."

"Why don't you tell us," Hazard said, "instead of guessing what we're thinking?"

Easy, Somers mouthed.

"You're mad because I called you the gay," Dudley said. "I didn't mean anything by it. Anyway you can't get mad, not when I asked you what you want to be called and you sat there like you're sucking an onion."

"Just tell us," Hazard said.

"It wasn't McAtee. Not the way you're thinking. And it wasn't the night shift, although that took its toll. It wasn't easy, you know. Working nights isn't easy on anybody. Your friends have jobs during the day; your boyfriend, he sticks it out as best he can, but he's got his own needs, not to talk like some of those Arkansas girls, but a man's got needs, and that's nothing but the truth. But that's not enough, you see. I'd found Jesus."

"Swimming in shit."

To his surprise, Dudley laughed. "That's right. And wasn't nothing going to tear me away from Jesus."

"Something did."

Go easy, Somers mouthed.

"Yes." Dudley brought both hands to her face, but instead of covering herself again, she slowly brought her hands down, as though wiping her expression clean. "Yes, something did."

"What happened?" Somers said.

"He never looked at me. McAtee. He never talked to me. He never wanted anything to do with me. I wasn't his type, and he made that clear, but he never went out of his way to do it. And when I was on night shift, he didn't come around raising hell. He didn't scratch up my car. He didn't say boo to a mouse, not around me. I didn't even see him for the first six or eight months because I was working nights.

"Then, one night, they brought in a girl for drunk and disorderly. There had been some kind of domestic out in the county, and most everybody had settled down, but this girl hadn't paused for so much as a breath. She was whooping and hollering when they brought her, and one of the deputies told me she'd smashed the headlights in the cruiser with a sledgehammer." Dudley's mouth thinned into a line; she stared past the two detectives, and when she spoke, her words were slow and particular. "She was pregnant. Just showing. On a bigger girl, on me, you wouldn't have seen it, but she was skinny enough that the bump was there. She was drunk. You're not supposed to drink when you're pregnant. I thought she'd be better off for a few nights in jail. Clean herself up, maybe help that babe a little. She didn't talk much to me that first night. She just hollered. And the next night, she was sleeping. She was still sleeping when Grant McAtee came in."

Again, that thrill ran through Hazard. "During your shift?"

"Yes, sir. He waltzed right in. He told me he wanted to speak to the prisoner—that's what he called her, like she was anything but a girl who'd gotten herself in the same trouble most girls get into—and walked right past me. Didn't so much as howdy-do, just walked past. All right, I said. All right, that's not my nose he's bending, I don't need to worry about that. And I heard them talking. He was angry, real hot, but talking low enough I couldn't hear. She was plenty loud, though. Said he ought to act like a real man. Said she was tired of Demetrius—I learned later that he was her boyfriend—said she was tired of Demetrius asking questions. She was getting hot too. She kicked the cell door to hell." Dudley's voice broke, and she wiped at her eyes. "She kicked and kicked and kicked."

Again, she stopped, and she looked like she might cover her face with her hands again. She didn't, though, and the tears trickled down the sides of her face.

"There was a girl who hanged herself," Somers said. "Last summer. They found her—" He stopped. "You found her."

"She'd kicked so hard she'd broken her big toe. I could tell just looking at it."

"You're saying Grant McAtee went into the county jail and murdered a girl," Hazard said. "You're saying he made it look like a suicide. And nobody cared. That's what you're telling us?"

Now Dudley did cover her face, and a silent sob shook her big, rawboned frame. When she spoke, though, her voice was surprisingly clear. "I ought to shoot that man. I ought to shoot all men, all of the lot."

Now Hazard noticed the nightstand next to the bed, with its layer of dust and with clean spaces in the dust marking where something—several somethings—had stood. "You could do it, too, couldn't you? You could make a shot like the one that killed the sheriff. Where'd you put the trophies?"

Drawing her sleeve across her face, Dudley snuffled and sat up. "How'd you know?"

"Who did you want to shoot? McAtee for what he did to that girl? Or the sheriff, who didn't listen to you and who put you out on the street when you wouldn't be quiet?"

"I told you I resigned. And it was on account of the drink. Now how'd you know?"

"You resigned, but only because the sheriff would have forced you out anyway. And you drink because of the murder and because you feel guilty for letting that girl die on your watch."

"For hell's sake," Somers said.

"Go on," Dudley said. "If that makes you feel tough, saying that to my face, go on then. It's nothing I haven't thought before. Let's hear it."

"I want to know where you were on Sunday at noon."

"I don't know. Drunk under the honeysuckle, in a stranger's bed, on the side of the road. I don't want to know, can't you get that?"

"Did you kill Sheriff Bingham?"

"I don't think so. I hope to God I didn't."

Hazard shook his head and sat back. For a minute, maybe two, none of them spoke.

"I was Miss 4-H," Dudley said, tracing a finger through the night stand's dust. "First girl from the county. Three years in a row. Riflery. That's what those trophies were, although I'll never know how you saw the truth of that." In the silence, the low hum of a vacuum picked up somewhere else in the house. "I never put my mind to it, never even meant to be good at it, but Pa took me hunting, and it just grew inside me. Not many boys want to date a girl who's Miss 4-H. Not many boys want to date a girl who's a better shot. They'd rather have a girl in the swimsuit competition."

"We're going to ask around," Somers said. "We'll make calls. You could help us by giving us some names. People you normally see. Places you like to drink. Where you crash when you don't come home."

Dudley nodded.

"Is there anything else you can tell us? About the sheriff, about the department, about yourself?"

"I hitched a ride home today," she said. "And don't go picking at this. Don't go prying. I'm not trying to get anyone in trouble."

"For giving you a ride?"

"This is a small county. People talk. I heard somebody sent the sheriff a death threat."

"All right."

"Is that true?"

"Why do you ask?"

"I think it's true." Lacing her fingers over her stomach, she seemed to consider something. "I saw that before. At his house."

"A death threat?"

"That's right."

"Why were you at his house?"

"I had to drop off something from work. It was a while back. A year, maybe more. Longer, I guess, because I was still working days. When I got to the house, he answered the door, and he asked me to come in. He said he was going to get us some drinks, and I didn't want to stay, but I didn't know how to go. He left me in the front room, and when he didn't come back, I wondered if I was supposed to follow. I found his office. He has a safe there, built into that big table against the wall. And it was open. And on the desk, there was this folder, and it had dozens of them. Maybe more."

"Can you describe them?"

"All different kinds of paper. The letters looked like something out of a movie—you know, when the bad guy cuts up the letters and pastes them onto the paper so nobody can identify his handwriting. That kind of stuff."

"Can you give me some specifics? The wording, the types of letters, the color of the paper?"

She shrugged. "He came into the room right then and tried to play it cool, but he kept looking at that folder like he wanted to rush over there and grab it up. After that, he got me out of that place pretty fast. It was weird, sure, but I didn't think about it again. Not until I heard about the death threat. You know what I think? I think he's been getting them for a long time. I think whoever did this, he's been planning it for a long time."

"You think it's a man."

"Dennis Rutter's on your list, isn't he?"

"You know I can't tell you that," Somers said.

"If that's right, well, you ought to know something. The Rutter family, they've never been right. You know that? Well, some of them are worse than others. And Dennis had this brother, name of Howie. Howard, I guess. And Howard was locked up in the county jail. This was before my time. I'm not saying anything else on account of it was before my time, and I don't want you picking at this and trying to figure out who said what to who. I'm just saying Howie Rutter went in there on his own two legs, and the next time his family saw him, they were putting him in the ground. And there's always been bad blood between the sheriff and that family." She paused. "You know what I'd do if I were smart? I'd go out there myself. I know Rutter all right. I could wrangle him, I think. I'd go out there, put a collar on him, and bring him back. That'd be something, wouldn't it?"

"You should leave this to us, Miss Dudley. There's no reason for you to get yourself in any trouble."

"I'd clear my name. I might even get my job back. Yeah, that'd really be something."

"That wouldn't be smart," Somers said. He pulled pen and paper and passed them to her. "Instead, why don't you help us with those names we were talking about? People, places, anything that might help us figure out where you've been."

And when she had, Dudley led them to the front door. Her mother was still running the vacuum in short, precise lines across the living room, and she didn't look up as they passed her. The hum of the small motor filled the house, and the detectives shook Dudley's hand in silence and left her framed by the storm door, the enormous Garfield t-shirt fluttering against her thighs.

"She could have done it," Hazard said in the car. "Black-out drunk is a convenient excuse."

"She didn't do it."

"She's the right size and height for the prints."

"She didn't."

"She's got motive. She's got opportunity. She's got means."

"She can shoot a gun. So can every boy over twelve in this county. Most of the ones under twelve too."

"Not every boy gets named Mr. 4-H and has trophies in riflery. Not every boy carries overwhelming guilt and a personal hatred for the man who stopped a murder investigation."

"Yeah: she feels guilty. That's exactly why she wouldn't go and kill someone. She's got too much of a conscience."

"Guilt makes people do crazy things. This guy in St. Louis, he killed his wife with a screwdriver. Walked right into the precinct. He still had the screwdriver in his hand, and he was sobbing like a baby."

"She wasn't sobbing."

"You feel sorry for her."

Somers blew out a breath. "Yeah. I do. And I also don't think she's our killer."

"I'm saying she could have done it. I'm not saying she did it."

The only sound between them was the Interceptor's tires beating the gravel.

"She's a smoker," Hazard said.

"For Christ's sake."

"Her nails were practically yellow. Did you see that?"

"All right. Fine. I agree. She could have done it. Is that enough?"

"Let's grab something to eat. I'm starving."

"Are you sure?"

"I haven't eaten since breakfast."

"It's just, well, you're trying to get Nico back. And I don't think he's going to want you if you can't fit into your pants." Somers frowned thoughtfully. "Although I suppose most of the time he wants you out of your pants, so maybe it'll be all right."

"You're possibly the stupidest person I've ever met."

"You've told me that before."

They turned onto the state highway towards Wahredua.

"Ree."

The Interceptor thrummed. Hazard stared at the trees. They were winter-dead, of course.

"Ree."

In the crown of an old oak, a bird had constructed a massive nest. A falcon, Hazard thought. Some kind of falcon for sure.

"Ree."

"For God's sake, what?"

"If you can't fit into your pants, I think Dudley would let you borrow that Garfield shirt."

CHAPTER TWENTY-THREE

FEBRUARY 13
TUESDAY
7:00 PM

SOMERS STRAIGHTENED HIS TIE. It didn't seem to help. If anything, it had made things worse. He had dressed nicely for dinner with Naomi, but the tie was askew. And the jacket was wrinkled. A little. He'd found it under the bed, and a crease under his arm was gray where dust had adhered to the fabric. The shirt needed ironing—just a quick job, just a couple of minutes, tops. But he hadn't ironed it.

He hadn't had time. That was all Hazard's fault. They'd come back from Dudley's house, and Hazard had stuffed his face with burgers from River Drive-In, and then he'd marched Somers up to the station to dig through files. Marched in the literal sense. They'd walked the ten blocks from River Drive-In to the station because Hazard wanted to talk about Cassella, about the case, and about their suspects. In the end, though, Hazard hadn't said anything that they hadn't already known: there was something fishy about Cassella, they still had three suspects who could have killed the sheriff, and they didn't have any hard evidence that might close the case. Hazard was convinced that they hadn't dug deep enough into their suspects' backgrounds, and Somers had left him at the station, his dumb, Neanderthal face blue in the monitor's glow.

And then Somers had quick-stepped it the whole ten blocks back to the Interceptor, and he'd raced home, and he'd changed, and now here he was, sitting outside Manzi's, adjusting the damn tie. He yanked it one final time and headed into the restaurant.

Manzi's wasn't haute cuisine. It was family fare. Italian, with a splash of urban design: lots of exposed brick, the vents and ducts overhead painted black, the traditional red-checked tablecloths laid over ultra-modern stainless steel tables. Naomi was already waiting; she was facing the door, and Somers took a seat opposite her.

Naomi Malsho shared some of her looks with Somers's wife. Both women were slender, dark-haired, and beautiful with a kind of waifish fatigue. Where Cora wore flannel and denim as often as not, Naomi looked like she never dressed in anything that hadn't come straight off a runway. Tonight was no exception: she wore something black and shimmering that made her eyes deep and dark as hell.

"I ordered a red. If you're going to have something else, at least try to pace yourself."

"It's nice to see you too."

"Where's your guard dog?"

Somers flipped open the menu. "What's good here?"

"So. You didn't let him come. Good. Did he throw a fit?"

Running a finger down the appetizers, Somers paused at the bruschetta. Roasted tomatoes. Goat cheese. Balsamic vinegar.

"He must have been furious. But he did what you told him to do, didn't he? He wagged his tail and got right into his crate and let you turn off the lights and leave him in the dark." Naomi laughed. "Oh my God. You know what? You really could make him sleep in a crate. He'd do it for you. You know that, don't you? He'd curl up like a dog if you so much as smiled at him."

Roasted tomatoes, Somers said to himself. Goat cheese. You need this bitch's help. You need her help and she's trying to get you riled, trying to get you off balance. She's trying to get you so you can't think straight. Goat cheese. Goat cheese. Balsamic fucking vinegar.

"What's it like, working with a morally degenerate sub-human? Can you tell why he's gay? I have a theory about that, you know. Natural selection. There's something off about him. Something messed up. And natural selection takes care of it. He's gay. No biological children. The unsuccessful traits aren't passed down."

"Are you here to talk about Dennis Rutter? Or are you here to spout batshit theories?" The waitress approached, and Somers said, "Tequila. Whatever you've got. And the goddamn bruschetta."

"We don't have—"

"A beer then. Just something."

The waitress, her young face filled with confusion, retreated.

Naomi was smiling. "You're scrambling. I enjoy it. Really, I do. I like watching you. It's like a hamster on the wheel. You run and run and you don't get anywhere. What's it like, John-Henry?"

165

"I get a lot of exercise."

"No, not that. What's it like having a secret?"

"I don't have any secrets," Somers said, but his heart had started to pound. "You made sure of that."

For a moment, she was silent. "You do. You're hiding something. Something you haven't admitted to yourself. Something you can't admit to yourself. What's that feel like? Is it under your skin? Does it make you want to tear yourself in half?"

Yes, Somers wanted to say. Yes, when I make him smile. Yes, when I look into his eyes for too long. Yes, when he bumps against me and growls and acts like it's my fault. Yes, all those times, it's under my skin, it's a wire in my gut, it's like I'm choking and I might not ever breathe. Yes.

What he said, though, was, "We need to talk to your client."

"I'm talking about my sister, you know. Do you want me to tell you your secret?"

"I don't have any secrets."

"Your secret, the one that you can't even admit to yourself, is that you don't love her. No, you don't have to convince me otherwise. I know. I see how you look at her. And she knows too, even though she pretends that she doesn't. Do you want me to tell you what you should do?"

"I'm taking dating advice from a neo-Nazi now?"

"You should let her go."

"Where's Dennis Rutter?"

"That's an interesting question. Why don't you tell me?"

"Because I don't have any goddamn idea. His whole family rabbited. Where are they, Naomi? Where did you stash him?"

"Why do you need to talk to him? I'm asking honestly, John-Henry. My client is the object of a witch-hunt. This is a power play by the mayor and his cronies. You've got nothing on him."

"Then he should come in to clear his name. That's the next step, Naomi. Otherwise I'm going to keep looking for him until I find him and get some answers."

"Let's play that game, John-Henry. You keep looking for him—your expression—and ask questions. He doesn't have to answer."

"Boy. I wonder what we'll do then."

"That's very interesting. Am I supposed to understand that you would willfully and maliciously persecute my client because you are convinced of his guilt regardless of the evidence? This is beginning to smell like harassment—harassment at the very least."

"Naomi, you said—"

"Tell you what, John-Henry. I'm feeling very fair, tonight. You've put me in a good mood. I've gotten to say things to you that I've wanted to say for years. So, I'll do you a favor: you tell me where you've already looked for my client, and I'll let you know if you should keep looking."

You're a bitch, Somers wanted to say. You're a real goddamn bitch.

"I'll even help," Naomi said, her voice light and mocking. "Have you been to the Rutter property?"

Somers looked over her shoulder; where was the bruschetta?

"Have you, John-Henry?"

"Good Lord, Naomi. Of course we have."

"Good. And he wasn't there?"

"No. He wasn't there."

"Have you tried motels in the area?"

Somers narrowed his eyes.

"I'm only asking because you're having such a hard time with such a simple task. Did you think he might not be registered under his own name?"

"I'm done with this game, Naomi. Let's talk about Dennis Rutter and the reasons he might want the sheriff dead."

"I'm not going to have this conversation with you. You're bumbling your way through this investigation, and you don't have any legitimate suspects. Unless—" Naomi arched one perfect eyebrow. "I could arrange for a meeting with my client. I know he'd be happy to cooperate, especially under certain conditions."

"You think we're going to give him immunity? That's insane."

"I wish I could help you, John-Henry. I'll urge my client to come in. You understand, though, that I have limited influence; Dennis Rutter is an independent man, and he has a particular hatred for the small-minded tyrants of an illegitimate government fostered by corporate bribery and liberal propaganda."

"It must be hell using so many adjectives. Fine, Naomi. Play your game. We'll find him, and we'll get answers out of him."

Behind Somers, the door chimed, and cold air curled around his ankles. Naomi stood, opened her handbag, and drew out a manila envelope. "I do have something for you, though. I don't want you to think tonight was a complete waste."

"If you're fundraising for the KKK, I'm not interested."

"Charming. Have a good night, John-Henry."

Naomi passed over the manila envelope and left. Somers sat for a moment, holding the envelope, his heart suddenly thudding strangely. Naomi was smart. Naomi was more than smart; she was clever. Naomi had brought him here for a reason, and Somers suddenly thought the reason had nothing to do with Dennis Rutter or the investigation into the sheriff's murder. It had to do with this, right here in his hand.

He could lean forward, touch the tip of the envelope to the candle's flame, and let it catch. He'd tilt the envelope, letting the flame race up the paper, and he'd drop it on empty plate and wait until it was ash. That's what he'd do. That was the smart thing to do.

The envelope wasn't sealed; it was just buttoned down by metal clasps, and the clasps bent easily, and he pulled out the sheaf of documents.

Divorce papers. He thumbed the stack, and two signatures glanced back at him from every page. His own signature, and Cora's. He'd sent this—how long ago? Eight months? Ten? Not quite a year? He'd sent this in a narrow window of time: after he'd stopped feeling guilty, but when he was still at rock bottom, when Cora wouldn't answer his calls, wouldn't come to the door, wouldn't let him see Evie. He'd done this because he'd wanted to hurt her. He'd done this because he'd thought maybe it'd give him a chance at seeing his daughter again.

And he'd never heard anything from Cora. In its own way, that had been worse because it had left him in limbo. Time had dragged by. Things had changed. Somers had changed. And then, just a few months ago—

—Emery Hazard had come back into his life—

—Cora had called him out of the blue, and she had wanted to reconnect, and first they had started talking, and then they had started laughing, and he had held Evie again, and he had thought things were moving—

—away from Hazard—

—towards some kind of resolution.

Now this. Now these pages, and their two signatures. And the experience shocked Somers because it was like having a splinter pulled: painful, especially because this went deep, and so it hurt like hell. But underneath it, so far down that he couldn't acknowledge it, not yet, relief.

Then he heard her laughter. Bright, thrilling, untouchable like silver shining behind glass. Somers turned, unable to help himself.

Cora stood in profile, while a handsome man helped her out of her long winter coat. Somers recognized the man. They'd gone to high school together. They'd gone to Mizzou together. Ethan Dorsey had become a CPA and now made six figures doing books for Tegula. He was saying something in Cora's ear, and she was still laughing, and he was so close, just so damn close to her, why didn't he just stick his tongue in her ear and get it over with already?

They still hadn't seen him. Somers swept the papers into the envelope and walked towards the back of the restaurant. Pushing through the kitchen, ignoring outraged shouts and a cry to stop and the bemused waitress carrying the bruschetta he'd ordered, Somers found the back door and knocked it open with his hip.

Behind Manzi's, the alley was cramped and cold and mercilessly illuminated by two lights set over the door. The brick on the building opposite was reddish-brown, and Somers took two steps towards it and swung a huge right hook.

At the last minute, he pulled the punch. Brick skinned his knuckles, and he shook the sting from his hand and kicked the Dumpster instead. It boomed, and the metal popped back.

The rational part of his brain was saying talk to someone. Call up one of your buddies. Call up a friend. Call up your mother, for Christ's sake, because she'll be over the moon. But he didn't do any of those things. He trudged out into the road, ignoring the blare of horns, and cocked his head one way and then the other and noticed that his knuckles were bleeding a little and that he'd left a trail of black marks in the snow, like commas on a fresh white page, and he shook his hand and then the commas were everywhere, crazy, and then he knew where he was going and headed up the street to get a drink.

CHAPTER TWENTY-FOUR

FEBRUARY 13
TUESDAY
7:00 PM

HAZARD WAS STALLING. He knew he was stalling. Behind the Jetta's wheel, he checked his watch. Again. It was seven o'clock. He needed to get out of the car, head up the stairs, and knock on Nico's door. At the same time, probably at some fancy restaurant with real tablecloths and a wine list as long as Les Mis, Somers wanted to sit down to dinner with his wife. Instead, he was meeting Naomi. But Somers wanted to spend the night with his wife. That's what he'd said in the car. That's what he wanted to be doing tonight. Fine. Good for him. That was perfect because Hazard was spending the night with his boyfriend.

His boyfriend who had said casually, dropping it at the end of their conversation like it was a bomb from ten thousand feet up, love you. Not even I love you. Love you. That was it.

The snow hadn't been that bad lately. The Jetta had half a tank of gas. Hazard could make it as far as Columbia. Jeff City. Hell, he could refuel and make it to St. Louis or KC. He could refuel again and make it to Des Moines. Or Chicago. Or Denver. He could catch a plane. He had some wiggle room on his Visa, and he could be in Paris. Or Beijing. Or whatever the farthest point on the globe was from Wahredua, MO.

The antipodes, a detached voice in his head reminded him. You're thinking of the antipodes. Like putting a finger on each side of the globe to mark an invisible line straight through the center.

Alone in the Jetta, Hazard allowed himself a groan, and then he kneed the door open and crunched through the snow. Love you. How the hell was he supposed to deal with that? He knew, of course. He knew he should walk away now. It was the right thing to do. A break up was coming down the line. But he couldn't bring himself to do it. He couldn't face what a break up would mean. Easier, for now, to bury that realization. Easier to pretend, for a little while, that things might be ok, that he could be happy by lying to himself a day at a time.

When he knocked, Nico opened right away. He was flushed, his eyes shiny, and he leaned in for a kiss that tasted like rosé. He was wearing his typical Nico ensemble: athletic shorts that came barely halfway down his long thighs, and a perfectly ripped t-shirt that showed smooth, flat muscle in all the right places. It was an outfit begging Hazard to rip it off the younger man. Nico knew what he was doing.

But in what had become more and more common over the previous weeks, Nico also quite obviously wanted Hazard to work for it. He led the way into the apartment; his suitcase, on its side, spilled the clothes and toiletries Nico had taken for his stay at Marcus's apartment. Dishes filled the sink—already, after less than a damn day. At least a half dozen pairs of socks trailed from the sofa to the bedroom.

"You wore all those socks?"

"What?" Nico perched on the arm of the sofa. "What's that supposed to mean?"

"Nothing."

"I don't want to fight."

"I'm not trying to fight. I asked if you wore all those socks."

"You want to get me angry. You think if we start fighting about the socks, I'll forget about what happened on Saturday. Then we'll just be fighting about socks, and that's a stupid thing to fight about, and I'll lose the fight."

"If you wore all those socks, just say so. That's the only thing I'm asking."

"This is exactly what Marcus said you'd try to do."

"Yeah? Did Marcus tell you that I was going to try to win? And that I was going to make you lose? Because that's messed up. Relationships aren't about winning and losing, Nico."

"I didn't mean that. The way I said it, that's not what I meant. I just meant that I want to talk about the real issues in our relationship. I don't want to get sidetracked."

"They're socks. Nobody wears that many goddamn socks in one day. One pair. Maybe two. That's not sidetracking. That's just an observation."

"Ok. Was it just an observation when you beat up that guy at the Pretty Pretty and put him in the hospital?"

"He was fine."

"He had a concussion. Marcus told me all about it. He had to stay overnight because they were worried there was internal bleeding."

"He's alive, isn't he?"

"And that makes it ok? Because he's alive, everything you did was ok? Is that what you're saying? If that's what you're saying, I want to hear you say it."

Hazard glanced over the apartment again. Seven pairs of socks. He had missed a pair balled up behind the television.

"So you're going to ignore me."

"I'm not ignoring you. You're being dramatic."

"Help me understand what's going on, Emery. You show up here, the first thing you want to do is pick a fight about my socks—"

"I wasn't picking a fight."

"—and now you're telling me that what you did at the Pretty Pretty, that was ok. I don't think I'm being dramatic about anything. And I don't like you making me feel silly and small and ridiculous."

Tension tightened Hazard's shoulders, pulling them almost to his ears. With Alec, their arguments had always ended with Hazard bruised, with sex mixing hate and passion and desire. With Billy, the arguments had been fewer. Almost nonexistent, in some ways. Billy had been the master manipulator. He had known how to pull Hazard's strings. And now here Hazard was again, backed into a corner. Nico was going to end things. Nico was going to kick Hazard out. And then Hazard would be alone again. At the back of his head, a vision flashed of Hazard alone while Somers moved in with Cora. Somehow that was worse, a million times worse, than anything else Hazard could imagine, and he shoved the thought away.

"I'm sorry."

"What?"

"I'm sorry for what I said. And for what I did."

"I can't hear you."

"I said I'm sorry for what I said to you. About being dramatic. And I'm sorry that I hit that guy at the Pretty Pretty." Hazard didn't want to look. He didn't want to see. But he forced himself to meet Nico's gaze. Hazard didn't have Somers's ability to read other people. But he knew what he was seeing in Nico's face because he'd seen it in Billy's, because he'd seen it in Alec's. It wasn't anything obvious. It wasn't anything huge. But Nico was happy. Nico knew, now, that he was in charge.

"Thank you for saying that. It means a lot to me." Nico took a breath. "But I'm worried that you're just saying it. I want to talk about why these things happened. I want to know what you were thinking. I want to be sure this isn't going to happen again."

Talk, Hazard thought, and he faced his watery reflection in the television's glass. Talk, talk, talk. "I wasn't being respectful at the club. You're a grown man. You know how to take care of yourself. I should have let you take care of that guy when he kissed you."

Nico was nodding. "I felt like you didn't trust me. That made me feel insecure about our relationship. And it made me feel afraid that you might do something like that to me."

"I wouldn't hit you."

"Emery."

"No, that's not fair. I've never so much as raised a fucking finger to you."

"Emery. You're not acknowledging my feelings. If that's how this is going to be, we might as well stop right here. I need to know that you recognize that my feelings are valid."

Hazard stared at his blurred reflection. Had he really worried about ending up alone? Alone? Who the hell cared about being alone? Get the hell out of here, he told the reflection. While you still can.

"Emery."

He made a non-committal noise.

"Fine. If you don't respect my feelings—"

"All right. They're valid. I recognize that. What do you want me to say?"

"Do you think I like this? Do you think I like having to coach you on what anybody else would do just because they cared about me? Do you think this is easy for me, the way you shut yourself down, the way you shut me down, the way you keep building walls between us? Do you, Emery?"

The buzz of Hazard's phone spared him from answering. He glanced at the screen. He didn't recognize the number. "This is probably work."

"We need to talk about that too."

"I have to take this."

"We need to talk about your priorities, Emery. About our priorities. And we need to talk about John-Henry. The way things are going—"

Hazard swiped at the screen to accept the call; so what if Nico was pissed? And just about anything was better than talking about Somers, especially with Nico. Maybe this was a phone call telling Hazard he had a terminal disease. Maybe somebody was calling to tell him he'd been drafted into the army. Maybe somebody just wanted to tell him to go fuck himself. All of those sounded a hell of a lot better than where things were going here.

"Is this Detective Hazard?"

"This is."

In the background of the call, glass shattered, and a familiar voice was shouting. Another, deeper crash echoed across the line. In the next lull, the man spoke again. "If you don't get your ass down to Saint Taffy's in the next five minutes, I'm calling this in. I don't care if he is a cop; nobody comes in here and trashes my place."

"I'm coming."

"Son of a bitch is about to tear the place down around my ears. Who do you think's paying for this? Not me."

"I said I'm coming. Just don't call him in."

Hazard ended the call. "I've got to go."

Nico pulled his knees to his chest. He didn't nod. He didn't so much as blink. "Tell me again that's about work."

"I've got to go handle this."

"So you've got that much decency left. You won't lie to me. Not to my face, anyway."

"Can we talk about this when I come back?"

"Why do you need to go? John-Henry got shit-faced. All right. That's his problem, not yours."

"I'm his partner."

"And I'm your boyfriend. I'm your boyfriend who's had it up to here with John-Henry. Every minute, Emery, every damn minute you're with him. I'm tired of it. I'm tired of you running off whenever he wants you to."

"He's my partner." Hazard got to his feet.

"That's not a work call. He's not your partner tonight. He's a fucking drunk. He's a miserable fucking drunk and he's doing this on purpose. He's doing this because he knows you're here and he wants to ruin this."

Heading towards the door, Hazard said, "We'll talk about this tomorrow."

"No." Hazard had only an instant to realize that Nico was coming after him, and then Nico clutched his arm and swung him around. Nico's face was drawn in harsh vertical slashes. Anger distorted his voice. "No. This is it. I'm—I'm putting my foot down. I'm done with this. I'm done with being second. I want somebody who will put me first. I deserve somebody who will put me first. If it's not you, there's somebody who will, Emery."

"Get off me. Now."

"This is the last time I'm going to say it. You're not going."

Without speaking, Hazard pried Nico's fingers loose and shook off the younger man.

"If you go out the door, we're done. We're fucking finished. I don't ever want to see you again."

And then Hazard saw it: what Somers had tried to point out to him, what had been lurking beneath the surface of Nico's jabs and barbed comments over the last few months. Not only Nico's basic jealousy but also his fear and the juvenile, knee-jerk reaction. Anger washed out of Hazard, and he suddenly felt tired and old and sad.

"I hope you'll take that back," Hazard said, and he walked out.

From the doorway, Nico watched him. He was breathing so loud that Hazard could hear him halfway down the hall. And then Nico loosed a wild shriek and slammed the door, and the sound chased goosebumps up Hazard's arms and knocked him out into the cold, dark night.

CHAPTER TWENTY-FIVE

FEBRUARY 13
TUESDAY
7:59 PM

THE BOTTLE EXPLODED AGAINST THE WALL, and Hazard jerked away. Beer wet his face, and glass tinkled to the floor. Somers stood at the bar, fending off several angry men with a pool cue, while he reached for another bottle to throw. He wavered on his feet, but when one of the men—Hazard recognized him as an employee—surged forward, Somers cracked him across the head with the cue fast enough, and the man stumbled back rubbing at his scalp.

Saint Taffy's, the cop bar on Market Street, was a wreck. Glass shards littered the floor, mixed with puddles of beer and liquor. Behind the bar, the old mirror with fogged glass had been shattered. Instead of the usual cool darkness, someone had turned up the lights, and a blue-white glare reached the corners of the room. A few customers still sat in their booths at the back, but the place had clearly been busier only a short time before; drinks still covered the tables, and a trio of wait staff huddled near the kitchen.

One of the three men trying to disarm Somers glanced at the door and noticed Hazard. "About goddamn time."

This drew Somers's attention. "Hey. Ree. How's it—" He swayed, latched onto the bar, and gestured airily with the cue. "How's it going?"

"You're wasted," Hazard said. He took the three steps down to the polished concrete and crossed towards Somers.

Somers took a step back. His hip bumped a stool, and the whole row clattered. "Stop. Stop right there. I don't want—I don't want—" He lanced the cue towards Hazard. "I'm having fun."

"You're shit-faced."

"Will you get him the hell out of here?" one of the men said.

"Let's go," Hazard said.

Somers shook his head.

"Come on." Hazard took a step forward, and Somers swung the cue. It whistled, and Hazard deflected it from his head. The blow stung all the way up his arm, and Hazard swore. "Drop the fucking act. Let's go."

In answer, Somers swung again. This time, the tip whistled just below Hazard's eye and clipped the bridge of his nose. Blood ran down Hazard's face. He was growling, he knew, but he was too angry to stop it. He backed up before the cue could catch him again. "Cut it out, you drunk motherfucker."

"Am I going to get paid?" a man said. Hazard thought he was the manager. Or maybe the owner. "Look at this place. He tore it apart. "Either he pays or I call the cops."

"Drop that thing," Hazard said, "or I'll break your goddamn arm."

Somers shook his head. "You're supposed to be at Nico's. That was the deal." He paused, blinking owlishly, and then said, "That was the deal. I see Naomi. You see Nico."

Fingers pressed to his bleeding nose, Hazard said, "Well I'm not at Nico's, am I? I'm here because you're a part-time alcoholic and turns out you're a real asshole about it."

"You." Somers swished the cue. "Love." It whistled through the air again. "Nico."

"For fuck's sake."

"I just want you to say it. Go on. Say it. And then—" Somers paused. His free hand covered his forehead, massaging his temples, and his eyes suddenly looked deep and blue, and Hazard thought he'd make a hell of a splash falling into those eyes. "And then I won't feel so fucked up all the time. Right? Then I wouldn't feel so goddamn fucked up. You say it. I want you to say it. They—" The cue whipped towards the three men and then back towards Hazard. "They've been laughing at me. You know that? This whole town laughing at me." And then Somers burst out laughing. "I've got horns." His free hand mimed horns, and he pretended to charge and then fell back against the bar laughing again. "This whole fucking town knew before me. Knew I had horns. I couldn't even feel them on my own head. So you go on and say it, and then we'll go back to the way we were. Come on. Say it."

"I've got no idea what you're talking about. But you touch me with that cue one more time, and you'll spend Valentine's in a coma."

"Say you love Nico." Somers's face reddened. "Say it!"

"Nico dumped my dumb ass tonight, you dumb motherfucker."

Somers took a step sideways, and the cue dipped. Blindly, he groped behind the bar until his hand closed over a bottle. He shook it, seemed pleased at the slosh of liquid, and pulled it towards his mouth. He took a long pull, and in his drunkenness, it took a moment before surprise registered on his face. A maraschino cherry hung between his teeth, and some of the juice dripped down his chin.

Hazard took advantage of the distraction and charged.

Somers reacted, but too slowly. The cue banged against Hazard's shoulder, and then Hazard was inside Somers's reach. Crashing into the smaller man, he drove him back against the bar. Somers tried to get another blow in with the cue, but Hazard clutched his wrist and applied pressure until Somers howled and dropped the cue. The fight might have ended there, but Somers had gone into a frenzy. Shouting, kicking, writhing in Hazard's grip, he had gone past any point of reason. He hurled the jar of cherries, and some of their syrup splashed Hazard's shoulder and neck. The jar cracked somewhere behind Hazard, and its sugary scent filled the bar.

"Enough," Hazard growled, getting a hold of Somers's collar and shaking him. "That's enough, all right?"

"Oh fuck," Somers said, sagging against the bar. Color washed out of his face. "Oh fuck, fuck, fu—"

He hinged at the waist and threw up. Some of it got Hazard's trousers. Most of it got his shoes. It went on for a while; Somers hooked an arm around Hazard's waist to support himself, and Hazard curled his fingers under Somers's collar. Hazard was going to stroke his hair, but those shoes had been expensive, and Hazard had a hell of a headache again. He settled for running his thumb along Somers's neck, where the skin was pink and hot.

When Somers had finished, Hazard pulled out the other man's wallet and tossed a credit card on the bar.

"Don't bring him back here," one of the men said, crabbing sideways towards the card. "He can't pull shit like this and come back here."

"Whatever that doesn't cover," Hazard said, "you can put on this." He slapped down his own Visa. "Think about what you just said. I'll let you sleep on it."

"I don't want him back here. Neither of you."

Hazard led Somers out to the street, where the air was clean and cold and smelled like water. They began walking towards the apartment at the Crofter's Mark. On the next block, Somers stumbled, his arm still hooked around Hazard's waist, and when Hazard dragged him upright Somers buried his face in Hazard's shoulder. Hazard waited for drunken tears, but

Somers only stood there, pressed against him. Somers turned his head fractionally. His lips were dry and chafed Hazard's neck.

"None of that."

Somers didn't press the issue. But he didn't pull back either.

"Let's get you off the street."

"I like it here." His lips tickled Hazard's neck when he spoke, and he snuggled closer.

"You're a cop. You don't want anyone to see you like this."

"I don't care." His fingertips found Hazard's collarbone and dusted along it. "I don't care about any of that anymore."

"I said none of that. Come on."

Hazard dragged Somers towards the Crofter's Mark. The street was silent and black except for the nimbus of street lights. Everybody else in the world might be gone, everybody but the two of them. Somers smelled like sea salt, like amber, like tequila and sweat and vomit. Hazard felt like his heart was stretching out across some unseeable distance. They had walked this way before: Somers drunk, Hazard carrying him. They had come, that October night, to the Crofter's Mark.

Emery Hazard had seen the world very clearly then. He had thought he knew where all the lines were drawn. He had thought he understood what he wanted. He had planned, that night, to confront Somers about what had happened to Jeff all those years ago. Hazard hadn't known how things would turn out. He hadn't known that Billy would leave him. He hadn't known that Somers would become an inextricable part of his life. He hadn't known that he would date Nico. He hadn't known that he would, against his best judgment, fall deeper and deeper in love with the boy who had haunted his dreams since high school. He hadn't known he could care so much for anyone, let alone John-Henry Somerset.

And that's what it was, wasn't it? Caring? Love? That's what this feeling was, when he wanted to thread his fingers through Somers's golden hair, when he wanted to clean him up and get him in bed, when he wanted to touch him, everywhere, all the time, when he wanted to mouth kisses across his chest, when he wanted to trace those dark lines of ink on Somers's muscles, when he wanted him to smile, when he wanted to be the reason that Somers smiled, when he did and said things just because he knew they would get a rise out of the blond man—all those things, all the different ways Hazard moved and talked and thought differently because Somers was near, that was love. Wasn't it?

Inside the Crofter's Mark, the elevator glided to the fourth floor. They swayed as it stopped, and Somers was heavy against Hazard's side. His fingers wormed behind Hazard's belt, gathering the cloth of his shirt, tugging it free. Chilly fingers found Hazard's belly, teasing the dark hair, drifting up, shadowing the swell of Hazard's pectorals, and Hazard realized he was making a sound, realized he was stumbling against the elevator's mirrored wall, saw his face flushed and his pupils blown in the wall opposite, his erection threatening to split his trousers.

Somers staggered against him, his lips finding Hazard's neck, kissing, biting, nipping at Hazard's collarbone. His fingers didn't stop. They wove through the dark bristles on Hazard's chest, circled his nipple, tightened until Hazard grunted and thought he might spill without Somers touching him anywhere else.

"Fuck," Hazard groaned, turning away from the touch, his hands cuffing Somers's wrists. "I said no. I said none of that."

The elevator door dinged and tried to close, and Hazard caught it with his heel.

"My bed," Somers said, tottering towards the door. "You can fuck me in my bed."

He didn't wait for an answer. Hazard, shaking, stumbled after him. It was Hazard who had to unlock the door, though, and as he dug out his keys, Somers was back at it again. He undid Hazard's belt, yanked open the fly, and grabbed at Hazard's cloth-covered erection.

The door sprung open, which was a mercy because Hazard knew he couldn't last much longer. Propelling Somers by the arm, he got the other man inside and locked them both in the apartment. Hazard, his back against the door, braced himself as Somers spun and came towards him again. Somers was already shrugging out of his shirt, dropping it to the floor, exposing hard planes of muscles—smooth, with only a glimmer of dark blond hair below his navel—and the swirling calligraphy that covered his chest and arms. He undid the buttons on Hazard's shirt easily. His mouth, wet now, found the top of Hazard's chest, and it sent a moan through Hazard. His hands slid along Hazard's shoulders. Somers's wedding ring scraped along Hazard's shoulder blade.

Now, Hazard heard a part of himself thinking. Just let it be now. You've waited so long. You've been patient. You've been good. You're free now, free to do what you want, free to do what you've wanted since you were sixteen. And he wants this. You can see it in his eyes. You can see it—another moan rippled through Hazard as Somers's teeth scraped skin—you can see it in his eyes, he wants this, he wants you to fuck the daylights out of him, and so let it be now, let this be the moment, even though he's drunk, even though he's married, so what? Doesn't anything you've done matter?

Doesn't any of the waiting, any of the hoping, any of the last twenty years, doesn't it count for anything? Let it be now. Let it be now. Let it be now, even if morning comes and he hates you—

Catching a handful of Somers's hair, Hazard pulled his head back, forcing Somers to meet his eyes. Somers mewled and lunged with need. His pupils had devoured the blue in his eyes, and again Hazard knew, with total certainty, that whatever he wanted, he could do; whatever he took, Somers wouldn't resist. Tonight. It could be tonight.

"John," Hazard said, and his voice broke, and he didn't know why, couldn't have said if he had a gun to his head, but he just knew it wasn't the only thing breaking. "John," more firmly this time, ignoring Somers's thrusts. "I asked you to stop. Not like this. Not because you're drunk. Not because you're lonely. Not when you're married."

The words cut through Somers's panting. For a moment longer, he stared at Hazard. Then, shaking himself loose, he tried to draw himself up with drunken dignity.

"John—"

"Get off me. Get the fuck off me." Somers shoved him, trying to break Hazard's grip. "You don't want to fuck me? Fine. But get the hell off me. I said get off. Get off, you big, stupid piece of shit. Get off. You don't want me? Fine. Cora doesn't want me? Fine. I don't care. I don't care about either of you. I don't give a good goddamn about either of you, I don't. Don't look at me like that. Don't. Get off. Get off. Get off!"

Hazard drew the other man against him, and for a moment longer, Somers fought him. Then, letting out a shuddering breath, Somers relaxed into Hazard. He was talking, Hazard realized. Something about dinner. Something about papers. Something about Cora. But he was crying, too, and he was drunk, and the words didn't mean anything.

It didn't matter. Somers kept talking. He talked about Cora. He talked about Evie. At some point, Hazard carried him to the sofa, and they lay there, Somers curled inside the length of Hazard's body, still talking. He talked about the past and what he'd done in high school. He talked about college. He talked about other men. He talked about Cora again and again, always Cora, always coming back to her. None of it made sense to Hazard, but he sifted Somers's hair, and he stroked the back of his hand along Somers's cheek, and at some point before dawn, Somers must have run out of things to say because he fell asleep, and then Hazard slept too, and Hazard remembered shifting during the night and feeling Somers inside his arms, and he remembered the heat from his body—not sexual, not completely, but not brotherly either—and he remembered at the edge of consciousness, in the moments before oblivion, that this was home, that this was maybe the only home he would ever know.

But in the morning, Hazard was cold, and Somers was gone.

CHAPTER TWENTY-SIX

FEBRUARY 14
WEDNESDAY
7:07 AM

SOMERS COULDN'T MEET HIS OWN GAZE in the cheap rectangle of the mirror, so he gripped the sink and stared down into the porcelain and wondered if he might not throw up again.

He had slept with Hazard.

There it was, that damn thought again circling back no matter how many times Somers chased it away. They hadn't fucked. They hadn't made love. They'd just slept, and something twisted painfully in Somers's gut, hurting even worse than the hangover, and he turned on the shower to mask his groan.

As Somers stripped, his heart fluttered as his mind played back snippets of the previous night. Dinner with Naomi. The divorce papers. Cora laughing while Ethan Dorsey just about sucked on her ear. And then the oh-so-fucking brilliant idea to get completely smashed. After that, things got blurry.

Naked, Somers sat on the floor of the shower, his chin on his knees as the hot water pounded his back. He'd made a mess of things at Saint Taffy's, that much he remembered. And he remembered Hazard—Jesus, had he hit Hazard? With a pool cue? Then they had walked home, and Somers remembered—aching with embarrassment and erect all the same—his advances on Hazard. Scrubbing at his eyes, Somers quashed the thoughts. There had been something at the end, something Hazard had said, and it tickled the back of Somers's mind. Then bitterness broke through: yeah, right at the end, when Hazard was busy rejecting him. Again.

Somehow, Somers showered and, wrapped in a towel, exited the bathroom. Hazard was on the sofa. Still asleep, if Somers had any luck. A fresh scab marked the bridge of his nose. Hazard had curled up after Somers left, and now Somers felt a pang. Why hadn't Somers thrown a blanket over him? Why couldn't he have done that much, at least? But Somers had been too startled—no, scratch that, terrified, he'd been terrified—and he'd sprinted to the bathroom and locked the door. Jesus, Somers thought, a blanket would have been nice, though.

At Somers's third step, Hazard's eyes opened.

"Morning." Cold air licked Somers's chest, and after the steamy shower he knew his nipples must have looked like goddamn icebergs. "Sorry."

"Why are you sorry?"

The blanket. Somers should have gotten a blanket for him. "I had to pee."

Hazard rolled onto his side; in the light, the scab across his nose looked worse, and Somers felt a pang of guilt. The sofa creaked under the bigger man. "And shower."

Somers laughed too loud at that. "Yeah. And shower."

They watched each other in silence, and then Somers scuttled towards his bedroom and shut the door. Pressed against the wood, he listened, and then the sofa springs creaked again, and footsteps came towards Somers's room. The steps grew louder. Closer. Somers's heart was pounding, the blackness darkened the edges of his vision. Breathe, he told himself. Just breathe. You've talked to him a million times. He's just going to ask if you're all right, and then he'll be Hazard again and go off and brood, and that will be the end of it.

But the steps stopped before they reached Somers's door, and then they moved away, growing quieter, and then, from the bathroom, came running water.

And somehow that was worse, much worse, than if Hazard had insisted they talk.

Somers wanted to slide to the floor. He wanted the floor to open up and he wanted to keep on sliding. Down to the cellar at least. Maybe farther. The earth's molten core might be nice. Instead, he dressed, found water and Tylenol, and told himself the worst of it was over.

Hazard emerged from the bathroom. His too-long hair was neatly combed and parted, a single wet curl already trying to escape. He was buttoned-up in shirt and tie and jacket, and another memory flickered inside Somers: running his hands between those buttons, the stiff hair on Hazard's chest springing under his touch.

"You're acting weird," Hazard said.

"I'm fine.

"We didn't fuck."

"God Almighty."

"You were pretty drunk; I thought you might be wondering."

"Is this how you talk to every boy you take home?"

"I don't take black-out drunk boys home." Hazard paused. "And you're not every boy."

"I'm fine. I said I'm fine, right? I promise, I am."

"You're not."

"Ree, come on. You know me. We're good. Everything between us is good."

"You're wearing two different shoes. And your shirt is inside out."

"Goddamnit." Somers kicked off his shoes and undid his shirt. "It's just the hangover. My head—well, I don't have to tell you. How's your head? That's more important."

"It hurts."

"You take your pills?

"They're at Nico's."

"We'll stop by."

"I'll get a new prescription."

"It'll take five minutes." Somers turned the shirt right-side out and slipped into it. "You can just run in."

"No."

"Ree, you're being stubborn. I promise if Cassella says something about us being late, I'll take the heat."

Hazard crossed his arms. "You don't remember."

"What?"

"Nico broke up with me. So I'm not going to pick up those goddamn pills. Will you drop it now?"

"Oh. Yeah. I'm really sorry."

"Just drop it."

They'd broken up, Somers was thinking. Hazard and Nico had broken up, and still Hazard hadn't wanted to—

A tiny flame of hope curled inside Somers's chest. Maybe Hazard wasn't ready. Maybe that's why. Maybe he needed time to get over Nico. Sure. That was all. Time.

"Will you stop that?"

"Huh?" Somers realized he had been whistling. "Oh. Right. Your head."

Hazard eyed him suspiciously, and Somers fought to hide his smile.

"We should get going." Somers dug out a matching shoe and tied the laces. "Do you want to talk about it? I don't mind, that's all I'm saying."

"We talked enough last night. You talked enough. You talked more than enough."

"Ree, you shouldn't bottle things up. We should talk. I know you think I don't like Nico—"

"You don't. You've told me countless times that you don't."

"—but I want to be here for you. As your partner. As your friend."

"I don't want to talk."

"I really think you should. You keep everything inside you; that's not good. It's not good for anyone. I swear, I won't say anything. Well, I won't swear very much. And you can tell me if I start crossing a line."

"All right."

"All right?"

"Maybe I do need to talk."

The flame inside Somers unfurled, hotter and brighter. "Yeah, go ahead. Whatever you want."

"Let's talk about Gina Torini."

"Uh."

"You told me about her at length."

"Look, I probably wasn't—this wasn't what I—"

"You didn't tell it in a straight line, but I think I got the gist of the story."

"We're not even talking about me. And anyway, nothing really happened. I'm not even sure I remember—"

"She was the girl in the windmill. The putt-putt course. She liked to use ropes. You spent half the night getting the worst blue balls of your life, and the other half you said she had this monster vibrator—"

Somers's phone rang. "Thank God," he breathed as he answered. "Hello?"

"Detective Somerset? This is Cassella."

"Yes?"

"I'd like to go over the crime scene with you. Let's meet first thing this morning. Can you be there in ten?"

"Yes."

"I'll see you there."

Somers disconnected. His face still felt hot. "We've got to meet Cassella at the sheriff's."

"A lot of guys like that stuff, you know. Ropes. It's nothing to be embarrassed about."

"Sweet Jesus."

"The vibrator on the other hand—"

"All right. Yeah. I think that's enough talking. We don't need to talk, Ree. We don't ever have to talk again."

If Somers hadn't known better, he would have thought he saw a smile—a very small, very subtle Emery Hazard smile—on his partner's lips. Somers was halfway to the car before his embarrassment faded enough for him to think clearly, and the realization made him stumble.

Emery Hazard had been flirting with him.

Suddenly, Somers forgot all about the hangover.

CHAPTER TWENTY-SEVEN

**FEBRUARY 14
WEDNESDAY
7:43 AM**

THEY PICKED UP BREAKFAST SANDWICHES from the Wahredua Family Bakery—once owned by the family of Hazard's tormentor, Mikey Grames—and drove on to the sheriff's house. Hazard had to work overtime to keep a grin off his face. Somers wasn't normally easy to rattle; he was too even-keeled, too self-possessed, too goddamn confident. This morning had been nice. More than nice. Dangerously more than nice, as Hazard caught himself thinking, for the hundredth time, of how Somers looked when he blushed, and his flustered embarrassment, and the way his full lips parted when he was trying to find a way to protest. Ropes, Hazard thought. They could have a lot of fun with ropes.

The sheriff's land sprawled ahead of them: the tall winter grass bending in the wind as though the house floated at the center of a rustling sea. Gravel crunched under the Interceptor's tires as they rolled to a stop behind a black Infiniti. Cassella swung himself out of the car, running a hand through his Kennedy hair, wearing what Hazard was pretty sure was another new suit.

"That's an expensive car," Somers said. His eyes drifted to Cassella.

Hazard shrugged.

"And an expensive suit." He was still staring at their temporary boss.

"He's got money. He's a lawyer."

"He's a special prosecuting attorney for the state. He's not working in-house for Facebook. I bet that haircut cost a hundred dollars. And he obviously spends a lot of time at the gym."

"You're spending a lot of time looking at him."

"Ree, come on."

"What?"

"Don't do that."

"I'm not doing anything."

"I just said he spends a lot of money on his hair."

"Yeah? Why don't you fucking ask him about it? It'll make a great icebreaker."

Without waiting for an answer, Hazard kicked open the Interceptor's door and dropped into the February cold. Somers followed a moment later, face like a martyr, and Hazard had to fight the urge to rearrange that face. Maybe rearrange it permanently. Rearrange it with a really hard right hook.

After Somers and Cassella exchanged pleasantries—Hazard ignored the offered handshake—Cassella nodded at the street. "I've been thinking about that one."

"Fukuma?" Somers said.

"What'd she say?"

"You know we talked to her?"

"No thanks to you," Cassella said, softening the words with a grin. "She came back home last night; I still had one of the patrol guys sitting outside. She didn't want anything to do with us. I guess she'd had enough after talking to you."

Somers filled Cassella in on their conversation with Fukuma, and when he'd finished, Somers said, "It seems pretty unlikely that she's our killer. Even if she is, there's not much we can do without a lot more evidence."

"People heard her threaten to kill the sheriff. That's a start."

"All right," Hazard said. "You want to take that in front of a grand jury? Go right ahead."

"Thank you, Detective Hazard, for your input."

"We're still working this case," Somers said. "And that means we've still got our eyes on Fukuma. But right now, that's how things stand."

"And I'm telling you, detectives, that we need to pick up the pace. We're going back to square one: the murder scene."

"This is bullshit," Hazard said. "You want to pick up the pace by starting from scratch?"

"Detective Hazard, if you don't want to be part of this investigation, I'm sure Detectives Swinney and Lender could handle it."

Hazard glared at the lawyer.

"Do you understand me?" Cassella said.

"Yes."

"We needed to come back here anyway," Somers said, turning sideways to place himself between the other two. "Deputy Dudley told us that she had seen death threats at the sheriff's home. She believed he'd received a number of them over an extended period of time."

"You found Dudley too?" Cassella said.

"Amazing how much you can find," Hazard said, "when you get off your ass."

"All right—" Cassella said, turning on Hazard

Somers slid between them. "Ree, go check on the safe."

"You go check on the safe."

"Just go, all right?"

Hazard left; he could feel Cassella's gaze hot on his back. Somers was already talking, smoothing things over the way he always did. Before Hazard reached the house, Cassella let out a laugh—an angry laugh but already softening.

It was one thing, Hazard thought as he let himself into the sheriff's home, it was one thing to have to deal with Somers practically drooling over the guy. It was one thing to watch Somers's eyes drop out of his head. But Hazard would jam his head through a paper shredder before he let the boy politician tell them how to do their job.

In the sheriff's study, Hazard found the safe in a rustic sideboard set along one wall. It was serious business: reinforced steel, fingerprint scanner, and the whole operation bolted to the floor. It'd be easier to rip out the floor joists than get that damn thing out of here. The door was shut and locked when Hazard tested it; so much for luck.

Footsteps announced Somers and Cassella. "Good," Somers said as they entered the study. "You found it."

"Is it open?" Cassella said.

"Yeah. It's open. I was just sitting here, keeping it closed until you guys got here."

"Jesus Christ," Somers muttered. Then, louder, "It's biometric?"

"You've got eyes, don't you? Or did they fall out back in the car?"

Somers muttered something else—*Lord help me*, it sounded like.

"We've contacted the manufacturer," Cassella said. "Waiting on them."

"How long?" Somers said.

Shrugging, Cassella spread his hands.

"That's perfect," Hazard said. "You know this town's got locksmiths, right? What are we waiting for?"

"Locksmith," Somers said. "Singular."

"I know," Cassella said. "We tried. He's out of town. He took his wife to Tan-Tar-A for Valentine's. He'll be back tomorrow and we'll get this open. Or the manufacturer might call us today. Either way, we'll get in there." A smile pulled at the corners of Cassella's mouth, and he added, "Who are you spending Valentine's with, Detective?"

"You think that's funny?" Hazard said, shooting to his feet.

"Whoa," Cassella said. "Did I touch a nerve? I just thought you might be spending it with that really good-looking boy, the one I saw you with."

Hazard's mind clicked and whirled as he processed possibilities. "You went to the Pretty Pretty again. Last night."

"I'm new in town. Motel rooms are boring. God, especially the Bridal Veil Motor Court. Do you have any idea—"

"You saw Nico there."

"That's right. That's his name. I noticed you weren't with him."

"Why don't we drop this?" Somers said. "Why don't we all take a breath?"

"You talked to him," Hazard said. He took a step. He was vaguely aware that Somers had a hand on his chest and was pushing him back—trying to push him, really, and it was comical, it was funny, it would have been hilarious if Hazard hadn't been focused on hitting Cassella so hard that he had to wipe his nose through his asshole.

"He was upset. A few of us bought him some drinks." Cassella shrugged. "Everybody talks after a few drinks."

"That's enough," Somers said. "Cassella, take a hike, would you?"

"Nico seemed lonely. Looking for companionship. Pretty guy like that, you know what—they always want somebody older. I guess you already figured that out though."

"Say his name," Hazard said. Somers had both hands on his chest now and was leaning into him, keeping Hazard out of arm's reach of Cassella. "Say it one more time."

"You know what I think he'd really be into—" Cassella began.

"All right," Somers said. "You made your goddamn point. Get out, Cassella. Now. Just get the fuck out."

Cassella blinked. The smile slid off his face, and he stretched like he might be winding up for a solid swing, but he just turned and left.

Hazard pushed at Somers's restraint, fighting to get past his partner.

"Do I have to put a goddamn leash on you?" Somers said, grabbing Hazard's tie and using it to jerk Hazard to the side. "Is that what I'm going to have to do?"

"Get off me."

"Why? So you can go beat him up because he likes how your boyfriend looks? What is this? High school?"

The tightness in Hazard's throat eased; a cool mixture of self-disgust and self-pity washed through him, and he eased away from Somers. Somers didn't let go of the tie, though.

"He's not my boyfriend."

"Oh yeah?"

"You know he's not."

"Well, you're sure as hell acting like he is."

"Cassella did that on purpose. To provoke me."

"And you gave him exactly what he wanted. Didn't you?"

Hazard's face was hot; he couldn't meet Somers's eyes.

Somers looped the tie around his hand, and Hazard was forced to take a step closer. Neither of them moved. Neither spoke. And then Somers tightened the loop again. Hazard could smell him now. Somers looped the tie around his hand once more. Less than an inch separated them. Kissing distance, and the thought sprinted through Hazard's mind like a high-speed train. When Somers's spoke, his breath was hot on Hazard's chin.

"Didn't you?"

"Yeah." Hazard yanked his tie free. "Now get the hell off."

"Are you going to act like you're a grown man?"

Hazard, flattening the wrinkles in his tie, moved to the french doors that overlooked the riverbank.

"We're not going out there again," Somers said, "until I know you can deal with Cassella. He's an asshole. Sure. You want me to say that? Fine. I'll write you a song about it if that's what you want. But we're not going out there until I know you're not going to do something stupid and get us kicked off this case."

Waterfowl—ducks, Hazard thought, and weren't they supposed to fly south?—spun up off the river, water sparkling in the February sun.

"Ree, he's going to go out. He's going to get smashed. He's going to screw some other guy that's not you. That's what happens after a breakup. It hurts, and it sucks, but that's what it is. And I'm really sorry about that."

As the ducks settled into their pattern, the last of the water falling from them dappled the river's surface, pocking it. Wherever they were going, Hazard hoped it was far away from here. Home. He hoped they were going home.

"Ree—"

"Don't you think it's strange that Cassella wanted to provoke us? Don't you think it's strange that he wants us off the case?"

"He doesn't want to provoke us. He wanted to provoke you. And that's because you crawled up his ass the minute we got here. You rode him pretty hard, and he was giving some of it back. It's over now, all right? Let's go do our jobs."

Hazard nodded, but he made the mistake of catching Somers's eyes—blue, so much bluer than the river, so blue that nothing, not the sky, not the ocean, nothing, could come close—and seeing worry there.

He's going to screw some other guy.

Why had Hazard held back last night? Why had he said no to Somers? That had been stupid. That had been the stupidest thing of Hazard's life. It was the kind of stupid you could win an award for—stupid like somebody winning a Darwin Award, one of those trophies they gave out for people who died cleaning out the human gene pool. John-Henry Somerset had been pressed up against Hazard, had wanted him, and Hazard had said no. The Darwin Award wasn't enough; this was too stupid, its own special degree of stupid. The Emery Hazard Award for Fucking Yourself. They could give it in memoriam.

Outside, Cassella had walked fifty paces up the gravel drive, and they joined him. When he spoke, his voice was neutral.

"She came down over there," his finger traced the slope of the land, "and made her way to the bluff. That's what the camera shows."

"That's what she told us too," Somers said.

"We didn't search over there."

Hazard felt a moment of disquiet.

"That's true," Somers said. "Damn it. We were so focused on the tracks that led to the river."

"If Fukuma was involved in this, then we might have missed something."

Somers was already nodding.

"Why her?" Hazard asked. "We've got three potential suspects. What makes you focus on Fukuma?"

"I'm not focusing on her. I think we missed something. We have no clue what route Dudley might have taken to get here. Rutter was on the river, and we've already searched there. We do know where Fukuma went, and we haven't searched there. I'm just checking boxes, Detective."

"We'll take a look," Somers said.

"When you're done, I want you to see what else you can run down about Fukuma and her run-in with the sheriff the other night. And keep working leads on Dudley; she's not clean just because she's too drunk to remember where she was. See if you can't catch up with Rutter, too. Detective Somerset, weren't you going to see if your contact inside the Ozark Volunteers—"

"That didn't pan out."

"Oh. All right. We'll have to track him down some other way; look into that, all right?"

Cassella waited a moment; when they didn't ask any questions, he left, and a moment later his Infiniti kicked up rocks along the drive.

"We start up at the road?" Somers asked.

Hazard trudged towards the top of the hill; Somers kept pace with them. It was cold, yes—a shattering kind of cold, like any fast movement, any loud noise might cause the air to crack. But the sun had risen, and that was warm on Hazard's face. It wasn't a day for worrying. Not today. Not with the early morning light pouring over the folds of Missouri countryside. It was a nice day. It might even be a beautiful day. Hazard could spend this whole day working the case. He would enjoy himself because he enjoyed his work. He didn't have to think about anything at all, didn't have to worry. Just because it was Valentine's Day—

He's going to screw some other guy.

"You sure you don't want to talk about it?"

"Don't do that."

"What?"

"Just don't do it, ok?"

Somers laughed. With one hand, he gathered the husks of seed pods from the tall grass, tearing them free as they walked. "It's not hard to guess, you know. You look like you're sucking on an exhaust pipe. I'm surprised steam doesn't shoot out your ears."

"I said I don't want to do this."

"Ok."

Hazard paused, studying the roadside grass. So far, it stood tall and unbroken, with no evidence of passage. He continued down the road.

"About this morning," Somers said.

"I thought we weren't going to talk about that."

"I should have gotten a blanket."

Hazard's head corkscrewed before he could stop himself; he forced himself to look straight ahead. That was what Somers wanted to apologize about: a blanket. That was the thing he was worried about: that Hazard might have been chilly. Not any of the rest of it. Not the fact that he'd practically ripped off Hazard's clothes. Not the fact that he'd picked a fight when Hazard turned him down. Not the fact that Somers had run away in the morning, hiding in the bathroom before Hazard could wake, so that Hazard woke up alone, a piece of himself gone and missing. None of that stuff. A blanket.

"Are you going to say something?"

"I had wool socks on."

Somers burst out laughing. He snagged another wavering stalk of grass and plucked it from the ground. "You had wool socks on."

"I wasn't cold."

"You were curled up on the sofa."

"Didn't bother me."

"You don't sleep like that normally. Normally you're sprawled out, taking up every inch you can."

"You don't know how I sleep."

"What about Windsor?"

Hazard felt the flush in his face. "I didn't take up the whole bed."

Somers, smirking, said, "But you wanted to."

"If you want to talk so much, let's talk about Cassella."

"Ree, let it go. You picked a fight. He came back at you. Hard. I don't like him for it, but—"

"There's something weird about him. About this whole case."

"Here we go."

"He was in town before the murder. And I'd bet money that he was still in town when the sheriff was shot."

"He's a politician in a conservative state."

"So?"

Peeling the grass into strips, Somers said, "So he probably doesn't go to gay bars in Jeff City. You don't shit where you eat."

"Why wouldn't he go to the gay bars? If he wants to win on the gay vote, and that's what it sounds like, then he damn well better go to gay bars. Hell, I wouldn't be surprised if he did some campaigning at the Pretty Pretty."

"He might want to win on the gay vote," Somers said, "but not until he's sure he can."

"What does that mean?"

"That means this is still a conservative state, and Cassella might not be out. Or he might not be out officially, which makes a big difference when it comes to campaigning. I bet he'll want to be absolutely sure of a win before he starts waving the rainbow flag."

Hazard snorted. "The important thing is that he sidelined us during the most important part of the investigation."

"It was a stupid move. It was a dick move. But he could have taken us off the case and he didn't. He's got us working it now. Why would he do that if he had something to hide?"

"Why are you defending him?"

"I'm not defending him."

Hazard stopped, planting hands on his hips. "What is it?"

"Nothing."

"Like fuck. What is it?"

"I think he's just a guy, that's all. Not a suspect."

All the gears and clockwork spun in Hazard's mind. Then he shook his head. "He said you were hot."

Red spots heated Somers's cheeks. "He didn't—" He swore and tossed away the shredded grass. "How the hell did you do that?"

Hazard shook his head again.

"He didn't say I was hot, all right?"

"What'd he say?"

Turning his face down, Somers spoke into the dirt. "He said I had a good face for politics."

"Jesus Christ."

"I'm not taking his side because he gave me one lousy compliment, you know."

"There's something weird about him, Somers. That's what I know. And I'm going to figure it out."

"Ree—"

"There." Hazard pointed out a section of grass matted by the weight of footsteps. "This is where she started. Come on."

"Ree?"

The grass rustled against Hazard's trousers; the cold had gotten into his fingers, stiffening them. He smelled the river, now, and the wet moldering of the trampled grass.

"Ree, I'm just asking if you think he might be right. I could do a lot of good—"

"I swear to God, Somers, I'm up to here with you right now."

For a moment, the only sound was the whisper of the grass against wool. Then Somers, in a voice pitched at the soles of Hazard's wingtips, said, "It's an important question, Ree."

"For the love of—"

"All right. All right. I'm dropping it."

They searched along the ridge, following it towards the dense stand of trees where someone had shot and killed Sheriff Bingham. Although days had passed, Fukuma's trail was easy to follow. Hazard didn't know if that was luck or the result of dry days and cold temperatures; the grass bent and snapped at the slightest pressure.

"Do you really think he's trying to set up Fukuma?" Somers asked.

"I don't know."

"Do you think he's wasting our time?"

"Maybe." Hazard turned over the question. "I think it's possible they missed something at the crime scene."

"Norman and Gross do good work. I know you don't like them, but they're solid on stuff like this."

"Norman and Gross couldn't find their asses with two hands."

"They've done fine in the past."

Hazard grunted. From what he'd seen about Norman and Gross, he wouldn't trust them to run up the police tape, let alone set foot in one of his scenes. It hadn't been Hazard's choice, though, and he knew Somers felt loyalty to the Wahredua PD.

Ahead of them, the trail curved along the ridge. Young growth thickened on one side of the detectives: slender aspens and oaks and maples, with plenty of sunlight pouring through their bare branches. By now, Hazard had worked up some heat, and he could smell his sweat and the wool of his coat. Grass crinkled as they moved. Somers breathed easily; for being such a lazy son of a bitch most days, the man was in perfect shape.

"Where it jinks to the right up there," Hazard pointed. "That's where they took the shot."

"Hold up."

They stopped. From where Hazard stood on the ridge, he had an excellent view of the river and the sandy stretch along its bank. Crime scene tape fluttered in the breeze, but the scene had been abandoned when the Ozark Major Case Squad left. There was nothing left to be found—or rather, nothing that they knew about.

Hazard's position also gave him an excellent view of the bluff where the killer had stood. He frowned. Fukuma had told them that she had seen Beverly Flinn kneeling over the sheriff and that she had seen the doctor running back from the house. But Fukuma also said that she hadn't seen the killer. That was a very narrow window: less than a minute, Hazard guessed, between when Fukuma heard the shot and when she saw Beverly turn the sheriff onto his back. What were the odds? It seemed too convenient that Fukuma would have arrived in time to see the early reactions to the sheriff's death but too late to see the killer.

"She said she stopped when she heard the gunshot," Somers said. "I doubt she got much farther than this—look, the grass up there is still standing."

"She might have gone through the woods. She might be lying."

Somers moved up to stand next to Hazard. He was so close that Hazard felt his heat, smelled his hair and the sea-salt notes of his cologne. Extending a hand, Somers held his index finger and thumb close together and mimed pinching something on the beach.

"What the hell are you doing?"

"You remember what Scott said?"

"He didn't say anything about you standing this damn close to me."

Somers didn't move, not exactly, but somehow the bastard was now leaning even closer, and Hazard fought the urge to clock him.

"Scott," Somers said, his breath tickling Hazard's neck, "said something about the killer looking down at them. Like they were ants. That's not quite how he said it, but do you remember?" Again, Somers mimed opening and closing his fingers. "Something about how he must have seen the sheriff. Not so big. Was that it?"

"I don't remember."

"You think that's why somebody did this?"

"What?"

Somers had somehow moved in even closer. His chin was practically resting on Hazard's shoulder, and his breath—warm, soft breath—was making Hazard want to jump out of his own skin. "Power. You feel big, you make the other person small. Somebody made Sheriff Bingham really small. So small all they had to do was move a finger—" Somers mimed closing his fingers again, as though crushing a bug, "—and poof."

Hazard wasn't enjoying the closeness. He wasn't appreciating it. Not exactly. It's just that it was so damn cold. And Somers did smell good. A little bit like the ocean. A little bit like sex. And if Hazard turned his head right now, their lips were already aligned, and—

"So what do you think?"

"Huh?" Hazard's voice came out like gravel on sheet metal.

"Do you ever listen to me? You think that's why somebody would want to kill the sheriff? Fukuma, for example. She seems like she's very concerned with power. She wants it. She doesn't want anybody else to have it. Gendered power dynamics." Somers leaned in even closer, whispering the next words: "And if you even pretend to be surprised that I know a phrase like gendered power dynamics, I'll push you down this hill."

"Did that come up a lot at frat parties?"

"God, you're an asshole sometimes."

"You might be right."

Somers chuckled.

"About the motive, I mean. Whoever wanted him dead planned it. Rutter might have wanted to feel powerful, killing the man who had murdered his brother—"

"If we take Dudley's story at face value."

Nodding, Hazard continued, "Or, as you said, Fukuma might have wanted power over a political figure who had made her feel powerless in the past."

"And Dudley," Somers said. "The sheriff put her in the jail. Made her work night shift. He's the one who made her an accessory to murder—that's how she sees it, anyway—and now she feels powerless to make it right."

Somers let out a thoughtful breath, and Hazard shivered. Right out of his skin; he was going to jump right out of his fucking skin if he had to feel that breath on his neck one more time. He took a step away, turned on his heel, and plunged between the trees.

The scraggly undergrowth thinned after a few feet, and Hazard stumbled into a clear space. He caught Somers by the arm as his partner followed, and Hazard indicated the clearing ahead of them.

"Look at that," Somers said.

Hazard was looking. He was looking at something very interesting. And in his mind, Hazard was already running backward through the events. She heard the shot. She saw the sheriff dead. She knew she was in trouble if she stayed, and she'd be in even more trouble if she were caught with something like this.

"Who do we know," Somers said, a lazy smile lighting up his face, "with a history of making these little gems?"

Hazard nodded. "Fukuma."

Then he bent down to pick up the Molotov cocktail.

CHAPTER TWENTY-EIGHT

FEBRUARY 14
WEDNESDAY
2:45 PM

WHEN THEY BROUGHT THE Molotov cocktail to Cassella, of course, he was ecstatic. He showered them with praise—Somers, mostly, who lapped it up like a goddamn cat. Hazard confronted Norman and Gross, and the two patrol cops blustered and bullshitted until Hazard got sick of them and left. Cassella stuck around long enough to tell everyone he was going to have one of the patrol boys lift prints from the bottle. Then he left to get a warrant for a DNA sample from Fukuma. This was enough, as far as Cassella was concerned, to take it to Judge Platter. As far as Hazard was concerned, Cassella wasn't just counting chickens before they hatched; he was counting before there were any goddamn eggs.

After that early discovery, however, Hazard's day began to go downhill. Cassella had reiterated his charge that Hazard and Somers continue investigating the other suspects, but the reality was that the Major Case squad had already done most of the work. Hazard and Somers spent a chunk of the day driving around, checking in with people who had previously been contacted, knocking doors, canvassing neighbors.

They even checked on the witnesses to the shooting, hoping that one of them might have remembered something. Eunice Moody, under a mask of face powder, was overseeing the setup for a charity auction. The South-Central Missouri Ladies Regional Ornamental Plantings luncheon—at least, that's what the banner said. Moody was snappy at a harried catering staff, most of them young men and women who were probably college students and trying to earn an extra buck.

"Sorry to interrupt you," Somers said, eyeing the ballet of chairs and tables and wait staff. "We'll only take a minute."

"They'll be fine," Moody said, flicking fingers at an acne-speckled young man, who turned around and ran. "I'm really only here to terrorize them. I wouldn't be here at all if half of our fundraising hadn't gone missing."

By all appearances, Hazard thought, she was doing a hell of a job at the terrorizing part.

"The ladies whatever it's called," Somers said. "You got robbed?"

"Something like that. Our treasurer, Pearl Warren, moved to some godforsaken spot in Kansas six months ago. Surprise, surprise, she isn't answering any phone calls."

"It wasn't a scramble?" Somers said. "Trying to throw this together?"

"Not really, dear. Your mother helped. She'll be here soon—why don't you stay and we'll all have tea?"

Somers looked like he'd rather drink poison. "Don't you need to stay? You know, to get everything ready?"

"No, dear. I told you: I'm really only here to raise hell. That's the secret to a good leader, I think. Wind them up like clockwork—wind them up until they think their heads are about to pop off. Then let them go. If you planned things right, it'll work out."

"Unless something unexpected happens."

"If you planned it right," Moody said, "you've already expected everything."

"Even if someone takes half the money," Hazard said.

"Look around you, Detective. As I said: I expect everything."

Unfortunately, she had nothing new to tell them, and when they left her, she clapped her hands and stalked towards a young woman. The poor girl spilled a tray of silverware and started sobbing.

They found Beverly Flinn, her bleached hair limp with sweat, at the community center. She spoke to them for a few minutes during a break in the rehearsal—it was a play Hazard had never heard of, but Beverly lit up at his question, and she began rattling off her description.

"It's like *Snapped* meets *King Lear*. God, it's a dream. You've got to see it. I'll get you comps."

But she didn't remember anything more, and they left her there.

Dr. Hayashi worked at an urgent care clinic—one of those revolving door facilities set in a washed-out strip mall. A mother and boy were the only ones waiting, and the boy had a serious case of chickenpox. It wasn't until Hayashi had a break that she spoke to them at the counter, her voice so low that Hazard wanted a shovel to scrape it off the ground.

"Oh. Um. Yes. I mean, it's very good of you to come. But, no. No, I don't remember anything. Um. No. No, I don't."

McAtee, they found setting a speed trap on the highway out of town. Somers's parked the Interceptor behind McAtee's cruiser, and they approached the passenger side door. Hazard didn't want to give McAtee any pretense for shooting them on accident. In the days since the murder, McAtee's eye had bruised from Somers's punch. Hazard found himself thinking about McAtee, about all that money squirreled away, about why McAtee's family would do a thing like that. McAtee didn't roll down the window until they'd knocked three times.

He cussed them up one side and down the other, but he hadn't remembered anything.

When Hazard and Somers got to Randall Scott's farm, Hazard was forcibly reminded that farming paid a hell of a lot better for some people than it did for others. Scott owned about as much land as the state of Rhode Island, and he had a house that wasn't much smaller. A small woman in a rayon blouse and stirrup pants led them through the house. Lots of trophies, lots of pictures of Thailand, lots of pictures of a boy—Scott's son, Hazard thought, and he remembered that the boy had died a long time ago. He remembered, too, the tragedy: a series of rapes, escalating in violence, and then someone had found the boy dead in a ditch. An angry brother or father or uncle, everyone said. Ugly, the kind of ugliness that stuck to a family.

They found Scott emptying the trunk of his car. He nodded to them, setting metal contraptions on the ground. Traps, Hazard realized. Big, nasty steel traps that looked big enough to take off a man's leg—anything smaller would likely just get snapped in half.

"Coyotes," Scott said. "Damn things get worse every year. You know what's hell about coyotes? They do damn well under pressure. If you lay into a pack of wolves, for example, start picking them off, you can knock them out pretty quick. I'm not speaking for myself; just speaking about how things were done. That's not true about coyotes, though. Damn things are mean as hell. You can't keep them down no matter how much you try, not without wiping them out completely." And that was all he could tell them, and Hazard wondered if Sheriff Bingham had been more of a wolf or a coyote. Had he been brought down because he'd lost his pack? Or had he been tenacious, too tenacious, and someone had wiped him out?

Lionel Arras, again, was nowhere to be found. They tried his office. They tried his home. They dragged Market and Jefferson, hoping to catch sight of him at one of the more popular restaurants in town. Nothing.

"He gave a statement," Somers said.

"After he ran out of the house. Now we can't find him again. That doesn't seem strange to you?"

"We'll find him."

"I didn't say we wouldn't find him."

"I didn't say you did."

When they left Scott's house, they drove south towards the Rutter compound. Somers insisted on playing that ridiculous twanging music. Once, after a particularly screechy section of strings, Hazard had failed to hide a dirty look, and then Somers had turned up the volume like a real bastard. After that, it was a matter of principle, and so Hazard gave Somers—and the radio—the dirtiest looks he could manage.

The sun cut through the last quarter of sky, and the light came from behind Hazard. Where it touched Somers, that golden light was perfect: gold on top of gold, shining on his jaw, his cheek, his hair, the beginning wrinkles at the corners of his eyes. In that light, the blond stubble on Somers's cheek gleamed and became visible. What would it be like to run his thumb over that? Rough, God, yes, Hazard knew it would be rough. It looked soft, but he'd felt it before, and it was scratchy as hell. But the scratch of it, that could be nice too in its own way. He could run the back of his hand down Somers's cheek. He could lean in. How would it feel against his lips? How would it feel against his tongue? He knew—Christ, he had to adjust his legs—he knew how it would taste.

And he's married, you worthless fuck, Hazard told himself. He's married, and he's got a daughter, and tonight he's going to dinner with his wife because he loves her. And the only decent thing you've done, the only worthwhile thing in your whole goddamn life, was keep him from screwing up his own life last night. So you can stare at him. You can think about catching those blond bristles between your teeth and tugging until he yelps—he shifted again, wondering how strong the zipper was, if his trousers would just split down the middle—yeah, you can think about that all day long, but the only good thing you ever did was not letting him ruin his shot at happiness.

"What are you thinking about?"

"Football."

"Nope. What, really?"

"Nothing."

"Come on."

"The sunlight."

And then they drove on in silence. When they reached the Rutter compound, the gate was still shut, and the signs on the gate still offered a range of unsolicited opinions about breeding, sexual proclivities, and and the temporal and eternal destinies of trespassers.

Now, though, there was a Ford Taurus with rusted wheel wells parked across the length of the gate. Somers let out a groan.

"You recognize it too?" Hazard asked.

"What the hell is she doing here?"

Behind the Taurus's steering wheel, Lisa Dudley's form was visible. She was staring through the gate, into the compound, and her big-boned body looked like it was strung on tight wires.

When Somers knocked on the glass, she jumped. "Easy," Somers said, motioning for her to roll down the window.

"Geez. Sorry about that; just about gave me a heart attack."

"Miss Dudley."

"I know, I know. We talked about this."

"We did."

"I'm not causing any trouble."

"You're parked so they can't get on their land. That's illegal."

"I wouldn't stop them if they showed up." Today, Dudley wore a long, ill-fitting shirt with a floral print; it had come off the rack in about 1987, Hazard guessed. She pulled at the lace neck and squirmed in her seat. "I would've moved."

"You can go on and move now," Somers said. "What are you doing here, Miss Dudley?"

"I just wanted to talk. I thought maybe if we talked, I could understand what was going on."

"You wanted to talk to Dennis Rutter?"

Dudley gave up on trying to make the shirt comfortable, and she clasped the steering wheel with both hands. "I'm not an idiot. You don't have to talk to me like I am."

"What are you really doing here?"

"I'm not a liar, either, sir. Ma would strip my hide if she thought I were a liar. I'm twenty-seven next month, and I've never seen a need to lie before."

"Just drink," Hazard said, "gamble, fuck around, sleep in ditches."

"All right," Dudley said.

"Real lady-like," Hazard said.

"All right." Pinpricks of sweat glistened on Dudley's forehead and darkened the floral print under her arms. "You like that, don't you? You like talking to a woman like that. Well, I've never so much as said a sour word to you, never so much as raised my voice. Ma says that's how the gays are, and I suppose she's right."

"Get home," Somers said. "And don't do something stupid like this again."

"I wasn't doing anything stupid. Ma didn't raise any stupid children. I'm here on account of Rutter. I thought it over, and I'm going to find him. I'll find him before you do."

"Get home, Miss Dudley. Right now, before I decide you're blocking private property and take you in to the station."

Lisa Dudley's tires threw up gravel as she tore away from the compound. Hazard watched her go; he was ignoring Somers.

It didn't work. Somers said, "You're hard on her."

"She was being stupid. And she's an adult."

"You rode her hard when we talked to her the first time."

"I don't pack her in cotton batting if that's what you mean."

"And I do?"

Hazard shrugged.

"What are you thinking?"

"You're not going to complain some more? You're not going to tell me I'm being a dick?"

"You are being a dick. You know you are. And you're doing it on purpose. Are you still worked up about last night? Because I thought we were over that. This morning, we got over that fast because we're adults."

"There's nothing to be worked up about."

"Sure." Somers gave a curt laugh. "All right, if that's what you say. So you're trying to get a rise out of Dudley. You're pushing her to see how fast she falls and which direction."

Hazard shrugged again, approaching the Interceptor.

As Somers swung up into the driver's seat, he said, "You think she did this?"

"She can't account for where she was. Nobody can. She's an excellent marksman."

"Markswoman."

"She got motive. She's got opportunity. She's got means. And she shows up at the Rutter compound."

"What's that got to do with it?"

"What would you do if you were the killer?"

"I don't know. What would you do?"

"I'd try hard as I could to pin it on somebody else. Somebody like Rutter."

Somers frowned. The sunlight surfed across the bridge of his nose, brightening the hollows of his eyes. "And if Rutter is dead, it's sure hard for him to make his own case. But why would she sit out here, plain as day? That's not real smart."

"She was a county deputy," Hazard said, nodding to the road so that Somers would start driving. "If she'd been smart, she would have been a cop."

CHAPTER TWENTY-NINE

**FEBRUARY 14
WEDNESDAY
4:15 PM**

THE STATION WAS BUSY as the shift change approached, and Hazard and Somers settled into their desks in the bullpen. Somers dragged a stack of reports across the desk, settled back in his seat, and began flipping through them.

"We've read those," Hazard said, powering up the behemoth of a computer that sat on his desk.

"Maybe we missed something."

"I didn't."

"We."

Hazard punched in his password.

"You could say we, Ree. We didn't miss anything."

"I don't know about you. I know about me."

"Blow me."

On the screen, Hazard pulled up a browser and began searching. Cassella. Salvatore Cassella. Salvatore Cassella campaign. Salvatore Cassella election. Salvatore Cassella donors. Salvatore Cassella fundraisers. On and on like that, digging deeper into the prosecutor's life. He found Cassella's LinkedIn page, his Facebook page—grotesquely wholesome, Cassella rigged up with running gear, jogging with a pair of Labradoodles—and then he started drilling into the Missouri Ethics Commission site.

After clicking his way through a maze of sub-pages, Hazard found himself scanning Cassella's most recent campaign finance report. The list of donors was impressive; Cassella had obviously made something of a name for himself, and plenty of political action committees, companies, and individuals wanted to get on Cassella's good side.

Many of the largest donations, Hazard saw, came from similar political action committees—organizations to elect other regional politicians. Hazard guessed it was something of a back-scratching game. Friends of John Smith, that kind of thing. Those politicians out there had a hell of a lot of friends.

Some of the donations, though, came from organizations with names Hazard didn't recognize. Missourians for Independence. Missourians for the Right to Liberty. Missouri Pride First. The Show-Me-State Independent Business and Real Estate Developers Committee. The Missouri Horse and Goat Veterinary Specialists. How did goat and horse specialists get ten thousand dollars for Cassella? And why were they giving it to him?

Hazard opened a new set of tabs, plunging deeper into the labyrinth, when Somers let out a huge sigh.

First things first, Hazard decided: work through the list. He'd start with Missourians for Independence.

Somers sighed again, more loudly, and tossed the folder onto the table.

With a few clicks, Hazard found himself staring at the organizational paperwork for Missourians for Independence. He googled the names he found. Farmers, mostly. And it sounded like the name was more literal than he had expected: they were all located around Independence, Missouri. All right; no red flags so far.

Stretching in his chair, Somers kicked his heels up onto the desk. His spine cracked like fireworks.

"What?" Hazard said.

"Huh?"

"Don't do that. You want something. What?"

"I was just stretching. It's this chair. We've been sitting here for so long."

Glowering at him, Hazard opened a new tab.

"I finished reviewing all the footage from the camera that picked up Rutter. There's nothing suspicious on it. Nothing that makes me think they tampered with it, anyway, or that it was staged."

"So we didn't get lucky."

"Now that we're talking," Somers said, "why don't you tell me what you're working on?"

"I'm busy. You should be too."

"Ree, there's nothing in these files. Nothing. We've gone through it."

"I told you."

"What about you?"

Hazard's mouse drifted towards the new tab, but then he shrugged and closed out the windows. He locked the computer just to be sure. "Let's take a walk."

Outside, the day had warmed considerably. Sunlight made it feel almost like spring, and the walk eased some of the tension that had been building in Hazard's core. They crossed the street and headed to the park, where the yellowing grass and the bare branches screened them from the rest of the world.

"All right," Somers said. "This is some real serious spy stuff."

"Cassella's got an election coming up."

"We had to walk out here for this?"

"He's running for state legislature. It's a big move for him. He's got a lot of money behind him."

"And you think—what? He came into town, murdered the sheriff, and stuck around because it would look good on his campaign posters?"

"I think something's weird. It's strange that Cassella was here the night before the shooting. It's strange that he coincidentally caught the case when the mayor insisted that someone else handle it. Hell, it's strange that the mayor kicked this down the road for the attorney general to handle. We've handled plenty of cases on our own."

"What do you have?"

"Evidence?"

"Yeah, you just about hammered that poor keyboard to death over the last couple hours. What do you have?"

"Cassella's finance reports."

"And?"

"I'm still working on it."

"So, just so I'm clear: at this point, all you have is evidence that Cassella is running for election and that he's properly documenting campaign contributions."

"You can be a real asshole sometimes."

"I'm not saying you're wrong, Ree. I'm just saying it feels like you're letting this become personal. He made you mad, and now you're digging into him with a grudge."

"This is all in my head. I'm seeing shadows because I don't like Cassella."

"That's not what I said."

"All right."

"Ree." Somers blew out a breath; he ran a hand through his short blond hair. "If you think there's something, there's probably something."

"Probably. Wow. Thanks."

"What do you want me to do?"

"Nothing, Somers. Not a damn thing."

The day didn't seem as warm now, and Hazard pulled his coat tighter and headed out of the park. He kicked gravel from the path into the street—on accident, sure—and thought fuck it and didn't stop. On the sidewalk, he took big paces that ate up the cement.

Somers caught up in the station parking lot. "I'm going to take off."

Glancing at his watch, Hazard said, "It's not even five."

"We're spinning our wheels, Ree. We started at the crack of dawn, and I'm exhausted; I didn't sleep—" Something on Hazard's face made Somers stop, and a flush surged under his golden skin, and he shook his head. "I've got stuff to do."

Then it made sense. "You've got dinner tonight. With Cora."

"I don't know."

"You don't know if you've got dinner tonight."

"I just—I don't know what's going on, all right?"

"Sure. It's Valentine's. You're having dinner with your wife." And as he was speaking, Hazard thought again about Nico and Somers's remark: he's going to screw some other guy.

"You know it's complicated."

"It's not, Somers. It's really not. She's your wife, isn't she?"

"Yeah."

"There you go. Clear as fucking day."

"Ree, what do you want—" Somers stopped. Something flickered in his expression—something that Hazard recognized but couldn't quite name, something that left him feeling unsettled. In high school, many times he'd walked into a room just as everyone went silent. He'd known why. He'd known they'd been talking about him. And this was like that, the tickling certainty that Hazard had been the butt of a joke that everybody knew except him. Then Somers's face cleared, and that trademark Somers grin split his face. "You want to come with us."

"Good Lord."

"You do."

"I'd rather eat a bullet."

Somers nodded knowingly. "You're hungry. You're carrying more weight these days. Your body needs more calories."

"It's a fucking expression you fucking moron."

"Ree, if you want to come to dinner, you can."

"Fuck you."

"But you're buying your own meal, Ree."

Hazard turned and started towards the station.

"I know you're upset," Somers called after him. "But remember, Ree: don't eat your emotions."

Hazard briefly entertained the thought of slamming Somers's head in a car door until the blond man stopped talking—Jesus, even a car door might not be enough—and tried to ignore Somers's laughter.

Making his way through the station, Hazard returned the cool nods from the other officers. James Murray, almost eighty, still worked the front desk. Miranda Carmichael, carrying one of her abundantly fragrant tomato-and-onion sandwiches, passed Hazard on her way out of the building. Norman and Gross were headed into the locker room to change, and Jonny Moraes passed them on the way out, already in street clothes. He was the only one to give Hazard a smile and a handshake.

Things were different in Wahredua than they'd been in St. Louis. Hazard was accepted here in a way that he'd never been in the city. Acceptance, though, wasn't the same as belonging. Somers belonged. The men and women in the station—in the city, for that matter—loved Somers. He was a part of them as much as they were a part of him. Hazard, for all that he had grown up here, was an outsider. He'd always be an outsider, and most days that didn't matter. But today was Valentine's, and Somers was having dinner with his wife.

Hazard shoved the thought aside as he settled into his desk. He rattled out his password, opened up the browser, and started searching through the PACs again. Budget lines, donor contributions, page after page of government forms blurred together. Somers was going to dinner. All right. Where? Somewhere fancy. Candlelight. Violin music. Somers would stuff a twenty in the guy's pocket and ask for—hell, something surprising, some obscure classical piece that would show, once again, that Somers had taste and charm and good looks, the whole goddamn package. And then the mental image stuttered, and it was Nico, only he was at the Pretty Pretty, grinding up against all the perfectly tan, perfectly coiffed, perfectly dressed boys. That frat boy would be there again. He'd have a big white bandage around his head just for the sympathy, and he'd buy Nico a drink, and the next thing, his tongue would be so far down Nico's throat that he could taste Nico's breakfast.

Hazard shook himself. Good. Good for both of them. At least somebody was having a nice Valentine's. At least somebody was going to enjoy himself. And anyway, what the hell did it matter who Somers had dinner with? Somers could have dinner with whoever he wanted. And Nico could screw whoever he wanted. Hazard didn't give a good goddamn about any of it. He was going to do his work. He was going to keep investigating — damn, which one was next? Hazard began typing. Show-Me-State Independent Business and —

Somers at dinner, candlelight, violin music, the selfish little piece of shit, while Hazard did all the work —

With the snap of plastic, the keyboard cracked down the center. On the screen, the letter j repeated in a long line.

"Goddamnit," Hazard muttered, yanking the cord loose from the USB port. He held the two pieces of the keyboard for a moment.

"What the hell happened there?" Cassella asked.

Hazard spun in his chair to face the other man, hoping his bulk would hide the computer screen. He raised the two pieces of the keyboard. "Defective."

"You're not kidding. You need another one?"

"I've got it."

"Everything all right?"

"Fine."

Cassella shrugged into his coat and collected his briefcase. "Emery — can I call you Emery?"

Hazard flexed the two pieces of keyboard. The broken plastic looked sharp, and there were wire filaments. Hazard guessed he could put the damn thing through Cassella's throat if he hit hard enough.

"Emery, I really want to apologize about this morning. What I said, the personal things, that was out of line."

Yeah, Hazard thought. Yeah, the plastic was plenty sharp. It would definitely be sharp enough to get the artery.

"We work together, and it means a lot to me that we have a good relationship." Cassella flashed a politician's smile, sticking out a hand. "Besides, guys like us ought to stick together. It's a new world out there. Lots of opportunities for us."

"Yeah," Hazard said. He proffered the keyboard as though it explained why he couldn't take Cassella's hand. "Guys like us."

Cassella's grin widened. Those teeth, they'd probably cost a few thousand dollars just in whitening. Hazard wondered what they'd look like all over the ground. He'd never broken teeth that expensive before.

"All right," Cassella said. "Glad we're on the same page."

"Definitely."

"Have a good night."

"You too."

"Oh, trust me. I'll make sure it's a good one." Cassella's eyebrows arched suggestively, and with a wave, he pushed out of the bullpen.

Hazard watched Cassella go. The man was everything a politician needed to be: friendly, good-looking, and smooth. It was the last one that bothered Hazard right then. Cassella was just too damn smooth. And that meant that Hazard needed an angle, an edge. He needed to find a way to get under all that smoothness and find the rough edges, the real Cassella, the stuff he was trying to keep out of sight.

Digging into the financial records was a good start, but it wouldn't be enough. Jeff City might have been a small pond on the national scale, but for Missouri politics, it might as well have been the Pacific. And Hazard wasn't a big enough fish to swim in the Pacific. He needed something a lot bigger. Something with teeth. He needed a shark.

And then he groaned because he knew what he had to do. He pulled out his phone and dialed. The phone rang seven times. Eight. Pick up, Hazard willed. Pick up the damn phone.

The voice was tired but clear. "Who is this?"

"Emery Hazard."

The police station, almost abandoned now, echoed with footsteps in the locker room. The computer fan whirred. Hazard's chair creaked as he adjusted his weight.

"What do you want?" Glennworth Somerset's voice had an edge in it, but the tone remained neutral. Somers's father was a lawyer, a philanthropist, and a shark in local politics. He'd gotten himself shot and almost killed a few months before, but it didn't sound like that had slowed him down much.

"Information."

"Does this have something to do with my son?"

"It has to do with a case we're working."

There was another long pause, and the silence in the station grew larger.

"He doesn't know you called me."

"He doesn't like asking for help."

Glenn's laugh was short and sharp and bitter. "No more than you do, I expect. But you still called. And you called me."

"I found who shot you, didn't I? You owe me."

"You didn't do it alone."

"Are you going to help me or not?"

"I want to know why me. And why my son doesn't know about this."

"Because you're a bastard, but I don't think you'd step on your son's neck. Not unless someone made it worth your while, anyway."

"And why didn't you tell my son you were going to call me?"

"Maybe I did."

"No. You didn't."

Hazard clutched the phone, its aluminum body slick in his hand. "He doesn't like asking for help."

"We both know that's bullshit. Why didn't you tell him? Why didn't he call me?"

"He thinks I'm digging into this because it's personal."

A white, staticky hiss filled the earpiece, and then Glenn's voice came louder, with amusement lacing the words. "It has to do with that boy you carry on with."

"That's enough. You can fucking forget I called." Hazard slid his thumb to disconnect the call.

"What do you want to know?"

Hazard hesitated. "Salvatore Cassella."

"I don't know him."

"He's in the Attorney General's office. He's here, a special prosecutor for the sheriff's shooting."

"All right," Glenn Somerset said, and Hazard could hear the interest in his voice like he'd just tasted blood in the water.

"Anything you can get on him. He's running for the state legislature; that may have something to do with it."

"With what?"

"Just find out whatever you can."

The next silence practically vibrated with Glenn's frustration, but all he said was, "I'll call when I have something."

As soon as the call disconnected, Hazard dragged Somers's keyboard into place and dropped the broken pieces of his own keyboard on Somers's desk. He returned to his investigation of Cassella's financials. A few minutes later, Hazard had pulled up the disclosures of the Show-Me-State Independent Business and Real Estate Developers Committee. He scanned the entries, googling individuals as he went—small business owners, mostly, scattered throughout the state. No pattern he could see. No red flags, nothing that—

Except there, buried in the list of donors. The amount wasn't extraordinary, so Hazard went back to the previous quarter's disclosure. And the same donor appeared. And on the previous quarter. Going back six years, InnovateMidwest had donated steadily to the Show-Me-State

Independent Business and Real Estate Developers Committee. Steadily, yes, but not in such extravagant quantities that they might draw undue attention. Hazard wondered, however, how much of the undisclosed contributions—the contributions recorded as under a hundred dollars, which did not need to be disclosed—had also come from InnovateMidwest, albeit indirectly.

This was it, the red flag that Hazard had been looking for. InnovateMidwest was a real estate development firm that had been involved in a number of questionable dealings throughout the state—and particularly in Wahredua. Wahredua's mayor, Sherman Newton, was one of the major shareholders in the firm. Over the last few months, Hazard and Somers had come to realize that the mayor and his investment firm were involved in more than just real estate. Hazard suspected, although he could not prove, that the mayor was behind several murders and attempted murders. More recently, he had tried to help cover up the death of a young girl.

And now here he was, tied to Cassella. Indirectly, yes, but still there—his money and influence percolating through strata of government documents until they reached the prosecutor handling the sheriff's murder investigation. This was what Somers had wanted to see, and now he wasn't here. Hazard found himself clutching the keyboard in frustration, and he forced himself to relax before he broke another one.

Had the mayor been involved in killing the sheriff? Had he planned it? Was he simply an accessory? Had he arranged with Cassella as part of some play to broaden his own reach? Having Cassella on his payroll inside the state legislature would be a nice addition to the mayor's influence.

Hazard printed everything. Every form he'd pulled up, every document, every page, all the stepping stones that led from Cassella to the mayor. Then he called Swinney.

"I'm in the bath," she said.

"It's barely five."

"Do you have any idea how boring Springfield is? I might as well be inside a Men's Warehouse. Just a bunch of empty suits." Her voice sharpened with interest. "What do you need?"

"You got anything for me?"

"No. Like I said, it's just empty suits up here. Cassella called and told me he's sending a DNA sample. Who is it?"

"Fukuma."

"No shit."

"It's a frame."

"Yeah?" Splashing noises came over the line, and then silence, and then Swinney spoke softly. "What's Lender up to?"

Swinney's partner, Lender, was on the take from the mayor. He had lied to keep Hazard and Somers trapped while a killer tried to eliminate them, and then he had killed a suspect to keep him from talking. Swinney knew the truth, and she had done her best to help Hazard and Somers, but she hadn't come forward to expose Lender. Like Hazard and Somers, she lacked hard evidence. And, Hazard suspected, she still held a deep, irrational loyalty to Lender. They were partners; they'd been partners a long time.

"That's what I wanted to ask you."

"Nothing. Not a word from him."

"Are you guys—"

"Things aren't normal between us. But they're not bad, either. This kind of quiet, it's standard for Lender." Swinney's breath whistled in the earpiece. "You think this is him?"

"Could be."

"If it's him, then you know it goes higher, right?"

"I know."

"Jesus. What about this guy, Cassella? What about him?"

"That's what I'm working on. You pick up anything about him? Chatter?"

"Chatter. I'm not some CIA spook, Hazard."

"Nobody's said anything about him."

"Oh yeah, I forgot. A bunch of us girls got together in the typing pool to talk about how dreamy the special prosecutor is."

Hazard waited.

"I'll ask around," Swinney said. "Do you ever laugh?"

"How do I get footage from traffic cameras?"

"It's on the cloud. Somers can give you the password."

"He's out."

"On a date?"

"What the hell do I know? Can you give me that password?"

"Cool it. Yeah, I'll give it to you."

"I need it now."

"You know what? Next time, have Somers call me."

"Text it to me now, Swinney. And if they run that DNA test, call me first."

"Do you ever say please?" And then she disconnected.

A moment later, Hazard's phone vibrated, and a text appeared. It had a link and a username and password. He stretched for the computer, but the phone buzzed again, and a number splashed across the screen. Hazard answered the call.

"Already?"

"That young man has quite a reputation. All I had to do was say his name and people were ready to talk."

"Ok."

"Sal Cassella is hungry. He's got a lot of pull inside the AG's office—God only knows how—and that means people are lining up to give him their spare change. From what I hear, he's well ahead of his opponent on fundraising. He's young, he's got charisma, but he's got to face an incumbent. The guy's been in the state house for twenty years. It's not easy to make an old dog roll over, even when you do have a lot of cash."

"So what's he doing here? Fundraising?"

"What else do you know about him?" The question had a barb in it, almost a leer, as though Glenn were telling an obscene joke and Hazard was the punchline.

"You mean that he's queer?"

"So you sniffed him out."

"I ran into him at a gay bar. Not very good cover for a closeted guy running for office."

"That's interesting."

"What?"

"Cassella is closeted. Well, technically. But that's about to change. His district has seen a lot of turnover in the last twenty years. A lot of young couples moving in. A lot of young money. And a lot of gays. My friends think that if Cassella is going to have a chance, he'll need those votes. And my friends have it on damn good authority that Cassella is going to come out soon."

"What do you think?"

The question seemed to catch Glenn by surprise. He hummed, the noise deep and tremulous on the line, and then said, "It's a different world. It's a good strategy, especially for him. But it's not enough."

"Yeah? What would you do if you were Cassella?"

"Get an endorsement. A big name, as big as I could. Probably someone mainstream, someone well established in local politics. I'd want the old-timers and the young vote. The old-fashioned folk and the gays. That's a powerful combination, and it would be hard to do, but Cassella's smart. He could swing it."

Hazard turned that over in his mind. "Someone like Mayor Newton?"

"Sure."

"What do you know about him and Cassella?"

"Nothing. Ever since you and my son . . . crossed paths with the mayor, I've been shoved to one side. If you want to know where he stands with Cassella, you'll have to ask him. Or Cassella."

"That's all for now," Hazard said.

"No, thank you? You're living up to your reputation."

"I'll call if I need anything else."

"Please do. And Detective Hazard? This was a favor because you found the bastard who shot me. In the future, though, understand that I don't give away anything for free." His voice turned to ice. "Especially not my son."

The call disconnected, and Hazard stared at the phone. What the hell had that last bit meant? He shoved Glenn's threat aside, though, and forced himself to focus. Mayor Newton, Wahredua's political patriarch, could bring a lot of clout to bear on Cassella's behalf. The money was there, transferred from InnovateMidwest and buried in the financial disclosures. Now Hazard just had to find the personal connection.

On the computer, Hazard logged into the cloud storage for the traffic cameras and began scrolling through the data. He didn't need to search through every single image. There were seven red light cameras around city hall and the government complex at the heart of Wahredua. There were three red light cameras near the freeway, as well as several speed cameras on the highway itself. There was also a police security camera near Big Biscuit, a greasy spoon favorite of the mayor's. He'd start with those.

Hazard found a filter for the range of dates and times. Cassella was a workhorse; he wanted to move up in the world, and he was doing a damn fine job of it so far. That meant he wouldn't leave work early, not if he could help it. And that meant he wouldn't take a day off, either—not if that put him outside Jeff City, and therefore outside the ambit of power. The earliest Cassella could have gotten into town was Friday night. Seven o'clock. Maybe six-thirty if he got a good clip going.

But the mayor wouldn't have met with Cassella that night. The mayor was old. And he was old money. And that meant he spent his evenings, especially his weekend evenings, at events and openings and galas and fundraisers. For a big fish, for someone with pull, Mayor Newton might have changed his plans. Cassella, no matter how promising, was still only a functionary in the attorney general's office. No, Mayor Newton wouldn't have changed plans for a kid like Cassella.

So that meant Saturday morning. And Saturday morning meant Big Biscuit. Hazard adjusted the date filters and opened that set of images. The police security camera hung at an intersection, and it gave a fish-eye view of the strip mall where Big Biscuit was located. The footage was color—state money had finally trickled down, and the cameras were being updated—but not spectacularly good quality. That was all right; Big Biscuit was a well-known diner, but that didn't make it haute cuisine. Most of the cars that came and went were American, with the sweeping steel forms that put them thirty or forty years out of date, and most of them looked like they should have been in junk heaps a long while since.

But at 9:45am, an Infiniti pulled into the parking lot. The man who stepped out of the car had his back to the camera, but Hazard recognized the expensive jacket and the Kennedy hair. Twelve minutes later, a Jaguar slanted across two stalls, and Mayor Newton got out of the car.

So there it was. Proof that the two had met the day before Sheriff Bingham was murdered, the day that Cassella had lied about twice: first, claiming that he had only come into town when he was assigned the case, and then adjusting his story and claiming that he, in fact, come to Wahredua on Saturday, but only that night, and only to visit the club.

Hazard printed the relevant photographs, collected them, and stored them with the rest of his research. He didn't have all the pieces, not yet. But he had the beginning of the trail. And Hazard knew, immediately, what his next step had to be: he needed to see what Salvatore Cassella was doing tonight.

CHAPTER THIRTY

FEBRUARY 14
WEDNESDAY
6:30 PM

SOMERS HAD TRIED TO IRON HIS SHIRT. He'd gotten the front all right, but somehow he'd managed to burn a hole straight through the armpit. He couldn't change. Everything else had been dirty. So, throwing on a jacket, he'd rushed out of the apartment.

And now he sat at a table at Tyrone's, staring at the bucks mounted on the wall, counting their points. Their eyes held a flat, dead light. Not glass, that much was for sure. Some kind of metal. The kind of eyes that made Somers wish he'd chosen somewhere else, anywhere else, than the famous steakhouse. He didn't need eyes like that staring down at him. Not tonight. Especially not when he had a draft up his armpit.

Cora liked Burgundy, and he'd ordered a pinot noir, something midrange that would go with the ribeyes. Had that been a mistake? Should he have waited? Was that a perfect example of his self-centered chauvinism? Or was it one of those things he was supposed to do? Was it thoughtful? Was it just common courtesy? He didn't know; he supposed that's why he was here, waiting for his estranged wife, waiting for the axe to fall.

"Hi," Cora said, bending to kiss his cheek from behind. Somers tried to stand, but she laughed and waved him back into his seat. She pulled out her own chair. It was the twenty-first century. Or was he being a pig? "Oh good." She sipped at the wine. "That's perfect."

"Hi," Somers said.

She was beautiful: slender, her dark hair short and curling, her features so starkly expressive and yet fragile. For a while, towards the end, it had been harder to see that beauty. They were with each other every day. They were with each other for the good times and, more often, for the bad. They were with each other working in the yard, with bad hair, when diarrhea struck, for all of it. And it hadn't made her less beautiful, but it had made it ... normal. Just one more part of every day. Now, when they saw each other once or twice a week, he could see her again. Distance. Perspective. Not the same girl he had fallen in love with in high school. Not the same kind of beauty. But stronger—both the girl and her beauty. Deeper. Richer. Some things only got better with age.

They talked then—small talk about the day, about Evie, about Tyrone's and the last time they'd been there. The small talk stretched out, and somehow that didn't help because then the talk sounded smaller and smaller. Around them, candlelight spilled over happy couples: young and old, of all races and persuasions, bent over the small tables, as though anything more than inches was an unbearable distance.

"We were like that once," Cora said, smiling and tilting her head. A young couple, very young, sat at a table in the back, crammed next to the kitchen door, which swung open every fifteen seconds and cracked against the young man's chair. He didn't mind. The girl didn't mind. God, they were on their own planet: young, in love, on Valentine's Day. They were in their own universe.

Somers realized he had waited too long. When he turned back, Cora was watching him, and she knew. He could tell by her face that she knew. That maybe she had known longer than he had.

Cora sipped at her wine and tried to smile. "It's all right, John-Henry. I'm not glass."

"I was at Manzi's last night. I wasn't following you. Kind of the opposite, actually. I had to talk to Naomi about this case, and she set the place."

"When you canceled—I wondered why she was so interested in my plans. I wondered why she kept pushing. I already had the sitter lined up for Evie. I didn't want to spend the night at home. And Naomi was right there, whispering in my ear, telling me I should see Ethan."

"Is it serious?"

"I don't know. I didn't know where you and I were."

"Did that matter?"

"Of course it mattered. I didn't give up on us, John-Henry."

"Naomi brought the divorce papers."

Cora bit her lip, and when she opened her mouth, a bead of blood glowed. "I did that a long time ago when I was still angry. And then I shoved them in a drawer and told myself to wait. And then I forgot about them."

"You didn't forget about them, Cora."

"I changed my mind."

"But you didn't tear them up."

The bead of blood had stained her teeth, and now it was the only color in her face. "No. I didn't."

"I didn't give up on us either. But everything's different now."

"Does Emery know how you feel about him?"

A wildfire ran through Somers, and he was surprised that the silverware didn't melt under his fingers, that the linen didn't combust. He kept his gaze steady. He tried to keep his voice steady. "You knew?"

"John-Henry."

"Does everyone know?"

She smiled, and he remembered the smile from when he'd been carrying the groceries and the bags had split, from when he'd tried to fix a light and knocked out the power, from when he'd taken her to Cancun and the hotel was a ratty strip of concrete on a stretch of grayish-brown water. He was surprised, again, at how much he loved that smile, how much he loved the woman behind that smile. "Does that matter? Does it really?"

"I can ask."

"I don't know. I don't think so. I only know because I—because I've seen it. How you've changed. When you're with him, especially."

Neither of them spoke.

"Do you feel better? Does it feel any better to have it out in the open between us?"

"It feels pretty fucking terrible, Cora."

Her hand found his, squeezed, and drifted away again. "You've known, though. We both have. And isn't it better to face it head on? Isn't it better than pretending?"

"I'm not pretending."

"So you told him?"

"He doesn't feel the same way."

"Oh, for heaven's sake."

"He doesn't."

"In one word, John-Henry: have you told him how you feel?"

"No."

"But you asked him how he felt?"

"Cora, you don't get it—"

"What I get, John-Henry, is that you haven't learned anything. This is classic you."

The waiter came then, and Somers lined up the silverware, and eventually Cora said something, and the waiter left.

"Do you remember when we went to prom?"

"Come on, Cora. Not this again."

"Do you remember?"

"I was seventeen."

"You spelled out my name with red Solo cups on the school fence." Somers couldn't help himself; he was smiling.

"And you bought me a bouquet of roses."

"I bought you eight bouquets. I didn't know you could buy roses by the dozen, so I just kept buying the mixes and pulling out the roses."

Hand to her mouth, Cora burst into laughter. "You never told me that."

"I used to have some dignity."

"And after prom, we drove out to Lake Palmerston, and you parked at the end of the quay. There was just that little sliver of moon, and then all those stars. I could hear the water." Some of the humor eased out of Cora's face. Her eyes were bright now. "You turned up the heater. I let the strap slide down my shoulder. And then you sat there."

"I was seventeen."

"You knew I liked you."

"I didn't have very smooth moves, Cora." He was fighting to paste a smirk on his face. "And you know I've gotten better."

"You never asked me."

"What?"

"You never asked me if I loved you."

"What are you talking about? You told me you loved me. And I love you."

"Yes, John-Henry. You did. You told me that after I told you."

"Cora, if you think that's why this didn't work out, I hate to break it to you—"

The first tear spilled from her eye, and she let it track the curve of her face. "Don't be silly. This didn't work out for a million reasons. Some of them are me. Some of them are you. Some of them are—I don't know. Chance, I guess. Bad luck."

"I'm sorry. I really am."

"You're a dummy, that's what you are. I'm trying to tell you that if you wait this time, if you think he's going to make the first move, you're going to lose him."

"Cora: he doesn't want anything to do with me. I'm not going to say anything else, but just trust me on that."

"Then you haven't seen how he looks at you. Even Naomi—"

223

"Jesus Christ—" Somers bit back the rest of it and forced himself to lower his voice. "Does everybody know?"

"Does it matter?"

Somers fiddled with the silverware again. Did it matter? Hell, nobody in the whole world could answer a question like that.

"Can I tell you something?" Cora asked. "You won't get angry?"

"I'll probably get angry, but I'll try not to yell again."

The rattle of dining continued around them, the low buzz of conversation, voices lilting with happiness.

"Go on," Somers said. "I promise I won't get angry."

"This thing with Ethan."

"Oh God."

"Never mind."

"No, go on."

Again, the sounds of waiters' voices, of cutlery against china, and then the pop of a cork.

"With Ethan, things feel new. I don't know how else to say it. I'm not trying to say anything bad about us, but I feel like I should tell you that. With Ethan, it's like I get to be someone else for a while."

Inside, Somers was thinking of his own words to Hazard, spoken weeks before. Like a part of me froze. Is that what he had said? Something like that. Something close to what Cora was saying now—that they had gotten together too young, that they had stayed together too long, that whatever growth they might have experienced had been funneled through that relationship. And Somers knew he could echo her words. He could say the same thing about Emery—that when he was with Hazard, he felt like someone new. Someone better.

But what he said was, "I didn't know you wanted to be someone else."

The pain showed in her face before anything else—before she could hide it, before she could paint on a smile. She gathered herself, preparing to stand.

"I'm sorry. I'm an asshole. I'm really sorry."

Another tear fell, slipping along the hollow of her cheek. "This is it, isn't it? We don't need to eat steak and drink wine and pretend."

"This is it." And suddenly the urge to cry, the need for it, was strong on Somers, and he cleared his throat and got to his feet.

"We're going to be okay, John-Henry. Both of us."

"I know."

But he didn't. When she had left, he paid for the pinot noir, and he drove the dark miles back to Wahredua. He turned off into the snow-crusted lot of a CVS; the red signage played bloody reflections on the ice. He didn't break into tears. A single, violent sob tore its way free, and he scrubbed at his eyes with his coat sleeve. Then a second sob shook him. And then it was a tipping point: either break down crying and never stop, or pull it together. So he pulled it together, tossed his wedding ring in the glove compartment, and with shaky hands eased the Interceptor back out into the night. He was thinking of prom. And about two miles later, he had something to say to Emery Hazard, something he'd needed to say for a long time.

And it was, after all, still Valentine's Day.

CHAPTER THIRTY-ONE

FEBRUARY 14
WEDNESDAY
7:44 PM

IN THE CHERRY-COLORED JETTA, Hazard watched and waited for Cassella. And Hazard was thinking about getting out of the car.

An interior monologue was explaining to him, in no uncertain terms, that Hazard was being a real grade-A moron. An imbecile. A fucking idiot. Following Cassella had been all right. It had been easy to find the man at the Bridal Veil Motor Court, and it had been easy to tail the Infiniti—God, a blind man could have tailed the Infiniti in Wahredua. Up until now, Hazard had been doing his job, he'd been doing good police work. But this, this next part, this was just stupid, and he knew it and was still going to do it.

His head was hurting. That was the explanation. The headaches, persistent since a killer had taken a baseball bat to Hazard's skull, had been better lately, but today, tonight, right now, it was hurting like a bitch. The headache was making it hard to think clearly—bullshit, that monologue said inside him—but more importantly, the headaches were the perfect excuse. Hazard would just knock on the door. He needed his pills, that's how he'd start, and then, when he saw Cassella, he'd push his way into the apartment. If they were already going at it, if Cassella had his dick hanging out, well— Hazard's head was about to goddamn split. He didn't know what he'd do, truth be told.

From the Jetta, Hazard eyed the Infiniti. And then he eyed Nico's apartment building. Sure, there was a chance that Cassella had gone inside to talk to somebody else. It was a decent-sized building. Probably thirty or forty apartments in there. Cassella could have gone to any of them. Maybe he was working his side of the investigation. Maybe he was meeting a friend.

The thought curved Hazard's mouth in a sickle-smile. Yeah. A friend. That's exactly what Cassella was doing: meeting his new friend, the hot boy with Argentine blood who was single and ready to mingle. God, Hazard thought through the headache, God, now he was thinking in cliches, and he blamed that on the headache too.

How long now? Fifteen minutes? No, seventeen. Seventeen minutes. They could have done anything in seventeen minutes. Seventeen minutes, and Cassella could have had his hands all over Nico. Could have blown him. Could have screwed him—or been screwed by him. Seventeen minutes. That was a long time. Too long for Cassella to just be saying hi. They were fucking, Hazard knew it. He reached for the door. He was distantly aware of the fact that he and Nico were no longer together, that it was no longer any of his business whom Nico decided to mess around with, that it was, in fact, exactly this kind of attitude that had gotten him into this mess in the first place. But those thoughts flickered at the edge of consciousness, tiny strobing lights that might as well have been on another continent. Nico, Cassella, that was right here, right now. That was something Hazard could deal with.

He opened the door.

The door swung halfway and stopped, and someone grunted, and Hazard reached for the .38 under his arm.

"For hell's sake," Somers said, kneeing the door back towards Hazard. "Would you watch what you're doing?"

"Get out of the way." Hazard shoved the door open again.

"Stay there." Somers slammed the door and shouted through the glass, "Stay there, I said." He came around the front of the car and dropped into the passenger seat. Suddenly the Jetta was crowded; Somers's knee brushed Hazard's, and their shoulders met between the seats. The smell of his hair filled the car. His face had lost its normal golden hue, and his eyes—

"Have you been crying?"

"Yeah, Ree. I pulled into a CVS lot and bawled my eyes out, and now I'm here."

Hazard studied him for a moment. "I can't tell if you're telling the truth."

"Oh for the love of—"

"I've got something to take care of, Somers. You better go home."

"Nico and Cassella?"

Hazard settled a hand on the door. His fingers grazed the pebbled plastic.

"You're not going in there. You might think you are. You might even really want to. But you're not."

"I'll do whatever I want."

"Let me guess: you found something on Cassella."

Hazard's hand trailed towards the latch.

"And you followed him here."

His fingers hooked the plastic lever. If he were fast, he could beat Somers to the apartment. And Hazard felt fast tonight. He could run like lightning if he needed to tonight.

"And now you know he's in there with Nico and you think you're going to be a great big ape and go up and there and pound your chest, is that about right? Get your hand off the fucking door before I cuff you to the steering wheel."

Hesitating, Hazard leaned back into his seat. On the street, a Ford F-250 rumbled past, and music with a heavy bass line pounded through the windows.

"You want to know why you're not going in there?"

"I'm not dating Nico. That's why."

"Jesus, do you believe that crap? Or do you just say it because you think you have to? You're not going in there because you have something on Cassella. Something real. And if you go in there, you're going to screw it all up. So you're going to be a good cop and do your job."

"A good cop." Hazard was suddenly tired. He slumped into his seat and tossed the keys onto the dash. "When the fuck has that ever worked out?"

"You want to know how I found you?"

"Because I'm a pathetic asshole."

"Maybe not always, but tonight you sure are. No. That wasn't how. You want to guess?"

Just down the block was a bakery that was closing its doors for the night. The girl was lowering the blinds in the front windows. A sign, obviously printed from a home computer, showed a heart and the words, *Today, buy something for someone you loaf.* Then the last of the blinds had dropped, and the girl was gone, and the door shivered when she turned the deadbolt, and Hazard wondered if she was going home to someone she loafed.

"You know what I said to myself? I wanted to know where you were, and you weren't answering your phone, and you know what I thought? I thought what's the absolute stupidest thing Emery Hazard could be doing right now? Where is the worst place on the whole planet he could be? That's what I asked myself. And you know what?"

"Here I am."

"Here you fucking are."

"You're angry at me."

"Not really."

"You sound angry. Why are you even here? Shouldn't you be at dinner? What happened to Cora?"

"Oh. So you remembered I had plans tonight. I wasn't planning on sitting in a car that should have been scrapped fifteen years ago."

Hazard turned to face his partner, surprised again by Somers's pallor, by the electric sheen to his eyes. Somers's hands scuttled across his legs, across the seat, across his arms, and now Hazard noticed that those hands were shaking.

"You're angry at me. You're angry because I'm here. Because of Nico."

"I'm not—"

"You know what? I know you don't like him. I don't—I don't even know if I like him. I mean, not the way he wanted me to. He said he loved me. Did you know that? Do you know how long it's been since somebody—you know what? It doesn't matter."

"It matters."

"Yeah, he and I had a fight last night. Pretty damn bad one. I thought I wanted it to be over. I thought I'd be better off alone. But being lonely sucks. I'm tired of being lonely. And yeah, I know I'm pathetic, sitting here, thinking I might go in there, thinking he might at least listen to me. I know what you think about me." Hazard tried to stop the flood of words, but they were coming too fast, and the pain inside his head was like splitting atoms, like fucking fission, and the words kept coming. "Most guys look at me. Maybe they want to screw around with a cop. Maybe they just want a top or a daddy. Whatever. That's fine, I can play that, I guess. But that's it, that's where it stops for them. Nico, at least he cared. At least he wanted to be with me. I know it wouldn't have lasted forever. These guys, they get to know me, and there's something that makes them take off. Or they stay, but they hate me, and that's even worse. Nico, at least he—Jesus, why am I even trying to tell you this?"

Somers's breathing had changed. It sounded like he had run a race. His face was still starlight pale, the same color as his high-gloss eyes, but his lips were red, and the long slashes in his cheeks were red, and God damn, that breathing, it sounded like he might pass out, like he might be having a goddamn heart attack.

"You're a fucking idiot," Somers said. Was he crying? God, was that what the breathing was? Or was he—maybe it was an allergic reaction, his throat swelling shut, maybe that's what it was. "You don't even know. Not a damn clue. If you had any idea—"

Movement at Nico's apartment distracted Hazard. Cassella emerged, bundled against the cold, and then Nico. Cassella slipped an arm around Nico; the wind stirred Nico's shaggy hair, and he leaned into Cassella, his head turning to catch something Cassella had said, his lips drawing back in a grin. They moved towards the Infiniti, and then they drove into the night.

Hazard scrabbled for the keys, his hands slapping at the dash, but a feeling of unease pricked the back of his brain. He glanced at Somers.

"What? What were you saying?"

"Follow them, you big dope. Let's go."

With a jerk, the Jetta launched into the street, and Hazard sped after the Infiniti. Somers laughed, his head rocking back from the force of the acceleration, one hand across his eyes like the whole thing was a joke, the best joke in the whole world, but he didn't sound happy. But by the time they took the first corner, Somers had stopped laughing, and by the time they hit the third block, Hazard had forgotten what they'd been talking about.

CHAPTER THIRTY-TWO

**FEBRUARY 14
WEDNESDAY
7:57 PM**

SOMERS GRIPPED THE JETTA'S DOOR as Hazard rounded another corner. They were keeping a safe distance behind Cassella's Infiniti, and Hazard wasn't driving particularly fast, but he was driving angry, and that made Somers grip the door harder.

With one part of his brain, Somers listened as Hazard laid out the facts that he had uncovered linking Cassella to Wahredua's mayor. The research was impressive, and Somers was struck, again, by Hazard's intelligence and resourcefulness.

The other part of Somers's brain, however, was thinking one thought, and it was so loud that it blotted out everything else. You could have told him. That's what was running through his mind, the simple, inescapable fact that Somers could have told Hazard. He could have told him what had happened with Cora. He could have told him how he felt about him. He could have told him—

—what he wanted from him—

—what he'd been hiding for all these years. You could have told him, Somers thought again, but you didn't because you're a coward. You could have grabbed his chin. You could have turned his head. You could have looked him in the eyes, right in those goddamn scarecrow eyes, and you could have told him everything. He would have stopped the car. He would have listened. He would have been pissed as hell, sure, but he would have listened.

It wasn't the right time, Somers insisted, although he wasn't sure who he was trying to convince. Himself, he supposed, and although Somers was pretty good at lying to himself, this time the lie rang out flat. I'll tell him, he thought. I will. I'll tell him when it's the right time.

"Well?" Hazard asked.

"I think you pretty much summed it up."

The Jetta clanked, rocking on its suspension as the car stopped at a red light. "You weren't listening."

"Sorry. I was distracted."

"Is he going to hurt Nico?"

"What? No. Why would he?"

"Because he's definitely in deep with the mayor. And I think he killed the sheriff, and now he's killing Nico to—"

"What? Do us all a favor?"

"This is a joke to you?"

"No, sorry, that was shitty. He's tied up with the mayor, all right. I believe that. But the rest, the idea that he killed Bingham, what do you have to support that?"

"He was in town; he lied about that."

"But why kill the sheriff?"

The light changed to green. Stomping on the pedal, Hazard accelerated, and the Jetta whined. Hazard's voice sped up along with the car. "Who the hell knows? Maybe the mayor wanted him out of the way."

"They were pretty tight, the two of them. Why would the mayor get rid of him now?"

"Maybe the sheriff knew something. Maybe something the mayor didn't want anybody else to know."

"Yeah, I'm sure he—Jesus, would you take it easy?" The Jetta careened around the next block, and Somers rocked into Hazard, smelling the bigger man's sweat, feeling his heat. "I'm sure the sheriff knew plenty. But both of them are so dirty that I don't think it mattered anymore. This wasn't about blackmail."

"What about those death threats, then? The ones that Dudley saw in the sheriff's safe?"

"What about them?"

"Somebody has wanted him dead for a long time, Somers."

"Yeah. That doesn't make it Cassella."

"Maybe he—"

"Ree, I get it. You're not over Nico. You don't like Cassella. We've got good reason to believe Cassella is all tangled up with the mayor. Now Cassella is taking your boy—"

"He's not my boy." Hazard punched the gas so hard that the Jetta actually jumped, rattling so that Somers waited for the mirrors to fly off. "And this has nothing to do with how I feel about him."

"Just because Cassella is meeting with the mayor, that doesn't mean anything. You're grasping, Ree. You want him to be guilty and you're grasping."

Hazard didn't answer, but the next turn took the Jetta onto two wheels.

"Real mature," Somers said.

"Open your mouth again."

Somers thought about it and decided not to tempt fate.

A few blocks ahead of them, Cassella's Infiniti pulled up to the curb in front of the Pretty Pretty. Wahredua's only gay bar was a testament to industrial design: concrete, massive steel plates, and neon pink lighting. Tonight, the velvet ropes lined the sidewalk, and a queue was waiting. Twenty years ago, when Somers and Hazard had been boys, Wahredua hadn't had a gay population—well, aside from Hazard. Times had changed. And on Valentine's Day, the change was visible.

Hazard yanked the steering wheel to the right, butted up against the curb, and killed the engine.

"There's a hydrant."

Hazard kicked open his door.

Somers trotted after him. "You're going to get towed."

Across the street, Cassella and Nico ignored the queue and headed straight towards the man at the door. Boos and catcalls came from the line— as well as a few suggestions of what Nico should do with the new guy—but Cassella passed something to the man at the door, and he checked it, waving them in before he'd even stuffed the green into his pocket.

"Graft," Somers said. "At a gay bar. I'm shocked."

"Just shut up, please."

"Honestly, I'm devastated. To think that capitalist corruption has invaded even the LGBT community, once a bastion of—"

"Somers, my head's about to fucking split, all right?"

They crossed the street at a brisk pace, and Hazard led them towards the front of the line. Men—and boys—called out to them, and more than a few grabbed at Somers's coat. One fellow, about three sizes bigger than Somers and with handlebar mustaches, got a good enough hold that Somers had to twist the guy's wrist halfway around before he'd let go. The guy had a grin as wide as a turnpike on his face.

Others in the crowd called to Hazard—and the calls were vicious.

"Get a fucking life."

"Go home. Leave him alone."

"We don't want you here, Hazard. Get lost."

"Nico doesn't want you here." To which somebody added, "Nobody wants you here."

"Damn," Somers said as he caught up with Hazard. "Sounds like word gets around."

Hazard didn't answer.

Somers, eyeing the huge man guarding the door, elbowed Hazard. "I got this."

"No, I—"

But Somers had already glided ahead, undoing his coat so it fell open, exposing the tight lines of his frame. He twisted the top button, and then the next, working at the cloth so that it exposed a triangle of chest under the hollow of his throat. He hoped the ink was showing—for some reason, that ink combined with vanilla good looks drove most guys—and gals—crazy.

But the bouncer wasn't smiling when Somers reached him. He wasn't frowning either. He was looking, though—taking plenty of time to admire Somers.

"Detective Somerset," and he flashed his badge. "My partner and I need to talk to someone inside."

The big guy—he wasn't bald, Somers noticed, in spite of all the stereotypes—looked like he was about to nod. Then he froze; his face went to ice, and he crossed his arms.

Hazard stepped up next to Somers.

"There's a line," the man said.

"Fuck that," Hazard said, shouldering past Somers.

The big guy got up, faster than Somers had expected, and planted himself between Hazard and the door. He laid into Hazard, a heavy, open-handed slap that caught Hazard's chest.

"Nobody wants you in there. Why don't you sniff for ass somewhere else?"

Hazard set his shoulders the way he always did when he was getting ready to punch. Somers knew how things would play out: Hazard would clobber this guy, wipe his ass with this guy, but things would get ugly. Nico and Cassella might run. Worse, they might stay. This would splash all over town, and judging by tonight's reception, Somers didn't think Hazard had much goodwill left in Wahredua. Word had definitely gotten around, and it looked like everybody had sided with Nico.

"Tell you what," Somers said, squeezing between Hazard and the bouncer. "You get out of our way right now, and nothing bad happens."

"Something bad's going to happen," the bouncer said. "You're damn right about that."

"I tried playing nice. I told you who I was. I showed you my badge. I let you know why we were going inside."

"Get the fuck out of my way," Hazard said, clutching Somers's shoulder.

Somers elbowed him back a step. "Now. You get out of our way right now. Otherwise, your boss loses his liquor license. Then you lose your job. Then, if I'm not wrong, whatever shit-hole you call home kicks you to the street. And then I'll let my partner come find you and see if you're still feeling like you want to take sides."

The big guy bunched his shoulders like he might just drop his head and charge, but after a lot of swearing, he dropped back onto his stool. Somers pushed through the Pretty Pretty's double doors, and they were inside.

He'd been here only a handful of times and always with Hazard. The place hadn't changed. Mirrors hung everywhere, throwing back reflected lights and the images of beautiful boys writhing on the dance floor. Mixed among the mirror, huge clusters of crystals cycled through pastel LED shades. Sweat and body-spray and cologne made the air musky and difficult to breathe; it got easier, Somers remembered, with time and with a drink. Music already filled the air, loud enough that Somers's bones shivered. He was partially surprised, again, to see women here—although they were almost exclusively paired with women. One of the blondes looked like Cynthia, Fukuma's hot piece from the cabin, but then the crowd shifted, and Somers lost track of her.

Beside him, Hazard scanned the crowd. Hazard was tall, and he raised up on his toes to see farther. He must have caught sight of Cassella and Nico because he lunged forward, but Somers caught his arm and hauled him to one side.

"They're getting drinks."

"Fine."

"Let go of me."

"Ree, why are we here? Because you're a jealous ex? Or because we're cops?"

The music dropped into a thudding base.

"I'm serious. Answer me."

"We're cops."

"So let's be cops."

For a moment, pain showed through Hazard's normal mask. "What the fuck are we going to do? Why am I even doing this?"

"Because you think there's something weird about Cassella. And you're right: there is. So let's do what we normally do: let's watch and wait." Somers studied the Pretty Pretty's massive space. Although a large portion of the room was given up to the dance floor, booths with vinyl banquettes lined the walls—some with curtains that could be drawn for privacy. The night was still young, and almost all of the booths were still empty. Somers nudged his partner towards the booth in the back corner, near a service door, where they could keep an eye on the bar.

"Everybody's going to see me," Hazard said as they reached the booth. "I'm lucky nobody's said anything yet."

"It's a big club. It's busy. And they're serving a lot of booze. Besides, by the time those guys from outside get in here, they're going to be so hopped up they won't remember their own names, let alone yours."

"I'm saying somebody will see me now, Somers. And they'll run straight over to Nico. This was stupid, this whole idea."

"Well, we're here now. Sit with your back to the bar."

As Hazard turned in the booth so that he was facing the wall, Somers slid across the table, wedging himself in the corner where he could watch the Pretty Pretty—and, most importantly, the stretch of the bar where Nico and Cassella were drinking and talking to an animated group of young men.

Hazard, twisted in his seat, resembled a pretzel.

"Stretch out your legs."

"Why?"

"So you don't give yourself back problems."

"You could have stayed on that side, you know."

"Sure. I could have." The song changed; something sugary, a pop song, came on, and Somers tapped the table in time with the rhythm. "So you're going to sit like that all night?"

Shifting his weight, Hazard stretched out one leg. Somers drew his feet up onto the banquette. From this angle, Hazard's legs looked massive. Tree trunks. Redwoods. And Somers's eyes ran up all that corded muscles towards the vee. He forgot, sometimes, how big Hazard was. And goddamnit, that was a lie, because he never forgot, not really.

"Tequila," Somers said to the blond waif hovering nearby. "A double. And a Guinness." The blond boy bobbed away. "What?"

"Nothing," Hazard said, but his other leg slid towards Somers, pinning him against the wall.

The crowd was huge tonight. Massive. Every gay in the area had turned out, it seemed, for the holiday. Hairy, muscled guys. Little blond twinkies. Everything in between, all of them grinding against each other, just a few centimeters shy of smashing on the dance floor. The music cranked up as the crowd's density increased, and the beat found a place in Somers's chest. His fingers continued their tattoo on the table. By now, sweat dampened his collar. Hazard was like a furnace. That was all it was, just the sheer number of bodies, just being squeezed between Hazard's legs. That's all.

Their drinks came. Hazard's fingers were pressed against his temple, and he sipped at the beer once and then ignored it.

"How bad's your head?"

Hazard ignored the question.

"Let me see your hand."

"Why?"

"Pressure points. It's good for a headache. Don't make that face, come on."

When Somers took Hazard's hand, it was bone dry. Lightly callused. The size of a catcher's mitt. Dark hairs across the back, along the knuckles. Hands like that, they could pick Somers up, toss him around. Hands like that could be all over him. Squeezing. Smacking. Pinching. Teasing. Still bone dry. Didn't the man ever sweat?

"You've never seen a hand before?"

"Asshole." Somers turned Hazard's hand, squeezing between the thumb and forefinger. "Better?"

Hazard grunted.

They stayed like that for a minute or two, but Hazard kept his other hand at his temple, and the furrows around his eyes didn't ease. Somers shrugged and loosened his grip.

"I didn't say let go," Hazard said. Those scarecrow eyes, like corn, like straw, like winter grass, like the last daylight slanting through leaves on the last day of the year. Somers ran his tongue under his lip. His hands were shaking, just his hands for now, but it was going to spread. This close to him, after this long, the shaking might never stop. Those goddamn catcher's mitts, those might stop it. If they really got a hold of him. If they held tight enough.

So you told him how you feel?

Damn Cora. Damn her for thinking she had any idea what she was talking about.

"Somers," Hazard said, his voice full of gravel.

"Yeah?"

"What now?"

What now? Now we go back to the apartment and fuck like nobody's ever fucked before. Now I tell you everything. Every single thing since that day I touched you in the locker room and knew—

—that I wanted you—

—how I felt. Now the rest of our lives begin, right now, right here, tonight.

"Nico," Hazard said. "And Cassella. What are they doing now?"

Somers dropped Hazard's hand and leaned back. It took him a moment to clear his throat.

"Somers?"

"Yeah. They're still drinking." He grabbed the double shot of tequila and pounded it down. It burned, and Somers winced, and he was almost too slow. "Shit, they're coming this way."

Hazard stiffened.

"No," Somers said. "Don't look. Just—" His mind flashed a series of possible escapes. Run onto the dance floor. No, too risky, they might be seen. Hide under the table. Yeah, fat chance with Hazard's huge ass down there. The service door—maybe, but it looked like that was exactly where Nico and Cassella were headed. They were close now, so close that if they looked in the right direction, they couldn't help but notice Somers. A gaggle of college-age boys, shirtless and gym-toned and gleaming, drifted into place like cloud cover, but that would only last for a moment. In another heartbeat, Cassella and Nico would be so close that they'd have to be blind not to notice—

"Kiss me."

"What the—"

Somers didn't give him time to finish. With one hand, he grabbed Hazard's long, wavy hair. With the other, he hauled him by the collar. Hazard came up out of his seat like a man rising from the dead. The kiss wasn't great, not at first; Hazard's mouth was stiff and unresponsive. Somers ignored his shock and kept going. He kissed harder, dragging Hazard on top of him, Hazard's weight crushing him against the vinyl. Just two guys fooling around. Just two guys getting hot and heavy in a booth. Nothing interesting. Nothing to look twice at, not in the Pretty Pretty, not on Valentine's.

It was the perfect cover. And that's all it had to be: cover. It didn't matter that Hazard was kissing like his jaw was wired shut. It didn't matter that his whole body was awkward lines of protest. Not a fuck, Somers didn't give a single fuck about any of that because this was about the case, it was about keeping out of sight, it was just good police work, and a part of his brain was screaming with laughter at the thought. Maybe they'd ask him to teach a course on this at the academy.

And then it wasn't just cover anymore. Hazard molded himself against Somers, his knees drawing up on either side, his hand snaking around to clutch the back of Somers's neck, his mouth softening—still firm, and the kisses almost painful with their brutal intensity, but softening—and his other hand undoing buttons, sliding under Somers's shirt, that mitt tightening on Somers's chest. Jesus, God, tight, tight enough that Somers knew he'd have bruises, and he didn't give a fuck about that either. What he cared about was the feel of Hazard, of his mouth, of the hardness of his erection as Hazard thrust against him, slowly, insistently, and Somers heard his whimpers underneath the kisses, heard the huskiness in Hazard's breathing, felt his own dick ready to pop, and he began to move against Hazard, straining for anything, for the roughness of fabric against him, for pressure, for weight, for stimulation to keep him at this perfect threshold. I'm going to come in my pants, Somers thought, I'm going to come in my pants like a goddamn thirteen-year-old.

But he didn't, somehow, although the intensity of the kissing continued. It went on a long time. Longer, for damn sure, than it needed to. Cover. This was just cover, right?

Hazard pulled back. His mouth was red, his lips chafed and slightly swollen, and those scarecrow eyes were unreadable. One of his hands had come to rest on the inside of Somers's thigh, and Somers fought the urge to moan, to press himself against that hand, to demand that Hazard finish what he'd goddamn well started.

"Guess it worked."

Somers let his head fall back, and a chuckle escaped. "I couldn't tell you. I got a little distracted. They might have stood around and taken pictures of the whole thing, and I wouldn't have a clue."

A smirk teased the corner of Hazard's mouth and vanished. "It was your idea."

"I'm a genius."

"A little distracted?"

"Don't get a big head. You're lucky I'm still breathing; your fat ass just about flattened me."

"I'm not fat. Say it."

"Will you get off me?"

Hazard's eyes narrowed. "I could make you say it."

In spite of himself, in spite of his bruised lips—goddamn, where had Hazard learned to kiss? With a bunch of goddamn cavemen?—Somers was grinning. "I'd like to see you try."

Leaning down, his lips brushing Somers's ear, Hazard said, "I know you would." Then he extricated himself from their tangle, drawing himself out of the booth, straightening his jacket and tie and frowning. "You popped a button on my collar."

Somers rolled his eyes and worked his way to his feet. "His fat ass breaks every bone in my body and he's worried about a button."

The Pretty Pretty's crowd had thickened, and now it filled the club to capacity—probably beyond capacity. If Nico and Cassella had returned, it would be near impossible to find them again.

Hazard must have had the same thought because he cocked his head toward the service door. After a short hallway, they found themselves outside in an alley.

"They came out here to fuck," Hazard said.

"You don't know that."

"Yeah, I do."

"Ree—"

"Nico thought it would be hot."

"Oh."

Hazard studied the alley for a minute, and Somers wondered what he was seeing. His ex-boyfriend pressed up against the concrete walls, balls out, getting screwed by the special prosecutor? Hazard had an uncanny eye for details. He could probably pick out the exact spot where they'd done it.

"Come on," Somers said. "There's nothing here."

In the Jetta, Hazard drove back towards Wroxall College and the faux-urban, trendy developments that had sprung up around the campus. When they reached Nico's apartment, he circled the block and then pulled up next to the Interceptor.

"There's no Infiniti parked out here," Somers said.

The Jetta rumbled and shook underneath them.

"What are you going to do?"

"It's late. Let's just call it a night."

"Bullshit. You're going to drive around looking for them."

Hazard's big hands drifted along the steering wheel. He fumbled with the radio. Classical music buzzed from a broken speaker. It might have been Bach. More like Bach being squeezed through a cheese grater.

"All right," Somers said. "Can we hurry up?"

"Get out of the car."

"No. And because I'm tired and because I'm pissed, I'm going to tell you why. If I get out of this car, you're still going to go look for them. And when you find them, you're going to do something stupid. So let's go find them, and then I'll let you beat up a brick wall or something, and once you've got it all out of your system, we'll go home."

Hazard snapped off the radio, and the dial came loose in his hand. He chucked it at the window. "Get out."

"The longer we sit here, the longer this is going to take."

No movement this time.

"Maybe they're playing backgammon. Or Parcheesi. Or shuffleboard."

"Jesus Christ," Hazard groaned, but he shifted the Jetta into drive, and they headed into the night.

The search didn't take long. Their next stop was also their last, and in the parking lot of the Bridal Veil Motor Court, they found Cassella's Infiniti. Somers didn't know which room belonged to the prosecuting attorney, but he had a good guess. Hazard was staring at room 1D with ferocious intensity, and the light was on behind the scrim of curtains, and two very vigorous people were putting on one hell of shadow play.

"You want to beat him up?"

Hazard grimaced, and the expression was so raw and so unusual that Somers felt a twist of compassion.

"If you want, I'll spank Nico's ass while you knock out Cassella's teeth."

It took a minute, but then a reluctant smile softened the worst of the despair. "Nah. He'd like that too much."

They drove back to the apartment at the Crofter's Mark, and they parted in the darkened living room. Hazard paused, and the light came on in his bedroom, silhouetting him against the door. His expression was lost in shadow, and his voice had its usual rigid control.

"Happy Valentine's, John-Henry."

"Happy Valentine's, Ree." And Somers thought maybe he was being a coward, maybe, or maybe it just wasn't the right time. Not yet. Maybe he'd missed his chance. Maybe not.

But lying in the dark, Somers didn't have any regrets. Not one. Not a damn one about the whole evening. And he wasn't thinking of the kisses. He wasn't even thinking about how things had gotten really hot and heavy, about what it had felt like to want to come under Hazard, about how that had just about blown Somers's brain out the back of his head. What he was thinking about in the darkness, what made him grin up at the ceiling, was that little smile on Hazard's face at the end. No, Somers didn't have any regrets. Not a damn one.

CHAPTER THIRTY-THREE

FEBRUARY 15
THURSDAY
4:14 AM

THE CALL DRAGGED HAZARD from his bed at ten to four, and twenty minutes later he was standing in the black February cold with Somers. Lynn Fukuma's house sat on the corner lot, a small, pleasantly domestic space that fit into the neat, middle-class neighborhood. So much, Hazard thought as he shivered, for Fukuma's legendary hatred of the bourgeoisie. This was about as boogie as it got.

Two black-and-whites sat in front of the house. Their lights were off, but one car's engine rumbled, warming the blonde who sat in the back seat. Moraes rubbed his hands against the cold; he was bundled up so that only the tip of his nose showed. His partner, Foley, stood next to him with his coat zipped only halfway, his fair skin flushed the same color as his red hair.

"Norman and Gross are inside," Moraes said. "Dr. Kamp already came by and took the body."

"He actually did something?" Hazard said.

"We got lucky." Moraes's eyes crinkled in amusement. "He was just the right degree of blitzed. After his drinks with dinner, but before he got hammered."

"What did he say?"

"Nothing official, but he said it looked like suicide."

"Start at the beginning," Somers said.

"The girl in the car claims she was partying all night," Foley said. "Alone. I guess the two—" He hesitated, and his eyes flicked to Hazard. Whatever he'd been about to say, he amended it. "The women were in a relationship, and the girl says they'd had a fight."

"Something like that," Somers said. "Her name's Cynthia."

"Well, she says she came over to make things right. We pressed her on that, and we'll keep pressing, but so far she's sticking to it. She said it just seemed like a good idea."

"Get her clothes," Hazard said. "Everything."

Foley nodded.

"You want to tell me how to tie my shoes, too?" Moraes said, his eyes bright with humor again.

"A couple of meatheads like you?" Somers said. "You need us to remind you not to piss into the wind. What'd the corpse look like?"

"Just like you'd think for someone who took a bullet to the head."

"Anything strange?"

"Yeah, something was off. Something right here." Foley tapped the right side of his head.

"Jesus, no wonder they've got you two working this shift." Somers softened the words with a smile. "Kamp didn't say anything?"

"Just the normal," Moraes said. "Bag and tag everything just in case. He doesn't explain. You know Kamp; unless he's telling you about a girl or about a drink, you can't get much out of him."

"Unless he's telling you about a girl or a drink, he's usually dead drunk already."

"Let's take a look," Hazard said.

But up at the house, Norman and Gross were still videotaping and photographing, and they wouldn't let the detectives into the scene.

"You mucked up the last one," Norman said. "You're not getting in here until we're done."

"It was sand," Somers said. "And anyway, that scene was a hot mess already."

"Come back when we're done," Gross said.

"The longer you stay here," Norman said, his pot-belly puffing, "the longer it's going to take us."

"How about some coffee?" Somers said

"That'd be real nice. You ladies get us some coffee."

"Ladies?" Hazard said as they left. "We're getting those bastards coffee?"

"Flies and honey, Ree. It's a small town, remember?"

Hazard did remember. It was hard to forget Wahredua was a small town. It was so small Hazard felt like he stubbed a toe every time he turned around. But they drove over to the Wahredua Family Bakery, which opened at five, and they got coffee and donuts. When they got back to Fukuma's, Moraes and Foley were sitting in the car. They accepted the paper cups and a few pastries; Cynthia declined. She looked like she was coming down pretty hard, and finding a suicide hadn't made it any easier.

Inside the house, Norman and Gross were packing up the videography equipment. The two balding men waddled over to the donuts, snagged coffee, and dropped into the chairs in Fukuma's living room. When Hazard asked about the firearm, they motioned to a table where they had started to collect the bagged evidence. Hazard found the revolver; it looked like the same one he had seen at Cynthia's cabin.

"See how helpful they're being?" Somers said as he pulled on paper booties and grabbed gloves. "Flies and honey."

Hazard followed his partner's example and led the way to the back of the house. Fukuma's study occupied a corner room with windows overlooking a swath of grass and a quiet suburban street. The air smelled like loose bowels and something worse, the smells that Hazard had come to associate with bodily cavities that had been violated. The smell of death, that's what it was. The walls were papered in blue-and-white stripes, and drying blood and brain covered an arc of one wall and the closet door.

Fukuma's desk was a mountain of papers and books—dense, academic tomes that Hazard wouldn't have minded poring over on a free afternoon. A Macbook sat open on the desk, the screen dark, with a wireless mouse to the left.

"She was working," Hazard said. "Working late at night on Valentine's."

"She'd lost her date." Somers stepped into the room, tugging on the plastic gloves. He eased open the closet door, glanced inside, and shut it again. "She seems like she preferred work to people anyway."

Hazard crossed to the desk. Several of the stacks of papers looked like student work: ill-formatted, derivative thinking, the pages slashed with red in a tight, furious script. Others, however, looked, like research. Forced castration. Male eugenics. One article, "The Sexual Liberation of Eunuchs," was dog-eared; apparently that had been a favorite. And then there were political pamphlets. Some were familiar to Hazard: progressive PACs, radical PACs, organizations that had national standing even if they only drew a fraction of the national audience. Others looked local, and although some of the names sounded familiar, Hazard didn't recognize them. A dozen copies of one pamphlet, for the LGBTQIA+ Anti-Federalist Union, were stacked to one side. A shredder sat next to the desk, the final destination for much of the paper in the room.

"She certainly was consistent," Somers said. "God damn, this whole stack is print-outs from castration fetish sites." Glancing at the top page,

Somers swallowed and shook his head. "Well, I'm never going to be able to forget that."

"Inspiration?"

"Christ. It's all about rubber bands. Just shoot me instead, all right?"

Hazard studied the scene. Mentally, he put himself in the chair, working on the laptop. The brains and blood spattered the wall to his left. That was consistent with what Foley had indicated when he tapped the right side of his head. So, Fukuma had been shot on the right. Hazard made a mental note to check with Norman and Gross about having the shell casing dusted for prints; he just didn't trust the two patrol officers to do it right, no matter what Somers said.

"She's sitting here, working," Somers said, "and she decides this is it. Boom." He shrugged. "I wouldn't have pegged her for suicide, but I guess it's possible."

"Why?"

"Maybe she's torn up about Cynthia. Maybe it's the stress of the investigation. Maybe she's been depressed for a long time. Maybe all those."

Hazard nodded. He examined the details of the office again. He doubted that Kamp had known Fukuma personally; Kamp's social life, outside of the morgue, consisted of buying cheap booze, drinking cheap booze, and occasionally doing those things at one of the roadhouses outside Wahredua, where he might get lucky enough to see a fistfight or two. No, whatever decision Kamp had made about Fukuma's death, it had been based on the preliminary forensics in this house. Most likely in this room. Hazard gritted his teeth; if they had to wait for an official report, they'd lose precious time, especially because Kamp was likely to drink himself into oblivion in the next few hours. That was the ME's standard procedure.

Touching the shredder's lid only at the edges, Hazard lifted it. The receptacle was full of paper ribbons. If Fukuma had been murdered, maybe the murderer had destroyed something. Another thing that he'd have to tell Norman and Gross to be careful with. They'd missed the Molotov cocktail at the first crime scene, after all.

After replacing the shredder's lid, Hazard lifted the machine and found a scrap of paper. It was small, and the edge was ragged. A few words printed in tiny font covered the piece of paper, and the color looked familiar. Hazard lifted it by the edges and studied it more carefully. Then he stepped over to the desk, opened one of the LGBTQIA+ Anti-Federalist Union pamphlets, and juxtaposed the two.

"What's that?"

"She had these in her office on campus too. These pamphlets. Someone tore one of them up."

"Sounds about right. They look batshit crazy."

"Someone tore it up and then tried to shred it. They missed this."

"Or they tore it up, threw away the pieces, and missed that one."

Hazard held out a hand, and Somers passed him an evidence envelope. "That's the smoking gun, Sherlock Holmes?"

"Could be."

"Norman and Gross would have gotten it."

Hazard made a disgusted noise.

At the laptop, Somers switched the mouse to his right hand, and the screen flicked to life. "If you're done sniffing along the baseboards, come look at this. No password on the screensaver. God. She definitely had a type." Somers pointed at the screen, where a naked blond lay with her legs spread, hands cupping her bare breasts and pointing them towards the viewer.

"She was murdered," Hazard said.

Frowning, Somers studied the nude girl on the screen. "She looks all right to me."

"Not her, you idiot. Fukuma. She didn't kill herself."

"What makes you say that?"

"I'm not sure."

"Dear God. Emery Hazard is relying on intuition."

"Don't be stupid. I'm proposing it as a hypothesis because I'm not convinced she killed herself."

"It looks like a suicide," Somers said. "At first glance, anyway. She's a suspect in a murder investigation, so maybe she killed herself because she was overwrought, because she was guilty, hell, because she can't face the idea of going to prison."

Hazard grunted. From the front of the house, footsteps reminded him that Norman and Gross were still around. Soon enough, they'd have licked the last of the frosting from the donut box and be back in the study, interfering as Hazard tried to work.

"If she didn't kill herself," Hazard said. "Run through it that way."

"She was sitting here working on something. An intruder gets into the house—"

"Stop."

Somers's eyes narrowed. "No signs of forced entry. So either this person has a key—"

"Cynthia."

"Or knocks on the door in the middle of the night and gets Fukuma to let him in."

"Again, possibly Cynthia."

"You think she did it?"

"I think she could have done it. I'd like to test her hands for gunpowder residue and her clothes for blood spatter."

Somers's handsome face was still tight with thought. "If someone did kill her, they did it for a reason."

"Bad breakup with Cynthia."

"Jesus, you're really pushing that angle."

Hazard shook his head. "I want to prove it wasn't Cynthia, but she keeps popping up."

"Whoever killed Fukuma had a reason," Somers said again. "Aside from romantic fallout, the most obvious thing would be the case."

"Exactly. Fukuma is a major suspect. If she's killed and it looks like a suicide, we presume she's guilty."

"If we're idiots."

"And this is all assuming that she isn't the real killer," Hazard said with a frown. "Maybe this will push up the Highway Patrol lab work. If we could get a DNA match between the cigarettes and Fukuma, that might put this to bed."

"We've got two possibilities," Somers said. "Fukuma killed herself. Fukuma was murdered. Either way, it doesn't put us any closer to solving the murder."

"Not until we get the DNA results."

"Damn it," Somers said. He scrubbed a hand through his blond hair. "You know what we've got to do, right?"

Hazard arched an eyebrow.

"We've got to assume she was murdered for now."

Hazard nodded.

"Because if we assume she killed herself, and that turns out to be true, we don't lose anything. On the other hand, if we assume she killed herself, but really she was murdered, we'll lose days, maybe more, before we finally start looking for a killer. By that point, we'll be too far behind."

"Bingo."

"Don't act so pleased. I'm not saying she was murdered, I'm just saying we have to act like she was."

"Good enough."

"If she was murdered," Somers said, glancing around, "why don't we take a look and see if there's a clue why."

Moving past Somers, Hazard examined the Macbook. Aside from the pornographic background, there was nothing on the screen.

"You have to move the mouse down here," Somers said, gesturing to the bottom of the screen. "That's where all the icons are. Yeah, like that. See, she has Safari open. And that, whatever that video camera icon is."

Hazard clicked on the Safari icon, and a browser ballooned onto the screen. It was the webpage for the LGBTQIA+ Anti-Federalist Union. The most recent entry was from the day before, and it had been posted by Lynk Fukuma.

"My recent persecution at the hands of the police," Somers read aloud, skipping lines, "my mistreatment at the hands of the patriarchy, the gross miscarriage of justice, truth will out, truth will set me free, witch hunt. God," he said, "she uses that phrase about ten times. Witch hunt."

"Doesn't sound like a guilty woman about to kill herself out of despair."

"No. No, it doesn't." Somers frowned. "Who else knew about the Molotov cocktail at the sheriff's house?"

"I don't know. It wasn't exactly a secret."

"Did you tell anyone?"

"No."

"Neither did I. I think Cassella shipped that thing off to the Highway Patrol lab as fast as he could. The rest of the department might not have heard about it. Not even Cravens, maybe."

Furrowing his brow, Hazard said, "And so the real killer might not know about that evidence. What does that mean?"

"I don't know."

Hazard nodded; something didn't feel right about that realization, but he couldn't put his finger on it. He browsed over to the video camera icon, and a video editing program came up. On the right, a box showed a preview of the video, while the rest of the screen was taken up with editing controls.

"You click here," Somers said, "to preview the video. This is what she was working on."

Another click, and the video began. It had been shot during the daytime, and although the video was clearly amateur, the quality was decent. It showed a crowd of people chanting, shouting, marching, cheering. They held signs, but Hazard couldn't read them. He recognized the event, though.

"The protest outside the sheriff's house."

Hazard nodded. The video advanced, showing more of the protest, including a rallying set of cheers. The camera panned left, as though the owner were trying to follow something, and then the video abruptly cut off.

"Weird," Somers said.

"What was she doing?"

"Try up here. Yeah, the trash can icon. Ok, drag that clip back over here like you're splicing the two together."

This time, the video was longer: when the camera panned left, the clip didn't end abruptly. Instead, it showed Fukuma emerge from the crowd. She was wearing the coat with white stripes, and she was crawling under the fence onto Sheriff Bingham's property. The camera held steady on her as she followed the rolling hill down. A roar went up from the crowd, and the protesters went wild waving their signs. At the edge of the video, Fukuma flinched and froze. And then she resumed walking, hurrying towards the bluff where someone had assassinated the sheriff. Then the video ended. The timestamp on the last frame read 11:50:49.

Hazard played the clip again. He watched it a third time.

"Why the hell did she try to cut out this part?"

Somers was frowning. "She was surprised."

"Yeah, all right. But there was something in this clip that she wanted to destroy. Something she didn't want anyone to see."

"Run it back again. Stop." Somers studied the frame and shook his head. "Never mind."

They watched it twice more, but neither of them could identify why Fukuma had pulled up this video clip or why she had tried to edit it.

"It doesn't make any sense," Hazard said. "If she killed the sheriff, the only reason to alter the evidence is so that she can avoid prosecution. But if that's what she was doing, why would she kill herself?"

"I thought we were going with the assumption that she was murdered. Provisionally."

"I know, damn it. I'm just trying to think this through. If she was guilty, though, and she was tampering with evidence, who would kill her? And why?"

"That's easy: an accomplice."

"Two people." Hazard frowned. "Fukuma and someone else. Someone big and heavy. Someone who would have left those tracks at the bluff."

Excited voices came from the front of the house, and Hazard and Somers went to see what was happening. A door in the kitchen was open, giving out onto Fukuma's garage. A blue Prius sat on the cement slab, its hatchback open. Norman and Gross stood a few feet back, waiting respectfully with cameras in hand.

Albert Lender stood at the hatchback. It was hard to reconcile the thick plastic frames of his glasses and enormous mustache with who Lender really was: a crooked cop, a murderer, a traitor. He looked like he spent nine hours a day behind a typewriter. He looked like he bought pocket protectors in bulk. He'd done his best to help the mayor try to kill Hazard and Somers before; Hazard had made it his policy not to turn his back on the man again. Ever.

"Took you two long enough," Lender said. He gestured to the trunk. "I thought I'd drop by and give a hand. Good thing I did; you guys might have spent the rest of the night inside."

They went around the back of the car to see what everyone was so excited about. There, folded neatly in the back of the Prius, was a set of heavy olive coveralls, just like what the sheriff's shooter had been wearing.

CHAPTER THIRTY-FOUR

FEBRUARY 15
THURSDAY
8:00 AM

IN CRAVENS'S OFFICE, things went from bad to worse.

"We've got her," Cassella said. He had kicked out his legs again, and he reclined in his chair, arms behind his head. Once again, he had on a suit that probably cost more than everything in Hazard's wardrobe. "The Molotov cocktail has her prints all over it. Then the suicide, the coveralls. We've got her."

"We've got some circumstantial evidence," Hazard said. "We've got nothing that puts a rifle in Fukuma's hands."

"Nothing except her history of terrorism," Cassella said. He fanned a stack of documents. "You wrote this up, remember? A few months ago, when Fukuma was one of your lead suspects. She shot up that construction site or hospital or whatever the hell it was."

"No one proved that. You're misrepresenting—"

"Listen, Detective Hazard, this is a win. For everybody, frankly. You and Detective Somerset did great work; you found Fukuma when nobody else could, and you dug up this background info, you even found her tampering with evidence the night of the murder. About the only thing you didn't do was find the coveralls, but you would have if Lender hadn't shown up."

"If she was the killer, tampering with evidence to try to make herself look innocent, why would she kill herself?"

Cassella's eyes got huge. "Are you kidding me? She's got a million reasons. She knows she can't get away with it, she knows Wahredua's finest are on to her, but she wants to fuck up the aftermath. How's that for starters?

Or what about this: she was crazy. How does that sound? For God's sake, you know the woman. Better than anybody, you know how wack she was."

"You're trying to pin this on her," Hazard said. "And I won't—"

"That's enough," Cravens said. Her matronly face had reddened, and one hand worked viciously at her ponytail. "Detective Hazard, you have made accusations like this before. I've been patient with you. I understand that you have a mixed history with certain people in the department. But I absolutely won't hear those accusations again without proof."

"If you're going to close your eyes to what's happening here—"

"Enough!" Cravens's hand cracked against the desk. "Get out. Both of you."

Hazard got up so fast that the chair rocked backward. He plunged into the bullpen; Somers followed a moment later. From inside Cravens's office, there was a burst of chatter, and then the door slammed shut.

"That went well," Somers said.

Hazard marched to his desk.

"You really handled that like a professional."

Hazard snatched up his coat.

"What I was wondering the whole time was, how does Hazard really feel about this?"

"Are you going to be a wise-ass or are you going to help me?"

Somers flashed a grin. "Normally I do both."

"Christ, why don't you just stay here?"

But, as usual, Somers refused to do as he was told. He tagged along, dragging on his coat as they moved towards the door.

Their departure, however, stalled when Hoffmeister and Lloyd paraded into the station. Hoffmeister, his sallow skin flushed with excitement, was hallooing, and Lloyd was waving a cowboy hat in one gloved hand.

"What's all this?" Somers said.

"Guess who found the sheriff's hat?" Lloyd fanned himself with it. Hazard inspected it as best he could while Lloyd continued to wave the hat, displaying it to the bullpen.

It was a derby hat, waterlogged, the felt flattened and shiny.

"That's not the sheriff's hat."

"It damn well is. We fished it out of the river, down near the pull-out. Well, Hoffmeister did," Lloyd made this acknowledgment gracefully, "but I spotted it."

"It's not his hat. His hat was a cattleman."

"Fuck do you know?" Hoffmeister said, and his styrofoam-colored face creased into a grimace. "Sheriff had a lot of hats. Could have been wearing any one of them."

"That pull-out is, what? A half-mile downriver? A mile? Jesus Christ, you two are morons. That hat could belong to anybody within fifty miles."

Lloyd's grin faded, and he shook his head. "Tell him, Hoff."

"Not a fucking chance."

"Go on and tell him."

"Tell me what?" Hazard asked.

"We already showed it to the witnesses. This is his hat. They all say so."

"What were you doing out there anyway?"

"Chief didn't like you finding that bottle, the one the chink professor dropped, and she put Norman and Gross in the doghouse for missing it. She sent us back to take another look."

Hazard gritted his teeth. "Will you get out of our way?"

"Poor as fuck loser," Hoffmeister said.

"You're not the only one who knows how to do police work," Lloyd said, giving the hat an admonitory wave in Hazard's direction.

Growling, Hazard shoved past the men, ignoring their shouts. Somers said something—Hazard didn't listen, he didn't care what Somers said—and he hit the cold face on, like cracking his head against a block of ice. Somers emerged from the building.

"What was that all about?"

"Nothing."

"It didn't look like nothing." A pair of cars cruised past the station, their tires humming against the asphalt, and when they were gone, a brindled dog nosed his way into the road.

"It's just a hat," Somers said. "If it's the sheriff's, maybe we'll get something useful off it."

"Can we go?" Hazard said, jerking his head at the Interceptor.

"So, I think it's safe to say that the case is closed," Somers said as they got into the SUV.

"The DNA evidence—"

"Ree, you've got to open your eyes. They might not run the DNA match. They might not ever run it now. Even if they do, even if it comes back not a match, what do you think is going to happen? Do you really think Cravens will say that the killer is still out there? No. She'll say that the cigarettes must have been from something unrelated. She'll say the most likely suspect is dead."

"Fuck." Hazard slammed a fist into the dash. "Fuck, fuck, fuck."

"As soon as Cassella wraps things up, Cravens will push us onto the next case. It doesn't matter if this one is officially closed or not; as long as Cassella and the mayor are happy, Cravens will box up the files herself just to have this off the table."

"This is wrong. They're doing this because it's easy. They don't care who killed—"

"Ree."

"They don't give a shit about any of it as long as they come out rosy. They—"

"Ree."

"What, goddamnit?"

"If you want to do something about it, let's do it now. If you want to bitch, go get in your own damn car."

"And exactly what the hell are we going to do, Somers?"

"Work this case."

Hazard dragged the seatbelt over his chest. "Well, fucking drive, then."

As Somers eased the car out of the parking lot, he said, "It's not your fault, you know."

Staring at the station building as they drove past, Hazard ignored him.

"You're just overflowing with charisma."

"Enough, Somers."

"You can't help it. I bet sometimes you want to be rude and you don't even know where to start."

"Fuck off."

"See? That's what I'm talking about. It's like you've got a silver tongue."

Putting a hand over his eyes, Hazard fought a smile. He lost.

"That probably explains why you're so good at relationships too."

"I get it, all right?" But the grin was getting bigger.

"Should we start with Dudley?"

"Do I have to say please?"

Somers laughed. "The day you say please, I'll probably just drop dead."

"I said I get it. I'm an asshole."

"Yeah," Somers said, "that's what makes you so great."

And Hazard had no idea in hell how to answer that.

255

CHAPTER THIRTY-FIVE

**FEBRUARY 15
THURSDAY
8:57 AM**

WHEN SOMERS PULLED UP in front of the tiny home halfway between Wahredua and St. Elizabeth, he noticed that the Ford Taurus with the rusted-out wheel wells was gone. The house itself was still. Curtains covered all the windows. Every noise Somers made was too loud: his breathing, the gravel under his feet, and the rap of his knuckles on the door.

On the second knock, the door opened, and it was Mrs. Dudley again, wearing a white rayon nightgown so shiny it looked like it had been waxed and polished.

"She's not here," Mrs. Dudley said through the storm door. She held the handle as though afraid they might try to open it.

"Good morning," Somers said.

"Lisa's gone off again." She worked her mouth like she was thinking about spitting. "You find her, you can keep her."

"Mrs. Dudley, do you have any idea where she might have gone?"

"Just about anywhere, I imagine. Took the car this time. I had church group. Bible study, and then we're selling candied pralines. I can't go now, but Lisa never minded making herself a bother to everything that breathes and walks." Her foggy eyes sharpened. "Do you want any candied pralines? That other man bought some."

"What other man?" Hazard said.

"He bought two pounds of them. For his mother, he said. He was a nice young man. Very polite. Very handsome." She blinked her eyes, and Somers had the disturbing sense that she was trying to be coquettish.

"Mrs. Dudley," Somers said. "Who came by the house?"

"He was looking for Lisa too. When he said he wouldn't mind a candied praline for his mother, I asked him inside. Now there was a nice young man. Two pounds, he bought. Two pounds just for his own sweet mother."

"Fine," Hazard said, drawing out his wallet. "Three pounds. Four. Whatever the hell you want. Who came by here?"

Mrs. Dudley blinked and smacked her lips. "I'll get the pralines. It'll just take me a hare's shake and I'll be back."

"You're kidding me, right?" Somers said.

"What were you going to do? Sweet talk her?"

"Four pounds, Ree. You're not eating four pounds of pralines."

"Of course I'm not going to eat them, you mental defective. I'm buying them so she'll talk to me. To us. Goddamnit, you know what I mean."

"I'm just saying, four pounds is a lot. You could have bought one. Or two."

"She kept saying two. She wanted us to buy more. You heard her."

"Right. It's just that, well, you can barely fit into your trousers as it is."

Hazard looked like he had a stroke building. "You son of a bitch. If you say one more thing about my weight—"

"Here we are," Mrs. Dudley chirped, cracking the storm door and passing through four ziplock bags. "Four pounds."

"Fine. Perfect. Who was the man?"

"I didn't get his name. He was in a hurry, you understand. He wanted those pralines, but he was in such a hurry. I asked him to sit down. I think a gentleman should sit when he comes into a home. But he just about walked the whole house before I got those pralines for him."

"You don't have a name?"

"He was in such a hurry."

"How about a description, Mrs. Dudley?" Somers asked. "What did he look like?"

She blinked. "Very handsome. Very fine, yes, a very fine young man. Dressed properly too, not like the young men who go around these days half-naked. That's Satan's work, you know. The fight with that old serpent is real as ever. We're doing our best at Bethany United, but the serpent is mighty strong these days."

"Fighting him with goddamn pralines," Hazard muttered. He folded bills together. "All right. Anything else you can tell us?"

"He was very polite," and she fixed him with a gaze that made her point clear.

"Fine. Thank you."

"Now you don't go eating all those yourself, you hear," she called after them. "Share with your friend. He's skin and bones."

Somers was grinning when they got into the Interceptor.

"Say one word," Hazard growled. "One."

With a smile that could have cut steel, Somers raised his hands innocently.

They must have driven ten miles before Somers did say something, and when he did, it was surprisingly relevant. "Do we go after Rutter now?"

"Nobody's had a glimpse of him since the shooting. I doubt he's going to show up now."

"Back to the station, then?"

Hazard shook his head. "Let's talk to our witnesses one more time. Something happened on that video Fukuma was watching. Let's see if they remember anything strange."

They found June Hayashi at home, a modest, albeit updated ranch. The doctor answered the door herself. Her skin was sallow, and dark circles ringed her eyes. She wore sweats and a UCLA hoodie, and she looked like she'd slept in the clothes more than once.

When they'd explained why they were visiting, Hayashi fixed them with an unblinking stare. "Oh. Um. Eleven-fifty?"

"That's right. Anything unusual that you can remember?"

"Mmm. No. Um. That was right before, well, you know. Before the sheriff was. You see. Shot."

"And you don't remember anything?"

"Hm. No, um. No. I don't."

She walked them to the door.

"Dr. Hayashi, are you well?"

"Yes. Yes, just a bug. Professional, um, hazard."

Their visit to Beverly Flinn was just as pointless. Flinn, too, was at home, although she lived in a small, Craftsman-style bungalow that looked like it needed another craftsman just to keep it on its feet. The porch sagged, the windows looked like they might be thirty years old, and the carpets inside had been installed by an amateur—they were coming up from the staples.

Beverly flitted from room to room, talking as she did so, putting jangling hoops in her ears, adjusting a necklace in the mirror, teasing out her short, bleached hair.

"Eleven-fifty?"

"Yes, Ms. Flinn."

She trilled a laugh. "Please, you're so formal. Just Beverly."

"Is there anything that stood out to you at that time? Anything, no matter how small?"

"No." She frowned. "We were shooting. It was all so much fun. And then—" Her whirlwind suddenly stopped, and she touched fingers to her eyes. "Oh God, it was just so horrible." She stood there, so still and silent that she might have gone to sleep. Then, in a tremulous voice, she asked, "Have you found anything?"

"I'm sorry, Ms. Flinn. We can't talk about the investigation. You understand."

Moody was at home, in a corset, and drunk. Somers glimpsed puffy white flesh crimped by the black undergarment before Moody pulled her dressing gown closed at the throat. Moody's face lacked its normal snowfall of foundation, and she looked surprisingly thin and wrinkled and vulnerable. In the background, show-tunes blared on an ancient CD player, and Moody bobbed her head in time to the rhythm.

"It's really not something that's done," she kept saying as she ushered them into chairs. "Showing up at a woman's home like this, unannounced. Fifty years ago, my father would have cut a switch and left you standing for a week."

"Thank God for small mercies," Hazard muttered. Somers elbowed him.

But Moody had heard. She settled herself on a blue-chintz chair, her eyes cloudy with drink, her head still wobbling along with the music.

"You know, Detective Hazard, one hears things about you."

"I'm sure one does."

"Miss Moody," Somers said, "we've really only got a few follow-up questions and then we'll let you get ready."

"Get ready?" Moody's eyes were wide and uncomprehending. Then she plucked at the dressing gown as though remembering it. Her eyes drifted back to Hazard. "One hears that you have a secret, Detective."

"If you mean I'm gay, it's not a secret."

A cruel smile hooked the corner of Moody's mouth. "No." She didn't say the word; she just mouthed it, shaking her head.

"Miss Moody," Somers tried again.

"What's it like, Detective? What's it like to have a secret that nobody can know? That nobody can ever know?"

Hazard's pale complexion had red splotches now, but his voice was low and steady. "That's the nature of a secret. Nobody knows."

"No. Most secrets are meant to be shared. With only a few people, true, but still, that's what makes them pleasurable. That's what makes them sweet. Some secrets, though—some are like shitting your pants, pardon my language. You can let it out, and you might feel a lot better, but it changes everything. What's it like, Detective?

The red had heightened in Hazard's face, and his jaw looked tense enough to crack.

Moody's eyes, glassy with drink, hadn't left Hazard's face. "Can you feel the pressure build? Can you feel it like a sickness, twisting in your stomach? How long can someone stand a feeling like that? A month? A year? How long before someone puts a knife to his throat or fumbles for pills in the night because that secret is growing inside him like a cancer?"

"That's enough," Somers said, and the words were so sharp he surprised himself. Moody blinked, drawing herself up in the chair, and Hazard's flush was almost purple. "We need to ask you what you remember from eleven-fifty on the day of the murder."

Moody looked like she might argue—her eyes were almost liquid now, and color infused her wrinkled cheeks, but she only said, "Before the shooting?"

"Yes."

"Why, I've already told you. We were down at the river. We were shooting."

"You don't remember anything else? Nothing strange that you saw or heard?"

Moody didn't, though. And when she walked them to the door, she took Hazard's hand awkwardly, her nails biting into his palm and the back of his hand, a bizarre grimace on her face. "I'll tell Nico you stopped by, Detective. He'll be very pleased, I think."

"She's a bitch," Somers said in the car.

Hazard, as usual, didn't say anything.

When they got to Randall Scott's home, they found him pulling out of the garage in a massive Dodge Ram. The engine, even at an idle, rumbled so loudly that Hazard could barely hear the man, but he understood that Scott was telling them he was busy and couldn't they come another time.

When Somers finally managed to ask the question, Scott frowned.

"Eleven-fifty? God, we were all down at the river. You know that. We talked through that whole damn day."

"We were hoping you might remember something that happened specifically at that time. Something unusual."

"Nothing unusual. Wind was low. Good shooting that day." Scott blanched, his weathered face showing his horror at the double meaning. "Christ, you know what I meant."

For a wonder, they found Lionel Arras at his office. Arras was a round man, with a round face, round eyes, and a hooked nose. Even his hair looked round—it was curly, and he wore it long, with the result that it made his head spherical. Someone, somewhere might have considered it beautiful. To Hazard, it just looked like Lionel Arras hadn't changed his hair since the seventies. Hell, it might have even been a perm.

"Haven't we done all this?" Arras asked, his voice high and grating. "Not the two of you, I mean, but the cops. I've talked to them. Told them the whole thing. I've got a business to run, things to do."

The two-room office was empty, aside from the three of them, and the phones were silent. Hazard raised an eyebrow, and Arras had the decency to blush.

"I wouldn't expect you to understand, but I've got a lot of work. Money." He mimed grabbing something from the air. "Here, and then gone. I've got to stay up with the markets. It all happens fast. I can't just sit around and talk."

"We'll just take a moment."

But Somers waited; Arras jittered with the papers on his desk. A bead of sweat rolled to the tip of his nose and clung there.

"We're between offices."

"We?"

"My secretary and I. She's not here today. The other office, it's being remodeled. She wanted pinks and blues, and I—what is this about, detectives?"

"We're sorry we didn't have a chance to talk with you the day of the shooting."

Arras snuffled, and the bead of sweat tumbled onto the blotter. "Terrible. That whole day was terrible. I couldn't just sit there. I'm—I'm a Taurus, you know? I just can't be still. Movement. Energy." His hands came up and grabbed fistfuls of damp hair. "I've got to use the bathroom."

He sprinted out of the room.

"I'll get the back door," Hazard said.

Somers walked through the small suite, listened at the bathroom door—Arras was sniffling like a crazy man, and the toilet flushed once, then again—and spotted Hazard leaning up against the back door. Then Somers went back to Arras's office. He pulled open the desk's center drawer and saw a mirror and a razor blade. Well, that explained some of it.

By the time Arras came back, he was wiping furiously at his nose, and his eyes darted from the desk to Somers to the desk. "Your partner can't be back there. He just can't. This is a private office."

"He won't bother anyone."

"That's not the point. I've got financial documents—"

"It's not a problem, Mr. Arras. Here he is now."

Hazard settled himself in the doorway, arms crossed.

"Now, we read over your statement about the shooting, and we just wanted to ask some follow-up questions."

"I already talked about this. Talk, talk, talk. That's all you cops want to do. Why don't you get out there and do something about it instead of talking? Where are those other cops, the ones I talked to the first time? Why aren't they here?"

"In your statement, you said that you were looking out over the river when the sheriff was shot. Is that right?"

Arras flinched. "Yes."

"So you didn't see the shooter?"

"No. Nothing."

"You didn't turn around? If someone were shot, the first thing I'd do would be look around. What'd you do?"

Arras lifted fingers to his cheek, not quite touching. "I just . . . stood there. I heard the shot. And I felt something—" He squeezed his eyes shut. "It was blood. On my cheek, his blood. Right here. I didn't look around. I didn't even move. If I moved, I was going to lose my fucking mind. So I didn't do anything."

"What about earlier?"

Blinking, Arras said, "Earlier? When? Who the fuck cares about earlier? I was a cowboy. I was a fucking cowboy that day. I stuffed my face at brunch. I had goddamn chaps on. Chaps. We went outside. I was joking. Joking about the goddamn OK Corral, or something like that. I don't even know, I was so—" He licked his lips. His dilated pupils danced from object to object. "I was so excited. And then boom. One shot, that was all, and I froze. Some kind of goddamn cowboy."

"Why were you dressed as a cowboy?"

Instead of discomfort or embarrassment, Lionel Arras radiated pride. "That's authentic gear. Do you realize that? Those chaps, I won those off a rodeo star in Vegas. It was a wicked game of poker, the kind of thing you see on TV. Guys betting their watches. He thought he was such fucking hot stuff, but I showed him."

"He bet his chaps," Somers said.

"Exactly. And the vest—Jesus, I don't even want to go into how much that thing cost. It's historic." He leaned forward, his voice dropping. "Jesse James."

"You own and wear a vest that once belonged to Jesse James?"

"Damn right I do. I bought it when I made my first million."

"That doesn't explain wearing it," Hazard said.

Arras's face darkened with anger, and Somers hurried to ask, "Do you remember anything happening at eleven-fifty? About ten minutes before the sheriff was shot if that helps."

"What? No. Why?"

"Nothing strange. No sounds. Nothing you might have seen."

"I was shooting skeet with everybody else. I couldn't have heard something if I'd tried."

"What about the hat?" Hazard asked. He was slouching against the doorframe.

"My hat? It's at the cleaners. It fell when I heard the shot."

"The sheriff's hat. We couldn't find it after the shooting."

"No, no. I already went over this."

"What? With who?"

"The cops, the ones that came to talk to me. I told them where it was."

"Did you take his hat?"

"Christ, no. Can you imagine—" Arras shivered. "When he—when he fell, the hat rolled into the river. It got caught up on the bank a few yards downstream. I thought about picking it up, but it had—" His face paled, and he gripped the desk to steady himself. "I couldn't. I just couldn't."

Hazard was as stone-faced as ever, but Somers could read the energy in those scarecrow eyes. Was Hazard pleased? Disappointed? It was hard to tell, but Somers knew that Hazard was intrigued.

"What can you tell us about finances?" Somers said.

"Excuse me?"

"You were the sheriff's financial planner, weren't you? I understand the next-of-kin has authorized you to talk to us about his recent financial history. Was the sheriff a wealthy man?"

"I don't know."

"That's a strange answer. How can you not know?"

Arras made another of those vague grabbing motions like a cat batting at string. "He was here. There. All over the place. One day he wanted to invest in real estate and started buying up mortgages. A few weeks later, he was done with that and wanted an aggressive mix of stocks. Some months he'd have deposits rolling in—small, but steady. Annuities he told me. I asked him one time, and that was one time too many. He made that really clear. Lately, the money flowed out. Fast. Really fast."

"So he was broke?"

"Did you see the statements I sent over?"

Somers nodded.

"So you know. He wasn't broke. Not yet. But he could have gotten there without breaking a sweat."

"Who was authorized to withdraw money from his accounts?"

"No. No, no, no. Don't even try that."

"Some financial planners have expensive tastes, Mr. Arras. What's to stop them—I'm asking hypothetically—from using some of their clients' money? Maybe it just looks like a bad investment. Maybe the market takes a tumble, that's all. It must be easy. If the sheriff found out, he would have gotten angry. Maybe somebody didn't want him to find out."

For the first time since the detectives had arrived, Arras seemed to pull himself together. He batted at that invisible string again. "You're thinking of Madoff, Ponzi schemes, shit like that. You're crazy. The government has cracked down on that stuff hard. And anyway, I couldn't have even if I wanted to."

"Why don't you tell us about that?"

"I don't have custody of the money." Arras must have read the Somers's expression correctly because he went on, "Custody means direct access. I don't have it. Most planners, brokers, advisors, whatever you call us, we don't have custody. We use third-party custodians. Fidelity, for example. Big firms. That way, there's no question about integrity."

"And you can provide documentation to prove this?"

"I already did. Not that you guys knew what you were looking for."

"And the only person who could have taken money out of that account was the sheriff?"

"You can double check the paperwork. He didn't have anybody else on the account."

"Did the sheriff tell you what he was doing with that money?"

"We didn't do that kind of talk."

"What kind of talk did you do?"

Grabbing at his damp hair again, Arras shook his head. "Look, he was throwing money around because of the petition. I don't know that I really liked Morris Bingham. He was—he was too much, sometimes. But I know he wasn't going down without a fight. That's where I think that money went."

"Bribing voters?"

"No. This is small-town politics. A lot of it is about swapping money, swapping donors, etc. My PAC gives to your PAC, vice-versa. My friends give to you, your friends give to me. It's like a shell game, and you're trying to guess where the money lands. Anyway, along with the money goes constituents, votes, etc. My guess is that Bingham was lining every pocket he could get a hand into."

"Did the sheriff and the mayor share friends?"

Arras snorted and batted, cat-like, at the air.

"Anybody else you know off hand?"

"That guy running for the state legislature, the one that's jimmied himself into every TV spot for the last two weeks. You know. He's down here. He's been mucking around for the last week or so."

"Sal Cassella."

"That's him. Real pretty-boy vibe, you know? But he knows how to play the game already. He came by here. Glad-handed me until I thought my arm would fall off, told me all the good things he'd heard about me from the sheriff, a goddamn quarter-hour of my life, that's what it cost me, and in the end he just wanted a donation. I sent him on his way. I don't have time for that shit."

Hazard's scarecrow eyes were practically sparking as he leaned into the room. "He'd talked to the sheriff?"

"It's all bullshit with those guys, you know? Someone probably mentioned that I did finance work for the sheriff, and Cassella took it and ran with it."

To judge by Hazard's face, he didn't believe that.

"This guy, Cassella, he's really worked the town over. You know that? He's hit just about everybody in town. Everybody that matters, anyway."

After that, they wrapped up the interview. Arras still jittered like he'd had a gallon of coffee before they'd arrived; he'd sweated all the way through his shirt by the time he ushered them out the door. Poor guy looked like he'd been swimming.

When they left Arras, Somers let the Interceptor idle. "He's a crackhead."

"Figured."

"That explains the shitty office, I guess. You think he was telling the truth about custody of the money, all that?"

Hazard shrugged. "We'll take a look at the paperwork, do some digging. What do you think?"

"I think he'd steal a kid's pocket change if he thought he could get away with it, but I don't think he stole from the sheriff. Did you know Cassella was that deep into politics?"

"I told you about his campaign, didn't I?"

265

"Yeah, sure, but he's working a case, isn't he? I mean, that's why he's here."

"Guys like Cassella do everything for one reason: to get ahead. And remember, he was here before the sheriff got killed."

"Doesn't make him the killer."

"I didn't say it did."

"But you've still got a hard-on for him."

"I'm just saying he was here, Somers. And he lied about it."

Somers shrugged, reversed the Interceptor, and started towards the city center. "Nobody remembers a damn thing about eleven-fifty. What the hell was Fukuma trying to hide?"

"Let's see if McAtee knows."

Before they'd passed Market Street, though, Hazard's phone rang. He answered, listened, and then swore as he disconnected.

"The Rutter compound," he said, checking the .38 under his arm. "Fast."

"What happened?"

"It looks like ex-deputy Dudley just had a shootout with Dennis Rutter."

CHAPTER THIRTY-SIX

**FEBRUARY 15
THURSDAY
9:48 AM**

WHEN HAZARD AND SOMERS REACHED the Rutter compound, the gates were open, and first responder vehicles formed a barricade. They ditched the Interceptor and proceeded on foot; a handful of deputies stood around, hands on their guns, but nobody tried to stop them.

"No police," Hazard said. All those deputies with their hands on their guns, just watching the two detectives. Hazard resisted the urge to check his .38 again.

"This is the county; it's their jurisdiction."

Aside from the addition of emergency vehicles, the Rutter compound looked unchanged: a collapsing log cabin; single- and double-wide trailers, their aluminum siding warped and nicked; a series of RVs and campers, as though guests had arrived for a visit and never left. The crowd of deputies and paramedics thickened around one of the double-wides, and Hazard charged in that direction.

Lisa Dudley lay on the ground, one hand over her stomach. She wore a billowy khaki button-up—not a deputy's uniform but definitely meant to look like one. Blood soaked the front of the shirt. Her flat-featured face stared emptily at the sky; her other hand clutched empty air a few inches from a revolver.

"God damn," Somers said.

As they approached the trailer, McAtee came out. His handsome features darkened when he saw them.

"This isn't police business."

"Rutter?" Somers said.

McAtee bared his teeth and cocked his head at the trailer. "Have at him."

Hazard knocked past McAtee, ignoring the deputy's swearing, and stepped into the trailer. His first impression was that he had stepped back in time. The pea-green shag carpet, the mustard-colored laminate counters, the TV the size of a small sedan. The TV was on, of course, and playing a game show. Judging by the hair and clothes and microphone, Hazard guessed the people on the screen were all as dead as disco now.

Much of the trailer's space was covered in trash: discarded clothing, mountains of two-liter bottles, pizza boxes trampled into flatness, plastic bags full of cans, paper plates, red plastic cups. On one wall hung a four-point buck, and a hiking boot with the sole torn off hung from the uppermost point. Someone had tacked a woman's crop top to the wall; the shirt had a camo print and the words *Camo Queen*. Someone—perhaps the same person who had hung the shirt—had then blasted it with paintballs.

Dennis Rutter had fallen onto a sofa; his legs hung up over the arm of it like he was a frat boy sleeping off a party. He wasn't a frat boy, though. Hazard had never seen the man before, but he didn't feel like he'd missed much: Rutter had short, straight hair, a patchy goatee, and a tattoo on the inside of his arm that said *Freedom is for the Brave*. He'd gotten the worse end of the fight: one of Dudley's shots had torn away most of his jaw, and another had taken him in the throat. His shirt said *Camo King*.

"You've got to be kidding me," Somers said.

"Not now."

They moved through the trailer carefully, and Hazard found what he had expected in the last room. Someone had set up a card table and a folding chair; magazines, newspapers, construction paper, paste, and scissors covered the top of the table. Hazard took a pen from his pocket and shifted some of the mess aside. A few layers down, a piece of red construction paper already had the word *Die* glued to it in cut-out letters.

"Look familiar?"

Somers grimaced and spoke in a low voice. "I'm supposed to believe this asshole had been sending death threats anonymously to the sheriff for years. Jesus Christ, Hazard. Dennis Rutter? The fucking Camo King? He's such a moron he'd be lucky if he licked a stamp and it didn't end up stuck to his tongue."

"What do you want to bet that once we do a little more digging, we find a box of .30-06 and a rifle that matches ballistics on the bullet that killed Sheriff Bingham?"

"No bet."

"Dinner."

"Not a chance."

Hazard shrugged.

Footsteps announced McAtee. "What are you two doing back here? This is a crime scene, you understand."

"Right."

"Then get the hell out of here. If we need you guys to do a coffee run, we'll tell you. Otherwise get your asses clear."

They let McAtee chase them from the trailer. As Hazard came down the steps, he eyed the other structures of the compound.

"Let's take a walk."

The trailers and campers and the old log cabin weren't set in anything resembling streets or even rows; it was all slap-dash, as though the Rutter clan had needed to throw up the next building as soon as possible and couldn't be troubled with minor details like clearance and proximity. Hazard weaved between the different structures, listening. Silence. No voices. No crying. No movement. The hairs went up on the back of his neck.

"Creepy," Somers said as they rounded the old cabin; it smelled like woodsmoke and mold.

"They're waiting," Hazard said. "They're expecting it."

"Trust me: the Rutters weren't expecting this."

"No, the deputies. They're waiting for the Rutter clan to start shooting."

Somers glanced up and down; his hand drifted an inch towards the Glock 22, a solid .40 caliber piece he kept holstered at the small of his back, but then it settled at his side again. "I almost said they wouldn't be that stupid, but that'd be wrong. They're plenty stupid."

Hazard nodded. "And the deputies know it. Let's get out of here."

As they worked their way towards the gate and their exit from the Rutter compound, though, Hazard slowed. A red Firebird had torn up the sod and was parked near the trailer where Dennis Rutter and Lisa Dudley had died. Flashlights were duct-taped to the side mirrors, and Hazard remembered Grant McAtee's story about the speeding ticket. Hazard eyed the deputies, but they all seemed more concerned with the crime scene and with the violent arrival of the Rutter mongrels. After dragging on a pair of gloves, Hazard reached through the open window and popped the trunk.

It was empty and clean—none of the usual debris that tended to accumulate in a trunk. Hazard ran a gloved finger across the carpet. Nothing. Then he stepped back, gaining a wider angle on the trunk.

"There," Somers said, pointing to a piece of plastic caught in the trunk's latch. "Hold on, I'll get evidence bags from the Interceptor."

Hazard pulled the plastic loose and examined it. It was heavy plastic, the kind that might have been used for a painter's dropcloth. He slid it into an evidence envelope. Then he touched the rubber seal that ran around the inside of the trunk door. When he pulled his glove away, rust-colored flakes dusted his fingertip.

"Damn," Somers said. "Here."

Depositing the glove with the flakes of dried blood in another evidence bag, Hazard closed the trunk and moved to the front of the car. There, in the Firebird's ashtray, he saw old cigarette butts. With the hand that still had a glove, Hazard gathered the butts and put them in a third evidence bag.

Holding them up to the light, he inspected the butts. One, only half-burned, still had a portion of the printed paper. He turned it towards Somers.

"Fortuna," Somers said. "Goddamn Fortuna, just like we found at the sheriff's."

CHAPTER THIRTY-SEVEN

**FEBRUARY 15
THURSDAY
10:30 AM**

HAZARD'S INVESTIGATION OF THE FIREBIRD had delayed them, and a rusted-out Chevy Silverado pulled into the compound as Hazard and Somers reached the Interceptor. The men who jumped out looked a lot like Dennis Rutter: slack-featured, with lank hair and patchy attempts at beards. They were some mixture of cousins and brothers and uncles, Hazard was pretty sure, and they all had rifles. Several of them had bump stocks.

"Sweet Jesus," Somers said. "This is going to be a massacre."

"We can stay or we can go."

McAtee emerged from the trailer, already shouting at the recently arrived Rutters and ordering them back into the truck. As McAtee moved towards the men, he had a hell of a lot of swagger, but he already had one hand on his service weapon.

"This is our land," one of the older Rutter men said. "You got no right to be on it."

"This is a crime scene. Take one more step, and I'll have all of you arrested. I swear to God, one more step." McAtee's jaw was set, and his grip on his revolver looked pretty damn tight.

The Rutter men were swearing, shouting, and threatening, but it was the one in the front, the older one, who was about to make things go one way or another. Either they'd go—and have one more complaint in their long list against government—or this would be the day they decided they'd had enough.

"Where's my boy?" the old man said. "He's here. I know he's here, and I want to talk to him."

That was when Hazard reached for the Smith & Wesson under his arm because he knew, after that question, there was only one way this would end.

"Hold on," Somers whispered, touching his arm.

At that moment, a Mercedes spun around the corner, skidding across the rutted dirt, throwing up clouds of dust behind it. The sedan slid to a halt at the compound gates, just behind the Silverado. Dust billowed and swirled around it, and the door swung open, and Naomi Malsho stepped out.

She was still beautiful, Hazard saw with a spark of irritation. More beautiful, in some ways, than her sister Cora. But today, that beauty was tempered by the fact that Naomi looked like she'd crawled out of a laundry hamper: yoga pants, a rumpled sweatshirt, and worn sneakers. Her hair was pulled back and up, and she wasn't wearing makeup. Or, at least, she wasn't wearing much.

"All right, Mr. Rutter," she said, waving her arms like she was trying to flag him down. "That's enough right there."

"They got my son—"

"Mr. Rutter, I'm telling you to get back in that truck, load these boys back in that truck, and turn around. Get out of here right now."

"Now you listen here, you wild slip, you listen to—"

Naomi leaned in, speaking so that her words didn't carry. Whatever she said, though, caught Pappy Rutter by the small hairs. His face went blank, then white, and then he tottered back a step. The rifle across his shoulder slipped, and he caught it without seeming to realize it.

Without another look at Naomi, he staggered to the truck. "Come on. Come on!"

The rest of the Rutter menfolk climbed into the truck's bed, and Pappy Rutter tore out of the compound. The deputies glanced at each other and at the bedraggled woman in yoga pants who had just averted a massacre.

"Miss—" McAtee began.

She ignored him and headed straight for Somers and Hazard. "We need to talk."

"That went pretty well," Somers said.

"This was an assassination, John-Henry. My client was gunned down by the Sheriff's Department. Is that what passes for justice in Dore County?"

"Lisa Dudley wasn't a deputy," Hazard said.

Naomi's cool eyes darted to Hazard and then back to Somers. "You know exactly what I mean."

"If I recall," Somers said, "I wanted to talk to you about this, and you refused to cooperate. You made sure that I knew exactly where you stood. On everything."

"You're acting like a child. This isn't about you. This is about an innocent man who was murdered."

"Spit it out, then," Hazard said. "Instead of talking in circles like you always do."

Naomi straightened; she was beautiful, even in disarray, and she was smart and dangerous, and Hazard wondered if he wasn't making a mistake just by listening to her. Her posture didn't change, but her eyes slashed sideways, taking in the closest deputy.

"I'll call you," she said, and without waiting for an answer, she climbed back into the Mercedes and sped off.

"God, she's a bitch," Hazard said.

Somers shrugged and got into the Interceptor.

As they headed back to Warhedua, Somers flicked on the stereo. Country music poured through the speakers. Banjo, Hazard thought. So much damn banjo.

"Do we have to?"

"I'm driving."

"Dennis Rutter wasn't shot at the trailer. I don't think Dudley was either, but I'm not sure."

"This doesn't make sense."

"There was blood on the inside of the trunk—"

"No, not that. Do you think I'm an idiot? Don't answer that." Somers pulled in a breath. "Someone went to a lot of trouble making it look like Fukuma killed herself this morning. Someone wanted it to look like Fukuma was guilty and was taking the easy way out. And it worked: the case is basically closed, we're moving on to other investigations. Then, a few hours later, they do the same thing: Rutter and Dudley manage to kill each other, which is maybe the most convenient scenario anyone could have ever imagined."

"We had three suspects for the sheriff's murder. And they're all dead."

"That's what doesn't make sense: choose one or the other. Why kill all three?"

Hazard shook his head. "Maybe all three knew something dangerous. Maybe they all knew the real killer and couldn't be trusted. It's possible that the killer simply wanted to make sure that the case had a dead end."

"What you said about the bullets, the gun, the death threats—someone planted those at Rutter's trailer. Someone wanted us to think he was the killer."

Hazard massaged his temples.

"Your head?"

"Fine." It wasn't though; this was one of the bad ones, one of the really bad ones. It hadn't hit, not yet, but it was coming. He could feel it like a thunderstorm on the horizon. It was coming, and it was going to hit like lightning in mid-summer.

"You don't want to say it. Fine. I'll call."

"What?"

Somers didn't answer; instead, he grabbed his phone and dialed, and then he spoke firmly into it. "Hey, Murray. You been at the desk all day? Yeah? Your knees, right? Well did you try that cushion we got you? I'm not poking fun, I'm just asking. Yes. I'm just asking about the damn cushion. Listen—no, hold on, I've got a question. Cassella, the prosecutor who's been around, is he there? No, don't get him. I'm just asking. He's there? He's been there since when? Goddamnit. All right. Thanks, Murray. Yeah, I know. Yeah. Your knees. All right, thanks."

Hazard leaned into the glass; the cold helped a little, and the pounding in his head receded.

"He's been there the whole goddamn morning. Sitting in the bullpen where every cop in the station has eyes on him." Somers blew out a breath, and his fingers danced along the steering wheel. "I'm not saying this to be a dick, but we've got to get our facts out: he was with Nico last night, so he's got an alibi for that too. Hell, we could practically alibi him."

"So it wasn't Cassella who did Fukuma. Or Rutter and Dudley."

"It wasn't Cassella directly. He could have hired someone, though. He could have pulled some strings. Hell, he might have asked the mayor to chip in."

The headache was really getting here now, really rolling in, one of those thunderstorms that took up horizon to horizon, black winds flattening the grass, one of those storms that ripped clotheslines free and shot your underwear straight into the sky. Jesus, God, it was just a headache, right? A headache couldn't hurt this much.

"Come here, all right?"

Hazard's eyes flicked open. His breath fogged the glass. "What?"

"Lean over this way."

Shifting in his seat, Hazard let his head flop back against the seat. A moment later, one of Somers's strong hands found the back of his neck. Fingers dug into flesh.

"Geez."

"Don't be a baby."

"I'm not, it's just—" Hazard lost what he'd been about to say. Goddamnit, how were Somers's fingers that strong? They were like iron. And it hurt, yeah, but it also felt—well, strangely good.

"We'll go to a CVS, pick up your meds. Then we'll work this."

Hazard tried to think, but it was like putting together a puzzle in a hurricane. Every time he thought he had a piece in place, that damn storm rushed in and knocked everything apart. The lightning bolts of pain illuminated fragments of memory: Lisa Dudley with her 4-H trophies; the cigarette butts in the Firebird; Beverly Flinn as Lady Macbeth; Dr. Hayashi, rushing to the house for her medical bag; Grant McAtee writing a ticket for driving without headlights; Randall Scott setting traps for coyotes; Lynn Fukuma flinching at eleven-fifty in the morning; Lionel Arras, his greasy curls flattened under a cowboy hat.

"Stop," Hazard said. In spite of Somers's best efforts, the headache had gotten worse, and now the pain turned Hazard's stomach. "Pull over."

He staggered out onto the road and threw up. It took him a while, and when he finished, he noticed Somers's hand on his back, the only warm spot in the whole damn universe. Well, except maybe that steaming pile of puke.

"Do you need to go to the hospital?"

"No. We need to go get the man who killed the sheriff. Right now."

Somers's eyebrows shot up. "Do you want to brush your teeth first?"

CHAPTER THIRTY-EIGHT

FEBRUARY 15
THURSDAY
11:28 AM

RANDALL SCOTT'S HOUSE WAS DARK and empty. The garage, however, held the old Dodge. The coyote traps were gone. Worry flickered inside Somers like a green strobe.

"He can't be too far," Hazard said.

"You need to see a doctor."

"I'm fine."

"You need your meds at the very least."

"He's killed three people already, Somers. He might kill more." Hazard paused. The next words cost him a lot. A hell of lot, Somers could tell. "I can do this."

Somers nodded and drew the Glock from his waist. "He's got a few horses, some chickens, but he's not a rancher. If he's out setting those traps, he'll be nearby."

"You're supposed to set traps near intersections: the corners of fields, railroad lines, culverts, anywhere a coyote might go. Look for places like that."

"How the hell do you know this kind of stuff?"

Hazard's face was paler than usual, almost translucent, and sweat shone on his brow, but he managed a smile. "Documentaries."

"Goddamnit."

"I'll go east and circle north. You go west and do the same."

"Ree, he's going to be armed."

With a nod, Hazard started east.

Somers went west. He didn't like this, splitting up. He didn't like not knowing how Hazard had decided that Scott was the guilty one. For most of the drive, Hazard had been too sick to talk, and what little he had managed to say didn't make sense. But Somers trusted his partner. He trusted Hazard. And goddamnit if Hazard wasn't the smartest person Somers had ever met. So for now, for the next few hours, Somers was going on faith. Pure, old-fashioned faith. And it made him feel like he was twerking on a high-wire.

Using what Hazard had told him, Somers followed the edge of the closest field, where corn stubble glinted like white gold in the sunlight. At the end of the field, he paused. An eddy of air stirred dry dirt, blowing it over the top of Somers's oxfords. He glanced up the strip of fence separating the fields; no sign of Scott. Hazard had said to circle north, so Somers turned and followed the fenceline.

The dead corn stalks rustled. The wind knocked over a watering can, and Somers spun on his heel, his heart hammering into his chest. There was a ditch up ahead, another place that Hazard had said to check. Scott couldn't know they were coming, but if he saw them, if he had even an idea of why they were here—

Movement at the corner of his eye, and Somers jinked right. Crows exploded out of the next field, a dark cloud hovering for a moment and then drifting towards the power lines. Jesus. Somers lowered the .40 caliber with a mocking grin for himself. Adrenaline wired him like the Hollywood sign. He felt too big for his skin. He felt like he could run for hours. Like he could jump and clear the next county. It was going to be hell when he came down, but for now, for this moment, he could smirk at his overreaction.

When he turned back towards the ditch, he was staring down the barrels of Randall Scott's shotgun.

Scott looked bad. His gnarled hands couldn't keep the shotgun steady, and chunks of yellow teeth showed between his lips, not quite a smile, not quite a grimace. The air stank like hair tonic.

"Randall."

"You're real jumpy today."

Scott knew. Somers could hear it in the words, could see it in the way those yellow teeth ground against each other.

"Put the gun down, Randall."

"The way you're jumping, I guess you know just about all of it."

"Drop the gun this instant. Right now. Then we'll talk."

"I didn't want any part of what they did to that girl. Dennis Rutter deserved a bullet or two, but that girl, she didn't have a drop of meanness in her."

"I know you didn't. I know a man like you wouldn't want anything bad to happen to her."

Scott's eyes were distant. "I made a mistake. I ought to have paid for that, and I guess I did. But I think I'd have been a different man if he'd let me."

"Why don't you tell me about that?" Somers was still staring into the shotgun barrels, staring into those two huge, black eyes where fire and death would come for him. He forced himself to jerk his gaze away; Hazard was climbing up from the ditch. Steady, Somers told himself. Don't react. Don't do anything that'll give him away.

But when he glanced at Scott's face, he realized he was too late.

"He's back there, is he? All right." Suddenly Scott didn't seem anything but tired. Tired and old. "You'd better go on and knock the barrel away because I'm about to pull the trigger. Go on, son. Right now."

Somers reacted more out of instinct and the age-old drive for survival. His arm came up, caught the barrel, and cracked the shotgun sideways. An instant later, Scott fired. The sound was enormous, deafening Somers. It was so loud that he didn't hear the second shot. Or the third. But Randall Scott gave a faltering step, and the shotgun dipped, and he opened his mouth and blood came out. He coughed once, and drops of hot blood caught Somers's chin, and then Scott folded at the knees and went down.

Hazard was running—a lumbering, wounded gait—and it was obvious that the big man was at the end of his limits. The .38 swung widely in his grip. He hit Somers so hard it was practically a tackle, but instead of carrying them both to the ground, Hazard wrapped his arms around Somers and pulled him tight against him.

Somers knew that Hazard was saying something. He couldn't hear the words because of the shotgun blast, but he could feel them buzzing in his chest. Are you ok? Over and over again, Hazard was shouting those words, his hands pulling at Somers, trying to get a look. And Somers was answering, saying, He wasn't going to shoot, he wasn't. And after a while he stopped saying it because he knew it would cause trouble. Hazard called in the incident, and they waited. The corn stubble tickled Somers's cheek. The wind carried away the smell of gunpowder. And Hazard kept his arm around Somers, tight enough that Somers could barely breathe until the first lights came into view.

CHAPTER THIRTY-NINE

**FEBRUARY 15
THURSDAY
3:30 PM**

THE REST OF THE DAY was a long blur. The paramedics checked them for injuries and released them. Lender took statements from each of them as part of the police-related shooting investigation that would follow. Cassella and Cravens wanted to know everything, but Somers managed to put them off until they could pick up Hazard's prescription. It wasn't until Hazard had rested and his head had cleared—at least somewhat—that Somers finally allowed Cassella and Cravens to start questioning. The added bonus was that by then some of Somers's hearing had come back, although his ears were ringing like he'd stuck his head up a belfry. It had also given Hazard and Somers time to do the research they needed to back up their theory.

"Why don't you take it from the beginning?" Cassella said. They were sitting in Hazard and Somers's apartment with the lights low and the blinds drawn. Hazard was trying to look tough, but mostly he still looked like he'd been hit by a truck. Or maybe two.

"They planned the whole thing very carefully," Hazard said. "I think some elements they'd been working on for years, but the details, the final version didn't come together until the recall petition. They needed a reason for all of them to be at his house together."

"They were his closest supporters," Cassella said. "I'm sure they'd met together dozens of times."

"Actually," Somers said, "they weren't his supporters at all. And they told us that in the initial interviews. We asked them why they were there. They made it clear they didn't like Bingham as a person, but they were willing to help with the recall petition."

"That sounds like support to me," Cravens said.

"They were helping him because he was blackmailing them."

Cravens and Cassella exchanged a glance.

"Scott told me that he'd made a mistake, but that Bingham wouldn't let him get past it."

"That's not much to go on," Cravens said.

"The sheriff has a reputation for blackmail," Hazard said. "He tried blackmailing me and Somers during our last case. And Lisa Dudley knew that the sheriff had blackmailed other people in the area."

"I'm not saying you're wrong," Cassella said, "but Miss Dudley is dead. All we have to go on is your word."

"I kept the blackmail note," Hazard said. "It'll match the other ones."

"The ones in the safe," Somers said.

"But we haven't even opened the safe yet," Cassella said. "The locksmith hasn't had a chance."

"Don't worry. They're in there. All those death threats that Dudley thought she saw? They weren't death threats. They were blackmail notes. And the sheriff wasn't receiving them; he was sending them. He kept records, too. Evidence. You'll find those in the safe as well. There was only one death threat, the one that you found, and that was left by McAtee. He made sure we found all the supplies used to make that death threat inside Rutter's trailer. Just more proof to make us believe Dennis Rutter killed the sheriff."

"You're telling me," Cravens said, "that when we open that safe, we'll find evidence that Sheriff Bingham had been blackmailing some of the town's most prominent citizens? The same ones, according to you, who conspired to murder him?"

"Not quite," Somers said. "You'll find blackmail material, but not for the ones who killed him."

"They already took that stuff out of the safe," Hazard said.

Cravens flushed. "It was locked, Detective. We still haven't gotten it open."

"Yes. But they did."

"They told us how, actually," Somers said. "They had to explain some of the irregularities in the crime scene, and so they told us without meaning to tell us, I suppose."

"All right, all right." Cassella raised his hands. "Like I said: walk through it from the beginning."

"Sheriff Bingham had been blackmailing people for years. We're not sure about all the crimes; we'll have to do more on that front."

Hazard spoke in a low voice. "Beverly Flinn killed her husband; I'm pretty sure of that. She told us that the sheriff took care of her. What she meant is that he covered up the murder and then blackmailed her."

"And Bingham had evidence that McAtee had abused inmates in the county jail. He might have even murdered one. Beyond the legal consequences, a bad reputation like that might have kept McAtee from ever getting his hands on the trust fund his parents left him."

"We think June Hayashi has a revoked medical license; something messy back West, and she ran here and hoped no one would figure it out. That's the only explanation for why she's working at a doctor-in-a-box clinic when she's got a degree from Stanford's med school."

"Randall Scott's son was a serial rapist; everyone thought it was an angry brother or uncle or father who finally tracked him down, and I guess in a way it was. Scott killed him. The others have similar stories. Moody embezzles from the charities she runs. Arras has a cocaine habit and steals from clients too stupid to know better."

"Good God," Cravens said. Her face was waxy. "You don't have proof—"

"We'll get to that. Bingham had been blackmailing these people for years. Bleeding them dry. Take Lionel Arras for example: he works in a tiny office. Part of that's his cocaine habit, but a lot of it was paying Bingham to be quiet. Then, all of the sudden, a series of events happens. Bingham's family falls apart. The recall petition gains momentum. The sheriff no longer looks invincible. They realize they might be able to get out from under his thumb."

Somers nodded and picked up the thread. "The recall petition gave them a perfect reason to be together—my guess is that Lionel Arras put it into the sheriff's head, and the sheriff thought it was his idea. The sheriff would get them together, squeeze whatever money he could out of them, and make it look like the town's most prominent citizens supported him. That was the most important part: he could squeeze them for money whenever he wanted, but what he needed was a show of support. They had to look happy, of course. They had to look like they were friends, or the rest of the town might not be swayed. So they had to do something fun, like a little skeet shooting. They even had a nice brunch."

"While the rest of the group kept the sheriff busy," Hazard said, "Randall Scott walked upriver, climbed the bluff, lined up a shot, and killed the sheriff. That was easy for him; about forty years ago, Scott was named Mr. 4-H. I should have realized what that meant when I learned about Dudley's riflery trophies from 4-H, but I didn't put it together until much later. Scott was a crack shot; he didn't need anything but a clean line of sight."

"He managed to miss Detective Somerset," Cassella said drily.

"The killing shot was at eleven-fifty," Somers said, eager to change the subject. "As soon as the sheriff was down, Beverly Flinn wiped his hands so they could get a clean print. She told us she was just grieving; she said she couldn't stand to see him like that. In fact, she put on quite the performance. Of course, she's an actress and a surprisingly good one. She didn't care that his face and hands were bloody except that the blood would interfere with the fingerprint. Once they got an impression of his fingerprint, Dr. Hayashi took it back to the house. She opened the safe, retrieved the relevant files, put them in her doctor's bag, and came back down to the river. Nobody thought to check her bag, even though her explanation of going to the house was fairly lame. After all, no one needed medical attention."

"By that point," Hazard said, "they had accomplished everything they needed. Scott was still on the bluff. He fired his gun a second time, exactly at noon. That was what everyone told us: the last shot, the killing shot, had been fired at noon. Then he went back the way he came, wading down the river. That's why there were prints on the bluff, but no prints leading from the riverbank up to the bluff. He told us he'd fallen in the water because he was so startled. He weighed down the gun and left it in the river; they were going to need it to frame someone, but they couldn't let us find it too quickly."

"Why the second shot?" Cassella said. "It's a small town, but not that small. They would have had a few minutes before the police responded."

"No," Cravens said. The waxiness had reached her lips. "There was a cop sitting in his driveway because of the protest. The response time was thirty seconds." She struggled to take a breath and then said, "That's all of them except Moody and McAtee."

"We'll get to McAtee in a moment."

"And Moody?"

"She planned it. That's what she's best at, isn't it? She told us herself: plan for everything, and then a plan never goes wrong. I guess the joke's on her."

"I don't buy it," Cassella said, leaning back in his seat. "They couldn't have planned it. Not all of it. They couldn't have guessed Fukuma would trespass and see them. If she'd been a minute earlier, she would have seen Scott take the shot. And they couldn't have planned that Dennis Rutter would be kayaking that exact stretch of river at the exact time. Or that Lisa Dudley would be MIA and have a serious grudge."

Somers cast a searching glance at Hazard, but Hazard didn't speak. After a moment, Somers said, "You're right. We don't think they planned for either Fukuma or Dudley to be involved. They had unexpected good luck. Fukuma made a likely suspect because of her politics, her criminal past, and her confrontation with the sheriff days before. Dudley, too, was lucky for them." Somers smiled. "I guess lucky isn't the right word; the sheriff had made a lot of enemies, so we were bound to have other suspects for his murder. But we do think that they knew, or anticipated, that Dennis Rutter would be kayaking. We think Deputy McAtee had been watching Rutter for some time, getting down his schedule. McAtee even told us that he'd been responsible for keeping tabs on Dennis after Dennis's brother died in the county jail; for a while, the sheriff was probably scared spitless and had McAtee tracking Dennis's every move. When it got close to the time for them to put their plan into action, McAtee had even gone to the trouble of stopping Dennis for driving without headlights. While he was writing him a ticket, he searched the car and collected some of Rutter's cigarette butts. Scott very considerately left those for us to find at the crime scene."

"From the beginning," Hazard said, "they had planned to have a fall guy. It was supposed to be Rutter. They had his cigarette butts; the DNA would be a match. Rutter had a personal vendetta against the sheriff because of his brother's death. And Rutter was going to be a candidate for sheriff—another reason Rutter might want Bingham dead."

"Why didn't Rutter come forward?" Cravens said. "Naomi Malsho is a damn good attorney; she would have dragged this case to a halt. Everything we had on Rutter was circumstantial. If he had just come in to talk to us, he probably would have walked free."

"I imagine he would have done exactly that; as you said, Naomi is a very good attorney. But he never had a chance. McAtee must have picked up Rutter as soon as he could. McAtee knew Rutter's favorite bars; it probably didn't take more than an hour or two."

"And he kept him this whole time?"

"Sure," Somers said. "It was easy. We weren't even looking for Rutter until Monday, really until Tuesday. McAtee had a full day to hide him somewhere we'd never look. I wondered why Naomi asked me to meet her; she was fishing. She wanted to know if we had any clue where her client was. She was worried that he really had killed the sheriff and that he was on the run."

"And then," Hazard said, "when it was time, McAtee shot Dennis Rutter and dragged him back to the compound. McAtee planted the death threat materials, the gun, and the box of .30-06. I'm right about that, aren't I?"

Cassella's eyes glided to Cravens. "We haven't gotten the ballistics back."

"But you will. And they'll match. And the Rutter compound was empty because we'd gone pounding on their gate one too many times, and McAtee knew he could trust us to scare them into hiding. It was easy for him to get in, do what he needed to do, and place an emergency call from — was it a payphone?"

"We'll have to check," Cravens muttered.

"What about Fukuma?" Cassella asked, tapping one finger on the coffee table. "What about Dudley?"

Again, Somers studied his partner's face. When Hazard spoke, his voice was taut with frustration. "We don't know."

"That's inconvenient."

"We think," Somers said, "that McAtee lured Dudley into the confrontation. When we first met with Dudley, she revealed that someone had been slipping her information about the investigation. We think it was McAtee. We also think McAtee put the idea in her head that if she could catch Rutter herself, she might have a chance at coming back into the Sheriff's Department. Mrs. Dudley told us that a cop came to the house looking for Lisa; my guess is that it was McAtee and that Mrs. Dudley didn't make a distinction between city police and the sheriff's deputies."

"And Fukuma?" Cassella pressed.

"We don't know," Hazard said again. "There might have been competing factions among the conspirators. Scott said that he hadn't wanted to harm Dudley. We think that maybe one of the conspirators thought Fukuma would make a more believable scapegoat and acted independently."

"I'm hearing a lot of 'we think' and 'maybe.' Here's what I don't get: if I were blackmailing somebody, I sure as hell would have a safety net. Like, I'd give copies of the blackmail to a lawyer with instructions to mail it out if anything happened to me. Something like that."

"I'm fairly sure that the sheriff did something like that. There was a car accident on Route 133 Saturday night. Pretty nasty one: the car went off the shoulder, rolled, and went into the river. The guy who died was a small-time lawyer in Honey Creek. Far enough that he wouldn't stick his nose into the sheriff's business, but close enough to hear if anything happened to him. I wouldn't be surprised if McAtee and a few of the others paid a visit to his office just to make sure those files were never found."

"This is a lot," Cravens said, rubbing at her eyes.

"The hat," Somers said.

"What?"

"Sheriff Bingham's cattleman hat," Hazard said. "It was missing after the shooting."

"Lloyd and Hoffmeister found it. It was caught up on some branches in the water. Something like that."

Shaking his head, Hazard said, "That wasn't his. That was Lionel Arras's hat. It's a derby. The sheriff wore a cattleman. They're significantly different; you can look at the photograph from that day and see them side by side."

"How the hell do you know that?"

"Documentary," Somers said drily. "Arras gave up his own hat and kept the sheriff's. That's his thing, I think. Makes him feel powerful. That's why he paid a million bucks or whatever the hell for Jesse James's vest. That's why he was so proud of winning the chaps off a rodeo cowboy. You'll find the hat at the cleaner's if Arras was telling the truth. Or he'll have it at his house. It's a trophy for him; he won't get rid of it. There's bound to be plenty of DNA evidence on it."

Hazard added, "They might have destroyed the blackmail files, but maybe not. Dr. Hayashi could still have them."

"Anything else?" Cravens got to her feet. Her face was red, her jaw set, and she glared from one detective to the other. "Any other twists and turns?"

Somers shook his head.

"Then I've got calls to make."

And with that, Cravens left, slamming the door behind her.

"It's a lot," Cassella said, his gaze thoughtful. "It's a hell of a lot to take in. But damn, you two did fine work."

Somers glanced at Hazard; his partner's eyes were drooping shut.

"I'll let you guys be. But I want to buy you a drink or two before I leave town." Cassella's smile was blinding as he shook Somers's hand. Hazard looked like he'd passed out, and after a watchful moment, Cassella didn't try to rouse him.

When Cassella had left, Somers put an arm under Hazard. "Let's get you to bed."

Groaning, Hazard shook his head. "Just give me a few minutes."

"He's a real asshole, you know?"

"Cassella?"

"Who else?"

"He's starting to get under your skin?"

"It's the way he looks at you. Like he's trying to figure if he should poke a bear."

Hazard grunted, but he didn't answer, and Somers left him. In his bedroom, Somers kicked off his shoes. His mind was racing with the events of the day. The early morning call, the moment of looking down Scott's shotgun and seeing his own death. Scott had wanted to die. Suicide by cop. Somers knew it; he hoped Hazard never did.

His mind went through those moments again and again: the knowledge that he was going to die, then the explosive sound of the shotgun, and Hazard loping towards him, crashing into him, arms crushing Somers against his chest. That was what it was like to feel alive. That moment, right then. Alive and in love.

Rolling onto his side, Somers punched his pillow. Fuck love, already.

Something about the day still bothered him. Fukuma's death. It didn't make sense. Yes, the theory Hazard had proposed of competing factions inside the group of murderers was possible. But it didn't feel right. Hazard would make fun of Somers for saying something like that; Hazard wanted facts, analysis, logic, reason. Somers wasn't smart like that. He just knew he trusted his gut, and his gut told him that something wasn't right about Fukuma's death. His gut also told him Cassella was a major asshole, but that wasn't any major revelation.

On a whim, Somers pulled up the LGBTQIA+ Anti-Federalist Union's website on his phone. To his surprise, there was a new post, dated from midday. It had been written by Fukuma. His heart pounded as he read it. Suddenly, Lionel Arras's comments made sense. The pamphlets in Fukuma's office, the ones Hazard had found, made sense.

"Ree."

In stockinged feet, Somers ran into the living room. "Ree, wake up. Ree. You've got to look at this."

Bleary-eyed and obviously grumpy at having been woken, Hazard accepted the phone. His expression transformed from sleepy to calculating.

"She wrote it last night," Somers said. "She wrote it and scheduled it to post today. This is what he was trying to stop. It had nothing to do with the video Fukuma was editing. Damn it, she probably wasn't even editing it; she was probably looking at it, realizing that the killing shot had been fired at eleven-fifty, when he showed up. After he killed her, he deleted part of the video just to throw us off and make us think she was trying to hide something."

Hazard tossed the phone back, dug out his own, and dialed. Somers didn't need to see the screen to know he was calling Nico.

"Are you with him?"

Whatever Nico answered—it sounded whiny and petulant—Hazard cut off by saying, "Answer me. Are you with him?"

Nico whined something else.

"Nico? Nico?" Hazard shouted and hurled the phone. It shattered against the wall.

"That's two," Somers said. "Now he's made you break two phones."

"Come on."

Somers glanced down at his phone one last time. The blog post that Fukuma had started writing, the blog post for which she had been killed, showed on the screen.

We, the directors of the LGBTQIA+ Anti-Federalist Union, urge all thoughtful and ethical people to vote against Salvatore Cassella in the upcoming election for the following fourteen reasons.

CHAPTER FORTY

FEBRUARY 15
THURSDAY
5:21 PM

SOMERS DROVE, AND THE INTERCEPTOR flew through Wahredua's streets, but to Hazard it felt like a crawl.

He'd been stupid.

He'd been blind.

He'd been jealous, and the jealousy had made him ignore what was right in front of him.

"He's fine, Ree. They're eating dinner or something. Cassella's not going to do anything to him."

It was obvious now, in hindsight. Cassella had come to town early. He had lied about being in town early. Not because he had killed the sheriff but because he had been testing the waters about running as an openly gay candidate. He had met with the mayor, the sheriff, and with the town's highly public, polarizing voice of the LGBT+ community: Lynn Fukuma. That was where Hazard had made his mistake. He had assumed that the only voice that mattered was Mayor Newton's. He hadn't thought about Fukuma's influence, what it might mean for Cassella. For hell's sake, Hazard had seen the damn pamphlets in Fukuma's campus office, and he should have known, then, that there was something strange going on. Cassella had met her on Friday night, maybe on Saturday. And he had taken one of the pamphlets. And he had carried that pamphlet into Fukuma's home, where they had argued again, and he had ripped it up, and a shred of it had fallen behind Fukuma's shredder. And maybe, just maybe, there was a fingerprint on it. For hell's sake, Hazard thought again, he'd seen the mouse on the left side of the computer and he still hadn't put it together. Hazard had told himself to ignore Cassella. He had told himself to turn a blind eye. He had told himself he was just being jealous. And now it might get Nico killed.

He wasn't sure why he thought Cassella might harm Nico. It wasn't logical. The safe thing for Cassella to do would be to leave town. As far as Cassella knew, nobody suspected him of anything. But Hazard clutched at the Interceptor's door and had his feet pressed to the floorboards as though he could somehow make the SUV go faster by sheer will.

When they reached Nico's apartment, there it was: the Infiniti snug against the curb. Hazard checked the .38. Gone; he'd handed it over after shooting Randall Scott.

"I'm going to circle the block," Somers said. "We can—"

"Give me your gun."

"Not a chance."

Hazard kicked open the Interceptor's door and dropped while the car was still rolling. Somers swore, and then a horn blared, and Hazard knew Somers would be too busy trying to avoid an accident to follow. Hazard took the stairs two at a time. He was distantly aware of the headache roaring back towards him, but he didn't care. All he cared about was getting to the apartment. Getting to Nico. Now.

When he hammered on the door, it opened, and Hazard barreled past Nico and into the apartment.

"What the hell?" Nico came after him. "Emery, you can't—"

Cassella was rising from the table, pushing back a bowl of rice. "Get down," Hazard shouted. "Get your hands in the air and get on the fucking ground."

Cassella, blinking, turned towards Nico. "What's going on? What's he—"

"I said get on the fucking ground—"

But before Hazard could reach Cassella, Nico interposed himself. He planted a hand on Hazard's chest, shook his dark, shaggy hair, and shoved. "Are you insane? Are you out of your damn mind, barging into my apartment like this, shouting, raising hell? What do you think you're doing?"

"Get out of my way."

"Why? Are you here to beat him up and stake your claim? We're over, Emery. You made that decision, not me. And if you think you can walk back into my life, disrespecting me like this, and expect me to—"

Hazard elbowed past Nico to meet Cassella's eyes. "Get on the ground."

"Am I under arrest?"

"You're goddamn right. For the murder of Lynn Fukuma."

"You're insane," Nico was shouting, grabbing Hazard's arm, trying to haul him towards the door. "I'm calling the cops. I'm calling the—"

"I was with Nico last night," Cassella said, hands on his waist. A power pose. This motherfucker was about to get arrested, Hazard thought, and he's trying a power pose. "Ask him. Nico, tell him."

"Yeah, Nico," Hazard said, shrugging off Nico's grip. "Tell me."

Nico was blushing. Or maybe he was just pissed off. "We spent the night together, you piece of shit. Now will you get out of here?"

"The whole night?"

"Yes, goddamnit. The whole night. Get out here, Emery. I'm serious: I'll call the cops."

"The whole night, Nico? Don't lie to me. Was he with you the whole night? He didn't leave for a minute?"

"Yes, he—" Nico hesitated, and in that hesitation, Hazard heard the answer. He risked a glance at Nico and saw the surprise in the boy's face, and then the expectation of hurt like he was bracing himself for a bell-ringer.

"He left, didn't he?"

"Nico," Cassella was saying. "Just think about this for a minute."

"He left and you don't know where he went."

"Nico, just hold on. He's trying to get inside your head."

"He left. How long? Half an hour? An hour?"

In a small voice, Nico said, "He went to get condoms. I said I had some at home, and he just laughed and told me to relax. He told me he'd be right back."

The pain on Nico's face was so much that for a moment, Hazard forgot everything else. He wanted to pull the boy against him, bury his face in Nico's shaggy hair, tell him it would be ok.

"That's nothing," Cassella said. "I was slow. I couldn't find a clerk at the CVS. It just took longer than usual, that's all. Nico, you don't honestly believe—"

"He's not wrong," Nico whispered. "He's never wrong."

Hazard was shaking his head, trying to think through the thunderstorm rolling in on him. "You fucked up, Cassella. You fucked up big. I don't know how you did it, but you talked your way into her house. You even brought the pamphlet. Was that what did it? Was that your show of good faith, and she believed you even though it was late? You told her you were interested in her ideas. Maybe you even told her you wanted to use them for your platform."

"This is crazy. Nico, come over here. Let me just talk to you."

Shaking his head, Nico stayed where he was.

"I don't know how you got her to stand still, but you did a good job. You got the right angle; the ME even believed it was suicide. Except you didn't consider one thing: you shot her in the right side of the head. Patrick Foley told me. The forensics at the scene back it up. But she was left-handed."

"Look, I didn't know her, but she was obviously sick. And I'm sorry she shot herself. It doesn't matter if she was left- or right-handed, though. She grabbed the gun, put it to her head, and boom. That was it. Nico, look me in the eyes. Honestly, you know Hazard. He's a sociopath. That's your word, sweetheart. He's here to screw things up between us."

"You thought you got rid of the pamphlet. Did she tear it up in your face? That's the kind of thing she'd do. Very dramatic. She liked big gestures. And you gathered up the pieces and put them through the shredder. Except one. One fell behind the shredder. And I'm going to lift your print off that piece of paper, and that's going to be it. That's the end." Something clicked, and Hazard suddenly felt staggered at how foolish he'd been. "Jesus Christ. Fukuma never took a Molotov cocktail to the sheriff's house. You planted it there after we'd finished with the crime scene, and then you led us back there just to rub our noses in it. You were putting all the pieces in place so we'd look at her more carefully. I bet you were smart enough to pay cash when you bought the booze, but we'll pull security video from the local liquor stores, and we'll find it. You'll be right on screen, buying that exact bottle of vodka. I hope you were smiling that day."

For a moment, Cassella's face registered nothing but shock and dismay: handsome, hundred-thousand-dollar shock and dismay. "Nico, if you'd just—"

Nico took a step back; Hazard met his ex's eyes, and he hated himself for what he'd just done, for ruining something that had made Nico happy, for taking another thing away from him.

"That's a fucking shame," Cassella said, and Hazard turned towards the lawyer just in time to see Cassella squeeze the trigger. The sound of the shot was deafening in the small apartment. Nico squeaked, clapped his hand to his waist, and tried to sit down. He hit the wall and slid, and behind him, he tracked a long, red streak.

Hazard wasn't sure how he reached Cassella. He had a vague impression of rushing movement, as though it was the world sliding past him instead of the other way around, and then he crashed into the lawyer and they hit the ground together. They rolled, once, and Hazard's head cracked against the floor. Then, storming in like a hurricane, came the headache, and it was all Hazard could do to keep from passing out.

He had a grip on Cassella's arm, and he was vaguely aware of Cassella gaining leverage. The lawyer was pushing himself upright, straddling Hazard, his eyes wide, his breathing heavy and ragged. Cassella's pistol began to turn, inching towards Hazard. Hazard bucked his hips, struggling to dislodge the other man, but he was tired and hurting and his head was blazing like a tire fire.

Neither man spoke. The only sounds were grunts of effort. Cassella's manic expression grew almost gleeful as the gun shifted again towards Hazard, and suddenly Hazard knew how it would play out: the jilted lover, the jealous ex, a murder-suicide. He could almost hear Cassella saying it. An old one, but the old ones are the best.

Cassella wrenched his other hand loose, gripped Hazard's hair, and slammed his head into the floor. The world went white and then black.

When Hazard came back from that blackness, he was surprised to find himself bouncing. Every bounce hurt. The bounces were irregular, unpleasant, and uncontrollable. He remembered being very small and being trapped on a trampoline with several older cousins. They'd jumped close to him, launching him into the air, and this was like that.

"Nobody's trying to bounce you, you big idiot," Somers said, his face looming out of the darkness. "Will you stop it already?"

Hazard hadn't realized he'd been speaking.

"It's these damn roads. Potholes all the way to the hospital."

"Nico?"

Somers glanced away. "They took him first."

"Cassella?"

"Safely on his way to the county jail. I asked him really nicely, and he decided he didn't want to have his head blown off."

"John." Hazard reached for Somers, found his hand, and squeezed. He couldn't seem to find any more words.

"I know, you big idiot. Will you just try not to have a brain hemorrhage?"

CHAPTER FORTY-ONE

**FEBRUARY 16
FRIDAY
11:15 AM**

SOMERS STUDIED THE SOLITAIRE HAND HE'D DEALT.
"You're not going to win."
Somers ignored his partner and turned over the next card.
"You never win."
Sighing, Somers leaned back. He needed an ace. Just one would be nice. His hands were perfectly steady as he ran through the cards. His hands had been perfectly steady for the last twenty-four hours. They were the only part of him that had been steady; the rest of him, everything inside, had been shaken to hell. He scooped up the cards. Behind his eyes, memory flashed: Hazard on the ground, pale, unmoving, as Cassella slammed his head into the ground. Somers shuffled. His hands were solid. Like fucking rocks. Behind his eyes, he was still seeing Cassella slam Hazard's head into the ground, and the fear that Hazard was dead, and three words like skywriting taking up every square inch of his brain: *I lost him.* That thought, those three little words, had shaken him into a million sharp-edged pieces. He dealt again, and his hands were still steady.
"You know they make card games for two."
"I know."
"You're being a real asshat."
Somers murmured his assent.
"I didn't mean to leave you behind."
"I just realized we're in a hospital," Somers said.
Hazard's face tightened with suspicion.
"So," Somers continued, "I could beat your ass and we'd have medical care right on hand."

The room was small, baby blue, and smelled faintly like fresh paint. Somers had cracked the window, but it had been too cold outside. Hazard jammed the buttons on a TV remote and tried not to look too ashamed. Somers figured he'd let his partner ride this out for another day or two before he let him off the hook. The man was a complete and utter moron, but his heart was in the right place. Unfortunately, that place happened to be a rather self-absorbed child named Nico, but Somers couldn't do anything about that.

"Cassella wouldn't have done anything, you know."

"We don't know that."

"If you hadn't gone charging in there like the Lone Ranger, he would have packed his bags and left town, and we never would have heard from him again."

Hazard grunted.

"You wouldn't be in here with your brain leaking out your ears."

"My brain isn't leaking."

"And Nico wouldn't be shitting in a bag."

Hazard didn't have a response to that. Twin red lines scratched his cheekbones, the only color in his pale face.

"He's going to be fine."

"You don't know that. Nobody knows that."

"He's going to be fine, Ree. He is."

They didn't talk much after that; Somers knew he was to blame. He didn't care.

After the doctor discharged Hazard, the dark-haired detective said he needed to check in on Nico. Somers followed Hazard, but he waited outside the room. He could hear them talking softly as the door swung shut, and then nothing. He found a sofa, stretched out, and waited. He dealt himself another game of solitaire and lost that one too.

An hour passed, and still no sign of Hazard, and that's when Somers had his answer. He swept up the cards, tossed them in the trash, and headed back to the apartment. He didn't need the cards anymore. He was playing solitaire for the rest of his life.

CHAPTER FORTY-TWO

**FEBRUARY 16
FRIDAY
10:21 PM**

OUTSIDE THE APARTMENT, the city had gone dark and silent and still. The Market Street lights spun gossamer across the river. Somers needed air, and he cracked a window, and all he got was a snort of cold, dry winter that made him think of snow, even though the sky was an empty slate, so he shut the window again.

Hazard didn't come home. Somers watched SportsCenter. Hazard still didn't come home. Somers tried CNN. By that point, for all Somers knew, maybe Hazard wasn't even in the same fucking state. He turned off the TV and changed into gym shorts and a tank and crawled into bed. The clock on the wall ticked past ten. A car honked outside once. And Hazard still didn't come home.

When the door clicked, a part of Somers's brain told him to stay in bed. Whatever had happened, his brain said, it had happened. Nothing he did tonight would change anything. Better to lie there and keep a scrap of dignity.

But he didn't just lie there. He thought of that skywriting on the back of his brain, those three huge words, *I lost him*. But the skywriting was different now. Something fundamental had shifted inside Somers, had moved, and it had happened when he saw Hazard pale and unmoving under Cassella. And the skywriting didn't say *I lost him* anymore. *I love him.* It said, *I love him* in huge white vapor-trails, white and puffy like smoke, which made sense because Somers was on fire, and all that smoke had to go somewhere. So he didn't just lie there. And the floor was cold under his bare feet as he padded into the kitchen.

It took a moment to locate Hazard. The lights were off, and the living room was dark. Where the shadows massed at one end, Hazard sat on the sofa, knees spread, head down, his long hair hanging loose and wild. No, Somers thought, his heart suddenly pounding again in his chest because his heart was a traitor. No, wild wasn't the right word. Savage. Brutal. Beautiful.

Which one of them was going to talk first? It was so dark, and Somers thought maybe that the whole city had lost power, maybe that's why it was so cold, maybe that's why he was shivering so hard he could barely keep from falling over.

Then Hazard's head came up. Those scarecrow eyes glowed, tiny chips of gold at the bottom of all that darkness.

"So," Somers heard himself saying. "You guys are back together?"

Slowly, Hazard shook his head.

"You want to talk?"

Again, that slow shake.

"Well, I'm freezing, so I'm going back to bed."

"Come over here."

"Why the fuck did you leave me waiting out there? I looked like an idiot, you know that? You could have told me you needed to talk to him."

"Come here."

"You could have told me I should go home, Ree. You could have told me just about anything and I would have understood. Instead, I sit around until I'm too damn embarrassed to do anything but leave, and then I sit around the apartment all day wondering if you're ok."

"Please."

That word, the sound of his voice, tightened every millimeter of John-Henry's skin. He took a few steps towards Hazard. "Tell me."

It was hard to tell in the darkness, but Somers thought he saw struggle in Hazard's expression. "He thought because of what happened—he thought we were together again."

"So you're going to wait. You'll tell him when he's better. I get it, Ree. You can't walk out on a guy after he got shot."

Hazard tilted his head; his dark hair spilled over his forehead, long waves of it cresting over his eyes. "Do you know how long I waited to come out after I realized I was gay?"

"What does this—"

"Fifteen seconds. Maybe less. I walked out of my room and told my parents. They had no idea what to do. What to say. God help them, they wouldn't have known if I'd given them a year to prepare, so I guess it didn't matter. But I didn't wait. I realized that was the truth about me, and then I acted on it."

"Look. I know I was shitty in high school. I know I told you that I figured things out when I got to college, when I started hooking up with guys—"

"Hold on. This isn't about you." A white sliver of smile opened in the darkness. "Not entirely, anyway. It's about me. Have you ever had something inside, something you knew was true—I don't know what to call it. A decision. A realization. A truth. Have you ever had that and not acted on it? It's shit." His hands shifted along his knees restlessly. "I knew, weeks ago, that I should end things with Nico. I knew it. Maybe not all the way in my brain, maybe not in words, but I knew. And I didn't say anything. I thought about it. A lot, in hindsight. But I didn't do anything about it. When we broke up the other day, it was because he broke up with me. I still kept my damn mouth shut because I was afraid. Even though I knew I needed to break up with him, it was safer to stay with him." His voice broke on the last word.

Somers was hearing him. He was seeing those sparks of gold staring back at him. But he was thinking about junior prom, when he had driven out to Lake Palmerston with Cora, when they had sat nervously side by side, clutching at each other's hands like centrifugal force might tear them apart, and how they'd settled for a few kisses with too much teeth and then he'd driven her home and hadn't asked her out again.

Somers thought about dinner with Naomi, and the serpent gleam in her eyes when she asked if Somers didn't have any secrets. He thought about dinner with Cora under the leaden eyes of dead beasts, while the young in love gleamed like crystal around them, and how she had known— she had known almost all of it—and Somers still hadn't been able to say it.

"Have I ever had something inside me," Somers said, pausing to lick his lips, "and not acted on it? Yes, Ree. Yes. Since I was sixteen years old and stupid and afraid, yes."

"Come here."

Those last few feet were the hardest; Somers didn't remember walking them. He just remembered standing in front of Hazard, close enough now to see the tracks running down his face, to see those scarecrow eyes, to see something new and terrifying in those eyes—no, Somers realized with a start. Not new. Terrifying, God, yes, but not new. This was old. He had seen this look before when he had stood naked in the locker room, the heat from the shower still flushing his skin, and kissed skinny Emery Hazard on the lips.

Hazard's hands caught Somers's wrists. Somers's pulse pounded there, trapped under Hazard's mitts. Then Hazard's hands slid down, enfolding Somers's fingers, turning Somers's palms up.

"You're not wearing your wedding ring."

All the air had gone out of the room. Somers said, "No."

"I'm a pretty poor fucking excuse for a detective, I guess." Then Hazard leaned down, kissing the one hand and then the other.

"I love you, Ree. You."

In answer, Hazard pulled him forward, so that Somers half-sat and half-fell into Hazard's lap. "I know," Hazard said, catching Somers's mouth with his, kissing him. He pulled back, a hand planted on Somers's chest, stopping him. "Still think I've got a fat ass?"

Growling, Somers leaned into the next kiss and managed to say, "You know I love your ass."

Through the thin gym shorts, Somers's erection slid along Hazard's chest, and Somers let out a groan. Hazard's huge hands gripped Somers's knees, spreading them, positioning Somers so that he could feel the length of Hazard's hardness trapped underneath him, so he could see the blush and the explosion of pleasure in Hazard's face as he rocked into Somers.

Somers started tearing at Hazard's shirt. Hazard's callused mitts crept up Somers's legs, a cascade of sensation and pleasure that made Somers shiver as he worked Hazard's shirt over his head. One of those big hands closed around Somers's dick, stroking once through the polyester mesh so that Somers thrust into his touch. Then, with a low, rasping chuckle, Hazard pulled his hand away.

"Tease me like that again," Somers said. "And I'm going to tickle you. I didn't forget." He ran his hands along Hazard's ribs, and Hazard squirmed before seizing both of Somers's wrists in one hand.

"Not a chance." Kiss. "Not tonight." Kiss, harder this time. "I've got big plans for tonight." Kiss, a kiss like Somers had his head knocked off.

"Ree," Somers was panting when he came up for air. "Ree, I fucking love you."

Hazard seized the tank with two hands and ripped. It came away like tissue paper. He whispered, "I know," and buried his face between Somers's shoulder and neck, the stubble on his cheek abrading sensitive skin, his teeth nipping, hard, and goddamn Somers hadn't known how much he would like that. Somers rubbed against Hazard again.

Two strong, callused fingers circled Somers's nipple. It was like someone had run jumper cables to his dick, and he cried out as Hazard pinched and twisted—and Somers was embarrassed at how easily the cry was pulled from him, and then no longer caring, no longer needing to care because he was giving himself up to Hazard, giving up every part of himself, all the things he'd held back for twenty years. His spine arched.

Hazard's free hand traced the hollow of it, tightening, pressing Somers against him, sliding the polyester mesh of the gym shorts across Somers's bone. Somers felt twenty-five again. Or maybe twenty-one. Eighteen, Christ—Hazard's hand closed around his dick again, and at the same time Hazard humped into Somers's weight, a groan coming from deep inside Hazard—no, sixteen, Somers felt like he was sixteen years old again, like sex was the only thing he'd been made for and he could do it for a full-time job.

Somers's pawed at Hazard's head, at his neck, at his back. He knew he should be doing something—anything—but his whole system was overloaded, and all he could do was arch his back until he thought his spine would snap. And then Hazard's mouth, warm and sucking, closed over a nipple, and teeth followed, and Somers cried out again.

"Jesus Christ, Ree, I fucking love you."

And Hazard pulled up, his mouth hot on Somers's lips, and between kisses he said, "I know." And then he pulled back, a smile crooked on his lips, and said, "I love you too."

Somers was breathing like he'd been running. A 5K? Fuck that. A ten? Not a chance. A marathon, like he'd been going the full distance. But he managed to smirk and say, "Of course you do."

Hazard's eyes widened with mock anger, and in one smooth movement he hauled down Somers's shorts and slapped his bare ass.

It was like Somers's whole body had turned to fire. He leaned in, his mouth kissing everywhere he could reach, begging Hazard, "Fuck me. Now, Ree. Right now."

Again, Hazard reared back. Those scarecrow eyes studied Somers, serious now. "I know this is new for you. Or mostly new. If you want to—"

"Ree, if you don't fuck my brains out right now, I'm going to cut your balls off. And I'm not even going to bother with Fukuma's research."

"John," and the way Hazard said that one word, that part of Somers's name that no one ever used by itself, sent a dangerous flush running through Somers. "John, I don't want you to—"

"Right now, you big brute." Somers shifted his weight, grinding down on Hazard's erection until the other man's breath caught in his throat and his pupils blew out. "I'm going to count down from five. Five."

Hazard looked like a man unhinged. He shot to his feet—not bothering to adjust Somers's weight, just wrapping two huge arms around him—and lurched towards his bedroom. He lowered Somers gently onto the bed. He touched his jaw, turned his face, kissed him. Softly. Barely brushing his lips.

"I love you, John."

Somers's eyes were wet, and he blinked them clear. Another smirk grew on his face. "Four."

They didn't make it to three. Even through the passion, there was a small knot of something that wasn't quite fear in Somers's stomach as Hazard spread his legs and retrieved a condom and a bottle of lube from the nightstand. Later, Somers would realize he never needed to worry. Hazard took his time. Those big, strong hands were surprisingly gentle. And when Hazard did enter him, there was some pain, and then there wasn't even pain, just pleasure rising like a wave, like a comber breaking the sea, like a tsunami, the waters carrying Somers higher and higher, until the air grew thin, higher until his vision was speckled with black, and then pleasure crashing down, obliterating everything, leaving Somers blank and sated and whole.

For a long time afterward they lay there, intertwined, Hazard's sweat pasting skin to skin, his long dark hair bedraggled against Somers's cheek. They talked the way new lovers talk: fragments that aren't quite sentences in a rhythm as smooth as their lovemaking, and the empty spaces between words didn't feel like silences. And at some point Hazard slept, his breath hot on Somers's neck, one arm loose across Somers's chest, as though afraid he might sneak off in the night the way he had the last time they had slept together.

Somers stroked the fine, dark hair on Hazard's arm, and his eyes roved around the room. He was seeing it from a new angle; he was seeing everything from a new angle, he thought, his heart slow and steady now, but he wanted to laugh at how silly and small that description sounded. A new angle, yes. A whole new goddamn world. He'd seen this place a hundred times. He could walk it in the dark. He could walk it blindfolded. And now, he was seeing it for what it really was, like one of those ambiguous images, where you can see a vase and then all of the sudden it's not a vase, it's a lady's face. Yes, Somers thought. Yes, yes, yes. It was exactly like that. He'd been seeing an apartment all this time.

Hazard stirred, grunted, and kissed Somers's cheek. In the citylight through the window, he frowned. He ran a finger through the tear track on Somers's cheek. "John, what's wrong?"

"Nothing."

"John?"

Somers kissed him and ran a hand through Hazard's thick, sweaty tangles of hair. "Nothing, promise. I'm just thinking."

Hazard's frown lingered, and Somers made a game of teasing it away with his fingers until Hazard buried his face in Somers's neck again, and a heartbeat later, his breathing evened into sleep.

Somers studied the room around them one last time before closing his own eyes. He'd been seeing an apartment, yes. And now he saw a home.

REASONABLE DOUBT

Keep reading for a sneak preview of *Reasonable Doubt*, the next Hazard and Somerset mystery.

CHAPTER ONE

**APRIL 21
SATURDAY
6:45 PM**

A BABY WASN'T A LOADED GUN. That's what Emery Hazard kept telling himself, anyway. He sat in a small living room while a dark-haired child played. She was sorting blocks, stacking them, and then smashing them to the ground. Her dark eyes came to rest on Hazard again and again, and Hazard found himself calculating how fast he could run, how long, how far. He could make it to the highway for sure. He could hitch a ride.

A baby wasn't a loaded gun. Not exactly.

The little girl had a mass of dark curls, longer in back and scanty in front, and that hair and those eyes were gifts from her mother. But her features, they were her father's features. Softened, yes. Hidden, to a degree, by baby fat and age. But they were there. The girl would be a knockout in fifteen years. Until then, she'd have to settle for being adorable.

Her father, John-Henry Somerset, was in the small house's even smaller kitchen, talking to his ex-wife. The conversation was low, but not heated. Casual. She was laughing, and then he was laughing, and the little girl's dark eyes stayed locked on Hazard like she was waiting for him to slip up, and then boom. He didn't know what boom might entail, but he knew it'd be bad. He could definitely run as far as the interstate. He knew he could make it that far.

And that conversation in the kitchen—like they were best friends. In some ways, Hazard thought, they were. Or they had been. But what the hell was Hazard supposed to do while they caught up? It was one thing to start dating the man he'd been drawn to since high school. It was one thing to date his partner, a cop, in a small town with the public spotlight narrowed to the two of them. It was one thing, even, to be the cause for Somers's divorce—he still thought of him as Somers, at least, most of the time. Not John-Henry. Not even John. Most of the time, he was Somers. But it was another thing entirely to sit in Somers's ex-wife's house, to smile, to let her kiss him on the cheek, to pretend that he hadn't ruined her life, torn apart her family, and to let her pretend too.

The blocks crashed to the ground again, and the dark eyes roved Hazard's face. Goddamnit. Didn't she ever look away? What was so goddamn fascinating about him? Was it a joke? A prank? Had Somers put something in Hazard's clothes? Hazard wasn't entirely sure about how babies worked. He understood the biology and physiology of reproduction. He'd seen a few documentaries on childbirth. If worse came to worst, he could probably get a woman through an easy labor. But the rest of it—were children like cats? Was there some toddler equivalent of catnip that Somers had sprinkled in Hazard's pockets? It seemed possible. Hell, right then, it seemed downright likely.

A baby wasn't a loaded gun. There were lots of differences. Lots. Hazard just couldn't put his finger on any. Not right then. He just needed a minute to think, that's all.

"You all right?" Somers stuck his head out of the kitchen. His blond hair mussed, his shirt wrinkled, the collar slipping to expose the dark ink along his collarbone: Somers was hot. There wasn't really any other way to put it. No other way to explain Hazard's reaction to him, to this man he loved. Amusement crinkled Somers's eyes.

"Just fu—"

The lines around Somers's eyes deepened as Hazard glanced at the little girl and swallowed the word.

"Yeah. Fine."

Somers didn't say anything, but he withdrew into the kitchen, and laughter exploded a moment later. Goddamn him. Goddamn both of them.

To Hazard's relief, Somers and Cora emerged from the kitchen a few minutes later. Cora looked as lovely as ever: her dark hair short, her skin luminous. She was beautiful the way movie starlets were beautiful sixty or seventy years before—like you couldn't touch her, and hell, you didn't need to. You could just look and enjoy. Even Hazard, who had never wanted anything more than a casual acquaintance with women, knew she was beautiful in a kind of knee-knocking way.

"Thank you again, Emery."

"It's fine."

"This really means a lot to me. I know you had plans."

"We were ordering pizza and watching a movie. We can do that here, right?"

Cora was already shaking her head. "Oh, God. I'm so sorry. Didn't John-Henry tell you? This house is gluten and dairy free. I hope that's not going to be a problem."

Hazard gritted his teeth. "No."

"And I really don't like any movies in the house that might affect the aura. Nothing violent or sexual. So, could you find something G-rated for the evening? Because of the aura."

Because of the aura. Because of the house's goddamn aura. Hazard fought back his first reaction. "Yeah. A lot of my favorite documentaries are unrated, but there's—"

Cora was already shaking her head.

"Ok," Hazard said. "Yeah. We'll figure something out."

A smile slipped to the corners of her mouth.

"You're bull—" Hazard stopped himself. "You're joking."

Nodding her head, Cora burst into laughter. "Emery, I'm sorry. John-Henry made me."

"Because you're sitting here like you're about to get your teeth pulled," Somers said, leaning against the wall, arms across his chest. "All of them."

"I'm sorry, Emery."

"No," he said. "It's fine."

"I shouldn't have teased you."

She really was beautiful, and she had this way of looking at Emery—at everyone, he guessed—that made him feel like he was important and interesting and the only one in the room. Some of the tension went out of him. "Don't worry about it. I'll take it out of Somers's ass."

"Language," Somers said with a grin.

Laughing again, Cora bent to kiss Hazard's cheek. "Thank you."

He grunted, unsure of what to say. She kissed Somers's cheek too, and then she left. Somers swooped down, catching up Evie in his arms. She squealed, her chubby legs flailed, and her arms went around his head. Pressing her face to his, she continued shrieking with delight. Hazard wondered if there was blood coming from his ears.

Then whatever enjoyment Evie found in being swung around by her father ended, and she screamed, "Down, down, down," and Somers, laughing, lowered her back to the floor.

"No," she said when he tried to snatch a block.

Somers just laughed again. He watched her as she settled back to work, her tiny face studious. You could have scribbled happiness in all his margins. He watched her for a long time, and Hazard watched him watching her. For many months, almost a year, she had vanished from his life. Cora had refused to allow Somers to see his daughter. Did he just want to hold her, Hazard wondered. Did he want to bury her in kisses? Did he wonder about those critical developmental stages that he had only glimpsed in passing or that he had missed completely? Some things, when you lost them, you could never get back. The thought struck a dark note inside Hazard, and he sensed a problem in a blind, scrabbling-in-the-dark way. A big problem like he was about to smack into a rock wall. But Somers didn't look like a man who'd lost anything, and he didn't look like a man with a problem. He looked like he'd hit the jackpot every time he dropped a quarter. Maybe more than that. More than lucky. Happy.

"You've got a way of looking at a guy that makes him think funny things," Somers said, his eyes still on his daughter.

Hazard sprawled on the couch. He kept looking.

Red mixed with the tan in Somers's cheeks, and his eyes flicked to Hazard. A smile pulled at Somers's lips.

"You're doing it on purpose."

"Doing what?"

"You know what."

Hazard spread his legs.

Somers moved over to straddle Hazard, his arms going round Hazard's neck and pulling him close.

"You're mad."

"I am not."

"Let's see."

Blond stubble glinted on Somers's jaw, and the smell of Dove soap came off him. He kissed Hazard lightly, and then harder, and then hard enough to make Hazard shift underneath him.

"Hm," Somers said, running his tongue over his upper lip. "Maybe you're telling the truth."

Hazard shrugged.

"You're amazing for doing this."

"I've always been a pretty good kisser."

Somers laughed, rolling sideways to sit next to him on the sofa. His hand found Hazard's. "Is this the most awkward night of your life?"

"No."

"Good."

"Top five, maybe."

"Ree, she doesn't hate you."

"All right."

"Hand to God."

On the floor, the little girl had lost interest in the blocks. With wobbly uncertainty, she pulled herself to her feet and tottered towards a toy box along the far wall.

"We'd been separated for almost a year, Ree. She was dating other guys. She was dating Ethan, and that's still going really well for her."

"I said all right."

"This was the right thing for both of us."

Enough was enough, Hazard decided. He grabbed the back of Somers's neck, pulled him in, and kissed him. Kissed the hell out of him.

When he let up, Somers was breathing like he'd just finished sprints. "I know this is weird and awkward, us being here, babysitting so she can go on a date. It's weird for me too."

Hazard kissed him again. He got a hand up under the t-shirt, and Somers leaned into his touch.

Panting, Somers said, "I promise, Ree, she's going to love you—"

This time, Hazard didn't let him finish.

When Somers came up for air this time, his eyes were owlish. "What was I saying?"

Hazard shrugged.

"You did that on purpose."

"It's the only way to shut you up." He kissed Somers again. His hand roamed the corded muscles on the other man's back. "I wish I'd figured it out fifteen years ago."

"I love you, Ree."

Kissing him one last time, Hazard leaned back. "Love you too." Then he wrinkled his nose.

Laughing, Somers twisted a handful of Hazard's shirt. "Come on, big boy. It's time you learn how to change a diaper."

CHAPTER TWO

APRIL 21
SATURDAY
11:59 PM

THE GRAY SMOKE-LIGHT OF THE CITY filled their bedroom without brightening it. In their small apartment in the Crofter's Mark building, Hazard lay with Somers curled against him, sweat cooling on his back and shoulders. The only movement was their breathing, unsynced but harmonious, and from time to time the individual beads of sweat would shift, pulled by gravity along slick skin, merging with the next drop, and the next, like rain after a storm. One bead, heavy and cold, slid to the hollow of Hazard's back, and he shivered.

"All right?" Somers said.

Hazard kissed his ear softly.

"You're sure tonight was ok?"

"You keep asking. Are you sure?"

Somers rolled to face him. He was beautiful. He was always beautiful, but tonight, buoyed up, weightless in the haze of light from the windows, he was more than that, something from a dream. Something from Hazard's dreams, from twenty years of restless dreaming. His eyes were the color of tropical water, warm, shallow, turquoise that might as well have been white as you splashed in it up to the ankles.

"I'm serious."

"I can do this now," Hazard said. He reached out, one thick finger finding the line of Somers's cheekbone and tracing it, then curving down along his jaw. Somers was the one who shivered this time. "And this." His finger found Somers's collarbone, gliding the length of his shoulder, then down to the dark calligraphy that inked Somers's torso. Seek justice. That's what Somers had said the script meant. More than that, too, but what

Hazard remembered, what he cared about, were those two words: seek justice. Those words, and what they said about Somers. "And this." He bent and kissed Somers on the lips. "Why wouldn't I be ok when I can do that?"

Frown lines scored Somers's forehead. "Do you want her to call you dad?"

"She's your daughter. What do you want her to call me?"

Somers stilled, and his hand rested softly against Hazard's chest. "What?"

"She's my daughter?"

"John."

"I know. I know. We don't have to figure it out now."

Hazard combed his fingers through Somers's short, textured hair.

"I just think about that. About stuff like that, I mean."

"All right."

"So you want her to call you that? Dad?"

"I'm saying all right. You think about stuff like that."

"And you don't?"

Hazard worked his fingers through the blond hair again.

"What do you want?"

"You."

Somers's lips quirked dangerously close to one of those sex-fueled smirks. "Yeah, you made that pretty damn clear. I mean, what else?"

"Do I want kids?"

"Sure. Do you want a family?"

"A family?"

"Yeah?"

"Why don't you just ask me if I want kids?"

"What's wrong with the word family?"

"Just ask me what you want to ask me."

"I thought that's what I did."

Letting his hand drop down to the dark whorls of ink on Somers's chest, Hazard shook his head. "You asked what I want. And you asked about a family."

"All right. Fine. I'm asking now. Do you want kids?"

"Do you?"

"That's not the point. I want to know what you want."

A growl was building in Hazard's chest. He pushed Somers onto his back and straddled him, the sheet sliding away, both of them naked to the gossamer light spun through the windows. Planting one hand on Somers's chest, pinning him to the mattress, he took firm hold of Somers's chin with

311

the other. Not too tight. Not hard enough to hurt. But damn sure that Somers wouldn't be able to turn away.

"I want you. If you want a kid, let's have a kid. If you're happy with Evie, so am I."

"Ree, I want to know—"

Shushing him, Hazard gave Somers's head a little shake, and he felt Somers hardening under him, and he heard the whisper of breath that was close to a moan. Hazard let a heartbeat pass and then leaned low. "If you want a million kids, I goddamn want them too. Understand?"

There were questions in Somers's eyes. And, to Hazard's surprise, a glimmer of what might have been pain. He kissed him, his tongue raking Somers's mouth, drawing a whimper from him. Somers bucked under Hazard's weight.

"Twice in one night?" Hazard said, grinning.

"You're such an asshole sometimes."

"Yeah?" Hazard slid a hand down Somers's taut stomach, over the bush of sandy blond hair, and to his dick. He squeezed. "Prove it."

Somers rolled, and Hazard moved with him, and then Somers was on top, kissing a line down Hazard's neck.

"I damn well will," Somers said, his voice mock-furious.

CHAPTER THREE

**APRIL 22
SUNDAY
10:11 AM**

IT SHOULD HAVE BEEN a perfect morning: waking late in bed together, a run along the river, brunch. Instead, two phone calls ruined it. The first call, the one about the murder, Hazard could have shrugged off. Murder was murder. Killers, for the most part, didn't care about brunch. The second call came while Hazard and Somers were en route to the crime, and that was what really screwed up his day.

"Who was that?" Somers asked as Hazard disconnected.

"Nobody."

"Nobody?"

They were driving along the old Missouri Pacific lines, heading east towards the part of town that used to cater to the railway. A hundred years ago, this part of the city had thrived: theaters, restaurants, tea houses, as well as the infrastructure for the rails themselves—homes for railroad workers, warehouses, light industry. What had once been prosperous and well maintained, however, had followed the same track as the rails: houses slumped towards the gutters; businesses folded like cheap suits; the only theater still open survived as a strip club, with the turn of the century decor torn out and replaced with mirrors and fog machines and a poorly-wired sound system.

"I don't think it was nobody, Ree."

"It was my dad. Can we drop it?"

"Is everything ok?"

"No, Somers. Everything is not ok. He's coming here. To Wahredua."

"Oh. What's wrong? God, your mom's not sick, is she?"

"What's wrong? I just told you: he's coming here."

The Interceptor bounced out of a pothole, and Hazard's head cracked against the glass. Nobody had repaired these streets in at least twenty years. Longer, Hazard guessed. Around them, the houses sagged inside their clapboard siding, and paint peeled from moldering frames. Maybe there was a hotel over here. Maybe he could stuff his dad somewhere over here, and in a day he'd be sick of it and turn around and head home.

"You're upset because he's coming here?"

"I don't want to talk about it."

Somers fiddled with the stereo, and a moment later, a woman's voice came across the speakers: raw, husky, with a slight twang. Hazard had listened to enough of Somers's music to recognize Gillian Welch. He punched off the radio.

"Jesus," was all Somers said, and they drove the rest of the way in silence.

Around them, the houses spread out, the postage-stamp lots growing larger, separated now by lines of willow and honeysuckle and lilac. Two patrol cars hugged the curb in front of a white, two-story farmhouse. A substantial fence had been raised around the property, and the wood looked new. Someone had also taken the time to replace the rotten siding on the front of the house and to slap on a fresh coat of paint. The place still looked like it might keel over, but if you took a picture from the front, with the right light, it might pass for decent.

Harold Lloyd, stockier than ever in his blue uniform, stood on the sidewalk, his hands resting on the small of his back like he'd just finished stretching. He nodded at Hazard and Somers as they stepped towards the house.

"Happy Sunday." Lloyd said it with his usual elfish smile. "You boys get off to a nice morning?"

Hazard ignored him; he spotted Lloyd's partner, Hoffmeister, behind the wheel of the car, and Hazard ignored him too.

"Who's inside?" Somers said.

"Norman and Gross. You know how they work. Couple of turtles."

"Thanks."

As they passed Lloyd, he called after them, "Sorry we had to interrupt your breakfast."

Hazard turned, but Somers caught his sleeve and tugged him towards the house.

"He's asking for it," Hazard said.

"We've been through this. They're assholes. You can't change that."

"If we sit back and take it—"

"When somebody says something straight out, we'll do something. If we get prickly every time there's a sideways comment, though, we start to look like the assholes."

"I could break his teeth. Then he wouldn't have anything clever to say. Not ever again."

Somers sighed, and his fingers ran down into Hazard's palm before he pulled away. "You're a Neanderthal. You know that."

Inside the front room of the house, they found the dead man still on the ground while Norman and Gross filmed the crime scene. The two beat cops weren't much to look at—they might have been brothers, although they weren't related, and they shared pot-bellies and bald heads. They looked like they hadn't spent fifty cents between them on clothing since 1985.

"Oh no," Norman said, lowering his camera and waving them back. "Not until we're done. You two always want to squirm in here and mess the whole thing up."

"What've you got?"

"A lot of work to do."

"We'll swing some coffee and donuts."

Norman glanced at Gross, who gave a decisive nod. Ambling towards them, Norman cocked his head at the body. "John Oscar Walden. Fifty-three. That's what's on his driver's license, anyway. He might not look like much now, but you've got the honor of being in the presence of the newborn Son of God, Jesus Christ himself, Brother Jeshua."

"What the hell?" Hazard said.

"Some kind of crazy religious get up. The house is empty, but we found some fliers on the kitchen table. Picture of Mr. Walden front and center. The damn things look so bad I doubt they dropped as much as a dollar on them at Kinko's. Probably don't have a dollar between them. You know what they're doing? They're spreading the good word that Christ Himself has come again, and he's living in Wahredua, Missouri. Did you know that?"

"I didn't," Somers said.

"Well, there's your Lord and Savior. Somebody put a knife in his belly so many times he's like a used kleenex down there. Dr. Kamp came by and took a quick look; he says Jesus has been dead at least twelve hours, probably more. Puts it around late afternoon yesterday. He'll have a better time after he gets him open."

"Who called it in?"

"Nobody. Lloyd and Hoffmeister were here; they had a bench warrant. Jesus Christ liked driving fast, but he didn't like paying his tickets. The door was open, and there he was."

"You haven't seen anybody?" Hazard asked.

"Not a soul. Not so much as an angel weeping holy tears." Norman had a smile the same color as his mustard slacks. "Who pulled you two out of bed?"

"Fuck off," Somers said.

Laughing, Norman headed back into the room to document the scene.

"What about the knife?" Hazard called.

"No sign of it."

"Guess we owe them coffee," Somers said. "Let's get Lloyd and Hoffmeister on doors, and then we'll see what we can find."

Lloyd and Hoffmeister, it turned out, did not want to knock doors and canvass the neighbors.

"I'm on duty right here," Hoffmeister complained. He was the color of old styrofoam, and he looked just about as strong. Right then, though, he was putting up one hell of a noise. "We're making sure nobody bothers Norman and Gross."

"Get walking," Hazard said. "Right now. I want you done with this street in the next half hour."

"Half hour?" That dampened Lloyd's quirky smile.

"If you don't move your asses, I'll move them for you. Half an hour."

"Who the hell can do this in half an hour?" Hoffmeister grumbled, but he turned and took one side of the street while Lloyd crossed. Hoffmeister's next words were delivered with venom—quiet, but meant to carry. "It's not as easy as cruising Shepherd Park."

"All right," Hazard said, rolling his shoulders as he took a step after Hoffmeister.

"Let him go," Somers said, catching Hazard's arm.

"Like hell."

Hoffmeister squeaked just like styrofoam and scurried up the street.

"Check the rest of the lot?" Somers asked. "Or get coffee?"

Hazard started around the house, Somers at his side. The back of the house was in even worse repair than Hazard had thought: a screened porch clung to the building, ready to collapse at any moment, and the clapboard had rotted away to splinters. Past the porch, a plot of bare earth showed recent efforts at cultivation. Weeds were stacked in a wheelbarrow, and someone had begun to till the soil. At the back of the lot, a red barn met the split-rail fence.

Somers nodded at the incipient garden. "What do you think?"

"Like most cults, they're already aiming at self-sufficiency. Cutting themselves off from the outside world is an essential part of proclaiming their uniqueness. It makes them special. People like to feel special. Hence, their own food supply."

"I meant, do you like gardening?"

"What does it matter?"

"Because I like learning things about you." The grass was still dewy underfoot as they approached the barn. "Do you?"

"What?"

Somers sighed. "Like gardening."

"I don't know."

"Do you want to live in a house or an apartment?"

"We already live in an apartment."

"But where would you like to live?"

"Somewhere I can pay off the mortgage in less than fifteen years."

"I'm talking about a family home. Not a house or an apartment. A place for your family. What do you want? What does it look like? Or what do you want it to feel like?"

"What's going on with you?"

Another sigh. "Never mind." A breeze carried in from the north, and it brought with it a fresh, green smell. "You think this is a cult?"

"They're proselytizing," Hazard said. "They're claiming their leader is Jesus Christ reborn."

"Norman said newborn."

"Norman couldn't tell his ass from a hole in the ground."

"Maybe they're right."

"That dead guy was Jesus Christ reborn?"

"What do you think?"

"They say third time's the charm."

Somers laughed, reaching out to touch Hazard's arm. That felt good. The sunshine, the breeze, the smell of green things, the dew shining like someone had captured the world in glass, and that touch. Hazard liked that touch.

The barn itself looked like old construction, its red paint peeling, the wood weathered and, in places, split with dry rot. A much newer staircase ran alongside the exterior wall, though, with a cherry-red door at the top.

"Loft apartment," Somers said. "Sometimes they call it a carriage house. It's an easy way to convert and rent out unused space, bring in a little cash."

"Your parents do this?"

"God, no. They wouldn't be caught dead. But it's popular on all those home renovation shows."

Hazard took the stairs two at a time; they were firm and held his weight without squeaking. At the top, he stopped. The door was a solid-core exterior model, with a latch and a deadbolt.

"Someone sure as hell doesn't want us getting in there," Hazard said, pointing to the deadbolt. The broken remains of a key were turned halfway in the lock. "We'll need a locksmith. Or we'll have to take the damn thing apart piece by piece."

Then, from within came a piercing cry.

"What the hell was that?" Somers asked.

Hazard braced himself against the rail and kicked. His heel drove into the door, and the frame creaked. Wood popped and splintered. He kicked again, and again, and again. On the next kick, fragments of wood sprayed his shoe, and a chunk of the frame ripped free. The door swung inwards.

From inside came the sounds of grunting, shuffling movement, the slap of flesh on flesh. Drawing his .38, Hazard stepped through the door.

The woman, on hands and knees on the bed, was facing him, and she let out a shriek. She had to be in her late forties, maybe early fifties, and she probably hadn't ever lacked for calories. The boy mounting her looked like he couldn't be more than sixteen. Red-faced, his narrow body slick with sweat, he slammed into her twice more before her shrieks penetrated his hormone-infused thoughts. Then he looked like someone had slapped him, and he slid backwards, ass-first onto the mattress.

Hazard made room for Somers. The older woman was scuttling through the bedding, hands grasping at an antique bra with enormous cones, still screaming.

"Be quiet," Hazard said.

She did, but she didn't stop moving until she'd tugged the straps over her shoulders and dragged a blanket over her legs. The boy—definitely no older than eighteen, and Hazard guessed even that was a stretch—hugged his scrawny chest. His face was almost purple, and Hazard guessed some of that was fear and a lot of that was frustration.

"Who are you?" Hazard asked.

"L-l-lazarus."

Hazard eyed the woman. Her stringy gray hair had fallen in front of her face, and she dashed it away from her eyes now. A little bit of courage had come back. Or maybe a little bit of pride. Something put an ounce of steel in her.

"Kelley Jane Walden. Who the hell are you?"

Hazard processed the last name, her age, and the compromising position, but as usual Somers beat him to the punch.

"Ah. That must make you Mrs. Jesus Christ."

Acknowledgments

My deepest thanks go out to the following people:

Cheryl Oakley, for the corrections in this revised edition.

Monique Ferrell, for her careful reading of a draft of this story, including her advice about MWOs. Any mistakes in the book are mine; anything I got right is due to her diligent research and gentle corrections. In addition to her comprehensive legal expertise, Monique consistently provided thoughtful responses to inconsistencies in the characters and the plot. Thank you for catching that dumb T-shirt and changing it to a coat!

Austin Gwin, for his editorial insight into what makes the book's ending work. That powerful final scene took on the shape that it has now thanks to a series of emails that Austin wrote, and I'm grateful to him for his sensitivity and insight into the characters and their relationship. More than anything else, Austin gave a name to the underlying fears that Hazard and Somers share, and he also saw a way for them to move past those fears (at least, to move past them initially!). As I've already mentioned to Austin, those boys will still manage to screw up a lot of things.

Sloan Jordan, for her unflagging support, for her patient encouragement for me to join the twenty-first century, and for reading a draft of this manuscript and catching critical errors.

And Tray Stephenson, for editorial insight on the characters and plot, for catching a multitude of errors, for good-natured support over weekly email, and for taking the time to keep me appraised of what's happening on (as he calls it) 'the crazy farm.'

Last, as always, the weekenders group, for friendship, encouragement, criticism, and for Diet Coke and frozen pizzas.

About the Author

For advanced access, exclusive content, limited-time promotions, and insider information, please sign up for my mailing list at **www.gregoryashe.com**.

Made in United States
North Haven, CT
15 June 2024

53677241R00193